LOUISE PENNY

A Rule
Against
Murder

HODDER

First published in Great Britain in 2008 by Headline Publishing Group
Published in 2011 by Sphere
This edition published in 2021 by Hodder & Stoughton
An Hachette UK company
Previously published as *The Murder Stone* in the UK

3

Copyright © Louise Penny 2008

Map by Rhys Davies

Excerpt from *The Cremation of Sam McGhee* by Robert Service
used with permission of the estate of John Masefield.

A CIP catalogue record for this title is available from the British Library

B format ISBN 978 1 529 38822 0
eBook ISBN 978 1 529 38824 4

Printed and bound in Great Britain by Clays Ltd, Elcograf S.p.A.

Hodder & Stoughton policy is to use papers that are natural, renewable
and recyclable products and made from wood grown in sustainable
forests. The logging and manufacturing processes are expected to
conform to the environmental regulations of the country of origin.

Hodder & Stoughton Ltd
Carmelite House
50 Victoria Embankment
London EC4Y 0DZ

www.hodder.co.uk

Louise Penny is the Number One *New York Times* bestselling author of the Inspector Gamache series, including *Still Life*, which won the CWA John Creasey Dagger in 2006. Recipient of virtually every existing award for crime fiction, Louise was also granted the Order of Canada in 2014 and received an honorary doctorate of literature from Carleton University and the Ordre Nationale du Québec in 2017. She lives in a small village south of Montreal.

Praise for Louise Penny and the series:

'Louise Penny is one of the greatest crime writers of our times' Denise Mina

'She makes most of her competitors seem like wannabes' *The Times*

'A cracking storyteller, who can create fascinating characters, a twisty plot and wonderful surprise endings' Ann Cleeves

'Outstanding . . . a constantly surprising series that deepens and darkens as it evolves' *The New York Times*

'No one does atmospheric quite like Louise Penny . . . a fantastic series' Elly Griffiths

'Louise Penny's writing is intricate, beautiful and compelling. She is an original voice, a distillation of both PD James and Barbara Vine at their peaks and a worthy successor to both' Peter James

'[An] atmospheric, distinctive series' Kate Mosse

'Penny is an absolute joy' *Irish Times*

'The series is deep and grand and altogether extraordinary . . . Miraculous' *Washington Post*

The Gamache series

A LETTER FROM LOUISE

When I was thirty-five, I thought the best was behind me.

I was lonely, and tired, and empty. Plodding through life. At thirty-five.

By the time I was forty-five, I was married to the love of my life, and my first book was about to be published.

And now I'm sixty. Living in a beautiful Quebec village, surrounded by friends, with thirteen books to my name. And counting.

This milestone birthday gives me a chance to look back in wonderment. And gratitude. And amazement. That I should be here, happy, joyous, and free.

No one quite appreciates, and recognises, the light like those who've lived in darkness. That awareness is what I try to bring to the books. The duality of our lives. The power of perception. The staggering weight of despair, and the amazement when it is lifted.

The gap between how we appear and how we really feel.

Those are foundations of the Gamache books.

Initially they were called the Three Pines books, which, of course, they are. Three Pines is the tiny hidden village in Québec. Not on any map, it is only ever found by those who are lost.

But, once found, never forgotten.

At their core, though, these books are about the profound decency of Armand Gamache, and the struggles he has to remain a good person. When 'good' is subjective, and 'decent' is a matter of judgement.

These books might appear, superficially, as traditional crime novels. But they are, I believe, more about life than death. About choices. About the price of freedom. About the struggle for peace.

Armand Gamache, of the Sûreté du Quebec, is inspired by my husband, Michael Whitehead. A doctor who treated children with cancer. Who spent his life searching for cures. Who saved countless young lives, boys and girls who now have children of their own.

Despite the dreadful deaths and broken hearts all around him, Michael was the happiest man alive. Because he understood the great gift that life is.

Michael gave that perception to Armand.

Michael died of dementia. And it broke my heart. But I still have Armand. And Clara, and Jean-Guy. Myrna and Gabri and Olivier. And crazy old Ruth.

At thirty-five, I thought the best was behind me.

As I celebrate my sixtieth birthday, I can hardly wait to see what happens next.

Ring the bells that still can ring
Forget your perfect offering
There's a crack in everything.
That's how the light gets in.

Welcome to the very cracked world of Armand Gamache and Three Pines. I am overjoyed to be able to share it with you.

Meet you in the bistro . . .

Louise Penny
March 2018

For my parents, in love and memory

Du Moulin

PROLOGUE

———

More than a century ago the Robber Barons discovered Lac Massawippi. They came with purpose from Montreal, Boston, New York, and burrowing deep into the Canadian wilderness they built the great lodge. Though, of course, they didn't actually dirty their own hands. What clung to them was something else entirely. No, these men hired men with names like Zoétique, Télesphore and Honoré to hack down the massive and ancient forests. At first the Québécois were resistant, having lived in the forest all their lives. They balked at destroying a thing of such beauty and a few of the more intuitive recognized the end when they saw it. But money took care of that and slowly the forest receded and the magnificent Manoir Bellechasse rose. After months of cutting and stripping and turning and drying the huge logs were finally stacked one on top of the other. It was an art, this building of log homes. But what guided the keen eyes and rough hands of these men wasn't aesthetics but the certainty that winter's bite would kill whoever was inside if they didn't choose the logs wisely. A *coureur du bois* could contemplate the stripped trunk of a massive tree for hours, as though deciphering it. Walking round and round, sitting on a stump, filling his pipe and staring until finally this *coureur du bois*, this man of the woods, knew exactly where that tree would sit for the rest of its life.

It took years, but finally the great lodge was completed. The last man stood on the magnificent copper roof like a lightning rod and surveyed the forests and the lonely, haunting lake from a height he'd never achieve again. And if that man's eyes could see far enough he'd make out something horrible approaching, like the veins of summer lightning. Marching towards not merely the lodge, but the exact place he stood, on the gleaming metal roof. Something dreadful was going to happen on that very spot.

He'd laid copper roofs before, always with the same design. But this time, when everyone else had thought it was finished, he'd climbed back up and added a ridge, a cap along the peak of the roof. He had no idea why, except that it looked good and felt right. And he'd had the copper left over. He'd use the same design again and again, in great buildings across the burgeoning territory. But this was the first.

Having hammered the final nail he slowly, carefully, deliberately descended.

Paid off, the men paddled away, their hearts as heavy as their pockets. And looking back the more intuitive among them noticed that what they'd created looked a little like a forest itself, but one turned unnaturally on its side.

For there was something unnatural about the Manoir Bellechasse from the very beginning. It was staggeringly beautiful, the stripped logs golden and glowing. It was made of wood and wattle and sat right at the water's edge.

2

It commanded Lac Massawippi, as the Robber Barons commanded everything. These captains of industry couldn't seem to help it.

And once a year men with names like Andrew and Douglas and Charles would leave their rail and whiskey empires, trade their spats for chewed leather moccasins and trek by canoe to the lodge on the shore of the isolated lake. They'd grown weary of robbery and needed another distraction.

The Manoir Bellechasse was created and conceived to allow these men to do one thing. Kill.

It made a nice change.

Over the years the wilderness receded. The foxes and deer, the moose and bears, all the wild creatures hunted by the Robber Barons, crept away. The Abinaki, who often paddled the wealthy industrialists to the great lodge, had retired, repulsed. Towns and villages sprang up. Cottagers, week-enders, discovered the nearby lakes.

But the Bellechasse remained. It changed hands over the generations and slowly the stunned and stuffed heads of long-dead deer and moose and even a rare cougar disappeared from the log walls and were tossed into the attic.

As the fortunes of its creators waned, so went the lodge. It sat abandoned for many years, far too big for a single family and too remote for a hotel. Just as the forest was emboldened enough to reclaim its own, someone bought the place. A road was built, curtains were hung, spiders and beetles and owls were chased from the Bellechasse and paying guests invited in. The Manoir Bellechasse became one of the finest *auberges* in Quebec.

But while in over a century Lac Massawippi had changed,

3

Quebec had changed, Canada had changed, almost everything had changed, one thing hadn't.

The Robber Barons were back. They'd come to the Manoir Bellechasse once again, to kill.

ONE

~

At the beginning of summer the guests descended on the isolated lodge by the lake, summoned to the Manoir Bellechasse by identical vellum invitations, addressed in the familiar spider scrawl as though written in cobwebs. Thrust through mail slots, the heavy paper had thudded to the floor of impressive homes in Vancouver and Toronto, and a small brick cottage in Three Pines.

The mailman had carried it in his bag through the tiny Quebec village, taking his time. Best not to exert yourself in this heat, he told himself, pausing to remove his hat and wipe his dripping head. Union rules. But the actual reason for his lethargy wasn't the beating and brilliant sun, but something more private. He always lingered in Three Pines. He wandered slowly by the perennial beds of roses and lilies and thrusting bold foxglove. He helped kids spot frogs at the pond on the green. He sat on warm fieldstone walls and watched the old village go about its business. It added hours to his day and made him the last courier back to the terminal. He was mocked and kidded by his fellows for being so slow and

5

he suspected that was the reason he'd never been promoted. For two decades or more he'd taken his time. Instead of hurrying, he strolled through Three Pines talking to people as they walked their dogs, often joining them for lemonade or *thé glacé* outside the bistro. Or *café au lait* in front of the roaring fire in winter. Sometimes the villagers, knowing he was having lunch at the bistro, would come by and pick up their own mail. And chat for a moment. He brought news from other villages on his route, like a travelling minstrel in medieval times, with news of plague or war or flood, someplace else. But never here in this lovely and peaceful village. It always amused him to imagine that Three Pines, nestled among the mountains and surrounded by Canadian forest, was disconnected from the outside world. It certainly felt that way. It was a relief.

And so he took his time. This day he held a bundle of envelopes in his sweaty hand, hoping he wasn't marring the perfect, quite lovely thick paper of the top letter. Then the handwriting caught his eye and his pace slowed still further. After decades as a mail carrier he knew he delivered more than just letters. In his years, he knew, he'd dropped bombs along his route. Great good news: children born, lotteries won, distant, wealthy aunts dead. But he was a good and sensitive man, and he knew he was also the bearer of bad news. It broke his heart to think of the pain he sometimes caused, especially in this village.

He knew what he held in his hand now was that, and more. It wasn't, perhaps, total telepathy that informed his certainty, but also an unconscious ability to read handwriting. Not simply the words, but the thrust behind them. The simple, mundane three-line address on the envelope told him more than where to deliver the letter. The hand was old, he could tell, and infirm. Crippled not just by age, but by rage. No good would come from this thing he held. And he suddenly wanted to be rid of it.

His intention had been to wander over to the bistro and have a cold beer and a sandwich, chat with the owner Olivier and see if anyone came for their mail, for he was also just a little bit lazy. But suddenly he was energized. Astonished villagers saw a sight unique to them, the postman hurrying. He stopped and turned and walked briskly away from the bistro, towards a rusty mailbox in front of a brick cottage overlooking the village green. As he opened the mouth of the box it screamed. He couldn't blame it. He thrust the letter in and quickly closed the shrieking door. It surprised him that the battered metal box didn't gag a little and spew the wretched thing back. He'd come to see his letters as living things, and the boxes as kinds of pets. And he'd done something terrible to this particular box. And these people.

Had Armand Gamache been blindfolded he'd have known exactly where he was. It was the scent. That combination of woodsmoke, old books and honeysuckle.

'*Monsieur et Madame Gamache, quel plaisir.*'

Clementine Dubois waddled around the reception desk at the Manoir Bellechasse, skin like wings hanging from her outstretched arms and quivering so that she looked like a bird or a withered angel as she approached, her intentions clear. Reine-Marie Gamache met her, her own arms without hope of meeting about the substantial woman. They embraced and kissed on each cheek. When Gamache had exchanged hugs and kisses with Madame Dubois she stepped back and surveyed the couple. Before her she saw Reine-Marie, short, not plump but not trim either, hair greying and face settling into the middle years of a life fully lived. She was lovely without being actually pretty. What the French called *soignée*. She wore a tailored deep blue skirt to mid-calf and a crisp white shirt. Simple, elegant, classic.

The man was tall and powerfully built. In his mid-fifties and not yet going to fat, but showing evidence of a life lived with good books, wonderful food and leisurely walks. He looked like a professor, though Clementine Dubois knew he was not that. His hair was receding and where once it had been wavy and dark, now it was thinning on top and greying over the ears and down the sides where it curled a little over the collar. He was clean-shaven except for a trim moustache. He wore a navy jacket, khaki slacks and a soft blue shirt, with tie. Always immaculate, even in the gathering heat of this late June day. But what was most striking were his eyes. Deep, warm brown. He carried calm with him as other men wore cologne.

'But you look tired.'

Most innkeepers would have exclaimed, 'But you look lovely.' '*Mais, voyons*, you never change, you two.' Or even, 'You look younger than ever,' knowing how old ears never tire of hearing that.

But while the Gamaches' ears couldn't yet be considered old, they were tired. It had been a long year and their ears had heard more than they cared to. And, as always, the Gamaches had come to the Manoir Bellechasse to leave all that behind. While the rest of the world celebrated the New Year in January, the Gamaches celebrated at the height of summer, when they visited this blessed place, retreated from the world, and began anew.

'We are a little weary,' admitted Reine-Marie, subsiding gratefully into the comfortable wing chair at the reception desk.

'*Bon*, well we'll soon take care of that. Now.' Madame Dubois gracefully swivelled back behind the desk in a practised move and sat at her own comfortable chair. Pulling the ledger towards her she put on her glasses. 'Where have we put you?'

Armand Gamache took the chair beside his wife and they exchanged glances. They knew if they looked far enough back in that same ledger they'd find their signatures, once a year, stretching back to a June day more than thirty years ago when young Armand had saved his money and brought Reine-Marie here. For one night. In the tiniest of rooms at the very back of the splendid old Manoir. Without a view of the mountains or the lake or the perennial gardens lush with fresh peonies and first-bloom roses. He'd saved for months, wanting that visit to be special. Wanting Reine-Marie to know how much he loved her, how precious she was to him.

And so they'd lain together for the first time, the sweet scent of the forest and kitchen thyme and lilac drifting almost visible through the screened window. But the loveliest scent of all was her, fresh and warm in his strong arms. He'd written a love note to her that night. He'd covered her softly with their simple white sheet then sitting in the cramped rocking chair, not daring to actually rock in case he whacked the wall behind or barked his shins on the bed in front, disturbing Reine-Marie, he'd watched her breathe. Then on Manoir Bellechasse notepaper he'd written, *My love knows no –*

How can a man contain such –
My heart and soul have come alive –

9

My love for you –

All night he wrote and next morning, taped to the bathroom mirror, Reine-Marie found the note.

I love you.

Clementine Dubois had been there even then, massive and wobbly and smiling. She'd been old then and each year Gamache worried he'd call for a reservation to hear an unfamiliar crisp voice say, '*Bonjour, Manoir Bellechasse. Puis-je vous aider?*' Instead he'd heard, 'Monsieur Gamache, what a pleasure. Are you coming to visit us again, I hope?' Like going to Grandma's. Albeit a grander grandma's than he'd ever known.

And while Gamache and Reine-Marie had certainly changed, marrying, having two children and now a grand-daughter and another grandchild on the way, Clementine Dubois never seemed to age or diminish. And neither did her love, the Manoir. It was as though the two were one, both kind and loving, comforting and welcoming. And mysteriously and delightfully unchanging in a world that seemed to change so fast. And not always for the better.

'What's wrong?' Reine-Marie asked, noticing the look on Madame Dubois's face.

'I must be getting old,' she said and looked up, her violet eyes upset. Gamache smiled reassuringly. By his calculations she must be at least a hundred and twenty.

'If you have no room, don't worry. We can come back another week,' he said. It was only a two-hour drive into the Eastern Townships of Quebec from their home in Montreal.

'Oh, I have a room, but I'd hoped to have something better. When you called for reservations I should have saved the Lake Room for you, the one you had last year. But the

Manoir's full up. One family, the Finneys, has taken the other five rooms. They're here—'

She stopped suddenly and dropped her eyes to the ledger in an act so wary and uncharacteristic the Gamaches exchanged glances.

'They're here . . . ?' Gamache prompted after the silence stretched on.

'Well, it doesn't matter, plenty of time for that,' she said, looking up and smiling reassuringly. 'I'm sorry about not saving the best room for you two, though.'

'Had we wanted the Lake Room, we'd have asked,' said Reine-Marie. 'You know Armand, this is his one flutter with uncertainty. Wild man.'

Clementine Dubois laughed, knowing that not to be true. She knew the man in front of her lived with great uncertainty every day of his life. Which was why she deeply wanted their annual visits to the Manoir to be filled with luxury and comfort. And peace.

'We never specify the room, madame,' said Gamache, his voice deep and warm. 'Do you know why?'

Madame Dubois shook her head. She'd long been curious, but never wanted to cross-examine her guests, especially this one. 'Everyone else does,' she said. 'In fact, this whole family asked for free upgrades. Arrived in Mercedes and BMWs and asked for upgrades.' She smiled. Not meanly, but with some bafflement that people who had so much wanted more.

'We like to leave it up to the fates,' he said. She examined his face to see if he was joking, but thought he probably wasn't. 'We're perfectly happy with what we're given.'

And Clementine Dubois knew the truth of it. She felt the same. Every morning she woke up, a bit surprised to see

11

another day, and always surprised to be here, in this old lodge, by the sparkling shores of this freshwater lake, surrounded by forests and streams, gardens and guests. It was her home, and guests were like family. Though Madame Dubois knew, from bitter experience, you can't always choose, or like, your family.

'Here it is.' She dangled an old brass key from a long keychain. 'The Forest Room. It's at the back, I'm afraid.'

Reine-Marie smiled. 'We know where it is, *merci*.'

One day rolled gently into the next as the Gamaches swam in Lac Massawippi and went for leisurely walks through the fragrant woods. They read and chatted amicably with the other guests and slowly got to know them.

Up until a few days ago they'd never met the Finneys, but now they were cordial companions at the isolated lodge. Like experienced travellers on a cruise, the guests were neither too remote nor too familiar. They didn't even know what the others did for a living, which was fine with Armand Gamache.

It was mid-afternoon and Gamache was watching a bee scramble around a particularly blowsy pink rose when a movement caught his attention. He turned in his chaise longue and watched as the son, Thomas, and his wife Sandra walked from the lodge into the startling sunshine. Sandra brought a slim hand up and placed huge black sunglasses on her face, so that she looked a little like a fly. She seemed an alien in this place, certainly not someone in her natural habitat. Gamache supposed her to be in her late fifties, early sixties, though she was clearly trying to pass for considerably less. Funny, he thought, how dyed hair, heavy make-up and young clothes actually made a person look older.

They walked on to the lawn, Sandra's heels aerating the grass, and paused, as though expecting applause. But the only sound Gamache could hear came from the bee, whose wings were making a muffled raspberry sound in the rose.

Thomas stood on the brow of the slight hill rolling down to the lake, an admiral on the bridge. His piercing blue eyes surveyed the water, like Nelson at Trafalgar. Gamache realized that every time he saw Thomas he thought of a man preparing for battle. Thomas Finney was in his early sixties and certainly handsome. Tall and distinguished with grey hair and noble features. But in the few days they'd shared the lodge Gamache had also noted a hint of irony in the man, a quiet sense of humour. He was arrogant and entitled, but he seemed to know it and be able to laugh at himself. It was very becoming and Gamache found himself warming to him. Though on this hot day he was warming to everything, especially the old *Life* magazine whose ink was coming off on his sweaty hands. Looking down he saw, tattooed to his palm, ǝℲi⅃. Life. Backwards.

Thomas and Sandra had walked straight past his elderly parents who were lounging on the shaded porch. Gamache marvelled yet again at the ability of this family to make each other invisible. As Gamache watched over his half-moon glasses Thomas and Sandra surveyed the people dotted around the garden and along the shore of the lake. Julia Martin, the older sister and a few years younger than Thomas, was sitting alone on the dock in an Adirondack chair, reading. She wore a simple white one-piece bathing suit. In her late fifties she was slim and gleamed like a trophy as though she'd slathered herself in cooking oil. She seemed to sizzle in the sun, and with a wince Gamache could imagine her skin beginning to crackle. Every now and then Julia would lower her book and gaze across the calm lake. Thinking. Gamache knew enough about Julia Martin to know she had a great deal to think about.

On the lawn leading down to the lake were the rest of the family, the younger sister Mariana and her child, Bean. Where Thomas and Julia were slim and attractive, Mariana was short and plump and unmistakably ugly. It was as though she was the negative to their positive. Her clothes seemed to have a grudge against her and either slipped off or scrunched around awkwardly so that she was constantly rearranging herself, pulling and tugging and wriggling.

And yet the child, Bean, was extremely attractive, with long blond hair, bleached almost white in the sun, thick dark lashes and brilliant blue eyes. At that moment Mariana appeared to be doing t'ai chi, though with movements of her own making.

'Look, darling, a crane. Mommy's a crane.'

The plump woman stood on one leg, arms reaching for the sky and neck stretched to its limits.

Ten-year-old Bean ignored Mommy and continued to read. Gamache wondered how bored the child must be.

'It's the most difficult position,' Mariana said more loudly than necessary, almost throttling herself with one of her scarves. Gamache had noticed that Mariana's t'ai chi and yoga and meditations and military callisthenics only happened when Thomas appeared.

Was she trying to impress her older brother, Gamache wondered, or embarrass him? Thomas took a quick glance at the pudgy, collapsing crane and steered Sandra in the other direction. They found two chairs in the shade, alone.

'You're not spying on them, are you?' Reine-Marie asked, lowering her own book to look at her husband.

'Spying is far too harsh. I'm observing.'

'Aren't you supposed to stop that?' Then after a moment she added, 'Anything interesting?'

He laughed and shook his head. 'Nothing.'

'Still,' said Reine-Marie, looking around at the scattered Finneys. 'Odd family that comes all this way for a reunion then ignores each other.'

'Could be worse,' he said. 'They could be killing each other.'

Reine-Marie laughed. 'They'd never get close enough to manage it.'

Gamache grunted his agreement and realized happily that he didn't care. It was their problem, not his. Besides, after a few days together he'd become fond of the Finneys in a funny sort of way.

'*Votre thé glacé, madame.*' The young man spoke French with a delightful English Canadian accent.

'*Merci*, Elliot.' Reine-Marie shaded her eyes from the afternoon sun and smiled at the waiter.

'*Un plaisir.*' He beamed and handed a tall glass of iced tea to Reine-Marie and a perspiring glass of misty lemonade to Gamache, then went off to deliver the rest of his drinks.

'I remember when I was that young,' said Gamache wistfully.

'You might have been that young but you were never that—' She nodded towards Elliot as he walked athletically across the manicured lawn in his tailored black slacks and small white jacket snugly fitting his lithe body.

'Oh, God, am I going to have to beat up another suitor?'

'Maybe.'

'You know I would.' He took her hand.

'I know you wouldn't. You'd listen him to death.'

'Well, it's a strategy. Crush him with my massive intellect.'

'I can imagine his terror.'

Gamache sipped his lemonade and suddenly puckered, tears springing to his eyes.

'Ah, and what woman could resist that?' She looked at his fluttering, watering eyes and face screwed into a wince.

'Sugar. Needs sugar,' he gasped.

'Here, I'll ask the waiter.'

'Never mind. I'll do it.' He coughed, gave her a mockingly stern gaze and rocked out of the deep and comfortable seat.

Taking his lemonade he wandered up the path from the fragrant gardens and onto the wide veranda, already cooler and shaded from the brunt of the afternoon sun. Bert Finney lowered his book and gazed at Gamache, then smiled and nodded politely.

'*Bonjour*,' he said. 'Warm day.'

'But cooler here, I notice,' said Gamache, smiling at the elderly couple sitting quietly side by side. Finney was clearly older than his wife. Gamache thought she was probably in her mid-eighties while he must be nearing ninety and had that translucent quality people sometimes got, near the end.

'I'm going inside. May I get you anything?' he asked, thinking yet again that Bert Finney was both courtly and one of the least attractive people he'd ever met. Admonishing himself for being so superficial, it was all he could do not to stare. Monsieur Finney was so repulsive he was almost attractive, as though aesthetics were circular and this man had circumnavigated that rude world.

His skin was pocked and ruddy, his nose large and

16

misshapen, red and veined as though he'd snorted, and retained, Burgundy. His teeth protruded, yellowed and confused, heading this way and that in his mouth. His eyes were small and slightly crossed. A lazy eye, thought Gamache. What used to be known as an evil eye, in darker times when men like this found themselves at best cast out of polite society and at worst tied to a stake.

Irene Finney sat next to her husband and wore a floral sundress. She was plump with soft white hair in a loose bun on her head, and while she didn't glance up he could see her complexion was tender and white. She looked like a soft, inviting, faded pillow, propped next to a cliff face.

'We're fine, but *merci*.'

Gamache had noticed that Finney, alone among his family, always tried to speak a little French to him.

Within the Manoir the temperature dropped again. It was almost cool inside, a relief from the heat of the day. It took a moment for Gamache's eyes to adjust.

The dark maple door to the dining room was closed and Gamache knocked tentatively, then opening it he stepped into the panelled room. Places were being set for dinner, with crisp white linen, sterling silver, fine bone china and a small arrangement of fresh flowers on each table. It smelled of roses and wood, of polish and herbs, of beauty and order. Sun was streaming through the floor-to-ceiling windows, which looked onto the garden. The windows were closed, to keep the heat out and the cool in. The Manoir Bellechasse wasn't air conditioned, but the massive logs acted as natural insulation, keeping the heat in during the bitterest of Quebec winters, and the heat out on the most sizzling of summer days. This wasn't the hottest. Low 80s, Gamache figured.

But he was still grateful for the workmanship of the *coureurs du bois* who raised this place by hand and chose each log with such precision that nothing not invited could ever come in.

'Monsieur Gamache.' Pierre Patenaude came forward smiling and wiping his hands on a cloth. He was a few years younger than Gamache and slimmer. All that running from table to table, thought Gamache. But the maître d' never seemed to run. He gave everyone his time, as though they were the only ones in the *auberge*, without seeming to ignore or miss any of the other guests. It was a particular gift of the very best maître d's, and the Manoir Bellechasse was famous for having only the best.

'What can I do for you?'

Gamache, slightly bashfully, extended his glass. 'I'm sorry to bother you, but I need some sugar.'

'Oh, dear. I was afraid of that. Seems we've run out. I've sent one of the *garçons* to the village to pick up some more. *Désolé*. But if you wait here, I think I know where the chef hides her emergency supply. Really, this is most unusual.'

What was most unusual, thought Gamache, was seeing the unflappable maître d' flapped.

'I don't want to put you out,' Gamache called to Patenaude's disappearing back.

A moment later the maître d' returned, a small bone china vessel in his hands.

'*Voilà!* Success. Of course I had to wrestle Chef Véronique for it.'

'I heard the screams. *Merci*.'

'*Pour vous, monsieur, c'est un plaisir*.' Patenaude picked up his rag and a silver rose bowl and continued his polishing while Gamache stirred the precious sugar into his lemonade.

18

Both men stared in companionable silence out of the bank of windows to the garden and the gleaming lake beyond. A canoe drifted lazily by in the still afternoon.

'I checked my instruments a few minutes ago,' said the maître d'. 'A storm's on the way.'

'*Vraiment?*'

The day was clear and calm, but like every other guest at the gracious old lodge he'd come to believe the maître d's daily weather reports, gleaned from his home-made weather stations dotted around the property. It was a hobby, the maître d' had once explained, passed from father to son.

'Some fathers teach their sons to hunt or fish. Mine would bring me into the woods and teach me about the weather,' he'd explained one day while showing Gamache and Reine-Marie the barometric device and the old glass bell jar, with water up the spout. 'Now I'm teaching them.' Pierre Patenaude had waved in the direction of the young staff. Gamache hoped they were paying attention.

There was no television at the Bellechasse and even the radio was patchy, so Environment Canada forecasts weren't available. Just Patenaude and his near mythical ability to foretell the weather. Each morning when they arrived for breakfast the forecast would be tacked outside the dining-room door. For a nation addicted to the weather, he gave them their fix.

Now Patenaude looked out into the calm day. Not a leaf stirred.

'*Oui.* Heat wave coming, then storm. Looks like a big one.'

'*Merci.*' Gamache raised his lemonade to the maître d' and returned outside.

He loved summer storms, especially at the Bellechasse. Unlike Montreal, where storms seemed to suddenly break overhead, here he could see them coming. Dark clouds would collect above the mountains at the far end of the lake, then a grey curtain of rain would fall in the distance. It would seem to gather itself, take a breath, and then march like a line of infantry clearly marked on the water. The wind would pick up, catching and furiously shaking the tall trees. Then it would strike. Boom. And as it howled and blew and threw itself at them, he'd be tucked up in the Manoir with Reine-Marie, safe.

As he stepped outside the heat bumped him, not so much a wall as a whack.

'Find some sugar?' asked Reine-Marie, stretching out her hand to touch his face as he leaned down to kiss her before settling back into his chair.

'*Absolument.*'

She went back to reading and Gamache reached for *Le Devoir*, but his large hand hesitated, hovering over the newspaper headlines. Another Sovereignty Referendum Possible. A Biker Gang War. A Catastrophic Earthquake.

His hand moved to his lemonade instead. All year his mouth watered for the home-made Manoir Bellechasse lemonade. It tasted fresh and clean, sweet and tart. It tasted of sunshine and summer.

Gamache felt his shoulders sag. His guard was coming down. It felt good. He took off his floppy sun hat and wiped his brow. The humidity was rising.

Sitting in the peaceful afternoon Gamache found it hard to believe a storm was on its way. But he felt a trickle down his spine, a lone, tickling stream of perspiration. The pressure was building, he could feel it, and the parting words of the maître d' came back to him.

'Tomorrow's going to be a killer.'

TWO

～

After a refreshing swim and gin and tonics on the dock the Gamaches showered then joined the other guests in the dining room for dinner. Candles glowed inside hurricane lamps and each table was adorned with simple bouquets of old English roses. More exuberant arrangements stood on the mantelpiece, great exclamations of peony and lilac, of baby blue delphinium and bleeding hearts, arching and aching.

The Finneys were seated together, the men in dinner jackets, the women in cool summer dresses for the warm evening. Bean wore white shorts and a crisp green shirt.

The guests watched the sun set behind the rolling hills of Lake Massawippi and enjoyed course after course, beginning with the chef's *amuse-bouche* of local caribou. Reine-Marie had the *escargots à l'ail*, followed by seared duck breast with *confit* of wild ginger, mandarin and kumquat. Gamache started with fresh roquette from the garden and shaved parmesan then ordered the organic salmon with sorrel yogurt.

'And for dessert?' Pierre lifted a bottle from its bucket and poured the last of the wine into their glasses.

'What do you recommend?' Reine-Marie barely believed she was asking.

'For Madame, we have fresh mint ice cream on an éclair filled with creamy dark organic chocolate, and for Monsieur a pudding *du chômeur à l'érable avec crème chantilly*.'

'Oh, dear God,' whispered Reine-Marie, turning to her husband. 'What was it Oscar Wilde said?'

'I can resist everything except temptation.'

They ordered dessert.

Finally, when they could eat no more, the cheese cart arrived burdened with a selection of local cheeses made by the monks in the nearby Benedictine abbey of Saint-Benoit-du-Lac. The brothers led a contemplative life, raising animals, making cheese and singing Gregorian chants of such beauty that they had, ironically for men who'd deliberately retreated from the world, become world-famous.

Enjoying the *fromage bleu* Armand Gamache looked across the lake in the slowly fading glow, as though a day of such beauty was reluctant to end. A single light could be seen. A cottage. Instead of being invasive, breaking the unspoiled wilderness, it was welcoming. Gamache imagined a family sitting on the dock watching for shooting stars, or in their rustic living room, playing gin rummy, or Scrabble, or cribbage, by propane lamps. Of course they'd have electricity, but it was his fantasy, and in it people in the deep woods of Quebec lived by gas lamp.

'I called Paris and spoke to Roslyn today.' Reine-Marie leaned back in her chair, hearing it creak comfortably.

'Everything all right?' Gamache searched his wife's face, though he knew if there was a problem she'd have told him sooner.

'Never better. Two months to go. It'll be a September baby. Her mother will be going to Paris to take care of Florence when the new one arrives, but Roslyn asked if we'd like to go as well.'

He smiled. They'd talked about it, of course. They were desperate to go, to see their granddaughter Florence, to see their son and daughter-in-law. To see the baby. Each time he thought about it Gamache trembled with delight. The very idea of his child having a child struck him as nearly unbelievable.

'They've chosen names,' she said casually. But Gamache knew his wife, her face, her hands, her body, her voice. And her voice had just changed.

'Tell me.' He put his cheese down and folded his large, expressive hands on the white linen tablecloth.

Reine-Marie looked at her husband. For a man so substantial he could be so calm and contained, though that only seemed to add to the impression of strength.

'If it's a girl they think they'll call her Geneviève Marie Gamache.'

Gamache repeated the name. Geneviève Marie Gamache. 'It's beautiful.'

Is this the name they'd write on birthday and Christmas cards? Geneviève Marie Gamache. Would she come running up the stairs to their apartment in Outremont, little feet thumping, shouting, 'Grandpapa, Grandpapa'? And would he call out her name, 'Geneviève!' then scoop her up in his strong arms and hold her safe and warm in that pocket of his shoulder reserved for people he loved? Would he one day take her and her sister Florence on walks through Parc Mont Royal and teach them his favourite poems?

> *Breathes there the man with soul so dead*
> *Who never to himself hath said,*
> *'This is my own, my native land!'*

As his own father had taught him.

Geneviève.

'And if it's a boy,' said Reine-Marie, 'they plan to call him Honoré.'

There was a pause. Finally Gamache sighed, 'Ahh,' and dropped his eyes.

'It's a wonderful name, Armand, and a wonderful gesture.'

Gamache nodded but said nothing. He'd wondered how he'd feel if this happened. For some reason he'd suspected it would, perhaps because he knew his son. They were so alike. Tall, powerfully built, gentle. And hadn't he himself struggled with calling Daniel 'Honoré'? Right up until the baptism his name was supposed to be Honoré Daniel.

But in the end he couldn't do that to his son. Wasn't life difficult enough without having to walk through it with the name Honoré Gamache?

'He'd like you to call him.'

Gamache looked at his watch. Nearly ten. 'I'll call tomorrow morning.'

'And what will you say?'

Gamache held his wife's hands, then dropped them and smiled at her. 'How does coffee and liqueur in the Great Room sound?'

She searched his face. 'Would you like to go for a walk? I'll arrange for the coffees.'

'*Merci, mon coeur.*'

'*Je t'attends.*'

Breathes there the man with soul so dead, Armand Gamache whispered to himself as he walked with measured pace in the dark. The sweet aroma of night-scented stock kept him company, as did the stars and moon and the light across the lake. The family in the forest. The family of his fantasies. Father, mother, happy, thriving children.

No sorrow, no loss, no sharp rap on the door at night.

As he watched the light flickered out, and all was in darkness across the way. The family at sleep, at peace.

Honoré Gamache. Was it so wrong? Was he wrong to feel this way? And what would he say to Daniel in the morning?

He stared into space, thinking about that for a few minutes, then slowly he became aware of something in the woods. Glowing. He looked around to see if there was anyone else there, another witness. But the *terrasse* and the gardens were empty.

Curious, Gamache walked towards it, the grass soft beneath his feet. He glanced back and saw the bright and cheerful lights of the Manoir and the people moving about the rooms. Then he turned back to the woods.

They were dark. But they weren't silent. Creatures moved about in there. Twigs snapped and things dropped from the trees and thumped softly to the ground. Gamache wasn't afraid of the dark, but like most sensible Canadians he was a little afraid of the forest.

But the white thing glowed and called, and like Ulysses with the sirens, he was compelled forward.

It was sitting on the very edge of the woods. He walked up, surprised to find it was large and solid and a perfect square, like a massive sugar cube. It came up to his hip and when he reached out to touch it he withdrew his hand in surprise. It was cold, almost clammy. Reaching out again, more firmly this time, he rested his large hand on the top of the box, and smiled.

It was marble. He'd been afraid of a cube of marble, he chuckled at himself. Very humbling. Standing back, Gamache stared at it. The white stone glowed as though it had captured what little moonlight came its way. It was just a cube of marble, he told himself. Not a bear, or a cougar. Nothing to worry about, certainly nothing to spook him. But it did. It reminded him of something.

'Peter's perpetually purple pimple popped.'

Gamache froze.

'Peter's perpetually purple pimple popped.'

There it was again.

He turned round and saw a figure standing in the middle of the lawn. A slight haze hung about her and a bright red dot glowed near her nose.

Julia Martin was out for her secret cigarette. Gamache cleared his throat noisily and brushed his hand along a bush. Instantly the red dot fell to the ground and disappeared under an elegant foot.

'Good evening,' she called merrily, though Gamache doubted she could possibly have known who was there.

'*Bonsoir, madame,*' said Gamache, bowing slightly as he came up beside her. She was slender and was wearing an elegant evening dress. Hair and nails and make-up were done, even in the wilderness. She wafted a slim hand in front of her face, to disperse the pungent tobacco smell.

'Bugs,' she said. 'Blackflies. The only trouble with the east coast.'

'You have no blackflies out west?' he asked.

'Well, not many in Vancouver. Some deerflies on the golf courses. Drive you crazy.'

This Gamache could believe, having been tormented by deerflies himself.

'Fortunately smoke keeps the bugs away,' he said, smiling.

She hesitated, then chuckled. She had an easy manner and an easy laugh. She touched his arm in a familiar gesture, though they weren't all that familiar. But it wasn't invasive, simply habit. As he'd watched her in the past few days he'd noticed she touched everyone. And she smiled at everything.

'You caught me, monsieur. Sneaking a cigarette. Really, quite pathetic.'

'Your family wouldn't approve?'

'At my age I've long since stopped caring what others think.'

'*C'est vrai?* I wish I could.'

'Well, perhaps I do just a little,' she confided. 'It's a while since I've been with my family.' She looked towards the Manoir and he followed her gaze. Inside, her brother Thomas was leaning over and speaking to their mother while Sandra and Mariana looked on, not speaking and unaware anyone was watching them.

'When the invitation arrived I almost didn't come. It's an annual reunion, you know, but I've never been before. Vancouver's so far away.'

27

She could still see the invitation sitting face up on the gleaming hardwood floor of her impressive entrance where it had fallen as though from a great height. She knew the feeling. She'd stared at the thick white paper and the familiar spider scrawl. It was a contest of wills. But she knew who'd win. Who always won.

'I don't want to disappoint them,' Julia Martin finally said, quietly.

'I'm certain you couldn't do that.'

She turned to him, her eyes wide. 'Really?'

He'd said it to be polite. He honestly had no idea how the family felt about each other.

She saw his hesitation and laughed again. 'Forgive me, monsieur. Each day I'm with my family I regress a decade. I now feel like an awkward teenager. Needy and sneaking smokes in the garden. You too?'

'Smoking in the garden? No, not for many years now. I was just exploring.'

'Be careful. We wouldn't want to lose you.' She spoke with a hint of flirtation.

'I'm always careful, Madame Martin,' said Gamache, careful not to return the flirtation. He suspected it was second nature to her and harmless. He'd watched her for a few days and she'd used the same inflection on everyone, men and women, family and stranger, dogs, chipmunks, hummingbirds. She cooed to them all.

A movement off to the side caught his attention. He had the impression of a white blur and for an instant his heart leapt. Had the marble thing come to life? Was it lumbering towards them out of the woods? He turned and saw a figure on the *terrasse* recede into the shadows. Then it reappeared.

'Elliot,' called Julia Martin, 'how wonderful. Have you brought my brandy and Benedictine?'

'*Oui, madame.*' The young waiter smiled as he handed her the liqueur off his silver salver. Then he turned to Gamache. 'And for Monsieur? What may I get you?'

He looked so young, his face so open.

And yet Gamache knew the young man had been lurking at the corner of the lodge, watching them. Why?

Then he laughed at himself. Seeing things not there, hearing words unspoken. He'd come to the Manoir Bellechasse to turn that off, to relax and not look for the stain on the carpet, the knife in the bush, or the back. To stop noticing the malevolent inflections that rode into polite conversation on the backs of reasonable words. And the feelings flattened and folded and turned into something else, like emotional origami. Made to look pretty, but disguising something not at all attractive.

It was bad enough that he'd taken to watching old movies and wondering whether the elderly people in the background were still alive. And how they died. But when he started looking at people in the street and noticing the skull beneath the skin it was time for a break.

Yet here he was in this peaceful lodge examining the young waiter, Elliot, and on the verge of accusing him of spying.

'*Non, merci.* Madame Gamache has ordered our drinks for the Great Room.'

Elliot withdrew and Julia watched him.

'He's an attractive young man,' said Gamache.

'You find him so?' she asked, her face invisible but her voice full of humour. After a moment she spoke again. 'I was just remembering a similar job I had at about his age, but

29

nothing as grand as this. It was a summer job in a greasy spoon on the Main, in Montreal. You know, boulevard Saint-Laurent?'

'I know it.'

'Of course you do. Forgive me. It was a real dive. Minimum wage, owner was all hands. Disgusting.'

She paused again.

'I loved it. My first job. I'd told my parents I was at the yacht club taking sailing lessons, but instead I'd get on the 24 bus and head east. Uncharted territory for Anglos in the Sixties. Very bold,' she said in a self-mocking tone. But Gamache knew the times and knew she was right.

'I still remember my first pay cheque. Took it home to show my parents. Do you know what my mother said?'

Gamache shook his head then realized she couldn't see him in the dark. '*Non*.'

'She looked at it then handed it back and said I must be proud of myself. And I was. But it was clear she meant something else. So I did something stupid. I asked her what she meant. I've since learned not to ask a question unless I'm prepared for the answer. She said I was privileged and had no need of the money, but someone else did. I'd as good as stolen it from some poor girl who actually needed the job.'

'I'm sorry,' said Gamache. 'I'm sure she didn't mean it.'

'She did, and she was right. I quit the next day, but I'd go back every now and then and look through the window at the new girl waiting tables. That made me happy.'

'Poverty can grind a person down,' said Gamache quietly. 'But so can privilege.'

'I actually envied that girl,' said Julia. 'Silly, I know. Romantic. I'm sure her life was dreadful. But I thought,

30

maybe, it was at least her own.' She laughed and took a sip of her B&B. 'Lovely. Do you think the monks at the abbey make it?'

'The Benedictines? I don't really know.'

She laughed. 'It's not often I hear those words.'

'Which words?'

'*I don't know*. My family always knows. My husband always knew.'

For the past few days they'd exchanged polite comments about the weather, the garden, the food at the Manoir. This was the first real conversation he'd had with any of them and it was the first time she'd mentioned her husband.

'I came to the Manoir a few days early, you know. To . . .'

She didn't seem to know what to say, but Gamache waited. He had all the time, and patience, in the world.

'I'm in the middle of a divorce. I don't know if you knew.'

'I had heard.'

Most Canadians had heard. Julia Martin was married to David Martin, whose spectacular success and just as spectacular fall had been chronicled relentlessly in the media. He'd been one of the nation's wealthiest men, making his fortune in insurance. The fall had started a few years ago. It had been long and excruciating, like sliding down the side of a muddy slope. It looked at each moment as though he might be able to stop the descent, but instead he'd just kept gathering mud and slime and speed. Until finally even his enemies found it hard to watch.

He'd lost everything, including, finally, his freedom.

But his wife had stood beside him. Tall, elegant, dignified. Instead of arousing envy for her obvious privilege, she'd somehow managed to endear herself to the people. They warmed to her good cheer and sensible comments. They identified with her dignity and loyalty. And finally they'd adored her for the public apology she'd made at the end, when it became clear her husband had lied to everyone, and ruined tens of thousands of life savings. And she'd pledged to pay back the money.

And now David Martin lived in a penitentiary in British Columbia and Julia Martin had moved back home. She'd make her life in Toronto, she'd told the media just before she'd disappeared. But here she was, in Quebec. In the woods.

'I came here to catch my breath, before the family reunion. I like my own space and time to myself. I've missed it.'

'*Je comprends*,' he said. And he did. 'But there is something I don't understand, madame.'

'Yes?' She sounded a little guarded, like a woman used to invasive questions.

'Peter's perpetually purple pimple popped?' Gamache asked.

She laughed. 'A game we used to play as children.'

He could see part of her face reflected in the amber light from the Manoir. The two of them stood silent, watching people move from room to room. It felt a little as though they were watching a play. The stage atmospherically lit, the different sets decorated and populated. The actors moving about.

And he looked again at his companion and couldn't help but wonder. Why was the rest of her family there, like an ensemble on the stage? And she was outside, alone in the dark. Watching.

They'd gathered in the Great Room, with its soaring

timbered ceiling and magnificent furnishings. Mariana went to the piano, but was waved away by Madame Finney.

'Poor Mariana.' Julia laughed. 'Nothing ever changes. Magilla never gets to play. Thomas's the musician in the family, like my father. He was a gifted pianist.'

Gamache shifted his gaze to the elderly man on the sofa. He couldn't picture the gnarled hands producing lovely music, but then they probably hadn't always been so twisted.

Thomas sat on the bench, raised his hands, and sent the strains of Bach drifting into the night air.

'He plays beautifully,' said Julia. 'I'd forgotten.'

Gamache agreed. Through the windows he saw Reine-Marie take a seat and a waiter deposit two espressos and cognacs in front of her. He wanted to get back.

'There's one more to come, you know.'

'Really?'

She'd tried to keep her tone light but Gamache thought he caught an undertow.

Reine-Marie was stirring her coffee, and had turned to look out of the window. He knew she couldn't see him. In the light all she'd see was the room, reflected.

Here I am, his mind whispered. *Over here.*

She turned and looked directly at him.

It was coincidence, of course. But the part of him that didn't worry about reason knew she'd heard him.

'My younger brother Spot is coming tomorrow. He'll probably bring his wife, Claire.'

It was the first time he'd heard Julia Martin say anything that wasn't nice and pleasant. The words were neutral, informative. But the tone was telling.

It was full of dread.

They walked back into the Manoir Bellechasse and as Gamache held open the screen door for Julia Martin he caught sight of the marble box in the woods. He could see just a corner of it and knew then what it reminded him of.

A grave marker.

THREE

⸺

Pierre Patenaude leaned against the swinging kitchen door and pushed just as a rumble of laughter came out. It stopped as soon as he appeared and he didn't know what upset him more, the laughter or its abrupt end.

In the middle of the room stood Elliot, one hand on a slender hip, the other raised slightly, his index finger erect and frozen, a look on his face both needy and sour. It was an exceptionally accurate caricature of one of their guests.

'What's going on?'

Pierre hated the stern disapproval in his voice. And he hated the look on their faces. Fear. Except Elliot. He looked satisfied.

The staff had never been afraid of him before, and they had no reason to be now. It was that Elliot. Since he'd arrived he'd turned the others against the maître d'. He could feel it. That shift from being at the very centre of the Manoir staff, their respected leader, to suddenly feeling an outsider.

How had the young man done it?

But Pierre knew how. He'd brought out the worst in him.

He'd pushed the maître d', taunted him, broken the rules, and forced Pierre to be the disciplinarian he didn't want to be. All the other young staff had been trainable, willing to listen and learn, grateful for the structure and leadership the maître d' provided. He taught them to respect the guests, to be courteous and kind even when faced with rudeness. He told them their guests paid good money to be pampered, but more than that. They came to the Manoir to be looked after.

Pierre sometimes felt like an emergency room physician. People streamed through his door, casualties of city life, lugging a heavy world behind them. Broken by too many demands, too little time, too many bills, emails, meetings, calls to return, too little thanks and too much, way too much, pressure. He remembered his own father coming home from the office, drawn, worn down.

It wasn't servile work they did at the Manoir Bellechasse, Pierre knew. It was noble and crucial. They put people back together. Though some, he knew, were more broken than others.

Not everyone was made for this work.

Elliot wasn't.

'I was just having some fun.'

Elliot said it as though it was reasonable to stand in the middle of the crowded, busy kitchen mocking the guests, and the maître d' was the unreasonable one. Pierre could feel his rage rising. He looked around.

The large old kitchen was the natural gathering place for the staff. Even the gardeners were there, eating cakes and drinking tea and coffee. And watching his humiliation at the hands of a nineteen year old. *He's young*, Pierre said to himself. *He's young*. But he'd said it so often it had become meaningless.

He knew he should let it go.

'You were making fun of the guests.'

'Only one. Oh, come on, she's ridiculous. *Excusez-moi*, but I think he got more coffee than I did. *Excusez-moi*, but is this the best seat? I asked for the best seat. *Excusez-moi*, I don't mean to be difficult, but I did order before they did. Where's my celery stick?'

Titters, quickly stifled, filled the warm kitchen.

It was a good imitation. Even in his anger the maître d' recognized Sandra's smooth, cool whine. Always asking for a little bit more. Elliot might not be a natural waiter, but he had an uncanny ability to see people's faults. And magnify them. And mock them. It was a gift not everyone would find attractive.

'Look who I found,' said Julia cheerfully as they stepped into the Great Room.

Reine-Marie smiled and rose to kiss her husband, holding out a bulbous cognac glass. The rest looked up, smiled, and returned to what they were doing. Julia stood uncertain on the threshold, then picked up a magazine and sat in a wing chair.

'Feeling better?' Reine-Marie whispered.

'Much,' Gamache said and meant it, taking the glass warmed by her hands and following her to a sofa.

'Bridge later?' Thomas stopped playing the piano and wandered over to the Gamaches.

'*Merveilleux. Bonne idée*,' said Reine-Marie. They'd played bridge most nights with Thomas and his wife Sandra. It was a pleasant way to end the day.

'Find any roses?' Thomas asked Julia as he walked back

to his wife. There was a rat-tat-tat of laughter from Sandra as though he'd said something witty and brilliant.

'Some Eleanor roses, you mean?' Mariana asked from the window seat beside Bean, a look of great amusement on her face. 'They are your favourites, aren't they, Julia?'

'I thought they were more along your line,' Julia smiled. Mariana smiled back and imagined one of the wooden beams falling and crushing her older sister. It wasn't as much fun having her back as Mariana had hoped. In fact, quite the opposite.

'Time for bed, old Bean,' said Mariana and put her heavy arm round the studious child. Gamache had never known a ten year old so quiet. Still, the child seemed content. As they walked by he caught Bean's bright blue eyes.

'What're you reading?' he asked.

Bean stopped and looked at the large stranger. Though they'd been together in the Manoir for three days they hadn't really spoken, until now.

'Nothing.'

Gamache noticed the small hands close more tightly over the hardcover book, and the loose shirt fold as the book was pressed closer to the childish body. Through the small, tanned fingers Gamache could read only one word.

Myths.

'Come on, slowpoke. Bed. Mommy needs to get drunk and can't before you're in bed, now you know that.'

Bean, still looking at Gamache, suddenly smiled. 'May I have a martooni tonight, please,' Bean said, leaving the room.

'You know you're not allowed until you're twelve. It'll be Scotch or nothing,' they heard Mariana say, then footsteps on the stairs.

'I'm not completely convinced she's kidding,' said Madame Finney.

Gamache smiled over to her but his smile faded as he saw the stern look on her face.

'Why do you let him get to you, Pierre?'

Chef Véronique was putting hand-made truffles and chocolate-dipped candied fruit on small plates. Her sausage fingers instinctively placed the confections in an artistic pattern. She took a sprig of mint from the glass, shook the water from it and clipped a few leaves with her nails. Absently she chose some edible flowers from her vase and before long a few chocolates had become a lovely design on the white plate. Straightening up, she looked at the man opposite her.

They'd worked together for years. Decades, come to think of it. She found it odd to think she was almost sixty and knew she looked it, though happily in the wilderness it didn't seem to matter.

She'd rarely seen Pierre so upset by one of the young workers. She herself liked Elliot. Everyone did, as far as she could tell. Was that why the maître d' was so upset? Was he jealous?

She watched him for a moment, his slim fingers arranging the tray.

No, she thought. It wasn't jealousy. It was something else.

'He just doesn't listen,' said Pierre, setting the tray aside and sitting across from her. They were alone in the kitchen now. The washing up was done, the dishes away, the surfaces scrubbed. It smelled of espresso and mint and fruit. 'He came here to learn, and he won't listen. I just don't understand.' He uncorked the cognac and poured.

'He's young. It's his first time away from home. And you'll only make it worse by pushing. Let it go.'

Pierre sipped, and nodded. It was relaxing being around Chef Véronique, though he knew she scared the crap out of the new employees. She was huge and beefy, her face like a pumpkin and her voice like a root vegetable. And she had knives. Lots of them. And cleavers and cast-iron pans.

Seeing her for the first time new employees could be excused for thinking they'd taken a wrong turn on the dirt road into the woods, and ended up at a lumber camp instead of the refined Manoir Bellechasse. Chef Véronique looked like a short-order cook in a *cantine*.

'He needs to know who's in charge,' said Pierre firmly.

'He does know. He just doesn't like it.'

The maître d' had had a hard day, she could see. She took the largest truffle from the tray and handed it to him.

He ate it absently.

'I learned French late in life,' Mrs Finney said, examining her son's cards.

They'd switched to the library and to French and now the elderly woman was slowly circling the card table, peering into each hand. Occasionally she'd reach out a gnarled finger and tap a certain card. At first she'd limited her help to her son and his wife, but tonight she'd included the Gamaches in her rounds. It was a friendly game, and no one seemed to mind, certainly not Armand Gamache, who could use the help.

The room was lined with books, broken only by the huge river-rock fireplace and the wall of French doors, looking into the darkness. They were open, to catch what little breeze the hot Quebec evening had to offer, which wasn't much. What it did offer was a constant trill of calls from the wild.

Worn oriental carpets were scattered about the old pine floor and comfortable chairs and sofas were grouped together for intimate conversations or a private read. Arrangements of fresh flowers were placed here and there. The Manoir Bellechasse managed to be both rustic and refined. Rough-hewn logs on the outside and fine crystal within.

'You live in Quebec?' Reine-Marie spoke slowly and distinctly.

'I was born in Montreal but now live in Toronto. Closer to my friends. Most left Quebec years ago, but I stayed. Back then we didn't need French. Just enough to speak to our maids.'

Mrs Finney's French was good, but heavily accented.

'Mother.' Thomas reddened.

'I remember those days,' said Reine-Marie. 'My mother cleaned houses.'

Mrs Finney and Reine-Marie chatted about hard work and raising families, about the Quiet Revolution in the 1960s, when the Québécois finally became '*maîtres chez nous*'. Masters in their own house.

'Though my mother still cleaned the houses of the English in Westmount,' said Reine-Marie, organizing her cards. 'One no trump.'

Madame Finney beetled over to look, nodding approval. 'I hope her employers were kinder to her. I'm ashamed to say I had to learn that too. It was almost as hard as the subjunctive.'

'It was a remarkable time,' said Gamache. 'Thrilling for most French Canadians, but I know it came at a terrible price for the English.'

'We lost our children,' said Mrs Finney, moving round

the table to peer into his hand. 'They went away to find jobs in a language they could speak. You might have become masters, but we became foreigners, unwelcome in our own home. You're right. It was terrible.'

She tapped the ten of clubs in his hand, his highest card. Her voice was without sentiment or self-pity. But with, perhaps, a bit of reproach.

'Pass,' said Gamache. He was partnered with Sandra, and Reine-Marie was playing with Thomas.

'I leave Quebec,' said Thomas, who seemed to understand French better than he spoke it, which was certainly better than the other way round. 'Went far to university and settle on Toronto. Quebec hard.'

It was remarkable, thought Gamache, listening to Thomas. If you didn't speak French you'd swear he was bilingual, so perfect was his accent. But the content lacked a certain *je ne sais quoi*.

'Three no trump,' said Thomas.

His mother shook her head and tsked gently.

Thomas laughed. 'Ah, my mother's tongue.' Gamache smiled. He liked the man and suspected most people would.

'Did any of your children stay here?' Reine-Marie asked Madame Finney. The Gamaches at least had Annie living in Montreal, but she missed Daniel every day, and wondered how this woman, and so many others, had done it. No wonder they weren't always comfortable with the Québécois. If they felt they lost their children for the sake of a language. And without thanks. In fact, often just the opposite. There remained a lingering suspicion among the Québécois that the English were simply biding their time, waiting to enslave them again.

'One stayed. My other son.'

'Spot. He and his wife Claire are coming tomorrow,' said Thomas, switching to English. Gamache looked up from his hand, which held nothing of interest anyway, and stared at the man beside him.

Like his sister Julia's earlier in the evening, Thomas's tone had been light and breezy when speaking of the missing brother. But something was drifting about beneath.

He felt a slight stirring in the part of his brain he'd come to the Manoir to turn off.

It was Sandra's turn to bid. Gamache stared across the table at his partner.

Pass, pass, he willed. *I have nothing. We'll be slaughtered.*

He knew bridge was both a card game and an exercise in telepathy.

'Spot,' huffed Sandra. 'Typical. Comes at the last minute. Does only the minimum, never more. Four no trumps.'

Reine-Marie doubled.

'Sandra,' said Thomas with a laugh barely hiding the rebuke.

'What? Everyone else comes days ago to honour your father, and he shows up at the last minute. Horrible man.'

There was silence. Sandra's eyes darted from her hand to the plate of chocolates the maître d' had placed on their table.

Gamache glanced at Madame Finney, but she seemed oblivious of this conversation, though he suspected she missed nothing.

His gaze shifted to Monsieur Finney, sitting on a sofa. Finney's wild eye roamed the room and his hair stuck out at odd angles so that his head looked like a damaged sputnik, fallen too fast and too hard to earth. For a man being honoured he was strangely alone. Finney's eye came to rest on a huge original Krieghoff painting of a rustic scene hanging over the fireplace. Québécois peasants were loading a cart and at one of the cottages a robust woman was laughing and carrying a basket of food to the men.

It was a warm and inviting scene of family and village life hundreds of years earlier. And Finney seemed to prefer it to his family in the here and now.

Mariana got up and walked over to the group.

Thomas and Sandra pressed their cards to their chests. She picked up a *Châtelaine* magazine. 'According to a survey,' she read, 'most Canadians think bananas are the best fruit for chocolate fondue.'

There was silence again.

Mariana imagined her mother choking on the chocolate truffle she'd picked up.

'But that's ridiculous,' said Sandra, also watching Madame Finney eat. 'Strawberries are the best.'

'I've always liked pears and chocolate. Unusual, but a great combination, don't you think?' Thomas asked Reine-Marie, who said nothing.

'So this is where you got to. No one told me.' Julia stepped lightly through the French doors from the garden. 'What're you talking about?'

For some reason she looked at Gamache.

'Pass,' he said. He didn't really know what they were talking about any more.

'Magilla here thinks bananas are best with melted chocolate.' Thomas nodded to Mariana. This brought much hilarity and the Gamaches exchanged amused but befuddled looks.

'Don't the monks make blueberries in chocolate?' asked Julia. 'I'll have to get some before we leave.'

For the next few minutes the game was forgotten while they debated fruit and chocolate. Eventually both Julia and Mariana retired to their corners.

'Pass,' Thomas declared, his mind back on the game.

Let it go. Gamache stared across at Sandra and sent the message. *Please, pass*.

'I redouble.' Sandra glared at Thomas.

What we've got here, thought Gamache, is a failure to communicate.

'Really, what were you thinking?' Sandra asked, her plump lips pursing as she saw the cards Gamache laid down.

'*Oui*, Armand.' Reine-Marie smiled. 'Six no trumps with that hand? What were you thinking?'

Gamache rose and bowed slightly. 'My fault entirely.' He caught his wife's eye, his own deep brown eyes full of amusement.

Being dummy had its advantages. He stretched his legs, sipped his cognac and walked the room. It was growing hotter. Generally a Quebec evening cooled off, but not this night. He could feel the humidity closing in, and loosened his collar and tie.

'Very bold,' said Julia, coming up beside him as he stared again at the Krieghoff. 'Are you disrobing?'

'I'm afraid I've humiliated myself enough for one evening.' He nodded to the table where the three bridge players were engrossed.

He leaned in and sniffed the roses on the mantelpiece.

'Lovely, aren't they? Everything here is.' She sounded wistful, as though she was missing it already. Then he remembered Spot and thought maybe for the Finneys this was their last pleasant evening.

'Paradise lost,' he murmured.

'Pardon?'

'Nothing, just a thought.'

'You were wondering whether it's better to reign in hell than serve in heaven?' Julia asked, smiling. He laughed. Like her mother, she didn't miss much. 'Because, you know, I have the answer to that. This is the Eleanor rose,' she said with surprise, pointing to a bright pink bloom in the bouquet. 'Imagine that.'

'Someone mentioned it earlier this evening,' Gamache remembered.

'Thomas.'

'That's right. He wanted to know if you'd found one in the garden.'

'It's our little joke. It's named after Eleanor Roosevelt, you know.'

'I didn't.'

'Hmm,' said Julia, contemplating the rose and nodding. 'She said she'd been flattered at first until she'd read the description in the catalogue. Eleanor Roosevelt rose: no good in a bed, but fine up against a wall.'

They laughed and Gamache admired the rose and the quote, though he wondered why it was a family joke directed at Julia.

'More coffee?'

Julia startled.

Pierre stood at the door with a silver coffee pot. His question was said to the room in general, but he was looking at Julia and blushing slightly. Across the room Mariana

46

mumbled, 'Here we go.' Every time the maître d' was in the same room as Julia he blushed. She knew the signs. She'd lived with them her whole life. Mariana was the fun girl-next-door. The one to grope and kiss in the car. But Julia was the one they all wanted to marry, even the maître d'.

Now Mariana watched her sister and felt blood rushing to her face, but for a whole different reason. She watched Pierre pour the coffee and imagined the huge, framed Krieghoff sliding off the wall and smashing Julia in the head.

'Look what you've done to me, partner,' moaned Sandra, as Thomas took trick after trick. Finally they pushed back from the table and Thomas joined Gamache, who was looking at the other paintings in the room.

'That's a Brigite Normandin, isn't it?' Thomas asked.

'It is. Fantastic. Very bold, very modern. Complements the Molinari and the Riopelle. And yet they all work with the traditional Krieghoff.'

'You know your art,' said Thomas, slightly surprised.

'I love Quebec history,' said Gamache, nodding to the old scene.

'But that doesn't explain the others, does it?'

'Are you testing me, monsieur?' Gamache decided to push a little.

'Perhaps,' Thomas admitted. 'It's rare to find an auto-didact.'

'In captivity, anyway,' said Gamache and Thomas laughed. The painting they were staring at was muted, with lines of delicately shaded beiges.

'Feels like a desert,' said Gamache. 'Desolate.'

'Ah, but that's a misconception,' said Thomas.

'Here he goes,' said Mariana.

'Not that plant story,' said Julia, turning to Sandra. 'Is he still telling that?'

'Once a day, like Old Faithful. Stand back.'

'Well, time for bed,' said Madame Finney. Her husband unfolded himself from the sofa and the elderly couple left.

'Things aren't as they seem,' said Thomas, and Gamache looked at him, surprised. 'In the desert, I mean. It looks desolate but it's actually teeming with life. You just don't see it. It hides, for fear of being eaten. There's one plant in the South African desert called a stone plant. Can you guess how it survives?'

'Let's see. By pretending to be a stone?' asked Julia. Thomas shot her an angry look, then his face fell back to its attractive, easy expression.

'You haven't forgotten the story, I see.'

'I haven't forgotten anything, Thomas,' Julia said, and sat down. Gamache took it all in. The Finneys rarely spoke to each other, but when they did their words seemed laden, heavy with a meaning that escaped him.

Thomas hesitated, then turned back to Gamache who was longing for his bed, though mostly longing for this story to be over.

'It pretends to be a stone,' said Thomas, his eyes boring into Gamache. The large man stared back, suddenly aware there was a significance to what was being said. Something was being communicated to him. But what?

'In order to survive it must hide. Pretend to be something it isn't,' said Thomas.

'It's just a plant,' said Mariana. 'It doesn't do anything on purpose.'

'It's cunning,' said Julia. 'A survival instinct.'

'It's just a plant,' repeated Mariana. 'Don't be foolish.'

Ingenious, thought Gamache. It doesn't dare show itself for what it really is, for fear of being killed. What had Thomas just said?

Things aren't as they seem. He was beginning to believe it.

FOUR

—

'I enjoyed this evening,' said Reine-Marie, slipping into the cool, crisp sheets beside her husband.

'So did I.' He took off his half-moon reading glasses and folded his book onto the bed. It was a warm evening. Their tiny back room had only one window, onto the kitchen garden, so there wasn't much of a through draught, but the window was thrown open and the light cotton curtains were billowing slightly. The lamps on their bedside tables provided ponds of light and the rest was in darkness. It smelled of wood from the log walls and pine from the forest, and a hint of sweetness from the herb garden below.

'Two days' time and it's our anniversary,' said Reine-Marie. 'July first. Imagine, thirty-five years together. Were we so young?'

'I was. And innocent.'

'Poor boy. Did I scare you?'

'Maybe just a little. But I'm over it now.'

Reine-Marie leaned back on the pillow. 'Can't say I'm looking forward to meeting the missing Finneys tomorrow.'

'Spot and Claire. Spot must be a nickname.'

'Let's hope.'

Picking up his book he tried to focus, but his eyes were growing heavy, flickering as he strained to keep them open. He gave up the fight, realizing it wasn't one he could win or needed to. Kissing Reine-Marie, he burrowed into his pillow and fell asleep to the chorus of creatures outside and the scent of his wife beside him.

Pierre Patenaude stood at the door of the kitchen. It was clean and orderly, everything in its place. The glasses lined up, the silverware in its sleeves, the bone china carefully stacked with fine tissue between each plate. He'd learned that from his mother. She'd taught him that order was freedom. To live in chaos was to live in a prison. Order freed the mind for other things.

From his father he'd learned leadership. On rare days off school he'd been allowed to go to the office. He'd sat on his father's lap, smelling cologne and tobacco, while his father made phone calls. Even as a child Pierre knew he was being groomed. Trimmed and shaped, buffed and burnished.

Would his father be disappointed in him? Being just a maître d'? But he thought not. His father had wanted only one thing for him. To be happy.

He turned out the light and walked through the empty dining room and into the garden to look once again at the marble cube.

Mariana unwrapped herself, veil after veil, humming. Every now and then she looked over to the single bed next to hers. Bean was either asleep or pretending to be.

'Bean?' she whispered. 'Bean, kiss Mommy goodnight.'

The child was silent. Though the room itself wasn't. Clocks filled almost every surface. Ticking clocks and digital clocks, electric clocks and wind-up ones. All set to go off at seven a.m. All moving towards that time, as they had every morning for months. There seemed to be more of them than ever.

Mariana wondered if it had gone too far. Whether she should do something. Surely it wasn't normal for a ten year old to do this? What had started as one alarm clock a year ago had blossomed and spread like an invasive weed until Bean's room at home was choked with them. The riot each morning was beyond belief. From her own bedroom she could hear her strange child clicking them all off, until the last tinny call to the day was silenced.

Surely this wasn't normal?

But then so much about Bean wasn't normal. To call in a psychologist now, well, it felt a bit like trying to outrun a tidal wave of odd, thought Mariana. She lifted Bean's hand off the book and smiled as she laid it on the floor. It'd been her own favourite book as a child and she wondered which story Bean liked the most. Ulysses? Pandora? Hercules?

Leaning down to kiss Bean Mariana noticed the chandelier and its old corded electrical wire. In her mind she saw a spark leap in a brilliant arc onto the bedding, smouldering at first then bursting into flames as they slept.

She stepped back, closed her eyes, and placed the invisible wall round Bean.

There, safe.

She turned off the light and lay in bed, her body feeling sticky and flabby. The closer she got to her mother the heavier her body felt, as though her mother had her own atmosphere and gravity. Tomorrow Spot would arrive, and it would begin. And end.

She tried to get comfortable, but the night was close and the covers collapsed and stuck to her. She kicked them off. But what really stood between her and sleep wasn't the stinking heat, the snoring child, the clinging bedclothes.

It was a banana.

Why did they always goad her? And why, at the age of forty-seven, did she still care?

She turned over, trying to find a cool place on the now damp bedding.

Banana. And she heard again their laughter. And saw their mocking looks.

Let it go, she begged herself. She closed her eyes and tried to ignore the banana and the clocks tsk, tsk, tsking in her head.

Julia Martin sat at the vanity and took off her single string of pearls. Simple, elegant, a gift from her father for her eighteenth birthday.

'A lady is always understated, Julia,' he'd said. 'A lady never shows off. She always puts others at ease. Remember that.'

And she had. As soon as he'd said it she knew the truth of it. And all the stumbling and bumbling she'd done, all the uncertainties and solitude of her teen years, had fallen away. Ahead of her stretched a clear path. Narrow, yes, but clear. The relief she felt was absolute. She had a purpose, a direction. She knew who she was and what she had to do. Put others at ease.

As she undressed she went over the events of the day,

making a list of all the people she might have hurt, all the people who might dislike her because of her words, her inflection, her manner.

And she thought of the nice French man and their conversation in the garden. He'd seen her smoking. What must he think of her? And then she'd flirted with the young waiter and accepted a drink. Drinking, smoking, flirting.

God, he must think she was shallow and weak.

She'd do better tomorrow.

She coiled the strand of pearls, like a young snake, onto its soft blue velvet bed then took off her earrings, wishing she could also remove her ears. But she knew it was too late.

The Eleanor rose. Why did they do it? After all these years, when she was trying to be nice, why bring up the rose again?

Let it go, she begged herself, it doesn't matter. It was a joke. That's all.

But the words had already coiled themselves inside her and wouldn't leave.

Next door, in the Lake Room, Sandra stood on their balcony surrounded by the wild stars and wondered how they could get the best table for breakfast. She was tired of being served last, always having to insist and even then getting the smallest portions, she was sure of it.

And that Armand, worst bridge player she'd ever seen. Why'd she been paired with him? The staff fawned over him and his wife, probably because they were French. It wasn't fair. They were staying in that broom closet at the back of the Manoir, the cheapest room. A shopkeeper almost certainly and his cleaning woman wife. Didn't seem right to have to share the Manoir with them. Still, she'd been courteous. They couldn't ask for more.

Sandra was hungry. And angry. And tired. And tomorrow Spot would arrive and it would get even worse.

From inside their splendid room, Thomas looked at his wife's rigid back.

He'd married a beautiful woman and still, from a distance and from the back, she was lovely.

But somehow, recently, her head seemed to have expanded and the rest shrunk, so that he had the impression he was now attached to a flotation device, deflated. Orange and soft and squishy and no longer doing its job.

Swiftly, while Sandra's back was turned, he took off the old cufflinks his father had given him on his eighteenth birthday.

'My own father gave me these, and now it's time to pass them to you,' his father had said. Thomas had taken the cufflinks, and the weary velvet pouch they came in, and shoved them into his pocket in a cavalier move he'd hoped would wound his father. And he could tell it had.

His father never gave him anything again. Nothing.

He quickly peeled off the old jacket and shirt, thankful no one had noticed the slight wear on the cuffs. Now Sandra was coming through the door. He casually tossed the shirt and jacket onto a nearby chair.

'I didn't appreciate your contradicting me over bridge,' she said.

'I did?'

'Of course you did. In front of your family and that couple, the shopkeeper and his cleaning woman wife.'

'It was her mother who cleaned houses,' Thomas corrected her.

'There, you see. Can't you just let me say something without correcting me?'

'You want to be wrong?'

It was a path worn through their marriage.

'All right, what did I say?' he finally asked.

'You know very well what you said. You said pears went best with melted chocolate.'

'That's it? Pears?'

He made it sound stupid but Sandra knew it wasn't. She knew it was important. Vital.

'Yes, pears. I said strawberries and you said pears.'

It was actually beginning to sound trivial to her. That wasn't good.

'But that's what I think,' he said.

'Come on, you can't tell me you even have an opinion.'

All this talk of warm chocolate dripping off fresh strawberries, or even pears, was making her collagen-filled mouth water. She looked around for the tiny chocolates hotels put on pillows. Her side of the bed, his side, the pillows, the night table. She ran to the bathroom. Nothing. Staring at the sink, she wondered how many calories there were in toothpaste.

Nothing. Nothing to eat. She looked down at her cuticles, but she was saving those for an emergency. Returning to the room she looked at his frayed cuffs and wondered how they'd frayed. Surely not by repeated touch.

'You humiliated me in front of everyone,' she said, transferring her hunger to eat into a hunger to hurt. He didn't turn round. She knew she should let it go, but it was too late. She'd chewed the insult over, torn it apart and swallowed it. The insult was part of her now.

'Why do you always do it? And over a pear? Why couldn't you just agree with me for once?'

She'd eaten twigs and berries and goddamned grasses for two months and lost fifteen pounds for only one reason. So that his family would say how lovely and slim she looked, and then maybe Thomas would notice. Maybe he'd believe it. Maybe he'd touch her. Just touch her. Not even make love. Just touch her.

She was starved for it.

Irene Finney looked into the mirror and lifted her hand. She brought the soapy cloth close, then stopped.

Spot would be there tomorrow. And then they'd all be together. The four children, the four corners of her world.

Irene Finney, like many very elderly people, knew that the world was indeed flat. It had a beginning and an end. And she had come to the edge.

There was only one more thing to do. Tomorrow.

Irene Finney stared at her reflection. She brought the cloth up and scrubbed. In the next room Bert Finney gripped the bed sheets listening to his wife's stifled sobs as she removed her face.

Armand Gamache awoke to young sun pouring through the still curtains, hitting their squirrelled-up bedding and his perspiring body. The sheets were kicked into a wet ball on the very end of the bed. Beside him Reine-Marie roused.

'What time is it?' she asked sleepily.

'Six thirty.'

'In the morning?' She got up on one elbow. He nodded

and smiled. 'And it's already this hot?' He nodded again. 'It's going to be a killer.'

'That's what Pierre said last night. Heat wave.'

'I finally figured out why they call it a wave,' said Reine-Marie, tracing a line down his wet arm. 'I need a shower.'

'I have a better idea.'

Within minutes they were on the dock, kicking off their sandals and dropping their towels like nests onto the warm wooden surface. Gamache and Reine-Marie looked onto this world of two suns, two skies, of mountains and forests multiplied. The lake wasn't glass, it was a mirror. A bird gliding across the clear sky appeared on the tranquil water as well. It was a world so perfect it broke into two. Hummingbirds buzzed in the garden and monarch butterflies bobbed from flower to flower. A couple of dragonflies clicked around the dock. Reine-Marie and Gamache were the only people in the world.

'You first,' said Reine-Marie. She loved to watch this. So did their kids when they were younger.

He smiled, bent his knees and thrust his body off the solid dock and into mid-air. He seemed to hover there for a moment, his arms outstretched as though he expected to reach the far shore. It seemed more of a launch than a dive. And then, of course, came the inevitable, since Armand Gamache couldn't in fact fly. He hit the water with a gargantuan splash. It was cool enough to take his breath for that first instant, but by the time he popped up, he was refreshed and alert.

Reine-Marie watched as he flicked his head around to rid his phantom hair of the lake water, as he'd done the first time they'd visited. And for years after that, until there was no longer any need. But still he did it, and still she watched, and still it stopped her heart.

'Come on in,' he called, and watched as she dived, graceful, though her legs always parted and she'd never mastered the toe-point, so there was always a fin of bubbles as her feet slapped the water. He waited to see her emerge, face to the sun, hair gleaming.

'Was there a splash?' she asked, treading water as the waves headed into the shore.

'Like a knife you went in. I barely even knew you dived.'

'There, breakfast time,' said Reine-Marie ten minutes later as they hauled themselves up the ladder back onto the dock.

Gamache handed her a sun-warmed towel. 'What'll you have?'

They walked back describing for each other impossible amounts of food they'd eat. At the Manoir he stopped and took her off to the side.

'I want to show you something.'

She smiled. 'I've already seen it.'

'Not this,' he chuckled and then stopped. They were no longer alone. There, at the side of the Manoir, someone was hunched over, digging. The movement stopped and slowly the figure turned to face them.

It was a young woman, covered in dirt.

'Oh, hello.' She seemed more startled than they. So startled she spoke in English rather than the traditional French of the Manoir.

'Hello.' Reine-Marie smiled reassuringly, speaking English back.

'*Désolée*,' the young woman said, smearing more dirt onto

her perspiring face. It turned to mud instantly, so that she looked a little like a clay sculpture, animated. 'I didn't think anyone was up yet. It's the best time to work. I'm one of the gardeners.'

She'd switched to French and she spoke easily with only a slight accent. A whiff of something sweet, chemical, and familiar came their way. Bug spray. Their companion was doused in it. The scents of a Quebec summer. Cut grass and bug repellent.

Gamache and Reine-Marie looked down and noticed holes in the ground. She followed their gaze.

'I'm trying to transplant all those before it gets too hot.' She waved to a few drooping plants. 'For some reason all the flowers in this bed're dying.'

'What's that?' Reine-Marie was no longer looking at the holes.

'That's what I wanted to show you,' said Gamache.

There, off to the side and slightly hidden by the woods, was the huge marble cube. At least now there was someone to ask.

'Not a clue,' was the gardener's answer to his question. 'A huge truck dropped it here a couple of days ago.'

'What is it?' Reine-Marie touched it.

'It's marble,' said the gardener, joining them as they stared.

'Well here we are,' said Reine-Marie eventually, 'at the Manoir Bellechasse, surrounded by woods and lakes and gardens and you and I,' she took her husband's hand, 'are staring at the one unnatural thing for miles around.'

He laughed. 'What are the chances?'

They nodded to the gardener and returned to the Manoir to change for breakfast. But Gamache found it interesting that Reine-Marie had the same reaction to the marble cube he'd had the night before. Whatever it was, it was unnatural.

The *terrasse* was mottled with shade and not yet scorching hot, though by noon the stones would be like coals. Both Reine-Marie and Gamache wore their floppy sun hats.

Elliot brought their *café au lait* and breakfasts. Reine-Marie poured Eastern Townships maple syrup onto her wild blueberry crêpe and Gamache speared his eggs Benedict, watching the yolk mix with the hollandaise sauce. By now the *terrasse* was filling with Finneys.

'It doesn't really matter,' they heard a woman's voice behind them, 'but if we could have the nice table under the maple tree that would be great.'

'I believe it's already taken, madame,' said Pierre.

'Oh really? Well, it doesn't matter.'

Bert Finney was already down, as was Bean. They both read the paper. He had the comics while Bean read the obituaries.

'You look worried, Bean,' the old man said, lowering the comics.

'Have you noticed that more people seem to be dying than are being born?' Bean asked, handing the section to Finney, who took it and nodded solemnly.

'That means there's more for those of us still here.' He handed the section back.

'I don't want more,' said Bean.

'You will.' And Finney raised the cartoons.

'Armand.' Reine-Marie laid a soft hand on his arm. She lowered her voice to a barely audible whisper. 'Is Bean a boy or girl?'

61

Gamache, who'd been mildly wondering the same thing, looked again. The child wore what looked like drugstore glasses and had shoulder-length blond hair around a lovely tanned face.

He shook his head.

'Reminds me of Florence,' he said. 'I took her up and down boulevard Laurier last time they visited and almost everyone commented on our handsome grandson.'

'Was she wearing her sun bonnet?'

'She was.'

'And did they comment on the resemblance?'

'They did, as a matter of fact.' Gamache looked at her as though she was a genius, his brown eyes wide with admiration.

'Imagine that,' she said. 'But Florence is just over a year. How old would you say Bean is?'

'Hard to say. Nine, ten? Any child reading the obituaries looks older.'

'Obituaries are ageing. I'll have to remember that.'

'More jam?' Pierre replaced their near empty containers with fresh jars of home-made wild strawberry, raspberry and blueberry *confitures*. 'Can I get you anything?' he asked.

'Well, I do have a question,' said Gamache and tilted his croissant towards the corner of the Manoir. 'There's a block of marble over there, Pierre. What's it for?'

'Ah, you noticed.'

'Astronauts would notice.'

Pierre nodded. 'Madame Dubois didn't say anything when you checked in?'

Reine-Marie and Gamache exchanged glances and shook their heads.

'Oh well.' The maître d' looked a little embarrassed. 'I'm afraid you'll have to ask her. It's a surprise.'

'A nice surprise?' asked Reine-Marie.

Pierre thought about it. 'We're not really sure. But we'll know soon.'

FIVE

—

After breakfast Gamache placed a call to his son in Paris and left a message with the number for the Manoir. Cell phones didn't work this deep into the woods.

The day meandered along pleasantly, the temperature slowly and inexorably climbing until before they realized it it was very hot indeed. Workers dragged Adirondack chairs and chaises longues about the lawns and gardens, seeking shade for their baking guests.

'Spot!'

The shout cut through the humid noon hour and into Armand Gamache's repose.

'Spot!'

'Strange,' said Reine-Marie, taking off her sunglasses to look at her husband, 'it's said with the same inflection you'd yell "Fire!".'

Gamache stuck his finger in his book and looked in the direction of the shout. He was curious to see what a 'Spot' looked like. Did he have floppy ears? Was he actually spotted?

Thomas was calling 'Spot!' and walking swiftly across the

lawn towards a well-dressed tall man with grey hair. Gamache took his sunglasses off and stared more closely.

'This is the end of our peace and quiet, I imagine,' said Reine-Marie, with regret. 'The odious Spot and his even more wretched wife Claire have materialized.'

Gamache put his glasses back on and squinted through them, not really believing what he was seeing.

'What is it?' Reine-Marie asked.

'You'll never guess.'

Two tall figures were converging on the lawn of the Manoir Bellechasse. Distinguished Thomas and his younger brother Spot.

Reine-Marie looked over. 'But that's—'

'I think it is,' he said.

'So where's—' Reine-Marie was flabbergasted.

'I don't know. Oh, there she comes.'

A rumpled figure appeared round the corner of the Manoir, a sun hat imperfectly screwed to her flyaway hair.

'Clara?' whispered Reine-Marie to Gamache. 'My God, Armand, Spot and Claire Finney are Peter and Clara Morrow. It's like a miracle.' She was delighted. The blight that had appeared imminent and unstoppable had turned into their friends.

Now Sandra was greeting Peter and Thomas embraced Clara. She was tiny in his arms and almost disappeared and when she pulled back she was even more dishevelled.

'You look wonderful,' Sandra said, eyeing Clara and happy to see she'd put on weight around her hips and thighs. And was wearing unbecoming striped shorts with a polka-dotted top. And she calls herself an artist, thought Sandra, feeling much better.

'I feel good. And you've lost weight. My God, Sandra, you have to tell me how you did it. I'd love to lose ten pounds.'

'You?' exclaimed Sandra. 'Never.'

The two women walked arm in arm out of the Gamaches' hearing.

'Peter,' said Thomas.

'Thomas,' said Peter.

They nodded brusquely to each other.

'Life good?'

'Never better.'

They spoke in semaphore, all punctuation unnecessary.

'You?'

'Great.'

They'd trimmed the language to its essentials. Before long it would just be consonants. Then silence.

From the dappled shade Armand Gamache watched. He knew he should be delighted to see their old friends, and he was. But looking down he noticed the hairs on his forearms sticking up, and felt a whispered cold breath.

On this shimmering hot summer day, in this pristine and tranquil setting, things were not as they seemed.

Clara made for the stone wall of the *terrasse*, carrying a beer and a tomato sandwich which dripped seeds, unseen, onto her new cotton blouse. She tried to fade into the shade, which wasn't difficult since Peter's family paid little attention to her anyway. She was the daughter-in-law, the sister-in-law, nothing more. At first it had been annoying, but now she found it a great advantage.

She looked out into the perennial garden and noticed if she squinted just so she could believe herself back home in

66

their little village of Three Pines. It wasn't actually all that far away. Just over the mountain range. But it seemed very distant indeed just now.

Each summer morning at home she'd pour a cup of coffee then walk barefoot down to the Rivière Bella Bella behind their house, sniffing roses and phlox and lilies as she passed. Sitting on a bench in the soft sun she'd sip her coffee and stare into the gently flowing river, mesmerized by the water, glowing gold and silver in the sunshine. Then she'd go into her studio and paint until mid-afternoon. Then she and Peter would get a beer and walk the garden, or join friends at the bistro for a glass of wine. It was a quiet, uneventful life. It suited them.

But one morning a few weeks earlier she'd gone as usual to check their mailbox. And there she'd found the dreaded invitation. The rusty door had shrieked as she'd opened it, and sticking her hand inside she'd known even before she'd seen it what was inside. She could feel the heavy vellum of the envelope. She'd been tempted to just throw it away, toss it in the blue recycling box so it could be turned into something useful, like toilet paper. But she hadn't. Instead she'd stared at the spider writing, the ominous scrawl that made her skin feel as if ants were crawling all over her, until she couldn't stand it any longer. She'd ripped it open, and inside was the invitation to the family reunion at the Manoir Bellechasse at the end of June. A month ahead of normal and just when Three Pines was taking down the Saint-Jean-Baptiste flags and preparing the annual July first Canada Day celebrations on the village green. It was the worst possible timing and she was about to try to get out of it when she remembered she was supposed to organize the children's games this year. Clara, who got along with children by pretending they were puppies, was suddenly conflicted and decided she'd leave it up to Peter. But there was something else included in the invitation. Something else would happen while they were all there. When Peter came out of his studio that afternoon she'd handed him the envelope and watched his handsome face. This face she loved, this man she longed to protect. And could, against most things. But not his family. They attacked from within, and she couldn't help him there. She saw his face, uncomprehending at first, and then he understood.

It was going to be bad. And yet, to her surprise, he'd picked up the phone and called his mother, and accepted the wretched invitation.

That was a few weeks ago, and now, suddenly, it was upon them.

Clara sat alone on the wall and watched as the rest of them sipped gin and tonics in the blinding sun. None wore sun hats, preferring sunstroke and skin cancer to spectacle. Peter stood talking to his mother, his hand to his brow to block out the sun, as though in a permanent salute.

Thomas looked regal and elegant while Sandra looked alert. Her eyes darted here and there, assessing portions, watching the weaving waiters, monitoring who got what when and how it compared to hers.

On the other side of the *terrasse*, also in the shade, Clara could just see Bert Finney. He seemed to be watching his wife, though it was hard to tell. She looked away just as his pilgrim eye caught hers.

Sipping her cool drink she grabbed a handful of thick hair, wet with perspiration, and peeled it off her neck. Then she flapped it up and down, to air out the area. Only then did she notice Peter's mother watching, her faded pink and white face crinkled and lovely, her Wedgwood eyes thoughtful and kind. A beautiful English rose inviting you to approach, to bend closer. Too late you'd realize there was a wasp buried deep, waiting to do what wasps do best.

Less than twenty-four hours, she said to herself. *We can leave after breakfast tomorrow.*

A deerfly buzzed around her sweating head and Clara waved her arms so wildly she knocked the rest of her sandwich off the stone wall and into the perennial bed below. The answer to an ant's prayers, except the ones it fell on.

'Claire hasn't changed,' said Peter's mother.

'Neither have you, Mother.'

Peter tried to keep his voice as civil as hers, and felt he'd achieved that perfect balance of courtesy and contempt. So subtle it was impossible to challenge, so obvious it was impossible to miss.

Across the scorching *terrasse* Julia felt her feet begin to burn in their thin sandals on the hot stones.

'Hello, Peter.' She closed her mind to her smouldering feet and crossed the *terrasse*, air-kissing her younger brother. 'You're looking good.'

'So're you.'

Pause.

'Nice weather,' he said.

Julia searched her rapidly emptying brain for something smart to say, something witty and intelligent. Something to prove she was happy. That her life wasn't the shambles she knew he thought it was. Silently she repeated to herself, *Peter's perpetually purple pimple popped.* It helped.

'How's David?' Peter asked.

'Oh, you know him,' said Julia lightly. 'He adjusts to anything.'

'Even prison? And here you are.'

She searched his placid handsome face. Was that an insult? She'd been away from the family so long she was out of practice. She felt like a long retired parachutist suddenly tossed out of a plane.

Four days ago, when she'd arrived, she'd been hurt and exhausted. The last smile, the last empty compliment, the last courtesy wrung from her in the disaster that had been the last year, during David's trial. Feeling betrayed, humiliated and exposed, she'd come back home to heal. To this cosy mother and the tall, handsome brothers of her magical, mystical memory. Surely they'd take care of her.

Somehow she'd forgotten why she'd left them in the first place. But now she was back and was remembering.

'Imagine,' said Thomas, 'your husband stealing all that money, and you not knowing. It must have been horrible.'

'Thomas,' said his mother, shaking her head slightly. Not in rebuke for the insult to Julia but for saying it in front of the staff. Julia felt the hot stones sizzling beneath her feet. But she smiled and held her ground.

'Your father,' Mrs Finney began, then stopped.

'Go on, Mother,' said Julia, feeling something old and familiar swish its tail deep inside her. Something decades dormant was stirring. 'My father?'

'Well, you know how he felt.'

'How did he feel?'

'Really, Julia, this is an inappropriate conversation.' Her mother turned her pink face to her. It was said with the tender smile, the slight flutter of those hands. How long had it been since she'd felt her mother's hands?

'I'm sorry,' said Julia.

'Jump, Bean, jump!'

Clara turned and watched as Peter's youngest sister leapt across the manicured lawn, feet barely touching the ground, and behind her ran Bean, beach towel tied at the neck, laughing. But not jumping. Good ol' Bean, thought Clara.

'Whew,' puffed Mariana, stepping onto the *terrasse* moments later, sweat pouring off her as though she'd run through a sprinkler. She took a corner of a scarf and wiped her eyes. 'Did Bean jump?' she asked the family. Only Thomas reacted, with a dismissive smirk.

Clara's bra itched in the heat and humidity. She reached down and tugged it. Too late, she looked over. Peter's mother was again watching, as though equipped with a special radar.

'How's your art?'

The question took Clara by surprise. She'd assumed it to be directed at Peter, and had occupied herself by trying to pick off the tomato seeds now baked to her breasts.

'Me?' She looked up into Julia's face. The sister she knew the least. But she'd heard the stories from Peter and was quick to put up her guard. 'Oh, you know. Always a struggle.'

It was the easy answer, the one they expected. Clara the failure, who called herself an artist but never sold. Who did ridiculous works like mannequins with bouffant hair and melting trees.

'I remember hearing about your last show. Quite a statement.'

Clara sat up straighter. She knew many people managed to ask the first, polite question. But it was the rare person who asked a second.

Perhaps Julia was sincere.

'Warrior Uteruses, wasn't it?' asked Julia. Clara searched her face for ridicule but found none.

Clara nodded. True, by economic measurements the series couldn't be considered a success, but emotionally it had been a triumph. She'd considered giving a Warrior Uterus to Peter's mother as a Christmas gift, but decided that might be a step too far.

'Didn't we tell you?' Peter walked over, smiling. Never a good sign at a family reunion. The more devious they got the more they smiled. Clara tried to catch his eye.

'Tell us what?' Sandra asked, sensing something unpleasant approaching.

'About Clara's art.'

'I'd like another beer,' said Clara. No one paid any attention.

'What about it?' asked Thomas.

'Nothing,' said Clara. 'Just lots of crap. You know me. Always experimenting.'

'She's been approached by a gallery.'

'Peter,' Clara snapped. 'I don't think we need to talk about it.'

'But I'm sure they'd like to hear,' said Peter. He took his hand out of his slacks pocket and it turned inside out, marring his otherwise perfect appearance.

'Clara's modest. The Galerie Fortin in Montreal wants to do a one-woman show. Denis Fortin himself came to Three Pines to see her work.'

Silence.

Clara's nails dug into her palms. A deerfly found the tender pale skin behind her ear, and bit.

72

'Marvellous,' said Peter's mother to Clara. 'I'm absolutely delighted.'

Clara, surprised, turned to her mother-in-law. She could barely believe her ears. Had she been too harsh all this time? Judged Peter's mother unfairly?

'So often they're too thick.'

Clara's smile faltered. Too thick?

'And not made with real mayonnaise. But Chef Véronique has outdone herself again. Have you tried the cucumber sandwiches, Claire? They're really very good.'

'They are good,' agreed Clara with maniacal enthusiasm.

'Congratulations, Clara. What good news.' The voice was masculine, jovial and vaguely familiar. '*Félicitations.*'

Across the lawn a powerfully built middle-aged man in a funny hat took easy strides towards them. Beside him was a small, elegant woman wearing the same floppy sun hat.

'Reine-Marie?' Clara peered, hardly believing her eyes. 'Peter, is that Reine-Marie?'

Peter was staring almost slack-jawed as the couple hurried up the steps.

'Oh, Clara, what wonderful news,' said Reine-Marie, taking her friend in her arms. Clara smelled Joy, the fragrance by Jean Patou, and felt the same way. It was like being saved from torture at the last moment. She pulled back from the embrace and stared at Reine-Marie Gamache, to make certain. Sure enough, the smiling woman was there. Clara could still feel the glares behind her, but it didn't matter as much. Not now.

Then Armand kissed her on both cheeks and squeezed her arm affectionately. 'We're thrilled for you. And Denis Fortin.' He looked into the fieldstone faces on the *terrasse*.

'He's the top art dealer in Montreal, as you probably know. A real coup.'

'Really?' Peter's mother managed to sound both dismissive and disapproving. As though Clara's coup was unseemly. And certainly this display of emotion, of elation, was unseemly. This was a rude interruption of a private family affair. And, perhaps worst of all, unmistakable evidence that Peter socialized with the people from the broom closet. It was one thing to play bridge when stuck in a remote lodge with them. That was simply being well bred. But it was quite another thing to choose their company.

Gamache walked over to Peter and shook his hand. 'Hello, old son.'

Gamache was smiling and Peter stared as though at something extraordinary.

'Armand? But how in the world did you come to be here?'

'Well, it is an inn after all.' Gamache laughed. 'We're here celebrating our anniversary.'

'Oh, thank God,' said Clara and stepped towards Reine-Marie. Peter also made to move towards them but the clearing of a small throat behind him stopped his progress.

'Perhaps we can talk later,' suggested Reine-Marie. 'You need time with your charming family.' She gave Clara another quick hug. Clara was reluctant to let go, but did, and watched as the Gamaches strolled across the lawn towards the lake. She felt a trickle down her neck. Reaching up to wipe the sweat away she was surprised to see blood on her fingers.

SIX

~

Finally, after a luncheon that lasted a thousand years, Clara was able to get away, and the first thing she wanted to do was go on the hunt for the Gamaches.

'I think Mother would prefer us to stay here.' Peter hovered on the stone *terrasse*.

'Come on.' She gave him a conspiratorial look and held out her hand. 'Be daring.'

'But it's a family reunion.' Peter longed to go with her. To take her hand and race across the perfect lawn, and find their friends. Over lunch, while the rest of the family either ate in silence or discussed the stock market, Peter and Clara had whispered urgently and excitedly about the Gamaches.

'You should've seen your face,' said Peter, trying to keep his voice down. 'You looked like Dorothy meeting the Great and Powerful Oz. All stunned and excited.'

'I think you're spending way too much time with Olivier and Gabri,' said Clara, smiling. She'd never actually smiled at a family reunion before. It felt odd. 'Besides, you looked like the Tin Man, all stunned. Can you believe the Gamaches are here? Can we sneak away and spend some time with them this afternoon?'

'I don't see why not,' said Peter, hiding behind a warm bun. The prospect of killing a few hours with their friends instead of enduring the family was a great relief.

Clara had looked at her watch. Two p.m. Twenty more hours. If she went to bed at eleven and woke up at nine tomorrow morning that would leave just – she tried to work it out in her head – eleven more waking hours with Peter's family. She could just about make it. And two hours with the Gamaches, that left just nine hours. Dear Lord, she could almost see the end coming. Then they could return to their little village of Three Pines, until another invitation arrived, next year.

Don't think about that.

But now Peter hesitated on the *terrasse*, as she secretly knew he would. Even over lunch she'd known he couldn't do it. Still, it had been fun to pretend. Like playing emotional dress-up. Pretending to be the brave one this time.

But in the end, of course, he couldn't do it. And Clara couldn't leave him. And so she walked slowly back inside.

'Why'd you tell your family about my solo show?' she asked Peter, and wondered if she was trying to pick a fight with him. To punish him for making them stay.

'I thought they should know. They're always so dismissive of your work.'

'And you're not?' She was pissed off.

'How can you say that?' He looked hurt, and she knew she'd said it to wound. She waited for him to point out that he'd supported her all these years. He'd put a roof over their heads and bought the food. But he stayed silent, which annoyed her even more.

As he turned to face her she noticed a small dot of whipped cream, like a whitehead, on his cheek. It might as well have been an aeroplane, so odd was it to see anything unplanned attached to her husband. He was always so splendid, so beautifully turned out. His clothes never wrinkled, the creases crisp, never a stain nor a fault. What was that thing on *Star Trek*? The tractor beam? No, not that. The shields. Peter went through life with his shields raised, repulsing attack by food or beverage, or people. Clara wondered whether there was a tiny Scottish voice in his head right now screaming, *'Cap'n, the shields are down. I canna git them up.'*

But Peter, dear Peter, was oblivious of the small, fluffy, white alien attached to his face.

She knew she should say something, or at least wipe it off, but she was fed up.

'What's wrong?' Peter asked, looking both concerned and a little afraid. Confrontation petrified him.

'You told your family about the Fortin gallery to annoy them. Especially Thomas. It had nothing to do with me. You used my art as a weapon.'

Cap'n, she's breakin' up.

'How can you say that?'

But he sounded unsure, something else she rarely heard.

'Please don't talk about my art with them again. In fact, don't mention anything personal at all. They don't care and it just hurts me. Probably shouldn't, but it does. Can you do that?'

She noticed his slacks pocket was still inside out. It was one of the most disconcerting things she'd ever seen.

'I'm sorry,' he finally said. 'But it wasn't Thomas, you know. Not any more. I think I've grown used to him. It was Julia. Seeing her again has thrown me.'

'She seems nice enough.'

'We all do.'

'Twenty more hours,' said Clara, looking at her watch then reaching up and rubbing the whipped cream off his face.

On their way up the footpath the Gamaches heard a voice calling to them, and stopped.

'There you are,' puffed Madame Dubois, holding a basket of herbs from the garden. 'I left a note at the front desk. Your son called from Paris. Said he'd be out this evening, but he'll try again.'

'*Quel dommage*,' said Gamache. 'We'll connect eventually. *Merci*. May I carry that?' He put out his hand for the basket and after a small hesitation the innkeeper handed it to him gratefully.

'It is getting hot,' she said, 'and I find the humidity wearying.' She turned and started up the path at a pace that flabbergasted the Gamaches.

'Madame Dubois.' Gamache found himself chasing after a woman in her mid-120s. 'We have a question.'

She stopped and waited for him.

'We were wondering about the marble cube.'

'What marble cube?'

'Pardon?' he said.

'Pardon?' said Madame Dubois.

'That big box of marble down there, on the other side of the Manoir. I saw it last night and then again this morning. Your young gardener doesn't know what it's for and Pierre told us to ask you.'

'Ah, *oui*, that marble box,' she said as if there were others.

78

'Well, we're very lucky. We're . . .' and she mumbled something then headed off.

'I didn't hear what you said.'

'Oh. All right.' She behaved as though they'd tortured her for the information. 'It's for a statue.'

'A statue? Really?' Reine-Marie asked. 'Of what?'

'Of Madame Finney's husband.'

Armand Gamache saw Bert Finney in marble in the middle of their beloved gardens at Manoir Bellechasse. Forever. His wretched face etched in stone and watching them, or God knows what, for eternity.

Their faces must have alerted Madame Dubois.

'Not this one, of course. The first one. Charles Morrow. I knew him, you know. A fine man.'

The Gamaches, who really hadn't given it much thought, suddenly understood a great deal. How Spot Finney had become Peter Morrow. His mother had married again. She'd gone from Morrow to Finney, but no one else had. In their minds they'd been thinking of them all as Finneys, but they weren't. They were Morrows.

That might explain, at least in part, how a reunion to celebrate Father seemed to ignore Bert Finney.

'Charles Morrow died quite a few years ago,' Clementine Dubois continued. 'Heart. The family's holding a little unveiling later this afternoon, just before the cocktail hour. The statue's arriving in about an hour. He'll make a wonderful addition to the garden.'

She looked at them furtively.

By the size of the marble pedestal the statue would be enormous, Gamache guessed. Taller than some of the trees,

79

though happily the trees would grow and presumably the statue wouldn't.

'Have you seen the sculpture?' Gamache asked, trying to make it sound casual.

'Oh, yes. Enormous thing. Naked, of course, with flowers around his head and little wings. They were fortunate to find red marble.'

Gamache's eyes widened and brows rose. Then he caught her smile.

'You wretched woman,' he laughed, and she chuckled.

'Do you think I'd do that to you? I love this place,' Madame Dubois said, as they walked her the rest of the way back to the swinging screen door into the cool Manoir. 'But it's getting so expensive to run. We needed a new furnace this year, and the roof will soon need redoing.'

The Gamaches tilted their heads back to look at the copper roof, oxidized green over time. Even looking at it gave Gamache vertigo. He'd never make a roofer.

'I've spoken to an Abinaki craftsman about doing the work. You know it was the Abinaki who built the Manoir to begin with?'

'No, I didn't,' said Gamache, who loved Quebec history. 'I assumed it was done by the Robber Barons.'

'Paid for by them, but built by the natives and the Québécois. Used to be a hunting and fishing lodge. When my husband and I bought it fifty years ago it was abandoned. The attic was filled with stuffed heads. Looked like an abattoir. Disgraceful.'

'You were wise to accept the Finneys' proposal.' He smiled. 'And their money. Better to have Charles Morrow in the garden and the repairs done than lose everything.'

'Let's hope he isn't naked. I haven't seen the statue.'

The Gamaches watched as she walked towards the kitchen.

'Well, at least the birds'll have one more thing to perch on,' said Gamache.

'At least,' said Reine-Marie.

The Gamaches found Peter and Clara on the wharf when they went down for a swim.

'Now, tell us what's been happening in your lives, starting with Denis Fortin and your art.' Reine-Marie patted the Adirondack chair. 'And don't leave out a thing.'

Peter and Clara brought them up to date on events in their village of Three Pines, then, after some more prompting, Clara told the story of the great art dealer showing up to their modest home there, his return visit with his partners, then the excruciating wait while they decided if Clara Morrow was, at the age of forty-eight, an emerging artist. Someone they wanted to sponsor. For everyone in the art world knew that if Denis Fortin approved of you, the art world approved. And anything was possible.

Then the nearly unbelievable news that after decades of trying to get someone, anyone, to notice her work, Clara was indeed going to have a solo show at the Galerie Fortin next year.

'And how are you feeling about this?' Gamache asked quietly, having left the women and wandered to the end of the dock with Peter.

'Wonderful.'

Gamache nodded and putting his hands behind his back he looked out to the far shore, and waited. He knew Peter Morrow. Knew him to be a decent and kind man, who loved his wife more than anything in the world. But he also knew Peter's ego was almost as large as his love. And that was enormous.

'What?' Peter laughed, after the silence had stretched beyond his breaking.

'You're used to being the successful one,' said Gamache simply. No use pretending. 'It would be natural to feel a little . . .' he searched for the right word, the kind word, 'murderous.'

Peter laughed again and was surprised to hear it magnified by the far shore.

'You do know artists. I've had a bit of a struggle over this, as I think you know, but seeing Clara so happy, well . . .'

'I'm not sure Reine-Marie would be pleased if I became a librarian, like her,' said Gamache, looking over at his wife talking animatedly with Clara.

'I can just see both of you working at the Bibliothèque Nationale in Montreal, seething resentments between the aisles. Especially if you got promoted.'

'That wouldn't happen. I can't spell. Have to sing the alphabet every time I look a number up in the phone book. Drives Reine-Marie crazy. But you want murderous feelings? Hang around librarians,' confided Gamache. 'All that silence. Gives them ideas.'

They laughed and as they walked back to the women they heard Reine-Marie describe the rest of their day.

'Swim, nap, swim, white wine, dinner, swim, sleep.'

Clara was impressed.

'Well, we've had all week to perfect it,' admitted Reine-Marie. 'You have to work on these things. What're you two doing?'

'Boating, unveiling, getting drunk, humiliating myself,

82

apologizing, sulking, eating, sleeping,' said Clara. 'I've had twenty years of reunions to perfect it. Though the unveiling is new.'

'It's a statue of your father?' Gamache asked Peter.

'The pater. Better here than our garden.'

'Peter,' said Clara mildly.

'Would you want it?' asked Peter.

'No, but I didn't really know your father. He was handsome enough, like his son.'

'I'm not at all like him,' snapped Peter in a tone so unlike him it surprised the others.

'You didn't like your father?' Gamache asked. It seemed a safe guess.

'I liked him about as much as he liked me. Isn't that how it normally works? You get what you give? That's what he always said. And he gave nothing.'

There was silence then.

'After Peter's father died his mother married again,' explained Clara. 'Bert Finney.'

'A clerk in my father's company,' said Peter, tossing pebbles into the calm lake.

He was slightly more than a clerk, Clara knew. But she also knew it wasn't the time to fine-tune her husband.

'I'll just be glad when this is over. Mother doesn't want us to see the statue until the unveiling so Thomas suggested we all go boating.' He cocked his head towards a green wooden rowboat tied to the dock. It was unusually long with two sets of oar holes.

'It's a *verchère*,' said Reine-Marie, amazed. She hadn't seen one in years.

'That's right,' said Peter. 'We used to go in the seven-in-a-*verchère* race at the local regatta. Thomas thought it would be a good way to pass the time. A sort of homage to Father.'

'Thomas calls you Spot,' said Gamache.

'Has most of my life.' Peter held out his hands. Reine-Marie and Gamache bent over, as though preparing to kiss a ring. But instead of a ring they found dots. Spots.

'Paint,' said Reine-Marie, straightening up. 'Turpentine'll get that out.'

'Really?' asked Peter with mock astonishment, then smiled. 'These are new. From this morning in the studio. But I've had them on my hands, my face, my clothing, my hair, all my life. When I was a kid Thomas noticed and started calling me Spot.'

'Nothing gets by Thomas, I'm guessing,' said Gamache.

'He's the original recycler,' agreed Peter. 'He collects conversations and events then uses them years later, against you. Recycle, retaliate, repulse. Nothing's ever wasted with our Thomas.'

'So that explains Spot,' said Reine-Marie. 'But what about your sister Mariana? Why is she Magilla?'

'Oh, some TV show she used to watch as a kid. *Magilla Gorilla*. She was fixated on it. Father used to get home from work right in the middle of the show and insist we all greet him at the door, like a big happy family. Mariana was always in the basement, watching TV. He'd have to yell at her. Every night she'd stomp up those stairs, crying.'

'So Thomas called her Magilla, after a gorilla?' Gamache was beginning to get a sense of the man. Peter nodded.

'And what did you call him?'

'Thomas. I was always the creative one in the family.'

They sat enjoying the slight breeze at the dock. Peter

listened as Clara talked again about Fortin visiting her studio this past spring and seeing the portrait of their friend Ruth, the old and withered poet. Embittered and embattled and brilliant. For some reason Peter couldn't hope to understand Clara had painted her as the Madonna. Not, of course, the dewy virgin. But an old and forgotten woman, alone and frightened and facing her final years.

It was the most beautiful work Peter had ever seen, and he'd stood in front of masterpieces. But never had he seen anything more extraordinary than in Clara's small back studio, cramped with rejected pieces and magazines and curled and crisp orange rinds, next to his pristine, professional, disciplined space.

But while he'd once again taken a common item and gotten so close it was unrecognizable then painted it as an abstract and called it *The Curtain*, or *Blade of Grass*, or *Transport*, Clara had squirrelled away in her little space and captured the divine in the face of their wizened, shrivelled, vicious old neighbour. Veined old hands clutched a faded blue robe to her withered neck. Her face was full of misery and disappointment, rage and despair. Except her eyes. It wasn't obvious. Just a hint, a suggestion.

It was there, in the tiniest dot in her eye. In the entire, huge canvas, Clara had painted a single dot, a spot. And in that spot she'd placed hope.

It was exquisite.

He was happy for her. Really.

A shriek broke into their reflections and in an instant all were on their feet turning towards the Manoir. Armand Gamache started forward just as a small figure shot out of the garden.

Bean.

The child raced screaming towards them down the lawn getting more hysterical with each panicked step, the swim towel snapping behind. And someone was chasing the child. As they came closer Gamache recognized the young gardener.

Peter and Clara, Gamache and Reine-Marie ran onto the lawn and put their arms out to stop Bean, who seemed strangely intent on avoiding them, but Peter caught the fugitive.

'Let me down,' Bean wailed and struggled in his arms, as though Peter was the threat. Wild eyed, the child looked back at the Manoir.

The lawn was filled with people, the Morrows, the Finneys and some of the staff following the now trotting gardener.

'Who are you running from, Bean?' Gamache quickly knelt down and took the child's trembling hands. 'Look at me, now,' he said kindly but firmly, and Bean did. 'Has someone hurt you?'

He knew he had until the others joined them to get an honest answer from Bean, and they were almost there. His eyes never left the frightened child.

Bean held out an arm. Welts were appearing on the tender skin.

'What have you done to my grandchild?'

It was too late. They'd arrived and Gamache looked up into the accusing face of Irene Finney. She was a formidable woman, Gamache knew. He admired, respected, trusted strong women. He'd been raised by one, and had married one. But he knew strength wasn't hardness, and a formidable woman and a bully were two different things. Which was she?

He looked at the elderly woman now, stern, unbending, demanding an answer.

'Get away from Bean,' she commanded, but Gamache stayed kneeling, ignoring her.

'What happened?' he quietly asked the child.

'It wasn't my fault,' he heard behind him and turned to see the young gardener standing there.

'That normally means it was,' said Mrs Finney.

'Irene, let the girl speak. What's your name?' Bert Finney spoke softly.

'Colleen,' said the gardener, edging away from the wild-looking old man. 'It was wasps.'

'It was bees,' snuffled Bean. 'I was riding round Olympus when they got me.'

'Olympus?' snapped Mrs Finney.

'The marble block,' said Colleen. 'And it was wasps, not bees. The kid doesn't know the difference.'

Gamache knelt down and held out his large hand. Bean hesitated, and while the family argued over the difference between bees and wasps he examined the three welts. They were red and warm to the touch. Peering closer he could see the stingers stuck under the skin, with small poison sacs attached.

'Can you get some calamine lotion?' he asked a member of the staff, who sprinted back up the lawn.

Holding Bean's arm firmly he quickly removed all the stingers and sacs, then watched for an allergic reaction, ready to scoop the child up and race for his car and the Sherbrooke Hospital. He looked over at Reine-Marie, who was obviously watching for the same thing.

Once a parent.

The arm remained angry but not lethal.

Reine-Marie took the bottle of peach-coloured liquid and kissing the welts first she dabbed the lotion on then straightened up. All around them the family was now arguing over whether calamine lotion really worked.

'The excitement's over,' declared Mrs Finney. Looking around she noticed the rowboat and walked towards the dock. 'Now, who'll sit where?'

After much discussion Peter and Thomas started hauling Morrows into the *verchère*. Peter stood in the boat and Thomas stood on the dock and between them they sat Mrs Finney, Mariana and Julia. Bean crawled carefully into the boat without help.

'My turn,' said Sandra, putting her arm out. Thomas handed her to Peter.

Clara stepped forward and reached for Peter, who hesitated.

'Excuse me,' said Thomas, and stepped beside Clara then into the *verchère*. Thomas sat and the entire boat stared at Peter, standing in front of the only seat left.

'Sit down before you tip us all,' said Mrs Finney.

Peter sat.

Clara lowered her arms. In the reflection of the water she saw the ugliest man alive standing beside her.

'Not everyone makes the boat,' said Bert Finney as the *verchère* left the dock.

SEVEN

'I didn't really want to go, you know,' said Clara, not looking at Reine-Marie. 'But I said I would because it seemed important to Peter. This is probably better.'

'Will you join us, sir?' Gamache walked up to Bert Finney, also looking out at the lake. Finney turned and stared at Gamache. It was a disconcerting look, not only because of his forbidding face and odd eyes but because people so rarely stared that openly for that long. Gamache held the stare and finally Finney's lips parted and his disarray of yellow teeth showed in what might have been a smile.

'No, *merci*. I believe I'll stay here.' He walked to the end of the dock. 'Seven mad Morrows in a *verchère*. What could possibly go wrong?'

Gamache took his floppy hat off and felt the full force of the sun. He couldn't remember a hotter day. It was stifling now. There was no breeze, nothing stirred, and the sun beat down on them relentlessly, bouncing off and magnified by the lake. Perspiration had plastered his fresh shirt to his skin. He offered the hat to the old man.

Very slowly Bert Finney turned round as though he was afraid of capsizing. Then an old hand, like twigs stripped of bark, reached out and held the gaily patterned sun hat.

'It's your sun bonnet. You need it.'

'I prefer to think of it as my helmet,' said Gamache, letting go of the hat. 'And you need it more.'

Finney chuckled and held the hat, his fingers stroking it slightly. 'A sun helmet. I wonder who the enemy is?'

'The sun?'

'That would be it, I suppose.' But he seemed unconvinced and nodding to Gamache he put the hat on his satellite head and turned back to the lake.

An hour later Peter joined them in the garden, his face red from sunburn, Clara was pleased to see. She'd decided to play it cool. Not show how she felt.

Gamache handed him a cold beer, ice slipping off the sides. Peter held it to his red face and rolled it on his chest.

'Have fun?' Clara asked. 'Get caught up with the family?'

'It wasn't too bad,' said Peter, sipping the drink. 'We didn't sink.'

'You think not?' said Clara and stomped away. Peter stared at Gamache then ran after her, but as he neared the Manoir he noticed a huge canvas blanket that seemed to hover in the air.

The statue had arrived. His father had arrived. Peter slowed to a stop, and stared.

'For God's sake, you can't even leave your family long enough to chase me,' yelled Clara from the other side of the Manoir, no longer caring that she was proving all the Morrow suspicions true. She was unstable, emotional, hysterical. Mad. But so were they.

Seven mad Morrows.

'God, Clara, I'm sorry. What can I say?' he said when he caught up with her. Clara was silent. 'I'm really fucking up today. What can I do to make this better?'

'Are you kidding? I'm not your mother. You're fifty and you want me to tell you how to make this better? You fucked it up, you figure it out.'

'I'm so sorry. My family's nuts. I probably should've told you sooner.'

He smiled so boyishly it would have melted her heart had it not turned to marble. There was silence.

'That's it?' she said. 'That's your apology?'

'I don't know what to do,' he said. 'I wish I did.'

He stood there, lost. As he always was when she was angry.

'I'm so sorry,' he repeated. 'There wasn't room in the boat.'

'When will there be?'

'I don't understand.'

'You could have left. Joined me.'

He stared at her as though she'd told him he could have sprouted wings and flown. She could see that. For Peter it was demanding the impossible. But she also believed Peter Morrow was capable of flight.

EIGHT

The unveiling ceremony was short and dignified. The Morrows sat in a semicircle facing the canvas-draped statue. It was late afternoon and the trees cast long shadows. Sandra batted a bee towards Julia who passed it on to Mariana.

Gamache and Reine-Marie sat under the huge oak tree next to the lodge, watching from a respectful distance. The Morrows dabbed dry eyes and moist brows.

Clementine Dubois, who'd been standing beside the statue, handed Irene Finney a rope and mimed a tugging movement.

The Gamaches leaned forward but the Morrows leaned, almost imperceptibly, away. There was a pause. Gamache wondered whether Mrs Finney was hesitant to pull the canvas caul off the statue. To reveal and release her first husband.

The elderly woman gave a tug. Then another. It was as though Charles Morrow was clinging on to the canvas. Unwilling to be revealed.

Finally, with a yank, the canvas fell away.

There was Charles Morrow.

All through the dinner service the statue was the talk of the kitchen. Chef Véronique tried to calm the giddy staff and get them to focus on the orders, but it was difficult. Finally, in a quiet moment, as she stirred the reduction for the lamb and Pierre stood beside her arranging the dessert service, she spoke to him.

'What's it look like?' she whispered, her voice deep and mellow.

'Not what you'd expect. You haven't seen it?'

'No time. Thought I might sneak a peek later tonight. Was it very awful? The kids seem spooked.'

She glanced at the young waiters and kitchen staff, huddled in small groups, some talking excitedly, others wide eyed and hushed as though sharing ghost stories around a campfire. And scaring each other silly, thought Pierre.

'*Bon*, that's enough.' He clapped his hands. 'Back to work.'

But he made sure to sound reassuring, not harsh.

'I swear it moved,' came a familiar voice from one of the groups. Pierre turned and saw Elliot, surrounded by other workers. They laughed. 'No, I'm serious.'

'Elliot, that's enough,' he said. 'Statues don't move and you know it.'

'Of course you're right,' said Elliot. But his tone was sly and condescending, as though the maître d' had said something slightly stupid.

'Pierre,' whispered Chef Véronique behind him.

He managed to smile. 'You haven't been smoking the napkins again, have you, young man?'

The others laughed and even Elliot smiled. Soon the maître d's squadron of waiters was out of the swinging door, crisply delivering food and sauces, bread and wine.

'Well done,' said Chef Véronique.

'Goddamned Elliot. Sorry,' said the maître d', shooting her an apologetic look. 'But he's deliberately scaring the others.'

She was surprised to see his hands tremble as he poured fresh sugar into a bone china bowl.

'Do we have enough now?' She nodded to the empty sugar sack in his hand.

'Plenty. Strange that we ran out. You don't think . . .'

'What? Elliot? Why would he?'

The maître d' shrugged. 'When something strange happens you can be sure he's behind it.'

Chef Véronique didn't disagree. They'd seen a lot of kids come and go over the years. Had trained hundreds. But there was only one Elliot.

He cares so deeply for the kids, she thought as she watched Pierre. As though they were his own. And she wondered, not for the first time, how much he missed being a father himself. He'd have been a good one. He gave these kids training and guidance. But even more than that, he gave them a stable environment and a kind home. In the middle of nowhere, they found what they needed. Good food, a warm bed and solid ground beneath their feet. Pierre had given up having his own children in exchange for a home in the wilderness and caring for other people and other people's children. They both had. But after almost thirty years had Pierre finally been pushed too far by one of them? Chef Véronique loved nature, and found plenty of time to study it, and she knew that sometimes something unnatural crawled out of the womb, out of the woods. She thought of Elliot, and wondered whether the charming, handsome young man was all, or perhaps more than, he appeared.

'What did you think of the statue?' Reine-Marie asked as they sipped their after-dinner espressos and cognacs on the lawn, the night broken only by a firefly flickering here and there. The Morrows were still inside, eating in near silence, and the Gamaches had the rest of the world to themselves.

Gamache thought a moment. 'I was amazed.'

'So was I,' she said, gazing over to where it stood. But the night was dark and she couldn't see the gaunt, weary face of Charles Morrow. A handsome man, gone to stone.

The wind had picked up steadily since the unveiling. But instead of being refreshing, the breeze seemed to drag even more heat and humidity with it.

Bach wafted from the open windows of the Great Room.

Armand loosened his tie. 'There. That's better. Did you see that?'

He pointed down the lake, though he didn't have to. In a night this dark the lightning was impossible to miss.

'Fork,' said Reine-Marie. 'Pierre was right. Storm's coming.'

Her husband was moving his lips, whispering numbers, counting the space between light and sound. And then, in the distance, a low rumbling. It built then broke, and rumbled some more.

'Long way off still,' he said. 'Might even miss us. Storms get caught in valleys sometimes.'

But he didn't think this storm would miss them. Soon all that was calm and peaceful would be disrupted.

'Paradise lost,' he murmured.

'The mind is its own place, monsieur,' said Reine-Marie. 'Can make a heaven of hell, a hell of heaven. This is heaven. Always will be.'

'This place? Manoir Bellechasse?'

'No.' She put her arms around him. 'This place.'

'Please take this in to the Great Room.' Pierre handed a silver tray with coffee, a Drambuie and chocolates to a waiter. 'It's for Madame Martin.'

'Here, I'll trade you. I'll take that.' At the door Elliot reached for the tray. 'I saw her go in the garden for a smoke. You can take mine. It's for Mrs Morrow.'

'The wild-haired one?' the waiter asked hopefully.

'No, the deflated one,' admitted Elliot. 'Sandra Morrow.' Seeing the other waiter's expression he lowered his voice. 'Listen, I know where Mrs Martin goes for a smoke. You'll be wandering all over trying to find her.'

'How d'you know where she goes?' the other waiter whispered.

'I just know.'

'Come on, man. I'm not going to take that to Mrs Morrow. She'll make me come back for more chocolates, or different chocolates, or a bigger coffee. Screw off.'

The waiter held on to his tray and Elliot reached for it.

'What's going on? Why're you both still here?'

They looked up and the maître d' was beside them. His eyes dropped to their hands, all four of them clasping the single silver tray for Julia Martin. In the background Chef

Véronique stopped arranging a tray with miniature *pâtisserie* and watched.

'Elliot, isn't that your tray?' The maître d' nodded to the tray sitting on the old pine sideboard.

'What's the big deal? We're just trading.'

'No we're not,' said the other waiter, yanking the tray away and spilling some coffee.

'That's it, that's enough. Get a fresh tray and coffee,' Pierre ordered the waiter, 'and you come with me.'

He took Elliot into a far corner of the kitchen. They couldn't escape the darting stares, but they could escape the ears.

'What's this about? Is there something going on between you and Madame Martin?'

'No, sir.'

'Then why cause this commotion?'

'I just can't stand Mrs Morrow, that's all.'

Pierre hesitated. He could understand that. He didn't much like her either. 'She's still our guest. We can't just serve the ones we like.' He smiled at the young man.

'Yes, sir.' But Elliot didn't smile back.

'*Bon*,' said Pierre. 'I'll take that.'

He took the refreshed tray for Julia Martin from the surprised waiter and left the kitchen.

'What'd the old man want?' a waitress asked Elliot as he picked up his tray and prepared to take it to Sandra Morrow, who'd no doubt complain it was late and cold.

'He doesn't want me to serve Julia Martin,' said Elliot. 'He wants her to himself. Have you seen the way he looks at her? I think he has a crush on her,' he sang in a childish falsetto.

The two took their trays through the swinging doors.

Elliot's words had a larger audience than he realized. Chef Véronique wiped her hands on a tea towel and watched as the door clacked back and forth until it was finally still.

'Home tomorrow,' said Clara to the Gamaches as they walked into the library from the *terrasse*. She could go to bed soon, sleep eight hours, have breakfast with her in-laws then head back to Three Pines. Really, only a couple more waking hours with these people. She looked at her watch for the umpteenth time. Only ten? How could that be? My God, could the Morrows stop time too? 'When do you leave?'

'Couple of days yet,' said Reine-Marie. 'We're celebrating our wedding anniversary.'

'That's right,' said Clara, embarrassed that she'd forgotten. 'Congratulations. When?'

'It'll be thirty-five years on July first. Canada Day.'

'Easy to remember,' said Peter, smiling appreciatively at Gamache.

'Was it love at first sight?' Clara sat beside Reine-Marie.

'For me, yes.'

'But not for you?' Peter asked Gamache.

'Oh yes. She means her family.'

'No, you had family problems too? In-laws?' asked Clara, eager to hear someone else's misery.

'Not exactly. They were wonderful,' said Reine-Marie. 'He was the problem.'

She nodded to her husband, leaning against the fireplace mantel, trying to pretend he was invisible.

'You? What happened?' asked Clara.

'Now you must remember I was young,' he warned her. 'And in love. And not very worldly-wise.'

'This is going to be good,' said Peter to Clara.

'Reine-Marie invited me round after mass on a Sunday for lunch, to meet her family. There were seventy-three siblings.'

'Nine,' his wife corrected him.

'I wanted to impress them, of course, so I spent all week trying to figure out what to take her mother. Nothing too big. Didn't want to show off. Nothing too small. Didn't want to appear cheap. I lost sleep. Couldn't eat. It became the most important thing in my life.'

'What did you take?' Clara asked.

'A bath mat.'

'You're kidding,' sputtered Peter. Gamache shook his head, unable to speak. As the others broke into howls of laughter he finally found his voice.

'Well,' he wiped away his tears, 'it never goes bad.'

'Or out of style, but doesn't it lack a certain *je ne sais quoi*?'

'His gift giving has improved,' admitted Reine-Marie.

'Soap dishes?' asked Clara.

'Toilet plunger?' asked Peter.

'Shhh,' whispered Gamache. 'That's a surprise for our golden anniversary.'

'And surprise it will be,' said Clara, laughing. 'But don't get us started on toilets.'

'Oh, please. Don't,' said Peter, trying to recover himself.

'Oh, no,' said Gamache, clasping Peter by the arm. 'Your turn, old son.'

'OK.' Peter relented and took a swig of Drambuie. 'When I first went away to school and was unpacking all my little socks and shoes and slacks, I found a note pinned to my blazer in my father's handwriting. It said, *Never use the first stall in a public washroom.*'

Peter, grown up and greying, stood in the room, but what Gamache saw was a serious little boy with spots on his hands holding the note. And memorizing it, as one might memorize a passage from the Bible. Or a poem.

Breathes there the man with soul so dead?

What kind of man was Charles Morrow that he'd write that to his son? Gamache was longing to ask Peter about the statue, but hadn't yet had the chance.

'Good advice,' said Reine-Marie and they all looked at her. 'If you're in a hurry, where do you go? To the first stall.'

She didn't need to say more.

Peter, who'd never decoded what his father had meant but knew in his heart it must be vital, wondered.

Was it that mundane? Was it really just practical advice after all? As a child, even as a teen, and even, dare he admit it, as an adult, he'd fantasized that it was a secret code. Given only to him. Entrusted to him. By his father. A code that would lead to treasure.

Never use the first stall in a public washroom.

And he hadn't.

Gamache was just about to ask Peter's opinion of the statue when Thomas strolled in.

'You were talking about public washrooms?' he said.

'Toilets?' asked Mariana, breezing into the room with Sandra. 'Bean'll be sorry to be in bed. It's the sort of conversation a ten year old is good at.'

'Hello.' Julia walked through the screen doors from the *terrasse* carrying a *demi-tasse* of espresso. 'There's lightning and thunder out there. I think a storm's coming.'

'No,' said Thomas sarcastically. 'Peter's been talking about toilets, Julia.'

'Not really,' said Peter quickly.

Julia stared at him.

'Men's or women's?' asked Mariana, with exaggerated interest.

'Probably men's,' said Thomas.

'That's it, that's enough.' Julia threw her coffee cup to the carpet, where it shattered. The action was so unexpected, so violent, everyone in the room jumped.

'Stop it,' she rasped. 'I've had enough.'

'Calm down,' Thomas said.

'Like you? You think I don't know?' She started to smile, or at least to show her teeth. 'Thomas the success, the talented one,' she hissed at him.

'And you.' She turned to Mariana. 'Magilla, the gorilla. The screw-up with the screwed-up child. Bean. Bean? What kind of a name is that? What kind of kid is that? You think you're so smart? Well I know. I know it all.

'And you. You're the worst.' She closed in on Peter. 'Gimme, gimme, gimme. You'd destroy anything and everything to get what you want, wouldn't you?'

'Julia.' Peter could barely breathe.

'You haven't changed. Cruel and greedy. Empty. A coward and a hypocrite. You all came here to suck up to Mother. You hated Father. And he knew it. But I know something none of you does.' Now she was up against Peter, tilting her face up to his. He didn't move, kept his eyes fixed on the painting above the fireplace. The Krieghoff. Lines and colour he understood. His sister's hysterics were unfathomable, terrifying.

'I know Daddy's secret,' Julia was hissing. 'I had to spend my life as far from you as I could get to figure it out, but I finally did. And now I'm back. And I know.'

She grinned malevolently and stared around the room. Her eyes finally came to rest on the Gamaches. For a moment she seemed confused, surprised to see them.

'I'm sorry,' she stammered, the spell broken, the rage gone. She looked down at the mess she'd made. 'I'm sorry.' She bent to pick it up.

'No, don't,' Reine-Marie said, stepping forward.

Julia stood up, holding a piece of the cup, a slight trickle of blood on her finger. 'I'm sorry.'

Her eyes filled with tears and her chin dimpled. All her rage dissolved. Turning, she ran out of the screen door leaving behind her family, who might have had their heads mounted on the old log walls. They'd been hunted, slaughtered, and put on display.

'She's cut her finger,' said Reine-Marie. 'I'll take her a bandage.'

'She's not hurt badly,' said Sandra. 'She'll be fine. Leave her.'

'I'll come with you,' said Gamache, grabbing the flashlight on the table by the door. He and Reine-Marie followed the bright spot of the flashlight as it played on the rough stones of the *terrasse* then the grass. They followed the light and the sobs and found Julia sitting on the lawn, near the edge of the forest. Near the statue.

'It's all right,' said Reine-Marie, kneeling down and putting an arm round her.

'It's. Not. All. Right.'

'Let me see your hand.'

All fight gone, Julia raised her hand. Reine-Marie examined it. 'The other one, please.' She found the small cut on Julia's finger and dabbed at the blood with a Kleenex. 'It's stopped bleeding. You'll be fine.'

Julia laughed, sputtering slime from her nose and mouth. 'You think?'

'We all get angry, we all shout and say things we don't mean,' said Reine-Marie.

Gamache handed Julia his handkerchief and she blew into it.

'I meant them.'

'Then things that didn't need to be said.'

'They did.' She was stuffing her innards back, sewing herself up, putting her skin, her make-up, her party frock back on.

'They'll never forgive me, you know.' She stood up, smoothed her dress, and wiped the tears and mucus from her face. 'Morrows have long memories for things like this. It was a mistake to come back. Foolish, really.' She gave a small snort of laughter. 'I think I might leave before breakfast tomorrow.'

'Don't,' said Reine-Marie. 'Talk to them. If you leave without seeing them it'll just get worse.'

'And you think talking would help? You don't know the Morrows. I've said way too much already.'

Gamache had been silent, watching and listening. And holding the torch. In the light he could just see her face, unnaturally pale, with harsh lines and shadows.

Not everything needed to be brought into the light, he knew. Not every truth needed to be told. And he knew she was right. He'd seen their faces as she'd fled. She'd said too much. He didn't understand it, couldn't see it, but he knew something foul had just come to light, come to life.

NINE

⁓

Gamache woke a few hours later to a rending, ripping sound as though something huge was tearing towards them. Then a sudden crash.

Thunder. Not quite on top of them, but close.

Drenched in sweat, the sheets tangled and soaking around his feet, he got up and quietly splashed cold water across his neck and on his face, tasting salt and feeling the stubble under his fingers and momentary relief from the sullen heat.

'Can't sleep either?'

'Just woke up,' he said, returning to bed. He turned his sodden pillow over and laid his head on the cool pillowcase. But within moments it too was hot, and damp with perspiration. Any moment now, he felt, the air must surely turn to liquid.

'Oh,' said Reine-Marie.

'What?'

'The clock just went out.' She stretched out and he heard a click, though nothing happened. 'The light's gone as well. Storm's knocked out the electricity.'

Gamache tried to fall back to sleep, but an image kept intruding. Of Charles Morrow, alone in the garden, illuminated by the flashes of lightning. Then in darkness again.

He'd expected the statue to be imperious, commanding. But as the canvas hood had slipped from the sculpture there'd been the most astonishing sight.

The statue was a deep undulating grey, and instead of holding his head high and proud he was bowed slightly. He looked off balance, as though about to step forward. But this Charles Morrow was not full of purpose and plans. This stooped, grey man hesitated on his pedestal.

There'd been silence when the canvas had collapsed to the ground and the Morrows looked once again upon their father.

Mrs Finney had walked up to the statue. One by one the children followed, circling it like nuts around a bolt, then Mrs Finney turned to the others.

'I think it's time for a drink.'

And that was that.

Once they'd gone inside Gamache and Reine-Marie had approached and looked up into that handsome face. Straight noble nose. Forehead high. Lips full and slightly pursed. Not in judgement, nor, Gamache thought, in sour reflection, but with something to say. But his eyes were the most striking. They looked ahead and what they saw had turned this man to stone.

What did Charles Morrow see? And why would the sculptor put that there? And how had the Morrows really felt? Gamache suspected that last question was the most difficult of all.

Light flashed for an instant into their bedroom. Instinctively he started counting. One one thousand, two one thousand.

Another rumble and another crash.

'Angels bowling,' said Reine-Marie. 'Mother told me.'

'Better than my answer. I actually thought it might be a storm.'

'Ignorant man. What kind of storm? Deciduous or coniferous?'

'Aren't those trees?'

'I believe you're thinking of the cumulous tree.'

'I have an idea,' he said, getting off the damp bed.

Minutes later, in their light summer dressing gowns, they'd snuck downstairs, through the living room and onto the screen porch. Sitting in the wicker rocking chairs they watched as the storm moved towards them down the lake. Reine-Marie picked plump purple cherries from a fruit bowl and Gamache ate a juicy peach. They were ready for whatever was coming. Or so they thought.

The silence was suddenly shattered as the wind picked up, keening through the trees and sending the leaves into wild, simpering applause for what was coming. Gamache could hear the lake too. Waves crashed against the dock and the shore, whitecaps breaking as the storm marched towards them. Gamache and Reine-Marie watched as the lightning bolted and approached, spearing its way down the bay.

It was a big one. The wind hit the porch, bowing the screens inward as though grabbing for them.

The lake and mountains flashed visible for an instant. Beside him Gamache could feel Reine-Marie tense as another huge fork of lightening shot into the forest across the lake.

'One one thousand, two—'

A huge explosion of thunder drowned their counting. The storm was less than two miles off, and heading straight for them. Gamache wondered if the Manoir had a lightning rod. It must, he thought, otherwise it would have been struck and burned years ago. Another lightning bolt lanced into the forest across the bay and they heard a huge rending crack, as an old-growth tree was destroyed.

'Perhaps we should go inside,' said Reine-Marie, but just as they rose a massive gust of wind hit the screen porch and with it a wash of rain. They stumbled inside, drenched and a little shaken.

'God, you scared me,' a small, quivering voice said.

'Madame Dubois, *désolée*,' said Reine-Marie. Any more conversation was drowned out by another blast of lightning and thunder. But in that flash the Gamaches saw figures running across the Great Room, like spectres, as though the storm had pushed the Manoir into the netherworld.

Then small spots of light began appearing in the room. Torrential rain pounded against the windows and doors could be heard banging furiously in the wind.

The spots of light began converging on them and they saw in an instant that Pierre, Elliot, Colleen the gardener and a few others had found flashlights. Within moments they'd swarmed away, closing storm shutters and locking doors and windows. There was no space for counting now between lightning and thunder. The storm was caught between the mountains, unable to escape. It hurled itself against the Manoir, over and over. Gamache and Reine-Marie helped and before long they were sealed into the log lodge.

'Do you have a lightning rod?' Gamache asked Madame Dubois.

'We do,' she said, but in the wavering light she looked uncertain.

Peter and Clara joined them and after a few minutes Thomas and Sandra appeared. The rest of the guests and staff were either sleeping through it, or too frightened to move.

For an hour or more the massive logs shuddered, the windows rattled, the copper roof pounded. But it held.

The storm moved on, to terrorize other creatures deeper in the forest. And the Gamaches returned to bed, throwing open their windows for the cool breeze the storm had left as an apology.

In the morning the power was restored, though the sun wasn't. It was overcast and drizzly. The Gamaches rose late to the seductive aromas of Canadian back bacon, coffee and mud. The smell of the Quebec countryside after a heavy rain. They joined the others in the dining room, nodding hellos.

After ordering *café au lait* and waffles with wild blueberries and maple syrup, and visiting the buffet, they settled in for a lazy, rainy day. But just as their waffles arrived they heard a faraway sound, something so unexpected it took Gamache a moment to recognize it.

It was a scream.

Rising rapidly he strode across the dining room, while the others were still looking at each other. Pierre caught up with him and Reine-Marie followed, her eyes on her husband.

Gamache stopped in the hallway.

The shriek came again.

'Upstairs,' said Pierre.

Gamache nodded and started up, taking the stairs two at a time. At the landing they listened again.

'What's above us?'

'The attic. There's a stairway hidden behind a bookcase. Over here.' They followed Pierre to a slight widening of the hall, where bookcases had been built in. One was swung open. Gamache peered up. There was an old staircase, dim and dusty.

'Stay here.'

'Armand?' Reine-Marie began, but stopped when he held up his hand. He ran up the stairs, disappearing round a bend.

A bare bulb swished from side to side. Dust floated in what little light it threw and cobwebs hung from the rafters. It smelled of spiders. Gamache forced himself to stop and listen. There was nothing but the thumping of his heart. He stepped forward and a floorboard creaked. Behind him came another shriek. He turned and plunged into a darkened room. Bending low, ready to leap to either side, he stared and felt a pressure in his own throat.

Hundreds of eyes were staring at him. Then he saw a head. And another. Eyes peered at him from decapitated heads. And just as his racing brain registered that, something flew at him from a corner and knocked him almost off balance.

Bean sobbed and clung, digging small fingers into Gamache's thigh. He prised them loose and held the child tight in his arms.

'What is it? Is someone else up here? Bean, you must tell me.'

'M-m-monsters,' Bean whispered, all eyes and dread. 'We have to get out. Pleeease.'

Gamache picked Bean up, but the child screamed as though scalded and writhed in his arms. He lowered Bean back to the ground and held the small hand and together they ran to the stairs and down. A crowd had gathered.

'You again. What have you done to Bean this time?' Mariana demanded, clawing at her child.

'Bean found the heads?' Madame Dubois asked. Gamache nodded. The old woman knelt down and put a wrinkled hand on the tiny heaving back.

'I'm so sorry, Bean. It was my fault. Those are just decorations. Animal heads. Someone shot them years ago and had them stuffed. I can see how they'd be scary, but they can't hurt you.'

'Of course they can't hurt you.' Another withered hand landed on Bean's back and the child stiffened. 'Now, no tears, Bean. Madame Dubois has explained it all. What do you say?'

'*Merci, Madame Dubois,*' was heard, muffled.

'No, Bean. You must apologize for trespassing. You must have known you shouldn't go there. You're old enough to know better.'

'*Non, ce n'est pas nécessaire,*' Madame Dubois protested, but it was clear no one was going anywhere until the child apologized for being frightened half to death. And eventually Bean did.

All returned to normal and within minutes the Gamaches were in their wicker rocking chairs in the screen porch. There was something deeply peaceful about a rainy summer day. Outside the rain was soft and steady and refreshing after the terrible heat and humidity. The lake was dull and small squalls could be seen marking the surface. Reine-Marie did crossword puzzles as Gamache stared out of the screen porch and listened to the rain drum steadily on the roof and drip to the grass from the trees. In the distance he heard the call of the 'Oh Canada' bird, and a crow. Or was it a raven? Gamache wasn't very good with bird calls, except loons. But this was like no bird he'd ever heard before.

He cocked his head to one side and listened more closely. Then he stood up.

It wasn't a bird calling. It was a cry, a shriek.

'It's just Bean again,' Sandra said, wandering into the porch.

'Just wants attention,' said Thomas, from the Great Room. Ignoring them Gamache walked into the hallway and ran into Bean.

'That wasn't you?' asked Gamache, though he knew the answer. Bean stared.

Another scream, even more hysterical this time, reached them.

'My God, what's that?' Pierre appeared at the door to the kitchen. He looked at Bean, then at Gamache.

'It's coming from outside,' said Reine-Marie.

Gamache and the maître d' hurried into the rain, not stopping for protection.

'I'll go this way,' yelled Pierre, motioning towards the staff cabins.

'No, wait,' said Gamache. Again he held his hand up and Pierre stopped dead. This man was used to giving orders and being obeyed, Pierre realized. They stood for what seemed an eternity, rain running down their faces and plastering their light clothes to their skins.

There was no more screaming. But after a moment Gamache heard something else.

'This way.'

His long legs took him quickly down the fieldstone walk and round the puddled corner of the old lodge, Pierre splashing and slipping after him.

Colleen, the gardener, stood on the sodden lawn holding her hands to her streaming face. She was whimpering and he thought she'd been stung in the face by wasps, but as he got closer he saw her eyes. Staring and horrified.

Following her gaze he saw it too. Something he should have noticed as soon as he'd turned the corner of the Manoir.

The statue of Charles Morrow had taken that hesitant step. Somehow the huge stone man had left his plinth and toppled over. He now lay deeply imbedded in the soft and saturated ground but not as deeply as he might have been, for something had broken his fall. Beneath him, barely visible, lay his daughter Julia.

TEN

———

The maître d' stopped dead.

'Oh, Christ,' he exhaled.

Gamache looked at Colleen, as petrified surely as Charles Morrow. Her hands covered her face and her bulging blue eyes stared out from between rain-soaked fingers.

'Come away,' Gamache said gently but firmly, standing in front of her to block the sight.

Her lips moved but he couldn't make out the words. He leaned closer.

'Help.'

'It's all right, we're here,' he said and caught Pierre's eye.

'Colleen.' The maître d' laid a hand on her arm. Her eyes flickered and refocused.

'Help. We need to help her.'

'We will,' Gamache said reassuringly. Together, he and the maître d' guided her through the rain to the back door into the kitchen.

'Take her inside,' Gamache instructed Pierre. 'Ask Chef

Véronique to make her hot sugared tea. In fact, ask her to make a few pots. I think we're going to need them. Earl Grey.'

'*Je comprends*,' said Pierre. 'What do I say?'

Gamache hesitated. 'Tell them that there's been a death, but don't tell them who. Keep everyone inside. Can you round up the staff?'

'Easily. On a day like today most are inside the main lodge doing chores.'

'Good. Keep them there. And call the police.'

'*D'accord.* The family?'

'I'll tell them.'

The door swung closed and Armand Gamache stood alone in the pelting rain. Then he made his way back to Julia Martin. Kneeling down he reached out and touched her. She was cold and hard. Her mouth and eyes were wide open, surprised. He half expected her to blink as the raindrops fell onto her open eyes. He blinked a few times in sympathy then his gaze continued down her body. Her legs were collapsed and invisible under the statue, but her arms were flung open as though to embrace her father.

Gamache stood for a long minute, rain dripping from his nose and chin and hands and running inside his collar. He stared at the surprised face of Julia Martin, and thought of the face of Charles Morrow, filled with sorrow. Then he turned slightly and stared finally at the white cube that had reminded him of a grave marker when first he'd seen it. How had this massive statue fallen?

Reine-Marie and Bean were sitting in the hallway of the Manoir playing I Spy when he returned. One look at his face told her all she needed to know, for now.

114

'Bean, why don't you get your book and we can read to-gether.'

'OK.' The child left but not before giving Gamache an appraising look. After Bean ran upstairs Gamache took his wife into the library and told her everything as he headed for the phone.

'But how?' she asked, immediately grasping the question.

'I don't know, yet. *Oui, bonjour.* Jean Guy?'

'You're not calling for advice again, are you, Chief? Eventually you're going to have to figure things out on your own.'

'Harrowing as that thought is, I do need your help.'

Jean Guy Beauvoir recognized this wasn't a social call from his long-time boss. His voice sharpened and Gamache could almost hear his chair fall back to the ground as his feet whisked off the desk.

'What is it?'

Gamache succinctly passed on the details.

'At the Manoir Bellechasse? *Mais, c'est incroyable.* That's the top *auberge* in Quebec.'

It always amazed Gamache that people, even professionals, thought Frette sheets and a superb wine list guarded against death.

'Was she murdered?'

And there was the other question. The two questions that had gotten up from the crime site and started to shadow Armand Gamache as soon as he'd seen Julia Martin's body: how had the statue tumbled down, and was it murder?

'I don't know.'

'We'll soon find out. I'm on my way.'

Gamache looked at his watch. Ten to eleven. Beauvoir and the rest of the team should arrive from Montreal by twelve thirty. The Manoir Bellechasse was buried south of Montreal, in an area known as the Eastern Townships, close to the American border. So close that some of the mountains he'd contemplated that misty morning were in Vermont.

'Armand? I think I hear a car.'

That would be the local Sûreté, he thought, grateful for the maître d's help.

'*Merci.*' He smiled at Reine-Marie and made for the hallway, but she stopped him.

'What about the family?'

She looked worried and for good reason. The thought that Mrs Finney would find out about her daughter from a waiter, or, worse, by perhaps wandering outside, was terrible.

'I'll just give the officers their instructions and go right in.'

'I'll go in and make sure they're all right.'

He watched her go, her step resolute, walking into a room filled with people whose lives were about to change forever. She could have sat quietly in the library and no one would have faulted her, but instead Reine-Marie Gamache chose to sit in a room soon to be overwhelmed with grief. Not many would make that choice.

Walking quickly outside he introduced himself to the officers, who were surprised to meet this renowned Sûreté investigator in the middle of the woods. He gave them directions, then motioning to one of them to follow he went inside to tell the Morrows.

'Something has happened. I have bad news.'

Armand Gamache knew it was never a kindness to prolong bad news.

But he knew something else.

If it was murder, someone in this room almost certainly did it. He never let that overwhelm his compassion, but neither did he let his compassion blind him. He watched closely as he spoke.

'Madame.' He turned to Mrs Finney, sitting composed in a wing chair, that day's *Montreal Gazette* folded on her lap. He saw her stiffen. Her eyes darted quickly about the room. He could read her nimble mind. Who was there, and who was missing?

'There's been a death.' He said it quietly, clearly. He was under no illusions about what his words would do to this woman. They were statue words, heavy and crushing.

'Julia,' she exhaled the name. The missing child. The one not there.

'Yes.'

Her lips parted and her eyes searched his, looking for some escape, some back door, some hint this might not be true. But he didn't blink. His brown eyes were steady, calm and certain.

'What?'

Thomas Morrow was on his feet. The word wasn't yelled. It was expelled across the room at him.

What. Soon someone would ask how and when and where. And finally the key question. Why.

'Julia?' Peter Morrow asked, standing. Beside him Clara had taken his hand. 'Dead?'

'I have to go to her.' Mrs Finney stood, the *Gazette* slipping to the floor, unattended. It was the equivalent of a scream. Mr Finney rose unsteadily to his full height. He reached for her hand then pulled back.

117

'Irene,' he said. Again he reached out, and Gamache willed with all his might that Bert Finney could go the distance. But once again the old twig hand stopped short and finally fell to the side of his grey slacks.

'How do you know?' snapped Mariana, also on her feet now. 'You're not a doctor, are you? Maybe she's not dead.'

She approached Gamache, her face red and her fists clenched.

'Mariana.' The voice was still commanding and it stopped the charging woman in her tracks.

'But Mommy—'

'He's telling the truth.' Mrs Finney turned back to the large, certain man in front of her. 'What happened?'

'How could she be dead?' Peter asked.

The shock was lifting, Gamache could see. They were beginning to realize a woman in her late fifties, apparently healthy, doesn't normally just die.

'An aneurysm?' asked Mariana.

'An accident?' asked Thomas. 'Did she fall down the stairs?'

'The statue fell,' said Gamache, watching them closely. 'It hit her.'

The Morrows did what they did best. They fell silent.

'Father?' asked Thomas, finally.

'I'm sorry.' Gamache looked at Mrs Finney, who stared as though stuffed. 'The police are with her now. She isn't alone.'

'I need to go to her.'

'The police aren't letting anyone close. Not yet,' he said.

'I don't care, they'll let me.'

Gamache stood in front of her and held her eyes. 'No, madame. Not even you, I'm afraid.'

She looked at him with loathing. It was a look he'd received often enough, and understood. And he knew it would get worse.

Gamache left them to their sorrow, taking Reine-Marie with him, but he quietly motioned the Sûreté officer into a corner.

Inspector Jean Guy Beauvoir stepped out of the car and looked at the sky. Unremitting grey. It would rain for a while yet. He looked down at his shoes. Leather. His slacks designer. His shirt. Casual linen. Perfect. Fucking middle of nowhere murder. In the rain. And mud. He slapped his cheek. And bugs. Flattened to his palm were the remains of a mosquito and some blood.

Fucking perfect.

Agent Isabelle Lacoste opened an umbrella and offered him one. He declined. Bad enough to be here, he didn't need to look like Mary Poppins.

Chief Inspector Armand Gamache came out of the *auberge* and waved. Beauvoir waved back then slapped his forehead. Gamache hoped it was a bug. Beside Beauvoir Agent Lacoste walked with an umbrella. In her late twenties, she was married and already a mother of two. Like most Québécoises, she was dark and petite with a comfortable flair and confidence. She wore a blouse and slacks that managed to be both sensible and *soignée*, even with rubber boots.

'*Salut, Patron*,' she said. 'How'd you manage to find the body?'

'I'm staying here.' He fell into step between them. 'The victim is a guest at the Manoir.'

'Hope she gets a discount,' said Beauvoir. They turned

the corner of the lodge and Gamache introduced the local Sûreté officers.

'Anyone come out?' he asked. Beside him Beauvoir was staring over at the scene, anxious to get there.

'Some older woman,' said a young female agent.

'English?' asked Gamache.

'No, sir. Francophone. Offered us tea.'

'Tall, with a deep voice?'

'Yes, that's her. Looked a little familiar, actually,' said one of the men. 'Suppose I've seen her in Sherbrooke.'

Gamache nodded. Sherbrooke was the nearest town, where the detachment was based.

'That would be the chef here, Véronique Langlois. Did she seem interested in the scene?' Gamache looked over to where the agents had encircled the site in yellow tape.

'Who wouldn't be?' The young woman laughed.

'You're right,' he said quietly. He turned sombre, kindly eyes on her. 'There's a woman over there who was alive hours ago. It might be an accident, it might be murder, but either way, this isn't the time or place for laughter. Not yet.'

'I'm sorry.'

'You're too young to be hardened and cynical. So am I.' He smiled. 'It's no shame to be sensitive. In fact, it's our greatest advantage.'

'Yes sir.' The young agent could have kicked herself. She was naturally sensitive but had thought she should hide it, that a certain cavalier attitude would impress this famous head of homicide. She was wrong.

Gamache turned to the scene. He could almost feel Beauvoir vibrating beside him. Inspector Beauvoir was the alpha dog, the whip-smart, tightly wound second in command who believed in the triumph of facts over feelings. He missed almost nothing. Except, perhaps, things that couldn't be seen.

Agent Lacoste also stared at the scene. But unlike Beauvoir she could become very still. She was the hunter of their team. Stealthy, quiet, observant.

And Gamache? He knew he was neither the hound nor the hunter. Armand Gamache was the explorer. He went ahead of all the rest, into territory unknown and uncharted. He was drawn to the edge of things. To the places old mariners knew, and warned, 'Beyond here be monsters.'

That's where Chief Inspector Gamache could be found.

He stepped into the beyond, and found the monsters hidden deep inside all the reasonable, gentle, laughing people. He went where even they were afraid to go. Armand Gamache followed slimy trails, deep into a person's psyche, and there, huddled and barely human, he found the murderer.

His team had a near perfect record, and they did it by sorting facts from fancy from wishful thinking. They did it by collecting clues and evidence. And emotions.

Armand Gamache knew something most other investigators at the famed Sûreté du Québec never quite grasped. Murder was deeply human. A person was killed and a person killed. And what powered the final thrust wasn't a whim, wasn't an event. It was an emotion. Something once healthy and human had become wretched and bloated and finally buried. But not put to rest. It lay there, often for decades, feeding on itself, growing and gnawing, grim and full of grievance. Until it finally broke free of all human restraint. Not conscience, not fear, not social convention could contain it. When that happened, all hell broke loose. And a man became a murderer.

And Armand Gamache and his team spent their days finding murderers.

But was this a murder at the Manoir Bellechasse? Gamache didn't know. But he did know that something unnatural had happened here.

'Take this in to them, *s'il vous plaît*.' Chef Véronique's large ruddy hand trembled slightly as she motioned to the trays. 'And bring out the pots already there. They'll want fresh tea.'

She knew this was a lie. What the family wanted they could never have again. But tea was all she could give them. So she made it. Over and over.

Elliot tried not to make eye contact with anyone. He tried to pretend he heard nothing, which was actually possible given the sniffles and snorts coming from Colleen. It was as though her head contained only snot. And too much of it.

'It's not my fault,' she sputtered for the hundredth time.

'Of course it's not,' said Clementine Dubois, hugging her to her huge bosom and readjusting the Hudson's Bay blanket she'd put on the young gardener for comfort. 'No one's blaming you.'

Colleen subsided into the soft chest.

'There were ants everywhere,' she hiccuped, pulling back but leaving a thin trail of mucus on the shoulder of Madame Dubois's floral dress.

'You and you,' said Chef Véronique, pointing to Elliot and Louise, not unkindly. The tea would be too strong if they waited much longer. The waiters were young, she knew, and had no experience with death. Unlike herself. Sending them in to wait on the Morrows was bad enough at the best of times, and this was far from the best of times. A room full of grief was even worse than a room full of anger. Anger a person got used to, met most days, learned to absorb or ignore. Or walk away from. But there was no hiding from grief. It would find you, eventually. It was the thing we most feared. Not loss, not sorrow. But what happened when you rendered those things down. They gave us grief.

All around the staff sat in easy chairs, perched on counters, leaned against walls, sipping strong coffee or tea, comforting each other. Murmured guesses, theories, excited speculation, filled the air. The maître d' had brought Colleen in, delivered her into their arms for comfort and dry clothing, then rounded up the rest of the staff. Once the family had been told he'd broken the news to the employees.

Madame Martin was dead. Crushed by that statue.

Everyone had gasped, some had exclaimed, but only one cried out. Pierre scanned the room, but didn't know who. But he did know the sound had surprised him.

Inspector Beauvoir finally stared into the hole. Only it wasn't a hole. It was filled with a human. A woman, wide eyed, surprised, and dead, a statue imbedded in her chest.

'Jesus.' He shook his head and slapped his arm, squishing a blackfly. In his peripheral vision he saw Agent Lacoste leaning in and putting her latex gloves on.

This was their new office.

Over the next few minutes more trucks and team members arrived and the Scene of Crime work got into full swing. Armand Gamache took it all in, as Beauvoir led the forensics.

'What do you think, Chief?' Lacoste removed her gloves and joined him under his umbrella. 'Was she murdered?'

Gamache shook his head. He was stumped. Just then the young Sûreté officer he'd placed in the Great Room with the Morrows appeared, excited.

'Good news, sir,' she said. 'I thought you'd like to know as soon as possible. I think we have a suspect.'

'Well done. Who?'

'The family was quiet at first, but after a while two of them started whispering. Not the artist fellow, but the other brother and sister. They seem pretty confident if it was murder she could only have been killed by one of two people.'

'Really?' Beauvoir asked. They might be able to get back to civilization sooner than he'd thought.

'*Oui.*' She consulted her notebook. 'The shopkeeper and his cleaning woman wife. Their names are Armand and Reine-Marie something. They're guests.'

Beauvoir grinned and Lacoste turned away briefly.

'My suspicions confirmed,' said Beauvoir. 'Will you come quietly?'

'I'll miss you,' said Agent Lacoste.

Gamache smiled slightly and shook his head.

Seven mad Morrows.

Six.

ELEVEN

'Peter,' Clara whispered.

She'd watched as he'd taken the Manoir notepaper and a pencil and then, grey head bowed, become lost as the pencil drew lines within ordered lines. It was mesmerizing and comforting, in the way the third martini was comforting. It felt good, but only because it numbed. Even Clara felt drawn in. Anything to escape the room filled with silent and solemn sorrow.

Across the Great Room Thomas's grey head was also bowed. Over the piano. The notes had been slow, tentative, but after a few moments Clara recognized them. Not Bach, for once. But Beethoven. 'Für Elise'. It was a spry and chipper tune. And relatively easy to play. She'd even managed to peck out the first few notes herself.

But Thomas Morrow played it as a dirge. Each note hunted for as though the tune was hiding. It filled the grieving room with an ache that finally brought tears to Clara's eyes. They burned with the effort of concealment, but the tears were out and obvious.

Sandra cried shortbread, scarfing the cookies one after another while Mariana sat beside Bean, a shawled arm round the child's shoulder as Bean read. They were silent now, though a few minutes earlier Thomas, Sandra and Mariana had been huddled together, whispering. Clara had approached, to offer her condolences, but they'd fallen silent and eyed her suspiciously. So she'd left.

Not everyone makes the boat, she thought. But HMCS *Morrow* was sinking. Even Clara could see that. It was a steamboat in the age of jets. They were old money in a meritocracy. The alarms were sounding. But even Peter, her lovely and thoughtful husband, clung to the wreckage.

Clara knew something the Morrows didn't. Not yet. They'd lost more than a sister and a daughter that morning. The police were at the door and the Morrows were about to lose whatever delusions had kept them afloat. And then they'd be like everyone else.

Peter's mother was sitting erect on the sofa, motionless. Staring.

Should she say something, Clara wondered. Do something? She racked her brains. Surely there was some way to offer comfort to this elderly woman who'd just lost her daughter.

What? What?

The door opened and Armand Gamache appeared. The music stopped and even Peter looked up. Behind Gamache came Inspector Beauvoir, Agent Lacoste and the young Sûreté officer.

'You bastard,' said Thomas, standing so abruptly the piano bench fell over.

He started towards Gamache.

'Thomas,' his mother commanded. He stopped. Mrs

Finney rose and walked a few paces into the centre of the room. 'Have you arrested this man?' She spoke to Beauvoir and nodded towards Gamache.

'I'd like to introduce Chief Inspector Gamache, the head of homicide for the Sûreté du Québec,' said Beauvoir.

The Morrows, except Peter and Clara, stared at the open door, expecting the great man to appear. Slowly, excruciatingly, their gaze fell back. To the large man in front of them. To the shopkeeper.

'Him?' said Mariana.

'Is this a joke?' With each word Sandra expelled shortbread crumbs onto the carpet.

'*Bonjour.*' He bowed solemnly. 'I'm afraid he does mean me.'

'You're a cop?' asked Thomas, trying to grasp that the chief suspect had become the Chief Inspector. 'Why didn't you tell us?'

'I didn't think it mattered. We were guests together, nothing more. Until this morning.' He turned to Mrs Finney. 'Would you still like to see your daughter? I couldn't allow it before because we had to secure the site. But I must warn you—'

'No need for warning, Chief Inspector. I know it won't be pleasant. Take me to Julia.'

She walked determinedly past him and Clara was impressed by her ability, even in grief, to change course. To accept Gamache as the Chief Inspector when Thomas and Mariana still stared, open mouthed and suspicious. And she, first among them, seemed to have accepted that Julia was indeed dead. But was it too quick, Clara wondered.

Gamache watched Mrs Finney move towards the door.

But he wasn't fooled any more. Earlier that morning, in the instant before he'd told her about Julia, he'd seen her avian glance, her flight around the room to see who was there, and who was gone. Which child was loved, now lost. He'd seen what she kept hidden.

'I'm going to have to ask the rest of you to stay here,' said Gamache, though no one else had made any move. Except Bert Finney.

He stopped a foot away from Gamache, his eyes focusing on a lamp and a bookcase. 'I'm afraid I have to insist,' the old man said.

Gamache hesitated. The face was craven, ashen, almost inhuman. But the action was noble. He nodded.

They left the young officer behind and Gamache wondered who'd got the more gruesome assignment.

As they approached the yellow circle of ribbon they were again joined by the notes of 'Für Elise'. The rain had all but stopped and a mist tugged at the mountains. Everything was shades of grey-green and between the notes they could hear rain dripping from the leaves.

Gamache had ordered the crime scene team to withdraw until after Mrs Finney had seen her daughter. Now they stood in a semicircle on the verge of the forest watching as the elderly woman, so tiny and pink, walked towards the hole in the ground.

As Mrs Finney approached she saw only the gaily fluttering police ribbon. Yellow. Julia's favourite colour. She'd been the feminine one, the daughter who'd loved dressing up, loved make-believe and make-up, loved the shoes and the hats. Loved the attention.

She saw then the semicircle of men and women in the forest, watching. And above them the bruised and swollen sky.

Poor Julia.

Irene Finney slowed as she approached. She wasn't a woman who understood the void, who'd given it any thought. But she knew, too late, she should have. She knew then that the void wasn't empty at all. Even now, steps away, she could hear the whisper. The void wanted to know something.

What do you believe?

That's what filled the void. The question and the answer.

Irene Finney stopped, not ready yet to face what she must. She waited for Bert. Not looking but sensing him there she took another step. One more and she'd see.

She hesitated then took it.

What she saw skipped her eyes completely and lodged right in her chest. In an instant she was pitched forward, beyond grief, into a wilderness where no anguish, no loss, no passion existed.

She heaved a breath up out of herself. Then another.

She used that breath to whisper the only prayer she could remember.

> *Now I lay me down to sleep,*
> *I pray the Lord my soul to keep.*

She saw Julia's hands outstretched. She saw the fingers, pudgy and wet, grasping her thumb in the bath in the old kitchen sink, in their very first apartment. Her and Charles. Charles, what have you done?

If I should die before I wake,
I pray the Lord my soul to take.

She offered the vesper to the void, but it was too late. It had taken Julia and now it took her. She looked up into the faces of the semicircle, but they'd changed. They were flat, like a reproduction. Not real at all. The forest, the grass, the Chief Inspector beside her, even Bert. All gone. Not real any more.

What do you believe?

Nothing.

Gamache walked them inside, remaining silent, respecting her need to be with her own thoughts. Then he returned to find the crane had arrived.

'Here comes the coroner.' Lacoste nodded to a woman in her early thirties wearing slacks, a light summer shell and rubber boots.

'Dr Harris.' Gamache waved then turned back to watch the removal of the statue.

Beauvoir directed operations, batting away blackflies. It was confusing for the crane operator who mistook his flailing for directions and twice almost dropped the statue back onto Julia Martin.

'Fucking bugs,' snarled Beauvoir, looking around at the rest of the team, working away steadily and methodically. 'Isn't anyone else bothered? Christ.' He whacked himself on the side of the head trying to crush a deerfly. He missed.

'*Bonjour.*' Gamache inclined his head towards the coroner. Sharon Harris smiled a small greeting. She knew how the Chief Inspector preferred decorum at the site of a murder, especially in the presence of the corpse. It was rare. Most murder scenes were filled with smart-ass and often gruesome comments, made by men and women frightened by what they saw, and believing sarcasm and rude remarks kept the monsters at bay. They didn't.

Chief Inspector Gamache chose men and women for his team who might also be afraid, but had the courage to rise above it.

Standing beside him and watching the statue sucked from the ground, and the woman, she caught the slight aroma of rosewater and sandalwood. His scent. She turned and watched the Chief Inspector for a moment, his strong face in profile. At rest, but watchful.

There was an old-world courtliness about him that made her feel she was in the company of her grandfather, though he was only twenty years older than her, if that. Once the statue was hovering over the flatbed truck Dr Harris put on her gloves and moved in.

She'd seen worse. Far worse. Horrible deaths that could never be avenged because there was no fault, except fate. This might be one, she thought, as she looked at the mangled body, then back at the statue. Then at the pedestal.

Kneeling down she examined the wounds.

'I'd say she's been dead twelve hours, maybe more. The rain makes it more difficult, of course.'

'Why's that?' Lacoste asked.

'No bugs. The amount and type of insect helps tell us how long a person's been dead. But the heavy rain kept the bugs home. They're like cats. Hate the rain. Now after the rain . . .'

She looked over at Beauvoir doing a mad dance and slapping himself.

'Here,' she pointed to a wound, 'see?'

Lacoste peered in. She was right. No bugs, though a few were beginning to hover.

'Now, this is interesting,' said Dr Harris. 'Look at that.'

On her finger was a smear of brown. Lacoste bent closer.

'Dirt?' she asked.

'Dirt.'

Lacoste raised her brows, perplexed, but didn't say anything. After a few minutes the coroner got up and walked to the Chief Inspector.

'I can tell you how she died.'

'A statue?' asked Gamache.

'Probably,' said the coroner, turning to look at the levitating statue then at its pedestal.

'That's the more interesting question,' said Gamache, reading her mind.

'We had quite a storm last night,' said Dr Harris. 'Maybe that knocked it down.'

'They're driving me crazy.' Beauvoir joined them, his face smeared with tiny freckles of crushed blackflies. He looked at Gamache, poised and comfortable. 'Don't they bite you?'

'No. It's mind over matter. It's all in your head, Inspector.'

That much was true, Beauvoir knew. He'd just inhaled a swarm of blackflies and he knew for certain a few had flown up his nose. A sudden buzzing in his ear warned him he was either having a stroke or a deerfly had just flown in.

Please, let this be an accident. Let me get home to my barbecue, my cooler of beer, my sports channel. My air conditioning.

He dug his little finger into his ear, but the buzzing only moved deeper.

Charles Morrow subsided onto the dirty truck. He lay on

his side, his arms out, his face sad, and smeared with his own flesh and blood.

Gamache walked alone to the edge of the hole in the ground. They all watched as he looked down. There was no movement, except his right hand, which clasped slowly closed.

Then he motioned to the team and there was a sudden flurry of activity as evidence was collected. Jean Guy Beauvoir took charge while Gamache returned to the large flatbed truck.

'Were you the one who put him on his pedestal?' he asked the crane operator.

'Not me, Patron. When was the job done?' the operator asked, securing and covering Charles Morrow for the trip to the Sûreté compound in Sherbrooke.

'Yesterday, early afternoon.'

'My day off. I was fishing in Lake Memphremagog. I can show you the pictures and the catch. I have a licence.'

'I believe you.' Gamache smiled reassuringly. 'Could someone else from your company have done it?'

'I'll ask.'

A minute later he was back.

'Called dispatch. Got the boss. He placed the statue himself. We do a lot of work with the Manoir, so when Madame Dubois called about this the boss decided it needed a special touch. No one's better than him.'

This was said with more than a little sarcasm. It was clear this man wouldn't mind if the boss turned out to have screwed up royally. And if he could help point the middle finger, so much the better.

'Can you give me his name and co-ordinates?'

The operator happily handed over a card with the proprietor's name underlined.

'Please ask him to meet me at the Sûreté detachment in Sherbrooke in about an hour.'

'Chief?' Dr Harris approached just as the driver got back in his rig and drove off.

'Could the storm have done this?' he asked, remembering the lightning bolts and the furious angels bowling, or crying, or pushing over statues.

'Knocked over the statue? Maybe. But it didn't.'

Gamache turned surprised brown eyes on the coroner. 'How can you be so certain?'

She held up her finger. Beside him Agent Lacoste grimaced. It wasn't just 'a' finger, it was 'the' finger. Gamache raised his brows and grinned. Then his brows lowered and he leaned in closer, staring at the brown smear.

'This was under her body. You'll see more when her body's moved.'

'It looks like dirt,' said Gamache.

'It is,' said Dr Harris. 'Dirt, not mud.'

Still the chief was baffled. 'What does it mean?'

'It means the storm didn't kill her. She was on the ground before the storm started. It's dry underneath her.'

Gamache was quiet, absorbing the information.

'Are you saying the statue fell off and crushed her before the storm hit?'

'That's a fact, Chief Inspector. The ground's dry. I have no idea how that thing came to fall, but it wasn't the storm.'

They all watched as the flatbed was slowly and carefully driven past them, a Sûreté officer in the passenger seat and the crane operator driving. They disappeared round a bend in the dirt road and into the thick forest.

'When did the storm hit?' He was asking himself as much as her. She was silent, pretending to think. She'd been in bed by nine with her Madeleine cookies, Diet Coke and *Cosmo*, though she'd rather not volunteer that information. She'd woken in the middle of the night to find her cottage shaking and the power out.

'We'll call the weather office. If they don't know the maître d' will,' he said, walking back to the hole. Staring in he saw what he should have noted in the first place. She was in the clothes he remembered from the night before.

No raincoat. No hat. No umbrella.

No rain.

She was dead before the storm had struck.

'Any other wounds on her body?'

'Don't appear to be. I'll do the autopsy this afternoon and let you know. Anything else before we take her away?'

'Inspector?' Gamache called and Beauvoir joined him, wiping his hands on his sodden slacks.

'No, we're finished. Dirt.' He looked at his hands and spoke as a surgeon might say 'germs'. Dirt, grass, mud, insects were unnatural to Beauvoir, for whom cologne and a nice silk blend were his elements.

'That reminds me,' said Gamache. 'There was a bees' or wasps' nest nearby. Be careful.'

'Lacoste, the nest?' Beauvoir jerked his head, but Lacoste continued to stare at the dead woman. She was putting herself in Julia's place. Turning. Seeing the statue do the impossible, the unthinkable. Seeing it fall towards her. And Agent Lacoste put her hands out in front of her, palms forward, elbows tucked into her body, ready to repel the attack. Turning away.

It was instinctive.

And yet Julia Martin had opened her arms.

The chief walked past her and stood in front of the pedestal. Reaching out he slid his hand over the wet marble. The surface was perfect, pristine. But that wasn't possible. A several ton statue would make scuffs, scratches, divots. But this surface was unmarred.

It was as though the statue had never been there. Gamache knew that was indulging his imagination. But he also knew he'd need his imagination if he was going to catch this killer. And there was a killer. Armand Gamache had no doubt. For all his magical thinking, Gamache knew statues didn't walk themselves off their pedestals. If magic hadn't done it, and if the storm hadn't, something else had. Some one had.

Somehow someone had managed to get a massive statue, weighing tons, to fall. And to land on Julia Martin.

She'd been murdered. He didn't know who, and he sure as hell didn't know how.

But he would.

TWELVE

Armand Gamache had never been in the Manoir kitchen but wasn't surprised to find it was large, with floors and counters made of gleaming dark wood and appliances made of stainless steel. Like the rest of the old lodge it was a mix of very old and very new. It smelled of basil and coriander, fresh bread and rich ground coffee.

As he entered bottoms slid from counters, the chopping stopped and the hum of conversation petered out.

Gamache immediately went over to Colleen, who was sitting beside the proprietor, Madame Dubois.

'Are you all right?' he asked.

She nodded, face bloated and blotched, but she seemed composed.

'Good. That was a pretty awful thing to see. Shook me too.'

She smiled, grateful he'd said it loud enough for everyone to hear.

Gamache turned to the room.

'I'm Chief Inspector Armand Gamache, head of homicide for the Sûreté du Québec.'

'*Voyons*,' he heard a loud whisper, 'I told you it was him.'

A scattering of 'Holy shit' was also heard.

'As you know, there's been a death. The statue in the garden fell and struck Madame Martin.'

Young, attentive, and excited faces looked at him.

He spoke with natural authority, trying to reassure, even as he broke the frightening news. 'We believe Madame Martin was murdered.'

There was stunned silence. He'd seen that transition almost every day of his working life. He often felt like a ferryman, taking men and women from one shore to another. From the rugged, though familiar, terrain of grief and shock into a netherworld visited by a blessed few. To a shore where men killed each other on purpose.

They'd all seen it from a safe distance, on television, in the papers. They'd all known it existed, this other world. Now they were in it.

Gamache watched as the young, fresh faces closed slightly, as fear and suspicion entered this room where just moments ago they'd known they were safe. And now these young men and women knew something even their parents probably didn't fully appreciate.

No place was safe.

'She was killed last night, just before the storm. Did any of you see Madame Martin after the coffee service? That would've been about ten thirty.'

There was a movement off to his left. He glanced over and saw Colleen and Madame Dubois sitting at the table. The young waiter Elliot was standing beside them and behind him was someone else. Given her age and costume it could only be the head chef, the famous Chef Véronique.

138

One of them had moved. Not a crime, but while everyone else was too stunned to budge, one of them wasn't. Who?

'You'll all be interviewed, of course, and I want to make something clear. You need to be honest. If you saw something, anything, you must tell us.'

The silence continued.

'Every day I look for murderers, and most of the time we find them. It's what we do, my team and I. It's our job. Your job is to tell us everything you know, even if you think it's not important.'

'You're wrong.' Elliot stepped forward.

'Elliot,' the maître d' warned, also coming forward, but Gamache stopped him with a raised hand and turned to the young man.

'Our job is to wait tables and make beds and serve drinks. To smile at people who insult us, who treat us like furniture. Our job isn't to help you find a murderer, and I sure as hell am not being paid enough to keep waiting on these people. I mean,' he appealed to the rest of the staff, 'one of them killed her. Do you want to stay and serve them? Did you ever?'

'Elliot,' said the maître d' again, 'that's enough. I know you're upset, son, we all are—'

'Don't call me son.' Elliot rounded on him. 'You're pathetic. These people won't thank you. They never do. They don't even know who you are. They've been coming here for years and has any of them even asked your last name? Do you think if you left and someone else took over they'd even notice? You're nothing to them. And now you'd risk your life to keep feeding them cucumber sandwiches? And you'd have us do the same?'

His face was bright red as though burned.

'It's our job,' repeated the maître d'.

'Ours is but to do and die, is that it?' Elliot offered a mocking salute.

'Pierre Patenaude's a remarkable man,' Chef Véronique said, speaking to Elliot but heard by all. 'You'd do well to learn from him, Elliot. And the first lesson could be knowing who's on your side. And who isn't.'

'You're right,' said the maître d' to Elliot. 'I will stay to feed them cucumber sandwiches or whatever they want and Chef Véronique makes. And I do it happily. Sometimes people are rude and insensitive and insulting. That's their problem, not mine. Everyone who comes here is treated with respect. Not because they've earned it, but because it's our job. And I do my job well. They're our guests, true. But they're not our superiors. One more outburst like that and you won't have to worry about staying on.' He turned to the rest of the room. 'If any of you want to leave I'll understand. I for one am staying.'

'So am I,' said Chef Véronique.

Gamache noticed Colleen's furtive glances at Elliot, then over to the maître d'.

'They're welcome to quit, Patron,' said Gamache, who'd found this exchange interesting, 'but they're not welcome to leave. You need to stay at the Manoir at least for the next few days.' He let this sink in then smiled reassuringly. 'If you have to stay, you might as well be paid.'

There were nods of agreement. Chef Véronique moved to the cutting board and handed bunches of herbs to a couple of the kitchen staff and soon the air was ripe with the scent of rosemary. A small murmur of conversation picked up. A few of the guys shoved Elliot playfully. But the young man wasn't ready to be jollied out of his rage.

Chief Inspector Gamache left the kitchen wondering about the scene he'd witnessed. He knew that behind rage was fear. That young waiter was very afraid, of something.

'So it was murder, Armand,' said Reine-Marie, shaking her head in disbelief. They were alone in the library and he'd just brought her up to speed. 'But how could someone push that statue over with their bare hands?'

'The family wants to know the same thing,' said Beauvoir, entering the room with Lacoste. 'I just told them we think it's murder.'

'And?' Gamache asked.

'You know what it's like. One moment they believe it, the next they don't,' said Beauvoir. 'Can't say I blame them. I've told them they can leave the Great Room, but not the grounds. And of course the crime site itself is out of bounds. Peter and Clara Morrow have asked to see you,' he said to the Chief Inspector.

'Good. I want to speak to them as well. Tell me what you know.'

Agent Lacoste sat in the wing chair across from Reine-Marie while the two men sat together on the leather sofa, heads almost touching as Beauvoir bent over his notebook and Gamache bent over him. They looked, Reine-Marie thought, a bit like Russian matrioshka dolls, nesting. Large powerful Armand hovering almost protectively over smaller, younger Beauvoir.

She'd spoken to their son Daniel while Armand had been supervising the crime site. He was anxious to speak to his father about the name they'd chosen for their child. He knew, as she did, what Honoré meant to his father. And while he'd never hurt his father, he was determined to use that name. But how did Armand feel about another Honoré Gamache? And his own grandson at that?

'How did the Morrows account for themselves last night?' asked Gamache.

Beauvoir consulted his notebook. 'The family was together all through dinner, sharing a table. After dinner they split up. Peter and Clara came in here and had drinks. They said you were with them.'

'Most of the time,' said Reine-Marie. 'We were on the *terrasse*. But we could see them through the window.'

Beauvoir nodded. He liked clarity.

'Monsieur and Madame Finney stayed at the table for their coffee.' Isabelle Lacoste picked up the story. 'Thomas and Sandra Morrow went into the Great Room. Thomas played the piano and Mariana took her child upstairs.'

'Bean,' said Reine-Marie.

'Been?' asked Beauvoir. 'Been what?'

'Bean Morrow, I suppose.'

They looked at each other, confused, then Reine-Marie smiled.

'Bean is the child's name,' she explained, spelling it for him.

'As in coffee?' he asked.

'If you wish,' said Reine-Marie.

He didn't. What he wished was that this would all go away. Jean Guy Beauvoir already suspected most Anglos were nuts. And now a Bean to prove it. Who called their child after a legume?

'And Julia?' asked Gamache. 'What did they say about her movements last night?'

'Thomas and Sandra Morrow say she went into the garden for a walk,' said Lacoste.

'She came into the library through the screen door from the garden,' Reine-Marie remembered. 'We were all in here by then. Thomas and Sandra Morrow had joined us. So had Mariana. The Finneys had just gone to bed.'

'Did they go to bed before or after Julia appeared?' Gamache asked his wife.

They stared at each other, then each shook their head.

'Can't remember,' said Reine-Marie. 'Does it matter?'

'Movements just before a murder always matter.'

'But you can't really think they killed Julia?' Reine-Marie asked, then regretted questioning her husband in front of his staff. But he didn't seem to care.

'Stranger things have happened,' he said, and she knew that was true.

'What was your impression of Julia Martin, sir?' Lacoste asked.

'She was elegant, sophisticated, well educated. She was self-deprecating and charming and she knew it. Is that fair?' He turned to his wife, who nodded. 'She was very polite. It made a contrast to the rest of her family. Almost too polite. She was very nice, kind, and I thought that was the impression she wanted to make.'

'Don't most people?' asked Lacoste.

'Most people want to make a good impression, it's true,' said Gamache. 'We're taught to be polite. But with Julia Martin it seemed more than a desire. It seemed a need.'

'That was my impression too,' said Reine-Marie. 'But

143

there was something manipulative about her, I felt. She told you that story, about her first job.'

Gamache told Beauvoir and Lacoste about Julia's first job and her mother's reaction.

'What a terrible thing to say to a daughter,' said Lacoste. 'Making her feel she has no role in life, except to be docile and grateful.'

'It was a terrible thing to say,' agreed Reine-Marie. 'Crippling, if you let it. But why is she still telling it forty years later?'

'Why do you think?' Gamache asked.

'Well, I find it interesting she told you, and not us. But then I'm not a man.'

'Now that's an interesting thing to say,' said Gamache. 'What do you mean?'

'I think like many women she behaved differently around men. And men seem hard wired to be sympathetic to a needy woman, even you. Julia was vulnerable. But she played on those things, I think. Probably had her whole life. And I think her tragedy wasn't that she had low self-esteem, though I think she had. Her tragedy was that she always found men to save her. She never had to save herself. She never knew she could.'

'From what I gather, she was about to find out,' said Agent Lacoste, understanding exactly what Reine-Marie Gamache was talking about. 'She'd left her husband and was starting a new life.'

'Yeah, right,' said Beauvoir. 'With millions of dollars. Not exactly a test of self-sufficiency. She is the Julia Martin who was married to that insurance man, the guy in a pen out west?'

'She is,' said Gamache.

'And what was the first thing she did?' asked Reine-Marie. 'She came here. To her family. Once again she wanted others to fix her.'

'Was it that?' asked Gamache, almost to himself. 'Or was she looking for something else from them?'

'Like what?' Beauvoir asked.

'I don't know. Maybe I was taken in by her, but I have a feeling there was something else behind her being here. She must have known her family weren't the supportive kind. I'm not sure she came here for that.'

'Revenge?' asked Reine-Marie. 'Remember last night?'

She told Inspector Beauvior and Agent Lacoste about the scene between Julia and her siblings.

'So you think she came here to unload?' asked Beauvoir. 'Having told the criminal husband to fuck off it was time to tell Mother and the rest?'

'I don't know,' admitted Reine-Marie. 'The problem was her outburst seemed so unplanned, so unexpected.'

'I wonder if it was,' said Gamache. He hadn't thought of it before but now he wondered. 'Is it possible one of them provoked that outburst? After all, who knows you better than your family?'

'What were you talking about?' asked Lacoste.

'Toilets,' said Gamache.

'Toilets?' asked Beauvoir. He'd been feeling a little intimidated by the surroundings but if that's what rich people and senior Sûreté officers on vacation talk about, hell, he'd fit right in.

The door opened and Clementine Dubois waddled in, followed by the maître d' and a couple of the staff, carrying trays.

'I thought you could use some refreshment,' the proprietor said. 'I've taken food and drinks in to the family as well.'

'How are they?' asked Gamache.

'Pretty upset. They're demanding to see you.'

Gamache looked down at a tray of frothy cold soups with delicate mint leaves and curled lemon rind floating on the top. Another tray held platters of open-faced sandwiches, roast beef, smoked salmon, tomato and Brie. The final tray held bottles of ginger beer, spruce beer, ginger ale, beer and a bucket with a light white wine on ice.

'*Merci.*' He accepted a ginger beer and turned to the maître d'. 'When did the storm start last night? Do you know?'

'Well, I'd done my last tour of the place and had just gone to bed. I was woken by a huge explosion, practically blew me out of bed. I looked over to my clock radio and it said one something. Then the power went out.'

'Did you see anyone before you went to bed?' asked Beauvoir, who'd taken a soup and a roast beef sandwich and was about to plop into a large leather wing chair.

The maître d' shook his head. 'No one was up.'

Gamache knew that wasn't true. Someone was up.

'I was woken by the storm too,' said Madame Dubois. 'I got up to make sure everything was properly shut and to secure the shutters. Pierre and a couple of the staff were already running around. You two were there. You helped.'

'A little. Were all the windows and doors shut?'

'They were shut before I went to bed,' said Pierre. 'I check on my last rounds.'

'But in the storm some blew open.' Gamache remembered the banging. 'Were they locked?'

'No,' Madame Dubois admitted. 'We never lock. Pierre's been trying to convince me for a few years that we should, but I'm a little hesitant.'

'Pig-headed,' said the maître d'.

'Perhaps a little. But we've never had a problem and we're in the middle of nowhere. Who's going to break in? A bear?'

'It's a different world,' said Pierre.

'Today I believe you.'

'It wouldn't have changed anything,' Gamache said. 'Julia Martin would still be dead no matter how many doors were locked.'

'Because whoever did this was already inside,' said Madame Dubois. 'What happened here last night isn't allowed.'

It was such an extraordinary thing to say it actually stopped the ravenous Beauvoir from taking another bite of his roast beef on baguette.

'You have a rule against murder?' he asked.

'I do. When my husband and I bought the Bellechasse we made a deal with the forest. Any death that wasn't natural wasn't allowed. Mice are caught alive and released. Birds are fed in the winter and even the squirrels and chipmunks are welcome. There's no hunting, not even fishing. The pact we made was that everything that stepped foot on this land would be safe.'

'An extravagant promise,' said Gamache.

'Perhaps.' She managed a small smile. 'But we meant it. Nothing would deliberately die at our hands, or the hands of anyone living here. We have an attic filled with reminders of what happens when creatures turn against each other. It scared that poor child half to death and well it should scare us all. But we've grown used to it, we tolerate the taking of lives. But it's not allowed here. You must find out who did this. Because I know one thing for sure. If a person would kill once, they'd kill again.'

She nodded briskly and left, followed silently by Pierre.

Gamache watched the door close. He knew the same thing.

THIRTEEN

﹏

'Mrs Morrow, would you like some lunch?'
'No, Claire, thank you.'

The elderly woman sat on the sofa next to her husband, as though her spine had fused. Clara held out a small plate with a bit of poached salmon, delicate mayonnaise and paper-thin cucumbers and onion in vinegar. One of Peter's mother's favourite lunches, she knew, from the times she'd asked for it at their place when all they had to offer was a simple sandwich. Two struggling artists rarely ran to salmon.

Normally when Mrs Morrow called her Claire, Clara was livid. For the first decade she'd presumed Peter's mother simply didn't hear well and genuinely thought her name was Claire. Sometime in the second decade of her marriage to Peter, Clara realized her mother-in-law knew perfectly well what her name was. And what her profession was, though she continued to ask about her job at some mythical shoe store. It was, of course, possible Peter had actually told his mother Clara worked in a shoe store. Anything, she knew, was possible with the Morrows. Especially if it meant keeping the truth from each other.

'A drink, perhaps?' she asked.

'My husband will look after me, thank you.'

Clara was dismissed. She glanced at her watch. Past noon. Could they leave soon? She hated herself for the thought, but she hated staying even more. And another thought she hated still more. That Julia's death was a massive inconvenience. More than that, it was a pain in the ass. There. She'd said it.

She wanted to go home. To be surrounded by her own things, her own friends. To work on her solo show. In peace.

She felt like shit.

Turning to look back she saw Bert Finney with his eyes closed.

Sleeping.

He's fucking sleeping. The rest of us are trying to deal with this tragedy and he's napping. She opened her mouth to invite Peter onto the *terrasse*. She longed for some fresh air, maybe a little walk through the mist. Anything to escape this stifling atmosphere.

But Peter had gone again. Into his own world. He was focused only on the movement of his pencil. Art had been his sanity growing up. The only place where nothing happened unless he made it happen. Lines appeared and disappeared according to his will alone.

But when does the lifeboat become the prison ship? When does the drug start working against you? Had her beloved, gentle, wounded husband escaped too far?

What was that called? She tried to remember conversations with her friend Myrna in Three Pines. The former psychologist sometimes talked about that. People who were delusional, disconnected.

Insane.

No, she shoved the shard of a word away. Peter was wounded, hurt, brilliant for having found a coping mechanism that soothed as well as provided an income. He was one of the most respected artists in Canada. Respected by everyone, except his own family.

Mrs Morrow was rolling in money and yet she'd never once bought a painting by her own son, even when they were all but starving. She'd offered to give them money, but Peter had side-stepped that mine.

Clara watched as Mariana Morrow wandered to the piano. Thomas had abandoned it and was now reading a newspaper. Mariana sat, swept her shawl over her shoulder and held her hands over the keys.

This should be good, thought Clara, awaiting the clunks and bangs. Anything to break the crackling silence. Mariana's hands hovered, bouncing slightly, as though playing air-piano. For God's sake, shouted Clara's mind. Can't they do anything for real?

Clara glanced around and saw Bean alone.

'What're you reading?' she asked, joining the serious child on the window seat.

Bean showed Clara the book. *Myths Every Child Should Know*.

'Wonderful. Did you find it in the library?'

'No, Mommy gave it to me. It was hers. See.' Bean showed Clara the first page, inscribed, *For Mariana on her birthday, from Mother and Father.*

Clara felt tears sting her eyes again. Bean stared at her.

'I'm sorry,' said Clara, dabbing her eye with a cushion. 'I'm being silly.'

But Clara knew why she wept. Not for Julia, not for Mrs Morrow. She wept for all the Morrows, but mostly for parents who gave gifts and wrote 'from'. For parents who never lost children because they never had them.

'Are you all right?' asked Bean.

It had been Clara's intention to comfort Bean.

'It's just very sad,' said Clara. 'I'm sorry about your aunt. How about you? Are you all right?'

Bean's mouth opened and music came out. Or so it seemed for an instant.

Turning round Clara stared at the piano. Mariana had dropped her hands to the keys, and they were doing the most remarkable thing. They were finding the notes. In the right order. The music was astonishing. Fluid and passionate and natural.

It was gorgeous, but it was also typical. She should have known. The untalented brother was a brilliant painter. The mess of a sister was a virtuoso pianist. And Thomas? She'd always presumed he was as he seemed. A successful executive in Toronto. But this family was fuelled by deceit. What was he, really?

Clara glanced around and saw Chief Inspector Gamache standing at the door, staring at Mariana.

The music stopped.

'I'm going to ask you all to stay at the Manoir for at least another day, perhaps longer.'

'Of course,' said Thomas.

'Thank you,' said the Chief Inspector. 'We're collecting evidence now and sometime today one of my agents will interview each of you. Until then feel free to wander the grounds. I'd like to speak with you. Will you walk with me?'

He gestured to Peter, who rose.

'We'd like to go first,' said Sandra, her eyes anxiously flitting from Peter to Gamache and back.

'Why?'

This seemed to surprise her. 'Do I need a reason?'

'It would help. If there's a pressing need then I'll ask the Inspector to get to you first. Is there one?'

Sandra, deflated and compressed by far too many pressing needs all her life, was silent.

'We don't want to speak to the Inspector,' said Thomas. 'We want to speak to you.'

'Flattering as that is, I'm afraid it'll be Inspector Beauvoir who'll interview you. Unless you'd prefer Agent Lacoste.'

'Then why does he get you?' Thomas jerked his head towards Peter.

'This isn't a competition.'

Thomas Morrow stared at Gamache with a look designed to wither. A look practised and perfected on secretaries who'd traded self-respect for a salary and trainees too young to know a bully from a boss.

As he headed out of the screen door Gamache looked back at the Morrows, staring after him like a *tableau vivant*. Out of that tableau, Gamache knew, a murderer would one day walk. And Gamache would be waiting for him.

Agent Isabelle Lacoste organized the officers from the local Sûreté detachment and handed out assignments. One team would search the staff rooms and outbuildings, another would search the Manoir and her team would handle the guest rooms.

She'd warned them to be careful. They were looking for

evidence, but they were also looking for a murderer. It was possible he was hiding on the grounds. Unlikely, but possible. Agent Lacoste was a cautious woman, by nature and by training. And now she conducted the search, always with the expectation that the monster was indeed under the bed or waiting in the wardrobe.

'Mariana Morrow?'

Inspector Beauvoir stepped into the Great Room, feeling a bit like a dental assistant. *Time for your filling.* And they looked at him with those same dental-patient eyes. Fear for those chosen, annoyance for those left to wait.

'What about us?' asked Sandra, standing up. 'We were told we could go first.'

'*Oui?*' said Beauvoir. No one had told him, and he thought he knew why. 'Well, I think I'll take Mademoiselle Morrow so she can get back to her . . .' Beauvoir looked over at the attractive blond child on the window seat, reading. 'Her child.'

He led Mariana into the library and sat her on a hard chair he'd brought in. Hardly torture, but he didn't like his suspects too comfortable. Besides, he wanted the big leather chair for himself.

'Mademoiselle Morrow—' he began.

'Oh, look, you have sandwiches. We've run out.' She got up and took a large tomato and thick-sliced maple ham sandwich without asking.

'I'm sorry about your sister,' he said, timing the barb so that her fat, greedy mouth was too full to answer. *Clearly, you're not*, he'd hoped to imply. But watching her shove the food into her mouth he thought his insult too subtle. He didn't like this woman. Of all the Morrows, even that impatient one, this one he liked least. Sandra he understood. He hated to wait too. He didn't like seeing others served first, especially when he'd arrived before them. He didn't like it when people butted into grocery lines, or cut in on the highway.

He expected people to play fair. Rules meant order. Without them they'd be killing each other. It began with butting in, with parking in disabled spaces, with smoking in elevators. And it ended in murder.

True, he had to admit, it was a bit of a stretch but it was descended from the same line. Trace it back far enough and a murderer probably always broke the rules, thinking himself better than the rest. He didn't like rule-breakers. And he especially didn't like them when they came wrapped in purple and green and scarlet shawls with children named Bean.

'I didn't know her well, you know,' said Mariana, swallowing and taking a spruce beer from the tray. 'Mind?'

But she'd opened it before he could say anything.

'Thanks. Yech.' She almost spat it out. 'Oh my God. Am I the first person to ever drink this stuff? Has anyone at the company tried it? It tastes like a tree.'

She opened and shut her mouth, like a cat trying to get something off its tongue.

'That's just disgusting. Like a sip?' She tilted it towards him. He narrowed his eyes and was surprised to see a grin on her unlovely face.

Poor woman, he thought. So ugly in a family so attractive. While he was no fan of the Morrows he could at least see that they were handsome. Even the dead woman, crushed, had retained some beauty. This one, whole, had none.

155

'No?' She took another sip and winced again, but didn't put it down.

'How well did you know her?'

'She was ten years older than me and had left home before I was twelve. We didn't have much in common. She was into boys, I was into cartoons.'

'You don't seem sorry she's dead. You don't even seem sad.'

'I've been raised in a family of hypocrites, Inspector. I promised myself I wouldn't be like them. I wouldn't hide my feelings.'

'Quite easy when there're none to hide.'

That silenced her. He'd won the point, but was losing the interview. It was never a good sign when the investigator was doing all the talking.

'Why show all your feelings?'

Her smiling face grew serious. It didn't make her more attractive. Now she looked glum and ugly. 'I grew up in Disney World. It looked good from the outside. It was meant to. But inside everything was mechanical. You never knew what was real. Too much courtesy, too many smiles. I grew frightened of smiles. Never a cross word, but never a supportive one either. You never knew how people really felt. We kept things to ourselves. Still do. Except me. I'm honest about most things.'

Interesting how important a single word could become.

'What do you mean, most?'

'Well, it'd be foolish to tell my family everything.'

She seemed suddenly coy, almost flirtatious. It was revolting.

'What haven't you told them?'

'Little things. Like what I do for a living.'

'What do you do?'

156

'I'm an architect. I design homes.'

Beauvoir thought he knew the kinds of homes she designed. Ones that impressed, that were all gaudy and shiny and big. Loud homes, that no one could actually live in.

'What else don't you tell them?'

She paused and looked around then leaned forward.

'Bean.'

'Your child?'

She nodded.

'What about Bean?' Beauvoir's pen hovered over his notebook.

'I haven't told them.'

'Who the father is?' He'd broken the cardinal rule of interrogation. He'd answered his own question. She shook her head and smiled.

'Of course I haven't told them that. There's no answer to that,' she said cryptically. 'I haven't told them what Bean is.'

Beauvoir felt himself grow cold.

'What is Bean?'

'Exactly. Even you don't know. But sadly Bean's nearing puberty and soon it'll be obvious.'

It took a moment for Beauvoir to appreciate what she meant. He dropped his pen and it rolled off the table to the carpeted floor.

'You mean you haven't told your family if Bean's a boy or girl?'

Mariana Morrow nodded and took a long pull on her spruce beer.

'It actually doesn't taste too bad. I guess you can get used to anything.'

Beauvoir doubted it. For fifteen years he'd been with the

Chief Inspector, investigating murders, and he'd never got used to the insanity of the Anglos. It seemed bottomless, and purposeless. What kind of creature kept the sex of her child a secret?

'It's my little homage to my upbringing, Inspector. Bean is my child and my secret. I can't tell you how good it feels in a family of know-it-alls to know something they don't.'

Fucking Anglos, thought Beauvoir. If he tried that his mother'd thrash him with a rolling pin.

'Can't they just ask Bean themselves?'

She roared with laughter, speckles of tomato hitting the pine table in front of him.

'Are you kidding? A Morrow ask a question? Admit ignorance?' She leaned forward conspiratorially and despite himself Beauvoir leaned forward to meet her. 'That's the brilliance of this. Their own arrogance is my best weapon.'

Beauvoir leaned back, then. Repulsed. How can a woman, a mother, do such a thing? His own mother would die for him, would kill for him. It was natural. This thing in front of him was unnatural.

'And what will you do when it's no longer a secret, mademoiselle? When Bean hits puberty, or volunteers the information one day?' He was damned if he was going to ask Bean's sex. He wouldn't give her the satisfaction of admitting he cared.

'Well, I always have Bean's name to torture her with.'

'Her?'

'My mother.'

Beauvoir could barely look at this woman, who'd given birth to a biological weapon aimed at her mother. He was beginning to think the wrong Morrow was murdered.

'Why would someone want to kill your sister?'

'By someone you mean one of us, don't you?'

It wasn't actually a question and now Beauvoir chose to stay quiet.

'Don't look at me. I didn't know her enough to kill her. She'd been gone for thirty years or more. But I can tell you one thing, Inspector. She could put as much distance between herself and us as she wanted, but she was still a Morrow. Morrows lie, and Morrows keep secrets. It's our currency. Don't trust them, Inspector. Don't trust a word they say.'

It was the first thing she'd said he'd no trouble believing.

'Julia had a falling out with Father,' said Peter. 'I don't know what it was about.'

'Weren't you curious?' asked Gamache. The two tall men had walked down the wet lawn of the Bellechasse and stopped at the shoreline. They looked onto the slate-grey lake and the mist that obscured the far shore. The birds were out, looking for insects, and every now and then a haunting loon called across the lake.

Peter smiled tightly. 'Curiosity wasn't something rewarded in our home. It was considered rude. It was rude to ask questions, rude to laugh too loud or too long, rude to cry, rude to contradict. So, no, I wasn't curious.'

'So she left home when she was in her early twenties. Thomas would have been a couple of years older and you were?'

'Eighteen,' said Peter.

'That's precise.'

'I'm a precise man, as you know,' said Peter, this time with a genuine smile. He was beginning to breathe again, feel

159

himself again. He looked down and was surprised to see crumbs on his shirt. He batted them off. Then he picked up a handful of pebbles. 'Julia would have loved today,' he said, skimming the stones.

'Why do you say that?' asked Gamache.

'It's a Vancouver day. She used to tell me how moody it was. Said it suited her.'

'Was she moody?'

Peter watched as his pebble took four skips before sinking. 'She was. But then I always think of her as twenty-one. I didn't see much of her after she left.'

'Why not?' Gamache watched his friend closely. There was a definite disadvantage to investigating a friend for murder. But there were advantages too. Like knowing when they were hiding something.

'We're not a close family. I sometimes wonder what'll happen after Mother goes. She's the one we come to see, the others are just there.'

'Maybe it'll bring you together.'

'Maybe. It might be a blessing. But I don't think so. I didn't choose to see Julia, but she didn't choose to see us either. She was happy in Vancouver with David and she forgot all about us. And frankly, months, years, would go by before I thought about her.'

'What would remind you?'

'Pardon?'

'What would bring her to mind? You say years could go by, but what would make her come back into your head?'

'Nothing much.'

'You do know I'm not just making conversation. These questions are important, even if they don't seem it.'

Gamache had spoken uncharacteristically sternly and it was true that Peter had forgotten he was speaking with the head of homicide for the Sûreté du Québec.

'I'm sorry. Why would I think of her?' He thought about it, then felt a pinch when he realized what the answer was. 'Because she'd call or write. We'd get postcards from all over. She and David travelled a lot.'

'She reached out to you,' said Gamache.

'Only when she wanted something. My sister might have appeared nice and kind but she was very canny. She almost always got what she wanted.'

'And what would she want? Not money, surely.'

'No, she had plenty of that. I think she just wanted to hurt. To make us feel guilty. It was her little game. Sending cards, phoning occasionally, but always making sure we knew she was the one who'd made the first move. We owed her. It was subtle, but we Morrows are nothing if not subtle.'

Not as subtle as you think, Gamache thought.

'We're a greedy family, Gamache. Greedy and even cruel. I know that. Why do you think I live with Clara in Three Pines? To get as far away as possible. I know salvation when I see it. And Julia? You want to know about Julia?' He heaved a stone as far as he could into the iron waters. 'She was the cruellest, the greediest, of us all.'

Sandra snuffed out her cigarette and smiled, smoothing down her slacks. They were tight, but Sandra knew country air made things shrink. Then she walked back into the Manoir. The dining room was empty. There, at the far end, was the dessert tray.

But a movement caught her eye.

161

Bean.

What was the child doing? Stealing the best desserts, probably.

The two stared at each other and then Sandra noticed something white and gleaming in Bean's hand. She moved closer.

It was a cookie. A chocolate-covered marshmallow cookie, with the chocolate eaten off, leaving just the mallow and the biscuit, and a guilty-looking child holding it.

'Bean, what've you been doing?'

'Nothing.'

'That means something. Now tell me.'

Just then an object fell and bounced on the floor between them. Sandra looked up. Dotted on the cathedral ceiling, between and sometimes on the old maple beams, were cookies. Bean had licked the marshmallow then tossed the cookies at the ceiling, sticking them there.

It was a constellation of cookies.

There must have been a pack and a half up there.

Sandra looked sternly at the odd child. And then, just as she opened her mouth to chastise, something else came out. Laughter. A small burp of amusement, then another. Bean, steeled for rebuke, looked surprised. But not half as surprised as Sandra, who'd expected to scold and instead had laughed.

'Want one?'

Bean held out the box and Sandra took one.

'You do thith, thee,' said Bean, sucking the chocolate cone off the top. 'Then you lick it.' Bean did. 'Then you toss it.'

Bean hurled the moistened cookie towards the ceiling. Sandra watched, breath held, to see if it stuck. It did.

'Try it. I'll show you.'

Bean, patient and clear, a born teacher, taught Sandra how to stick cookies to the ceiling. Granted, Sandra was a natural, and before long the dining room ceiling was covered, a form of insulation undreamed of by the Robber Barons or the Abinaki. Or Madame Dubois.

Sandra left the room, smiling, having forgotten why she went in. She'd never wanted children, too much work. But sometimes, in the company of an extraordinary child, a kind child, she felt an ache. It was inconceivable that fat, stupid, lazy Mariana had managed to have a baby. It gave Sandra some comfort to think Bean was screwed up. But then sometimes she forgot to hate Bean. And terrible things happened.

'Where were you?' Mariana asked when Sandra returned. 'The police want you.'

'I was taking a walk. I heard Peter talking to that Chief Inspector and he said the oddest thing.' She noticed her mother-in-law and raised her voice slightly. 'He said he thought if his mother died it would be a blessing.'

'He didn't,' said Mariana, clearly delighted. 'Really?'

'There's more. He said Julia was greedy and cruel. Imagine that. She's barely gone and already he's badmouthing her, and to a stranger. But maybe I misheard.'

'What was that?' Mrs Finney spoke from across the room, her soft pink face turned to them.

'I'm sure he didn't mean it. Forget I said anything.'

'He said Julia was greedy and cruel?'

Mrs Morrow saw again her daughter's white hand reaching out. So typical of Charles, to do such damage. Especially to Julia. But he'd damaged them all.

And now Peter was continuing his father's work.

'I won't have it. Julia was the most kind, the most sensitive, of all the children. Certainly the most loving.'

'I'm sorry,' said Sandra, and she was beginning to mean it.

'Who would want to kill your sister?'

Across from Beauvoir sat Thomas Morrow, a man in command even in the wilderness. He smoothed his linen slacks and smiled charmingly.

'She was a lovely woman. No one would want her dead.'

'Why not?'

'Shouldn't you be asking why?' But he was suddenly nonplussed.

'Why?'

'Huh?' asked Thomas, lost now. 'Look, this is ridiculous. My sister is dead, but she can't have been murdered.'

'Why not?'

Back there again. Beauvoir loved rattling witnesses.

'Listen, she lived most of her life in Vancouver. If she angered anyone enough to kill her they'd be there, not here, and sure as hell not in the middle of nowhere.'

'You're here.'

'What's that supposed to mean?'

'I heard all about what happened last night. In this very room. That must be the coffee stain.' He walked over and looked down. He'd found it before, but he liked the drama of this 'sudden' discovery.

'She wasn't herself, she was upset.'

'What upset her?'

'She'd been flustered all day. Father's unveiling. She and Father had had a falling out. It was emotional for all of us to see that statue, but probably more so for her. It's a difficult time for her. She's just been through a very public and messy divorce. Her husband was David Martin, you know.'

His grey-blue eyes slid over to Beauvoir, to make sure he'd understood. Beauvoir already knew about David Martin but was interested in Morrow's manner. He'd spoken with both malicious pleasure and pride. Pleasure that his little sister had screwed up and married a felon, and pride that the felon was one of the wealthiest men in Canada, even after paying back all that money.

'Who would want your sister dead?'

'Nobody. This was a family reunion, a happy time. No one wanted her dead.'

Beauvoir slowly turned his head to look into the misty day and was silent but even a Morrow couldn't miss his meaning. A hole in the ground outside those windows put the lie to Thomas Morrow's words.

Don't believe a thing they say, Mariana Morrow had said. And Beauvoir didn't.

'Did Julia have any children?' Gamache asked as he and Peter emerged from the woods and headed slowly back to the Manoir.

'None. Don't even know if they tried. We're not a big family for kids,' said Peter. 'We eat our young.'

Gamache let that join the mist around them. 'What did you think of the statue of your father?'

Peter didn't seem fazed by the non sequitur. 'I didn't give it any thought. I had no reaction at all.'

'That's not possible. Even as an artist you must've had an opinion.'

'Oh, well, as an artist, yes. I can see the merit. Obviously the person who did it has some technique. It wasn't bad. But he'd never met Father.'

Gamache just kept walking, his large hands clasped behind his back, his gaze alternately on his soaking feet and on the ever growing Manoir.

'My father never looked like that. Never looked sad or whatever that was on his face. He only ever scowled. And he never, ever stooped. He was huge and, and . . .' Peter gestured with his arms, as though sketching the world. 'Huge. He killed Julia.'

'His statue killed Julia.'

'No, I mean before she left, he killed her. He took her spirit and he crushed her. He crushed us all. That's what you've been dying for me to say, isn't it? Why do you think we have no children, any of us? Look at our role models. Would you?'

'There is one child. Bean.'

Peter harrumphed.

Again, Gamache was quiet.

'Bean doesn't jump.'

Gamache stopped, arrested by this unlikely string of words from his companion.

Bean doesn't jump.

'Pardon?' he asked.

'Bean doesn't jump,' Peter repeated.

He might as well have said, 'Toaster picture bicycle,' for all the sense he made.

'What do you mean?' Gamache asked, suddenly feeling very stupid.

'Bean can't leave the ground.'

Armand Gamache felt the damp seep into his bones.

'Bean's feet never leave the ground, at least not together. The child can't or won't jump.'

Bean can't jump, thought Armand Gamache. What family produces a child so earthbound? Mired. How does Bean express excitement? Joy? But thinking about the child, and the family, he had his answer. So far, in ten years, that hadn't been an issue.

Armand Gamache decided to call his son as soon as he was back at the Manoir.

FOURTEEN

⁓

'Daniel?'

'Hi, Dad, *enfin*. I was beginning to think I'd imagined you.'

Gamache laughed. 'Mom and I are at the Manoir Bellechasse, not exactly a telecommunications hub.'

As he spoke he looked out of the French doors of the library, across the mint-green wet grass and to the misty lake beyond. A low cloud clung softly to the forest. He could hear birds and insects, and sometimes a splash as a feeding trout or bass jumped. And he could hear the wah-wah of a siren and the irritated honking of a horn.

Paris.

The City of Light mingling with the wilderness. What a world we live in, he thought.

'It's nine p.m. here. What time is it there?' Daniel asked.

'Almost three. Is Florence in bed?'

'We're all in bed, I'm embarrassed to admit. Ah, Paris.' Daniel laughed his deep, easy rumble. 'But I'm glad we finally connected. Here, wait, let me just get to another room.'

Gamache could see him in their tiny flat in Saint-Germain-des-Prés. Moving to another room wouldn't guarantee either privacy for him or peace for his wife and child.

'Armand?' Reine-Marie stood at the door of the library. She'd packed her bags and a porter was just taking them out to the car. They'd talked about it, and Armand had asked her to leave the Bellechasse.

'I will, of course, if that's what you want,' she'd said. But she searched his face. She'd never seen him on a case before, though he talked about his work all the time and often asked her opinion. Unlike most of his colleagues, Gamache hid nothing from his wife. He didn't think he could keep so much of his life from her and not have it come between them. And she was more important than any career.

'I'll worry less if you're not here,' he said.

'I understand,' and she did. She'd feel the same way, if roles were reversed. 'But do you mind if I don't go far?'

'A pup tent on the edge of the property?'

'You are intuitive,' she'd said. 'But I was thinking of Three Pines.'

'What a good idea. I'll just ring Gabri and get you into his B&B.'

'No, you find out who murdered Julia and I'll call the B&B.'

And now she was ready to go. Ready but not happy. She'd felt a pain in her chest as she'd watched him negotiating the first steps of the investigation. His people so respectful, the officers from the local detachment so deferential and even frightened of him, until he'd put them at ease. But not too much at ease. She'd watched her husband take command of the situation, naturally. She knew, and he knew, that someone needed to be in charge. And he was by temperament more than rank the natural leader.

She'd never actually witnessed it before, and she'd watched with surprise as a man she knew intimately exposed a whole new side of himself. He commanded with ease because he commanded respect. Except from the Morrows, who seemed to think he'd tricked them. They'd seemed more upset by that than by the death of Julia.

But Armand always said people react differently to death, and it was folly to judge anyone and double folly to judge what people do when faced with sudden, violent death. Murder. They weren't themselves.

But privately Reine-Marie wondered. Wondered whether what people did in a crisis was, in fact, their real selves. Stripped of artifice and social training. It was easy enough to be decent when all was going your way. It was another matter to be decent when all hell was breaking loose.

Her husband stepped deliberately into all hell every day, and maintained his decency. She doubted the same could be said for the Morrows.

She'd interrupted him. She could see he was on the phone and began to leave the room. Then she heard the word Roslyn.

He was speaking to Daniel and asking after their daughter-in-law. Reine-Marie had tried to speak to Armand about Daniel, but it had never seemed the right time and now it was too late. Standing on the threshold she listened, her heart pounding.

'I know Mom told you about the names we've chosen. Geneviève if it's a girl—'

'Beautiful name,' said Gamache.

'We think so. But we also think the boy's name is beautiful. Honoré.'

Gamache had promised himself there'd be no awkward silence when the name was said. There was an awkward silence.

> Breathes there the man with soul so dead
> Who never to himself hath said,
> 'This is my own, my native land!'

The words of the old poem, spoken as always in the deep, calm voice in his head, filled the void. His large hand clasped gently shut as though holding on to something.

> Whose heart hath ne'er within him burned,
> As home his footsteps he hath turned
> From wandering on a foreign strand?

Daniel was in Paris, so far away, but he also felt Daniel was in danger of making a very serious mistake that could propel him further still.

'I think that might not be the best choice.'

'Why?' Daniel sounded curious, not defensive.

'You know the history.'

'You told me, but it is history, Dad. And Honoré Gamache is a good name, for a good man. You more than anyone know that.'

'It's true.' Gamache felt a twinge of anxiety. Daniel wasn't backing down. 'But more than anyone I also know what can happen in a world not always kind.'

'You've taught us we make our own world. What was that Milton quote we were raised with?

'The mind is its own place, and in it self
Can make a Heav'n of Hell, a Hell of Heav'n.

'It's what you believe, Dad, and so do I. Remember those walks in the park? You'd take Annie and me and recite poetry all the way there. That was one of your favourites. And mine.'

Gamache felt a fizzing in his throat as he remembered walks, tiny, pudgy fingers in what seemed a massive hand. Not so much holding as being held.

'One day soon it'll be my turn. I'll be taking Florence and Honoré to Parc Mont Royal blabbing poetry all the way.'

'Blabbing? Don't you mean reciting in a strong yet musical voice?'

'Of course. *Breathes there the man with soul so dead.* Remember that one?'

'I do.'

'All the ones you taught me, I'll teach them, including Milton, including that the mind is its own place and we make our own reality, our own world. Don't worry,' Daniel continued, his voice full of reason and patience. 'Honoré will know the world starts between his ears and is his for the making. And he'll be taught as I was what a beautiful name that is.'

'No, Daniel, you're making a mistake.' There, he'd said it. The one thing he'd promised himself not to say. Still, Daniel had to be made to see it, had to be stopped from making this well-intentioned but tragic mistake.

In his peripheral vision he saw a movement. Reine-Marie had taken a step into the room. He looked at her. Her body was composed but her eyes were filled with surprise and anxiety. Still, it had to be done. Sometimes parenting was standing up and doing what was unpopular. Risking censure. Daniel must not be allowed to name his son Honoré.

'I'd hoped you'd feel differently, Dad.'

'But why would I? Nothing's changed.'

'Time has changed. That was years ago. Decades. You need to let it go.'

'I've seen things. I've seen what wilful parents can do to a child. I've seen kids so deeply wounded—' they can't even jump, he almost said. Their feet never leave the ground. No leap for joy, no skipping rope, no jumping from the dock, no dangling in the arms of a loving and trusted parent.

'Are you accusing me of hurting our child?' Daniel's voice was no longer full of reason and patience. 'Are you really suggesting I'd hurt my son? He isn't even born yet and you're already accusing me? You still see me as a screw-up, don't you?'

'Daniel, calm down. I never saw you as a screw-up, you know that.'

Across the room he could hear Reine-Marie inhale.

'You're right. Always right. You get to win because you know things I don't, you've seen things I haven't. And you seem to know I'm so wilful I'd give our child a name that will ruin him.'

'Life can be hard enough without giving a child a name that will lead to abuse, to bullying.'

'Yes, it could lead to that, but it could also lead to pride, to self-worth—'

173

'He'll find his own self-worth no matter what name you give him. Don't handicap him.'

'You'd consider Honoré a birth defect?' Daniel's voice was dangerously distant.

'I didn't say that.' Gamache tried to pull back but knew it had gone too far. 'Look, we should talk about this in person. I'm sorry if I seemed to say you'd deliberately hurt your child. I know you wouldn't. You're a wonderful parent—'

'Glad you think so.'

'Any child would be fortunate to be born to you. But you asked how I feel, and it's possible I'm wrong but I think it would be unfair to name your son Honoré.'

'Thanks for calling,' said Daniel and hung up.

Gamache stood with the phone to his ear, stunned. Had it really gone so far wrong?

'Was it bad?' Reine-Marie asked.

'Bad enough.' Gamache hung up. 'But we'll work it out.'

He wasn't worried, really. He and Daniel argued sometimes, as he did with his daughter Annie. Disagreements were natural, he told himself. But this was different. He'd hurt his son in a place he himself knew. He'd questioned his ability as a father.

'Oh good, you're back.'

Beauvoir swung into the room, narrowly avoiding a technician carrying a huge box. 'Agent Lacoste's just finishing her search of the guest rooms. They've been all over the buildings. Nothing. And I've interviewed Thomas, Mariana and just now Sandra. They're not exactly the Waltons.'

Equipment was arriving and the old log library was being transformed into a modern incident room. Desks were cleared, computers hooked up, blackboards and foolscap put up on easels, ready for Inspector Beauvoir's facts, for witness lists and movement charts. For evidence lists and clues.

'We have a problem, Chief.' This came from a technician kneeling beside a computer.

'I'll be right with you. Did you get through to the B&B?'

'All arranged,' said Reine-Marie.

'Inspector, will you join me? We'll drive over to Three Pines with Madame Gamache then head on to the Sherbrooke detachment. We're meeting the crane operator there in an hour.'

'With pleasure,' said Beauvoir, adjusting an easel and fishing in a box for magic markers.

'What's the problem?' Gamache stood over the technician.

'This place. Hasn't been rewired in years, sir. I don't think we can plug these in.' She held up the plug for a computer.

'I'll find the maître d',' said Beauvoir, heading to the dining room.

Fucking country. Middle of nowhere. He'd been doing quite well until now. Trying to ignore the mosquitoes and blackflies and no-see-'ems. At least in Montreal you see what's coming at you. Cars. Trucks. Kids jonesing on crack. Big things. Out here everything's hidden, everything's hiding. Tiny bloodsucking bugs, spiders and snakes and animals in the forests, rotten wiring behind walls made from tree trunks for God's sake. It was like trying to conduct a modern murder investigation in Fred Flintstone's cave.

'*Bonjour?*' he called. No one.

'Anyone there?' He poked his head into the dining room. Empty.

'Hello?' What, was it siesta time? Maybe they were out shooting dinner. He swung open a door and stepped into the kitchen.

'Oh, hello. Can I help you?'

A voice, deep and sing-song, came from a walk-in cold room. Then a woman walked out, carrying a roast. She wore a white apron round her neck and tied at her thick waist. It was simple, no-nonsense. Nothing cute written on it. She marched towards him, her eyes keen and enquiring. She was six feet if she was an inch, Beauvoir guessed. Far from young and far from slim. Her hair was curly, black and grey, short and unbecoming. Her hands were huge, indelicate.

'What can I do for you?' The voice sounded as though she'd swallowed it.

Beauvoir stared.

'Is something wrong?' the throaty voice asked, as the roast was slapped down on the maple cutting block.

Beauvoir was all tingles. He tried to stop staring, but couldn't. Instead of feeling his heart racing, he actually felt it slow down. Calm down. Something happened and all the tension, all the excess energy, all the insistence, left.

He relaxed.

'Do I know you?' she asked.

'I'm sorry.' He stepped forward. 'I'm Inspector Beauvoir. Jean Guy Beauvoir, with the Sûreté.'

'Of course. I should have known.'

'Why? Do you know me?' he asked, hopeful.

'No, I know Madame Martin was killed.'

He was disappointed. He wanted her to know him. To explain this familiarity he suddenly felt. It was disquieting.

Beauvoir looked at the woman who had done this to him.

She must have been almost sixty, was built like an oak, moved like a trucker, spoke as if she'd swallowed a tuba.

'Who are you?' he managed to get out.

'I'm the chef here. Véronique Langlois.'

Véronique Langlois. It was a lovely name but it meant nothing. He felt sure he knew her.

'What can I do to help?' she asked.

What could she do to help? Think, man, think.

'The maître d'. I'm looking for him.'

'He's probably through there.' She pointed to swinging double doors from the kitchen. Beauvoir thanked her and walked out in a daze.

Through the French doors he saw the maître d' talking to one of the waiters on the deserted *terrasse* outside.

'You think this job is so difficult? Try planting trees or working in a mine, or cutting lawns at a cemetery all summer.'

'Look, I don't care what you did at my age. It doesn't interest me. All I know is Julia Martin's dead and someone here did it.'

'Do you know anything about her death, Elliot?'

There was silence.

'Don't be foolish, boy. If you know something—'

'You think I'd tell you? She was a decent person and someone killed her. That's all I know.'

'You're lying. You spent time with her, didn't you?'

'Time? What? All the spare time you give us? I work twelve hours a day, when would I have time to spend with anyone?'

'Are you going to go through life complaining?'

'Depends. Are you going to go through life bending over?'

Elliot turned and stomped away. Beauvoir held back,

curious to see what the maître d' would do when he thought no one was watching.

Pierre Patenaude stared after Elliot, grateful no one had heard their conversation. It'd been a mistake to tell Elliot about his own summer jobs, he could see that. But it was too late now. Then he remembered his father's words, spoken in the boardroom, surrounded by ancient, serious men.

'Everyone gets a second chance. But not a third.'

He'd fired a man that day. Pierre had seen it. It was horrible.

This was Elliot's third chance. He'd have to fire Elliot. Once the investigation was over and the police gone. It was no use doing it before that, since Elliot had to hang around anyway. The maître d' hadn't had to fire many people, but every time he did he thought of that day in the boardroom, and his father. And he thought of what his father did later.

Years after the firing his father had quietly invested hundreds of thousands of his own dollars in helping the man he'd fired start his own company.

He'd given him a third chance after all. But then he suspected his father was kinder than he was.

Turning round, Pierre was startled to see a man watching through the doors. Then he waved as the Inspector joined him on the stone *terrasse*.

'I've arranged accommodations for you and the other officer. We've put you in the main building, not far from the Chief Inspector.'

Beauvoir swatted a mosquito. More swarmed.

'*Merci, Patron.* Quite a kid.' Beauvoir gestured towards Elliot's retreating back.

'You heard that? I'm sorry. He's just upset.'

Beauvoir had thought the maître d' heroic for not punching the kid but now he wondered if Pierre Patenaude wasn't just weak, letting others, even kids, walk all over him. Beauvoir didn't like weakness. Murderers were weak.

They left the maître d' and the technicians to sort out the electrical problems while Gamache, Reine-Marie and Beauvoir headed to Three Pines. Beauvoir sat in the back seat. Behind Mom and Dad. He quite liked the thought. Ever since his encounter with the chef he'd felt strangely relaxed.

'Do you know the chef at the Manoir?' he asked casually.

'I don't think I've met him,' said Reine-Marie.

'Her,' said Beauvoir. 'Véronique Langlois.' Just saying her name calmed him. It was the oddest sensation.

Reine-Marie shook her head. 'Armand?'

'I met her for the first time this morning.'

'Strange that we haven't met her,' said Reine-Marie. 'I thought chefs loved to take bows. Maybe we met her and forgot.'

'Believe me, she's not easily forgotten,' said Gamache, remembering the massive, confident woman. 'Agent Lacoste will have interviewed the staff by the time we get back. She'll know more about her then. You know, I had the feeling I knew her.'

'Me too.' Beauvoir sat forward between the two front seats. 'Have you ever been walking down the street and smelled something, and suddenly you're someplace else? It's as if the smell transports you.'

With anyone other than the Chief Inspector he'd feel foolish saying that.

'I do. But it's more than that,' said Gamache. 'A feeling

goes with it. I'll suddenly feel melancholy or at ease or calm. For no reason, except the scent.'

'*Oui, c'est ça*. Especially an emotion. That's what I felt when I walked into the kitchen.'

'Was it just the smells of the kitchen, do you think?' Reine-Marie asked.

Beauvoir considered. 'No. I didn't have that feeling until I saw the chef. It was her. It's frustrating. It's as if it's just beyond my grasp. But I know her.'

'And how did you feel?' asked Madame Gamache.

'I felt safe.'

He'd also felt an almost overwhelming desire to laugh. A sort of joy had bubbled up in his chest.

He thought about that as the Volvo splashed along the muddy roads towards the village of Three Pines.

FIFTEEN

⌐

The Volvo came to rest on the crest of the hill. All three
got out and walked to the edge, looking down on the
tiny village. It sat in a gentle valley, surrounded by forested
hills and mountains.

Gamache had never seen Three Pines in summer. The
leaves of the maple, apple and oak trees obscured slightly
the old homes round the village green. But that made them
all the more magical, as though half hiding their beauty only
added to it. Three Pines revealed itself slowly, and only to
people with the patience to wait, to sit quietly in one of the
faded armchairs in the bistro, sipping Cinzano or *café au lait*,
and watch the changing face of the venerable village.

To their right the white spire of the chapel rose, and the
Rivière Bella Bella tumbled down from the millpond then
meandered behind the homes and businesses.

In a semicircle at the far end of the village green the shops
sat in a small brick embrace. Myrna's new and used bookstore,
Olivier's Bistro, with its bold blue and white umbrellas
protecting the assortment of chairs and tables on the sidewalk.

Next to that Sarah's Boulangerie. An elderly, erect woman was just leaving, limping and carrying a sagging net bag. She was followed by a duck.

'Ruth.' Gamache nodded. Rosa the duck was a dead giveaway. They watched as the embittered old poet went into the general store. Rosa waited outside.

'If we hurry we can miss her,' said Beauvoir, turning for the car.

'But I don't want to miss her,' said Reine-Marie. 'I called her from the Manoir. We're having tea together this afternoon.'

Beauvoir stared at Madame Gamache, as though for the last time. She was about to be devoured by Ruth Zardo, who ground up good people and turned them into poetry.

Villagers walked dogs and ran errands or, more precisely, strolled errands. Some could be seen with their floppy gardening hats and gloves and rubber boots kneeling in the moist gardens, snipping roses for bouquets. Each home had an abundant perennial bed. Nothing designed, no new species, none of the latest horticultural offerings. Nothing that wouldn't have been found in gardens by soldiers returning home from the Great War. Three Pines changed, but it changed slowly.

Back in the car they drove slowly down rue du Moulin and came to a stop at Gabri's B&B. The large, rumpled man in his mid-thirties stood on the wide porch, as though waiting for them.

'*Salut, mes amis.*' He walked down the wooden stairs and grabbed Reine-Marie's case from Gamache after giving them all, even Beauvoir, an affectionate hug and kiss on both cheeks. 'Welcome back.'

'*Merci, Patron.*' Gamache smiled, enjoying being back in the little village.

'Olivier and I were so sorry to hear about Peter's sister,' Gabri said as he showed Reine-Marie to her room in the inn. It was warm and inviting, the bed a dark, rich wood, the bedding in clean, luxurious white. 'How're they doing?'

'It's a shock,' said Gamache, 'but they're coping.' What else could he say?

'Terrible.' The large man shook his head. 'Clara called and asked me to pack a bag for them. She sounded a bit stressed. Do you clog?' he asked Reine-Marie, mimicking the old dance, a rustic cross between tap and Celtic.

It wasn't the next obvious question and she stared.

'I've never tried,' she said.

'Well, Mary Queen of the World, you're in for a treat. In a few days we have the Canada Day celebrations on the village green and we're putting together a clogging demonstration. I've signed you up.'

'Please take me back to the place with the murderer,' Reine-Marie whispered in her husband's ear as she kissed him goodbye at the car minutes later, smelling his slight rosewater and sandalwood scent. As he drove away she waved, still in the world of his scent, a world of comfort and kindliness and calm, and no clogging.

Chief Inspector Armand Gamache walked into the Sûreté offices in Sherbrooke and introduced himself. 'Perhaps you can direct us to your evidence area.'

The agent behind the desk leapt to his feet. 'Yessir. The statue's through here.'

They followed the agent to the back of the station and

into a large garage. Charles Morrow was leaning against a wall as though ordering a huge drink. An agent sat in a chair in front of the statue, guarding it.

'I thought it best to be sure no one interfered with it. I know you took blood and soil samples. We've sent them to the lab by courier, but I took some more, to be sure.'

'You're very thorough,' said Gamache. Their feet echoed across the concrete floor of the garage. Gamache had the impression Charles Morrow was waiting for them.

He nodded to the agent guarding the statue and dismissed him, then reached out a hand and touched the stone torso. He held it there, not really sure what he expected to feel. A distant pulse, perhaps.

And Gamache indeed felt something unexpected. He moved his hand to another position, this time on Morrow's arm, and rubbed up and down.

'Jean Guy, look at this.'

Beauvoir leaned closer. 'What?'

'Feel it.'

Beauvoir put his hand where the chief's had been. He'd expected to feel it cool to the touch, but it was warm as though Charles Morrow, the miser, had sucked the warmth from the chief.

But he felt something else. Drawing his brows together he moved his hand to Morrow's torso and stroked. Then he leaned even closer so that his nose was almost touching the statue.

'But this isn't stone,' he said at last.

'I don't think so either,' said Gamache, stepping back.

Charles Morrow was grey. A deep grey in some places, a lighter grey in others. And his surface undulated slightly. At first Gamache thought it was an effect somehow achieved by the sculptor, but touching the statue and looking more closely he realized it was ingrained. The waves, like sagging skin, were part of whatever Charles Morrow had been sculpted from. It was as though this was a real man, a giant. And the giant had petrified.

'What is it? What's it made of?'

'I don't know,' said Gamache. He was saying that a lot in this case. He looked up into the face of Charles Morrow. Then he took another step back.

The face had bits of earth and grass still clinging to it. He looked like a dead man dug up. But the face, beneath its layer of earth, looked determined, resolved. Alive. The arms, held loosely at the waist, palms up, looked as though he had lost something. Traces of blood, now dried, coloured Charles Morrow's head and hands. His slight stride looked hesitant.

Taken in parts he gave the impression of a sullen, impatient, greedy, certainly needy, man.

But taken as a whole Gamache had an entirely different impression. The sum of his parts spoke of longing, of sadness, of resignation mixed with resolve. It was the same feeling he'd had about Charles Morrow the moment the canvas caul had been whisked away at the unveiling. And now Gamache had the impression he was back in a familiar garden in Paris.

Where most visitors went to the Louvre, the Tuileries, the Tour Eiffel, Armand Gamache went to a quiet courtyard garden behind a tiny museum.

And there he paid his respects to men long dead.

For that was the *musée* of Auguste Rodin. And Armand Gamache went to visit the Burghers of Calais.

'Does the statue remind you of anything?'

'Horror movies. He looks as though he's about to come alive,' said Beauvoir.

Gamache smiled. There was something otherworldly about the statue. And it had killed once, after all.

'Have you ever heard of *Les Bourgeois de Calais*? The Burghers of Calais?'

Beauvoir pretended to think.

'*Non.*' He had the feeling he was about to. At least the chief wasn't quoting poetry. Yet.

'He reminds me of them.' Gamache stepped back again. 'Auguste Rodin sculpted them. They're in the Musée Rodin, in Paris, but there's also one outside the Musée des Beaux Arts in Montreal, if you want to see it.'

Beauvoir took that as a joke.

'Rodin lived about a hundred years ago, but the story goes back much further, to 1347.'

He had Beauvoir's attention. The chief's deep, thoughtful voice spoke as though reciting a tale and Beauvoir could see the events unfold.

The port of Calais almost seven hundred years ago. Bustling, rich, strategic. In the middle of the Hundred Years War between the French and the English, though of course they didn't call it that then. Just war. Calais was an important French port and it found itself under siege by the mighty army of Edward III of England. Expecting to be relieved by Philip VI of France the townspeople settled in, unconcerned. But days stretched to weeks stretched to months and hope stretched to breaking. And beyond. Eventually starvation was at the door, through the gate and in their homes. Still they held on, trusting relief would come. That surely they wouldn't be forgotten, forsaken.

Eventually Edward III made an offer. He'd spare Calais, if six of its most prominent citizens would surrender. To be executed. He ordered that these men present themselves at the gate, stripped of their finery, with ropes round their necks and holding the key to the city.

Jean Guy Beauvoir paled, imagining what he'd do. Would he step forward? Would he step back, look away? He imagined the horror of the town, and the choice. Listening to the chief he felt his heart pounding in his chest. This was far worse than any horror film. This was real.

'What happened?' Beauvoir whispered.

'A man, Eustache de Saint-Pierre, one of the wealthiest men in Calais, volunteered. Five others joined him. They took off all their clothes, down to their undergarments, put nooses round their own necks, and walked out of the gates.'

'*Bon Dieu*,' whispered Beauvoir.

Dear God, agreed Gamache, looking again at Charles Morrow.

'Rodin did a sculpture of that moment, when they stood at the gate, surrendering.'

Beauvoir tried to imagine what it would look like. He'd seen a lot of official French art, commemorating the storming of the Bastille, the wars, the victories. Winged angels, buxom cheering women, strong determined men. But if this statue reminded the chief of those men, it couldn't be like anything he'd seen before.

'It's not a regular statue, is it?' said Beauvoir, and thought maybe he'd find out where the Musée des Beaux Arts was in Montreal.

'No, it's like no other war statue you're likely to see. The men aren't heroic. They're resigned, frightened even.'

Beauvoir could imagine. 'But wouldn't that make them even more heroic?' he asked.

'I think so,' said Gamache, turning back to Charles Morrow. Who wore clothing, who had no chains or ropes or noose. At least, not visible. But Armand Gamache knew Charles Morrow was bound as surely as those men. Roped and chained and tied to something.

What was Charles Morrow seeing with those sorrowful eyes?

The owner of the crane company was waiting for them at the reception desk. He was small and square and looked like a pedestal. His steel-grey hair was short and stood on end. A red ridge cut across his forehead where a hard hat had sat, that day and every working day for the past thirty years.

'It wasn't my fault, you know,' he said as he stuck his square hand out to shake.

'I know,' said Gamache, taking it and introducing himself and Beauvoir. 'We think it was murder.'

'*Tabarnac*,' the man exhaled and wiped his beading brow. 'For real? Wait till the boys hear that.'

'Did your worker tell you what happened?' Beauvoir asked, as they took the man into the garage.

'He's a horse's ass. Said the block had shifted and the statue fell off. I told him that was bullshit. The base was solid. They'd poured a concrete foundation with sona tubes sunk six feet into the ground, below frost level, so it doesn't shift. Ya know what I'm talking about?'

'Tell us,' said Gamache.

'You have to dig down at least six feet around here when

188

you do construction, below the frost line. If you don't, whatever you build will heave when the ground thaws in the spring. Get it?'

Gamache understood what the worker had meant about his boss. The man was a natural lecturer, though not a natural teacher.

'Madame Dubois at the Manoir never does anything unless it's done right. I like that. I'm the same way myself. And she knows a thing or two about building.' It was his highest compliment.

'So what did you do?' asked Beauvoir.

'Keep your condom on, *voyons*. I'm getting there. She asked us to put in sona tubes so that the statue wouldn't fall over, so we did. That was about a month ago. The thing hasn't even been through a winter yet. Couldn't have shifted.'

'You sunk the shafts,' said Beauvoir, 'then what?'

A murder investigation, thought Beauvoir, was for the most part asking 'then what happened?' over and over. And listening to the answers, of course.

'We poured the concrete, waited a week. It set. Then we put down that damned base, and yesterday I put the statue on. Huge fucking thing. Had to lift it carefully.'

The men were treated to a fifteen-minute explanation of how hard his job was. Beauvoir replayed the baseball game from the night before, thought about whether his wife would be angry again about his being away from home, had a small argument with the caretaker of his building.

Gamache listened.

'Who was there when you placed the statue?'

'Madame Dubois and that other fellow.'

'Pierre Patenaude?' asked Gamache. 'The maître d'?'

'Don't know who he was. In his forties, dark hair, overdressed. Must have been dying in the heat.'

'Anyone else?'

'Lots of people came by to see. Couple of kids were working in the gardens and watching. The hard part is getting it on right. Don't want it facing the wrong way.' The operator laughed then launched into another five-minute monologue about positioning. Beauvoir treated himself to a fantasy involving Pierre Cardin and a shopping spree in Paris. But that got him thinking about the men of Calais, and that got him thinking about Charles Morrow and that brought him back to this long-winded bore.

'. . . put the canvas thing over him that Madame Dubois gave me, and left.'

'How could the statue have come off the pedestal?' Gamache asked the question as he might ask any, but everyone in the room knew it was the key question. The operator shifted his gaze to the statue, then back.

'The only way I know is with a machine.' He was unhappy with his answer, and looked guilty. 'I didn't do it.'

'We know you didn't,' said Gamache. 'But who did? If it wasn't done by a machine then how?'

'Maybe it was,' said the operator. 'There coulda been a crane there. Not mine, but someone else's. Maybe.'

'It's a possibility,' said Gamache, 'but I suspect Julia Martin would have noticed.'

They nodded.

'What did you think of the statue?' Gamache asked. Beauvoir looked at him with amazement. Who the hell cares what the crane operator thinks? Might as well ask the fucking pedestal.

The crane operator also looked amazed, but he thought about it.

'Wouldn't want it in my garden. Kinda sad, you know? I prefer happy things.'

'Like pixies?' asked Beauvoir.

'Sure, pixies or fairies,' the crane operator said. 'People think they're the same, but they're not.'

Dear God, not a lecture on pixies and fairies.

Gamache shot Beauvoir a warning look.

'Course, the bird helped.'

The bird?

Gamache and Beauvoir looked at each other.

'What bird, monsieur?' asked Gamache.

'The one on his shoulder.'

His shoulder?

The crane operator saw their confusion.

'Yeah, up there.' He stalked across the floor, his muddy boots thudding on the concrete. Stopping at the statue he pointed.

'I can't see anything,' said Beauvoir to Gamache, who also shook his head.

'You got to be close to see it,' said the crane operator, looking around the garage. Spotting a ladder he brought it over and Beauvoir climbed.

'He's right. There's a bird carved here,' he called down.

Gamache sighed silently. He'd hoped the crane operator had hallucinated. But no. There had to be a bird and it couldn't be on Morrow's foot. Beauvoir descended and Gamache stared at the ladder, knowing he had to see for himself.

'Want a hand?' smirked Beauvoir with the ease of a man who hadn't yet found his phobia.

'*Non, merci.*' Gamache tried to smile, but knew he probably looked maniacal. Eyes bright, hands shaking slightly, lips still trying to form a lie of a smile, he started up the ladder. Two, three, four rungs. Hardly high, but it didn't have to be. Maybe, like Bean, I'm afraid to leave the ground, he thought with surprise.

He was face to face with Charles Morrow, staring into that grim visage. Then he dropped his eyes and there, etched into the left shoulder, was a tiny bird. But there was something odd about it. Every nerve in his body was begging him to get down. He could feel waves of anxiety wash over him and thought perhaps he'd let go, fling himself off the ladder. Drop onto Beauvoir. Crush him, as Morrow had crushed Julia.

'You all right up there?' Beauvoir asked, slightly anxious now.

Gamache forced himself to focus, to see the bird. And then he had it.

No longer trying to appear composed Gamache raced down the ladder, jumping the last two rungs and landing inelegantly at the crane operator's feet.

'What kind of a bird is it, do you know?' Gamache asked.

'Course I don't know. It's a fucking bird. Not a jay, that's all I know.'

'Does it matter?' asked Beauvoir, who knew the chief never asked a question without a reason.

'It has no feet.'

'Maybe the guy forgot,' suggested the operator.

'Or maybe it was his signature, you know?' said Beauvoir. 'The way some artists never do eyes.'

'Like Little Orphan Annie,' said the crane operator. 'Maybe this guy never does feet.'

All three dropped their eyes. Charles Morrow had feet.

They put the ladder away and walked together to the door.

'Why do you think the bird's there?' asked the crane operator.

'Don't know,' said Gamache. 'We'll have to ask the artist.'

'Good luck,' said the operator, making a face.

'What's that supposed to mean?' Beauvoir asked.

The crane operator looked uncomfortable. What could make a man perfectly willing to admit to a fondness for pixies and fairies uncomfortable, Beauvoir wondered.

The crane operator stopped and looked at them. The younger guy was staring, like a ferret. All eager to pounce. But the older one, the one with the greying moustache and balding head, and the kind, smart eyes, he was quiet. And listening. He squared his shoulders and spoke directly to Gamache.

'Madame Dubois gave me the address yesterday morning to pick up the statue. Over Saint-Felicien-du-Lac way. I got there in plenty of time. I'm like that. Went to the coffee shop . . .'

Here we go, thought Beauvoir, and shifted on his feet.

The crane operator paused then plunged. 'Then I went to the atelier to get him, the statue I mean. Madame Dubois said it was an artist's studio, but it wasn't.'

He stopped again.

'Go on,' said Gamache quietly.

'It was a graveyard.'

SIXTEEN

~

Véronique Langlois was preparing one of the reduction sauces for the dinner service. It was almost five and things were running behind schedule, and destined to get even further behind if the young Sûreté agent continued to ask questions.

Agent Isabelle Lacoste sat at the scrubbed pine table in the warm kitchen, not wanting to leave. The kitchen had the most wonderful aromas, but more than anything it smelled of calm. Odd, she thought, for a place so filled with activity. Assistants in crisp white aprons were chopping herbs and cleaning early vegetables taken from the kitchen garden or dropped off by the local organic farmer, Monsieur Pagé. They baked and kneaded, they stuffed and stirred. It was a regular Dr Seuss book.

And Agent Lacoste did her job. She probed.

So far she'd interviewed all the outside staff, now back to cutting the vast stretches of lawn and weeding the endless flower beds. The place crawled with them. All young, eager to help.

Pierre Patenaude, whom she was currently interviewing, had just explained that the staff changed almost every year, so it was necessary to train most of them.

'Do you have trouble holding on to staff?' she asked.

'*Mais, non,*' Madame Dubois said. Agent Lacoste had already interviewed her and told her she could leave, but the elderly woman continued to sit, like an apple left on the chair. 'Most of the kids go back to school. Besides, we want new staff.'

'Why? It seems a lot of extra work for you.'

'It is,' agreed the maître d'.

'Here, taste this.' Chef Véronique shoved a wooden spoon under his nose and he pursed his lips as though kissing it, just the lightest of contacts. He did it by rote, a thing he'd done many times before, Lacoste realized.

'Perfect,' he said.

'*Voyons*, you always say that,' the chef laughed.

'Because it's always perfect. You can't do anything but.'

'It's not true.'

Agent Lacoste could tell she was pleased. And was there something else? Something in the instant the spoon touched his lips? Even she had felt it. An intimacy.

But then cooking was an intimate act. An act of artistry and creation. Not one she herself enjoyed, but she knew how sensual it could be. And she felt as though she'd just witnessed a very private, very intimate moment.

She looked at the chef with new eyes.

Towering over her young assistants, her apron-wrapped torso was thick, almost awkward in its movements, as though she only borrowed her body. She wore sensible rubber-soled shoes, a simple skirt and an almost severe blouse. Her iron-grey hair was chopped with less attention than the carrots.

She wore no makeup and looked at least sixty, maybe more. And she spoke with a foghorn voice.

And yet there was something unmistakably attractive about her. Isabelle Lacoste could feel it. Not that she wanted to sleep with the chef, or even lick her spoon. But neither did she want to leave this kitchen, this little world the chef created. Perhaps because she seemed so totally oblivious of her body, her face, her clunky mannerisms, there was something refreshing about her.

Madame Dubois was her opposite. Plump, composed, refined and beautifully turned out, even in the Quebec wilderness.

But both women were genuine.

And Chef Véronique Langlois had something else, thought Lacoste, watching her gently but clearly correct the technique of one of her young assistants, she had a sense of calm and order. She seemed at peace.

The kids gravitated to her, as did Pierre Patenaude and even the proprietor, Madame Dubois.

'It was a commitment my late husband made,' Madame Dubois explained. 'As a young man he'd travelled across Canada and supported himself by working in hotels. It's the only job untrained kids can get. And he spoke no English. But by the time he got back to Quebec he spoke it very well. Always with a heavy accent, but still it stayed for the rest of his life. He was always grateful to the hotel owners for their patience in teaching him his job, and their language. His dream from then on was to open his own *auberge* and do for young people what was done for him.'

That was the other ingredient of the Manoir, thought Lacoste.

It was filled with suspects, it was filled with Morrows, huffing and silent. But more than that, it was filled with relief. It was like a sigh, with structure. Guests relaxed, kids found an unexpected home at a job that could have been agony. The Manoir Bellechasse might be built of wood and wattle, but it was held together by gratitude. A powerful insulator against harsh elements. It was filled with young people revolving through, learning French, learning hospital corners and reduction sauces and canoe repair. Growing up and going back to PEI and Alberta and the rest of Canada with a love of Quebec, if not the subjunctive.

'So, all your workers are English?' asked Agent Lacoste. She'd noticed that the ones she'd interviewed were, though some seemed confident enough to conduct the interview in French.

'Almost all,' said Pierre. 'Diane over by the sink's from Newfoundland and Elliot, one of our waiters, is from British Columbia. Most are from Ontario, of course. It's closest. We even get some Brits and a few Americans. Many of them are sisters and brothers of kids who worked here before.'

Chef Véronique poured iced tea into tall glasses, giving the first to Patenaude, her hand just brushing his, unnecessarily and apparently unnoticed by the maître d'. But not unnoticed by Agent Lacoste.

'We're getting sons and daughters now,' said Madame Dubois, expertly snipping a sagging snapdragon from the beaker of flowers on the table.

'Parents trust we'll look after their children,' said the maître d'. Then he stopped, remembering the events of the day. Thinking of Colleen, from New Brunswick, standing in the rain, her large, wet hands covering her plain face. Her scream would follow him, Pierre knew, for ever. One of his staff, one of his kids, in terror. He felt responsible, though there was no way he could have known.

'How long have you been here?' Agent Lacoste asked Pierre.

'Twenty years,' he said.

'That's a round figure,' Lacoste pointed out. 'I need it exact.'

The maître d' thought. 'I came right out of school. It started as a summer job, but I never left.'

He smiled. It was something Lacoste realized she hadn't seen. He always looked so serious. Granted, she'd only known him for a few hours, after a guest had been brutally murdered in his hotel. Not much opportunity for hilarity. But he smiled now.

It was a charming smile, without artifice. He wasn't what she'd call an attractive man, not someone you'd pick out at a party or notice across a room. He was slim, medium height, pleasant, refined even. He carried himself well, as though born to be a maître d', or a multi-millionaire.

There was an ease about him. He was an adult, she realized. Not a child in adult's clothing, like so many people she knew. This man was mature. It was relaxing to be around him.

He ran his Manoir in much the same way Chief Inspector Gamache ran homicide. There was order, calm, warmth about the Manoir Bellechasse, radiating from the three adults who ran it, and impressing the young adults who worked there. They learned more than another language from these people, Lacoste knew. Just as she learned more than homicide investigation from Chief Inspector Gamache.

'How long ago did you come here?' she asked again.

'Twenty-four years.' The number surprised him.

'About the same time the chef arrived.'

'Was it?'

'Did you know each other before coming here?' she asked the maître d'.

'Who? Madame Dubois?'

'No, Chef Véronique.'

'Chef Véronique?' He seemed puzzled and suddenly Agent Lacoste understood. She stole a look at the chef, large, powerful, cubing meat with fast, practised hands.

Her heart constricted as she felt for this woman. How long had the chef felt this way? Had she lived almost a quarter-century in this log lodge on the edge of Lac Massawippi with a man who didn't return her feelings? What did that do to a person? And what happened to a love that was spread over time and in such isolation? Did it turn into something else?

Something capable of murder?

'How're you doing?'

Clara put her arms around her husband. He bent down and kissed her. They were dressing for dinner and it was their first chance to talk.

'It seems incredible,' Peter said, flopping into a chair, exhausted. Beauvoir had dropped off the suitcase from Gabri filled with underwear, socks, Scotch and potato chips. No real clothes.

'We might as well have asked W. C. Fields to pack,' Peter said, as they sat eating chips and drinking Scotch in their clean underwear. But, actually, it felt good.

Clara had found a Caramilk bar Gabri had thrown into their case and now ate it, discovering that chocolate really went quite well with Scotch.

'Peter, what do you think Julia was getting at last night when she said she'd figured out your father's secret?'

'She was ranting. Trying to cause an upset. It meant nothing.'

'I don't know.'

'Honestly, Clara, let it go.' Peter got up and rummaged through their own carrying case. He pulled out the shirt and slacks he'd worn the night before. Unfortunately they'd scrunched up their clothes and shoved them into the overnight case, expecting not to need them again.

'Thank God Armand Gamache is here,' said Clara, eyeing her powder-blue linen dress, her good one. It looked like seersucker.

'Yeah, what luck.'

'What's the matter?'

He turned to her, his hair mussed, his clothing dishevelled. 'Someone killed Julia. And Gamache will find out who.'

'Let's hope.'

They stared at each other, not with strain or animosity, but each waiting for the other to explain.

'Oh, I understand,' said Clara. And she did. Armand Gamache would find out who killed Peter's sister. How had she not thought of this earlier? She'd been caught on the barbed hook of Julia's murder, thrashing over that shocking event. She hadn't looked beyond why. To who.

'I'm so sorry.' Her normally composed, immaculate husband was falling apart. His stuffing seemed to be coming out. She looked at Peter, trying to find his necktie in the bottom of their case.

'Found it.' He held it up. It looked like a noose.

A few doors away Mariana Morrow gazed at her reflection. Yesterday she'd seen a free spirit, a creative, dashing, age-defying woman. Amelia Earhart and Isadora Duncan bound together, before they crashed to earth, of course. Mariana flung her scarf once more round her throat and gave it a little tug. Just to see how being throttled might feel.

Now she saw someone else wrapped and trapped in there. Someone tired. Someone worn. Someone old. Not as old as Julia, but then Julia had stopped ageing. Fuck her. Always ahead of her time. The one who'd married well, the one who was rich and thin. The one who got away. And now the one who'd never get old.

Fuck Julia.

Someone else was indeed bound up in there, with Amelia and Isadora. Someone just peeping out from the layers of too flimsy material.

Mariana tied a scarf to her head and imagined the huge iron chandelier in the dining room crashing down on top of all of them. Except Bean, of course.

'Must you wear that?' Thomas asked his wife.

She looked perfectly fine, but that wasn't the point. Was never the point.

'Why not?' she asked, looking at herself in the mirror. 'It's sombre but tasteful.'

'It's just not right.'

He managed to convey the sense it wasn't the dress that

201

was wrong. Nor was it necessarily Sandra. But her up-bringing. Not her fault. Really. Darling.

It was in the pauses. Never the words, but the hesitations. Sandra had spent the first few years ignoring it, agreeing with Thomas that she was just too sensitive. Then she'd spent a few years trying to change, to be slim enough, sophisticated enough, elegant enough.

Then she'd entered therapy and spent a few years fighting back.

Then she'd surrendered. And started taking it out on others.

Thomas went back to struggling with his cufflink. His large fingers fumbled at the tiny silver clasp which seemed to have shrunk. He could feel his tension rising, the stress starting at his toes spreading up his legs and through his loins and exploding in his chest.

Why wouldn't this cufflink go in? What was wrong?

He needed them tonight. They were his crucifix, his talisman, his rabbit's foot, his stake and hammer and garlic.

They protected him, and reminded the others who he was.

The eldest son, the favourite son.

He finally got the post through and secured the cufflink, noticing it gleaming next to the frayed cuff. Then they made their way down the hall, Thomas in a snit and Sandra brightening up, remembering the cookies plastered to the dining room ceiling, like stars.

'I don't think you need do that, my dear,' said Bert Finney, hovering behind his wife. 'Not tonight. Everyone will understand.'

She was dressed in a loose-fitting frock, her earrings in, her pearl necklace on. Only one thing missing.

Her face.

'Really.' He reached out and almost touched her wrist, but stopped just in time. They locked eyes in the harsh bathroom mirror. His bulbous nose pocked and veined, his hair thinning and unkempt, his mouth full of teeth as though he'd chewed them but hadn't yet swallowed. But for once his eyes, liquid almost, were steady. And trained on her.

'I must,' she said. 'For Julia.'

She dipped the soft round pad into the foundation. Bringing her hand up she hesitated for a moment, looking at her reflection, then began applying her mask.

Irene Finney finally knew what she believed. She believed Julia to be the kindest, most loving, most generous of her children. She believed Julia loved her too, and came back just to be with her. She believed had Julia not died they'd have shared their lives. Loving mother and loving daughter.

Finally, a child who wouldn't disappoint and disappear.

With each savage stroke of her make-up, Irene Finney filled the void with a child not loved then lost, but first lost, then loved.

Bean Morrow sat alone at the table. Waiting. But not alone or lonely. Bean had brought Hercules, Ulysses, Zeus and Hera. And Pegasus.

Alone in the dining room of the Manoir Bellechasse, feet planted on the ground, Bean climbed aboard the rearing, mighty stallion. Together they galloped down the grass of the Bellechasse and just as lawn turned into lake Pegasus took off. Together they circled the lodge then headed out across the lake, over the mountains. Bean wheeled and soared and swung, high in the sunlit silence.

SEVENTEEN

~

A table was set in the corner of the library, by the windows, and there the three officers sat to eat. They hadn't dressed for dinner, though Chief Inspector Gamache always wore a suit and tie during investigations and still wore it.

As the various courses arrived they went over their findings.

'We now believe Julia Martin was murdered last night shortly before the storm. That would be sometime between midnight and one a.m., is that right?' Gamache asked, sipping his cold cucumber and raspberry soup. There was a bit of dill in it, a hint of lemon and something sweet.

Honey, he realized.

'*Oui*. Pierre Patenaude showed me his weather station. Between his readings and a call to Environment Canada we can say the rain began about then,' Agent Lacoste confirmed as she sipped her *vichyssoise*.

'*Bon. Alors*, what were people doing then?' His deep brown eyes moved from Lacoste to Beauvoir.

'Peter and Clara Morrow went to bed shortly after you left the room,' said Beauvoir, consulting the notebook beside him. 'Monsieur and Madame Finney had already gone up. The housemaid saw them and wished them goodnight. No one saw Peter and Clara, by the way. Thomas and Sandra Morrow stayed in the library here with his sister Mariana discussing the unveiling for about twenty minutes then they went to bed too.'

'All of them?' Gamache asked.

'Thomas and Sandra Morrow went straight up, but Mariana stayed for a few minutes. Had another drink, listened to some music. The maître d' served her and waited until she'd gone to bed. That was about ten past midnight.'

'Good,' said the Chief Inspector. They were getting the skeleton of the case, the outline, the facts, who did what when. Or at least what they said they did. But they needed more, much more. They needed the flesh and blood.

'We need to find out about Julia Martin,' said Gamache. 'Her life in Vancouver, how she met David Martin. What her interests were. Everything.'

'Martin was in the insurance industry,' said Beauvoir. 'I bet she was insured to the gills.'

Gamache looked at him with interest.

'I imagine you're right. Easy enough to find out.'

Beauvoir lifted his brows then looked behind him. The large comfortable sofas and leather chairs had been rearranged and now a couple of tables were shoved together in the centre of the library. Three sensible chairs sat round the tables, and in front of each, neatly arranged, was a notepad and pen.

This was Agent Lacoste's solution to the computer problem. No computers. Not even a telephone. Instead they each had a pen and a pad of paper.

'I'll start training the pigeons to carry the message. No wait, that's silly,' said Beauvoir. 'There must be a pony express stop nearby.'

'When I was your age, young man—' Gamache began, his voice creaky.

'Not the smoke signal story again,' said Beauvoir.

'You'll figure it out.' Gamache smiled. 'I want to go back to last night. The family gathered here.' Gamache got up from the dinner table and walked to beside the fireplace. 'Before Julia came in we got to talking.'

Gamache replayed the scene in his head and now he saw them all. Saw Thomas making an apparently innocuous statement to his sister about their conversation. And Mariana asking something, and Thomas replying.

'He told Julia we were talking about men's toilets,' said Gamache.

'Were you?' asked Lacoste.

'Does it matter?' asked Beauvoir. 'Men's, women's, it's all the same.'

'People get arrested for thinking that,' said Lacoste.

'It seemed to matter to them,' said Gamache. 'We hadn't specified. Just public washrooms.'

There was silence in the room for a moment.

'Men's toilets?' Lacoste drew her brows together, considering. 'And that made Julia explode? I don't get it. Sounds harmless enough.'

Gamache nodded. 'I agree, but it wasn't. We need to find out why Julia reacted like that.'

'It'll be done,' said Lacoste, as they sat down again.

'Perhaps you'd like to chisel it into a stone so you don't

forget,' said Beauvoir. 'Though I think I saw some papyrus lying around.'

'You interviewed the staff,' Gamache said to Lacoste. 'It was a hot night, could some of them have snuck away for a swim?'

'And seen something? I asked and none admitted to it.'

Gamache nodded. It was what worried him the most. That one of the young staff had seen something and either was too afraid to come forward or didn't want to 'tell'. Or would do something foolish with the information. He'd warned them, but he knew kids' brains didn't seem to have receptacles for advice, or warnings.

'Did you find the wasps' nest by the murder site?' Gamache asked.

'Nothing,' said Lacoste, 'but I warned everyone. So far no problems. Maybe they drowned in the storm. But I did find something interesting while searching the guest rooms. In Julia Martin's room.' She got up and brought back a packet of letters, tied with a worn yellow velvet ribbon.

'They've been fingerprinted, don't worry,' she said when the chief hesitated to touch the bundle. 'They were in the drawer by her bed. And I also found these.'

Out of an envelope she brought two crinkled pieces of Manoir Bellechasse notepaper.

'They're dirty,' said Gamache, picking them up. 'Were they also in the drawer?'

'No, in the fireplace grate. She'd balled them up and tossed them in.'

'On a hot night, with no fire? Why wouldn't she just put them in the wastepaper basket? There was one in the room?'

'Oh yes. She'd used it to throw away that plastic wrap from the dry cleaners.'

Gamache smoothed out the two pieces of paper and read them as he took a sip of red wine.

I enjoyed our conversation. Thank you. It helped.

Then the other one.

You are very kind. I know you won't tell anyone what I said. I could get into trouble!

The writing was in careful block print.

'I've sent off a copy for handwriting analysis, but they're printed. Makes it more difficult, of course,' said Lacoste.

The Chief Inspector laid his linen napkin over the finds as the main course was brought in. Lobster for him, *filet mignon* for Beauvoir and a nice Dover sole for Lacoste.

'Would you say the same person wrote both?' asked Gamache.

Beauvoir and Lacoste looked again but the answer seemed obvious.

'*Oui*,' said Beauvoir, taking his first forkful of steak. He imagined Chef Véronique handling the meat, whisking the béarnaise sauce. Knowing it was for him.

'Wonderful meal,' said Gamache to the waiter as the plates were swept aside a few minutes later and a cheese tray arrived. 'I wonder where Chef Véronique studied.'

Beauvoir sat forward.

'She didn't, at least not formally,' said Agent Lacoste, smiling at the waiter whom she'd interviewed about murder just hours earlier. 'I spoke with her this afternoon. She's sixty-one. No formal training, but picked up recipes from her mother and travelled a bit.'

'Never married?' Gamache asked.

'No. She came here when she was in her late thirties. Spent

almost half her life here. But there's something else. A feeling I had.'

'Go on,' said Gamache. He trusted Agent Lacoste's feelings.

Beauvoir didn't. He didn't even trust his own.

'You know how in closed communities, like boarding schools or convents or the military where people live and work at close quarters, something happens?'

Gamache leaned back in his chair, nodding.

'These kids might have been here for weeks, maybe a couple of months, but the adults have been here for years, decades. Alone. Just the three of them, year in, year out.'

'Are you saying they have cabin fever?' demanded Beauvoir, not liking where this might be going. Gamache looked at him, but said nothing.

'I'm saying strange things happen to people who live on the shores of a lake together, for years. This is a log cabin. No matter how large, no matter how beautiful. It's still isolated.'

> *'There are strange things done 'neath the midnight sun*
> *By the men who moil for gold.'*

They looked at Gamache. Rarely when the chief spouted poetry did it clarify a situation for Beauvoir.

'Moil?' said Lacoste, who generally loved listening to the chief recite.

'I was agreeing with you.' Gamache smiled. 'So would Robert Service. Strange things are done on the shores of isolated lakes. Strange things were done here, last night.'

'*By the men who moil for gold*?' asked Beauvoir.

'Almost always,' said Gamache and nodded to Lacoste to continue.

'I think Véronique Langlois has developed feelings for someone. Strong feelings.'

Gamache leaned forward again.

What killed people wasn't a bullet, a blade, a fist to the face. What killed people was a feeling. Left too long. Sometimes in the cold, frozen. Sometimes buried and fetid. And sometimes on the shores of a lake, isolated. Left to grow old, and odd.

'Really?' Beauvoir leaned forward himself.

'Don't laugh. There's a big age gap.'

Neither man looked likely to laugh.

'I think she's in love with the maître d',' Lacoste said.

Clara thought the Morrows were Olympian in their ability to avoid unpleasantness, while being very unpleasant themselves. But never would she have believed them capable of ignoring the murder of their own sister and daughter.

But so far they'd whizzed through the soup course and no mention of Julia. Though Clara had to admit she wasn't anxious to bring it up herself.

'More bread? Too bad about Julia.'

How do you say it?

'More wine?' Thomas tilted the bottle down the table. Clara declined but Peter accepted. Finally Clara couldn't take it any more. Across the table Mrs Morrow straightened her fish fork. She'd joined in the conversation, but without interest and only to correct a misinterpretation, a mispronunciation or a flat-out mistake.

'How are you feeling?' Clara asked.

It fell into a lull in the conversation and now all faces turned to her, except Bert Finney and Bean. Both were looking out of the window.

'Are you speaking to me?' her mother-in-law asked.

Clara was pretty sure her skin had just been sliced, by the look if not the tone.

'It's been a terrible day,' said Clara, wondering where this suicidal instinct had sprung from. Maybe the Morrows were right. Maybe talking about it made it worse. She suddenly felt like a sadist, whipping this tiny, elderly grieving woman. Forcing her to confront the horrible death of her daughter. Forcing her to talk about it. Over *vichyssoise*.

Who was unreasonable now?

But it was too late. Her question was out there. She stared at Peter's mother, who looked at her as though seeing her daughter's murderer. Clara lowered her gaze.

'I was remembering Julia,' said Mrs Morrow. 'How beautiful she was. How kind and loving. Thank you for asking, Claire. I wish one of my own children had thought to ask. But they seem to prefer to talk about American politics and the latest show at the National Gallery. Do you care about those things more than your sister?'

Clara had gone from feeling like crap to feeling like a hero to feeling like crap again. She looked across the table at Peter. His hair was standing straight out at the sides and he'd dropped a small dribble of soup, like pabulum, onto his shirt.

'But then Julia was always the most sensitive of you. I understand you told the Chief Inspector Julia was greedy and cruel.'

Her gentle Wedgwood eyes focused on Peter. There was

no movement now. Even the waiters seemed afraid to approach.

'I didn't say that,' he stammered, reddening. 'Who told you that?'

'And you told him my own death might be for the best.'

Now there was an audible gasp and Clara realized they'd all inhaled in shock, including herself. She was finally in the boat. Great timing.

Mrs Morrow fiddled with the stem of her wine glass.

'Did you say that, Peter?'

'No, I didn't, Mother. I'd never say such a thing.'

'Because I know when you're lying. I always know.'

This wasn't difficult, Clara knew, since in her company they always lied. She'd taught them that. Their mother knew where all their buttons were, and why not. She'd installed them.

Peter was lying now. Clara knew it, his mother knew it. The maître d' knew it. The chipmunk Bert Finney was staring at probably knew it.

'I would never say that,' repeated Peter. His mother glared.

'You never disappoint me, you know. I always knew you'd come to nothing. Even Claire is more successful than you. A solo show with Denis Fortin. Have you ever had one?'

'Mrs Morrow,' said Clara. Enough was enough. 'That's not fair. Your son's a fine man, a gifted artist, a loving husband. He has lots of friends and a beautiful home. And a wife who loves him. And my name is Clara.' She stared along the table to the elderly woman. 'Not Claire.'

'And my name is Mrs Finney. You've called me Mrs Morrow for fifteen years, long after my marriage. Do you know how insulting that is?'

Clara was stunned into silence. She was right. It'd never occurred to her that Peter's mother was now Mrs Finney. She'd always just been Mrs Morrow.

How had it come to this? Here she was yelling at Peter's mother when she meant to comfort her.

'I'm sorry,' she said. 'You're right.'

And then she saw something almost as horrifying as what the young gardener must have witnessed that morning. But instead of a crushed middle-aged woman, Clara saw a crushed elderly woman. In front of her, in front of them all, Peter's mother put her head in her hands and started to cry.

Mariana shrieked and jumped up, just as the ceiling collapsed. Or at least, something landed on her from above, and bounced.

It was a cookie.

The sky was made of marshmallow, and it was falling.

Over coffee Chief Inspector Gamache put on his half-moon glasses and read the bundle of letters, handing each to Beauvoir as he finished. After a few minutes he lowered his glasses and stared out the window.

He was beginning to know Julia Martin. To know her facts, her history. He felt the rich, thick notepaper in his hands.

It was almost nine in the evening and still bright. They'd only just passed the summer solstice. The longest day of the year. The mist was disappearing, though some hovered lightly over the calm lake. The clouds were breaking up and a hint of red and purple was in the sky. It was going to be a magnificent sunset.

'What do you think?' he asked, tapping his glasses on the stack of letters.

'They're the strangest collection of love letters I've ever seen,' said Beauvoir. 'Why'd she keep them?'

Agent Lacoste picked up the letters and the velvet ribbon.

'They were important to her, for some reason. More than important, they were crucial. So much so she kept them with her. But . . .'

She seemed lost for words and Gamache knew how she felt. The notes spanned more than thirty years and seemed simply a collection of thank yous for parties, or dances or gifts. Various people telling Julia Martin she was kind.

None an actual love letter. Her father had written to thank her for a tie. There was an old one from her husband before they married, asking her to meet him for dinner. It was pleasant, complimentary. All of them were. Affectionate, grateful, polite. But no more.

'Why did she keep them?' Gamache mumbled, almost to himself. Then he picked up the more recent notes, the ones crumpled and found in the grate. 'And why did she throw these away?'

As he read them again something struck him.

'Do you notice something unusual about this note?' He pointed to one.

You are very kind. I know you won't tell anyone what I said. I could get into trouble!

Beauvoir and Lacoste studied it, but saw nothing.

'Not in the words, but in the punctuation,' said Gamache. 'The exclamation mark.'

They looked at him blankly and he smiled. But he also knew there was something there. Something important. As so often happened, the message wasn't in the words but in how they were put.

214

'I found something else in my search,' said Agent Lacoste, getting up from the table. 'I'd like to show you before the Morrows finish dinner.'

All three climbed the stairs to the guest rooms and Isabelle Lacoste led them to the Garden Room. Knocking, she waited a moment then opened the door.

Gamache and Beauvoir stepped forward then stopped.

'Have you ever seen anything like it?' Agent Lacoste asked.

Gamache shook his head. In thirty years as an investigator he'd certainly seen more disturbing things, more frightening things, more grotesque things. But he'd never seen anything quite like this.

'Why would a child have so many clocks?' asked Beauvoir, surveying Mariana and Bean Morrow's room. There were clocks on every surface.

'How do you know they're Bean's?' asked Gamache.

'Because the kid's screwed up. Wouldn't you be if your name was Bean and nobody knew if you were a boy or girl?'

They stared at him. He hadn't told them this yet.

'What do you mean?' asked Lacoste.

'Mariana Morrow's kept Bean's sex a secret.'

'Even from her mother?'

'Especially from her mother. From everyone. How fucked up is that?'

Gamache picked up a Mickey Mouse clock and nodded. What parents did to their kids, he thought, looking at the room and listening to the ticking, ticking, ticking. He examined Mickey then picked up a few other clocks.

Why had Bean set them all for seven in the morning?

EIGHTEEN

⌒

Peter Morrow stood alone just outside the yellow ribbon. The ground held a Julia-sized indent.

In life she'd torn the family apart and now she was doing it in death. Selfish, greedy and yes, cruel. He'd meant every word.

His mother had cried for her. Had only good things to say about Julia. She'd become perfect Julia, beautiful Julia, kind and loving Julia. Well, who'd stayed and looked after Mother? Who visited her and had her for dinners? Who phoned her and sent cards and gifts?

He stared at the hole and tried to feel something. Tried to remember Julia as a girl. His older sister. Born between the boys, like being born between the wars. Trodden upon and mauled as the boys tried to get at each other. They'd squashed and trampled her in the middle. Flat.

And now Dad had done it too.

There'd been four of them all their lives. Thomas, Julia, Peter, Mariana. Four wheels, four walls, four seasons, four elements, four corners of the earth.

But now they were three. Strange as their world had been, it at least made sense, to them. What happens when one corner is removed?

All hell breaks loose. And the first trumpet was heard tonight. His mother's cry.

'Peter?'

He stood still, not daring to turn round, to show his face to anybody.

'Is it all right that I'm here?' he asked.

'As long as you go no closer, but you know that,' said Gamache.

The two men stared at the scene, though both were actually staring at the pedestal of hard marble. Gamache had come into the garden for some fresh air, to walk off his dinner and try to put order into the pile of evidence they were collecting. But mostly he'd wanted to come here again, to look at the white block. The thing he'd first mistaken for a grave marker. And now it was.

But what troubled him was why the block wasn't marred. It showed absolutely no sign of the statue's ever being on it, and certainly no signs of it scraping off. Not a scratch, not a blemish. It was perfect. And it was impossible.

'My mother used to read us stories when we were children,' Peter said. 'My father would play the piano and we'd all cram onto the sofa and Mother would read. Our favourite was always from a book on myths. I still remember most of them. Zeus, Ulysses. Thomas loved that one. Always wanted it read. Over and over we heard about the lotus-eaters and the sirens.'

'And Scylla and Charybdis,' said Gamache. 'I loved it too. That terrible choice Ulysses faced, to aim his ship for the whirlpool or for the six-headed monster.'

'He chose the monster and it killed six of his men. They died and he sailed on,' said Peter.

'What would you have done?' asked Gamache. He knew the myth well. Ulysses returning from the Trojan War, his long perilous journey. Trying to get home. Coming upon that terrible strait. On one side a whirlpool that sucked every ship and soul into it. And on the other side Scylla. A six-headed monster. On one side certain death for everyone on the ship, and on the other certain death for six of his men.

Which path to take?

Peter felt the tears then. For little Julia, crushed by her brothers, crushed by her mother, crushed by her husband. And finally, just as she'd returned home, crushed by the one man she trusted. Her Ulysses. Her father.

But mostly he was weeping for himself. He'd lost a sister today, but worse, far worse, he felt he'd just lost his mother. A mother who'd decided the dead sister was perfect, and he was a monster.

'Let's walk,' said Gamache, and the two men turned their backs on the dented earth and the harsh white cube beside it. Gamache clasped his hands behind his back and they fell into step, walking silently across the lawn and towards the lake. The sun was just setting, filling the evening sky with spectacular lurid colour. Purples and pinks and golds, it seemed to change every moment.

The men stopped and stared.

'That was a lovely image of your family gathered around your mother as she read.'

'You're mistaken,' said Peter. 'We weren't gathered around her. We were on the sofa, all four of us. She was across the room in her wing chair.'

Suddenly the image that had been so natural, heart-warming even, that had finally allowed him to see the Morrows as a family, disappeared. Like the sunset, it shifted into something else. Something darker.

Four small children by themselves staring across the straits to their mother, upright and proper and reading about terrible choices. And death.

'You said Ulysses was Thomas's favourite. What was yours?'

Peter had been thinking of the square of white marble looming over the place where Julia died. Four corners, four walls.

'Pandora's box,' he said.

Gamache turned away from the sunset and looked at Peter. 'Is something bothering you?'

'You mean beyond the murder of my sister?'

'I do mean that. You can tell me.'

'Oh really? Well someone told my mother what I said to you this afternoon. Yes, look surprised, but can you imagine how I felt? You demand I tell you the truth, I tell it, and get practically kicked out of the family for it. I bet it's always been easy for you. So sure of yourself. Always fitting in. Well try being an artist in a family of intellectuals. Try being tone deaf in a family of musicians. Try being taunted all the way to class, not by other kids, but by your own brother, yelling "Spot, Spot".'

Peter felt the last restraints tear apart. He wanted to warn Gamache, to tell him to run, to flee from him, to hide in the forest until this riot had passed. Until the writhing, stinking, armed escapees had burned and violated everything in sight and moved on to another target. But it was too late, and he knew the man in front of him would never run.

Morrows ran and hid in smiling cynicism and dark sarcasm. This man stood his ground.

'And your father?' Gamache asked, as though Peter hadn't sprayed his face with spittle. 'What did he say to you?'

'My father? But you already know what he said. Never use the first stall in a public washroom. Who fucking says that to a ten year old? You know the other lesson we were taught? Beware the third generation.'

'What does that mean?'

'The first generation makes the money, the second appreciates it, having witnessed the sacrifice, and the third squanders it. We're the third generation. The four of us. Our father hated us, thought we'd steal his money, ruin the family. He was so afraid of spoiling us he never gave us anything, except stupid advice. Words. That was all.'

Was that the burden Gamache had seen etched in that stone face? Not sacrifice, but fear? Was Charles Morrow afraid his own children would betray him? Had he created the very thing he was so afraid of? Unhappy, unloving, ungrateful children? Children capable of stealing from their father, and killing each other?

'Who do you think killed your sister?'

It took Peter a minute to be able to speak again, to change direction.

'I think it was Bert Finney.'

'Why would he kill Julia?' It was almost dark now.

'For money, always for money. I'm sure my mother's the beneficiary of her insurance. He married my mother for money and now he'll get more than he dreamed.'

They continued their walk down to the dock and the two Adirondack chairs reclining on the grey, weathered wood.

Peter was drained. Their feet echoed on the slats and water gently lapped against the wharf.

As they approached one of the chairs moved. The men stopped.

The wooden chair grew before their eyes, outlined against the last of the light.

'Monsieur Gamache?' the chair said.

'*Oui.*' Gamache took a step forward though Peter reached out to grab him back.

'Armand Gamache? That is your name, didn't you say?'

'*Oui.*'

'I knew your father,' said Bert Finney. 'His name was Honoré. Honoré Gamache.'

NINETEEN

⁓

After dropping his bombshell Bert Finney had simply departed, jerking past the two men without another word.

'What did he mean by that?' Peter asked. 'He knew your father?'

'They'd be of an age,' said Gamache, his mind hurrying. He'd picked it, and his heart, up from the dock and shoved them back into his body.

'Has your father ever mentioned him? Bert Finney?' As though Gamache didn't know who'd spoken.

'My father died when I was a child.'

'Murdered?' Peter asked.

Gamache turned to him. 'Murdered? Why would you say that?'

Peter, who'd bunched up into Gamache's personal space in an effort to hide, took a step back. 'Well, you're in homicide, I thought maybe . . .' Peter's voice tailed off. There was silence then, except the gentle lap of the water. 'He must have been young,' Peter finally said.

'He was thirty-eight.' And five months, and fourteen days.

Peter nodded, and though he longed to leave he stayed with Gamache while the large man stared out into the lake.

And seven hours. And twenty-three minutes.

And once all the light had gone, the two men walked back to the Manoir, in silence.

Gamache's alarm went off at five thirty the next morning and after a refreshing shower he dressed, picked up his notebook and left. The summer sun was just up and wandering in the lace-curtained windows. Nothing stirred, except a loon calling across the lake.

As he descended the wide stairs he heard a noise in the kitchen. Poking his head in he saw a young woman and the waiter Elliot going about their work. The young man was arranging plates and she was putting bread in the oven. There was a smell of strong coffee.

'*Bonjour, monsieur l'inspecteur,*' said the girl in French with a thick English accent. She must have been fairly new, Gamache thought. 'You're up early.'

'And so are you. Hard at work already. I wonder if I might have some coffee?' he said slowly and clearly in French.

'*Avec plaisir.*' The girl poured him an orange juice and he took it.

'*Merci,*' he said, and left.

'Monsieur Gamache,' he heard behind him as he walked out of the swinging screen door and into the new day. 'I believe you wanted this.'

Gamache stopped and Elliot walked up to him, a bodum of coffee with cream and rock sugar on a tray with a couple of cups. He'd also placed some warm croissants in a basket with preserves.

'She's from Saskatchewan. Just arrived. Very nice, but you know.' Elliot, a man of the world, shrugged. He seemed to have recovered his equanimity, or at least his charm, and had resigned himself to continue working despite his flare-up with the maître d'. Gamache wondered, though, how much was genuine acceptance and how much was an act.

A hummingbird zoomed past and stopped at a foxglove.

'*Merci.*' The Chief Inspector smiled and reached out for the tray.

'*S'il vous plaît,*' said Elliot, 'I'll carry it. Where would you like to sit?' He looked around the deserted *terrasse*.

'Well, actually, I was going to the dock.'

The two walked across the lawn, their feet making a path through the light morning dew. The world was waking up, hungry. Chipmunks raced and yipped under the trees, birds hopped and called and insects buzzed quietly in the background. Elliot placed the tray on the arm of the second Adirondack chair, poured a delicate bone china cup of coffee and turned to leave.

'There is one thing I've wanted to ask you.'

Did the lithe back tighten in the trim white jacket? Elliot paused for a moment then turned back, an expectant smile on his handsome face.

'What did you think of Madame Martin?'

'Think? All I do here is wait tables and clean up. I don't think.'

Still the smile, but Gamache had the answer to his earlier question. Anger seethed under the charming exterior.

'Stop playing the fool with me, son.' Gamache's voice was steady but full of warning.

'She was a guest, I'm an employee. She was polite.'

'You talked?'

Now Elliot really did hesitate and colour slightly. With time, Gamache knew, his blush would disappear. He'd be confident instead of cocky. He'd be beyond embarrassment. And he'd be far less attractive.

'She was polite,' he repeated, then seemed to hear how lame he sounded. 'She wanted to know if I liked working here, what I planned to do after the summer. That sort of thing. Most guests don't see the staff, and we're taught to be discreet. But Madame Martin noticed.'

Was there an invisible world, Gamache wondered. A place where diminished people met, where they recognized each other? Because if he knew one thing about Julia Martin it was that she too was invisible. The sort others cut off in conversation, cut in front of in grocery lines, overlook for jobs though their hand might be raised and waving.

Julia Martin might be all that, but this young man was anything but invisible. No, if they had something in common it wasn't that. Then he remembered.

'You and Madame Martin had something in common,' he said.

Elliot stood on the dock, silent.

'You're both from British Columbia.'

'Is that right? We didn't talk about that.'

He was lying. He did it well, a skill that came with practice. But his eyes instead of shifting met Gamache's and held them, too long, too hard.

'Thank you for the coffee,' said Gamache, breaking the moment. Elliot was perplexed, then smiled and left. Gamache watched his retreat and thought of what Elliot had said.

Madame Martin noticed. And he thought that was probably true.

Is that what killed her? Not something buried in the past, but something fresh and vigorous? And deadly. Something she'd seen or heard here at the Manoir?

Settling into the chair on the wooden dock Gamache sipped coffee and stared at the lake and the forested mountains all around. He cradled the delicate cup in his large hands and let his mind wander. Instead of forcing himself to focus on the case he tried to open his mind, to empty it. And see what came to him.

What came to him was a bird, a footless bird. Then Ulysses and the whirlpool, and Scylla, the monster. The white pedestal.

He saw young Bean, earthbound and trapped among the stuffed heads in the attic. They might have been Morrows, meant more as trophies than children. All head, all stuffed and staring.

But mostly he saw Charles Morrow, looming over this case. Hard, burdened, bound.

'Am I disturbing you?'

Gamache twisted in the chair. Bert Finney was standing on the shore, at the foot of the dock. Gamache struggled out of the chair and lifted the tray, indicating the seat next to him. Monsieur Finney hobbled forward, all gangling arms and legs like a puppeteer's poor first attempt. And yet he stood erect. It looked an effort.

'Please.' Gamache pointed to the chair.

'I'd rather stand.'

The old man was shorter than the Chief Inspector, though not by much and Gamache thought he'd probably have been taller before age and gravity got him. Now Bert Finney pulled himself even more erect and faced Gamache. His eyes were less wilful this morning, and his nose less red. Or perhaps, Gamache thought, I've grown accustomed to him as one grows accustomed to chipping paint or a dent in a car. For the first time Gamache noticed there was a pair of binoculars hanging like an anchor round Finney's bony neck.

'I'm afraid I shocked you last night. I didn't mean to.' Finney looked directly at Gamache, or at least his wandering eyes paused on him.

'You surprised me, it's true.'

'I'm sorry.'

It was said with such dignity, such simplicity, it left Gamache speechless for a moment.

'It's been a while since I've heard people talk about my father. Did you know him personally?' Gamache again indicated the chair and this time Finney bent into it.

'Coffee?'

'Please. Black.'

Gamache poured a cup for Monsieur Finney and refreshed his own, then brought over the basket with croissants and rested it on the generous arm of his chair, offering one to his unexpected guest.

'I met him at the end of the war.'

'You were a prisoner?'

Finney's mouth twisted into what Gamache thought was a smile. Finney stared across the water for a moment then closed his eyes. Gamache waited.

'No, Chief Inspector, I've never been a prisoner. I wouldn't allow it.'

'Some people have no choice, monsieur.'

'You think not?'

'How did you know my father?'

'I'd just returned to Montreal and your father was giving speeches. I heard one of them. Very passionate. I spoke to him afterwards and we struck up an acquaintance. I was so sorry to hear he'd been killed. Car accident, was it?'

'With my mother.'

Armand Gamache had trained his voice to sound neutral, as though delivering news. Just facts. It was a long time ago. More than forty years. His father was now dead longer than he'd lived. His mother as well.

But Gamache's right hand lifted slightly off the warming wood and curled upward, as though lightly holding another, a larger, hand.

'Terrible,' said Finney. They sat quietly, each in his own thoughts. The mist was slowly burning off the lake and every now and then a bird skimmed the surface, hungry for insects. Gamache was surprised how companionable it felt, to be alone with this quiet man. This man who knew his father, and hadn't yet said what most people did. This man, Gamache realized, who would be almost exactly his father's age, had he lived.

'It feels like our own world, doesn't it?' Finney said. 'I love this time of day. So pleasant to sit and think.'

'Or not,' said Gamache and both men smiled. 'You came here last night too. You have a lot to think about?'

'I do. I come here to do my sums. It's a natural place for it.'

It seemed an unnatural place for counting to Gamache. And Finney didn't seem to have a notebook or ledger. What had Peter said the night before? The old accountant had married his mother for the money, and killed Julia for money as well. And now the elderly man was sitting on a dock in a remote lake, counting. Greed didn't lessen with age, Gamache knew. If anything it grew, fuelled by fear of not having enough, of things left undone. Of dying destitute. Though it might not be money he was counting. It might be birds.

'You birdwatch?'

'I do,' said Finney, bringing his hand up to finger the binoculars. 'I have quite a life-list. Sparrows, of course, and cardinals. Black-crested bulbul and white-throated babbler. Marvellous names. I've seen most of the birds here before, but you never know what you might find.'

They sipped their coffee and ate their croissants, batting away hungry flies. Dragonflies skimmed the water around the dock, graceful and bright as the sun caught their wings and luminous bodies.

'Do you know of a bird without feet?'

'Without feet?' Instead of laughing Finney considered the question carefully. 'Why would a bird have no feet?'

'Why indeed?' said Gamache, but chose not to elaborate. 'Who do you think killed your stepdaughter?'

'Besides Charles?'

Gamache remained silent.

'This is a difficult family, Chief Inspector. A complicated one.'

'You called them "seven mad Morrows in a *verchère*" the other day.'

'Did I?'

'What did you mean? Or were you just angry about being left behind?'

As Gamache had hoped, that roused the elderly man who up until that moment had seemed perfectly at ease. Now he turned in his chair and looked at Gamache. But not with annoyance. He looked amused.

'I remember I told Clara that not everyone makes the boat,' said Finney. 'What I didn't say is that not everybody wants to make the boat.'

'This is a family, Monsieur Finney, and you've been excluded. Doesn't that hurt?'

'Hurt is having your daughter crushed to death. Hurt is losing your father, your mother. Hurt is all sorts of things. It isn't being forced to stand on a shore, especially this shore.'

'The surroundings aren't the issue,' said Gamache quietly. 'The interior is. Your body can be standing in the loveliest of places, but if your spirit is crushed, it doesn't matter. Being excluded, shunned, is no small event.'

'I couldn't agree more.' Finney leaned back again into the deep Adirondack chair. Across the lake a couple of Oh Canada birds called to each other. It was just after seven.

Bean's alarms would have gone off by now.

'Did you know that Henry David Thoreau and Ralph Waldo Emerson were friends?'

'I didn't,' said Gamache, staring straight ahead, but listening closely.

'They were. Thoreau was once thrown in jail for protesting some government law he believed violated freedom. Emerson visited him there and said, "Henry, how did you come to be in here?" Do you know what Thoreau replied?'

'No,' said Gamache.

'He said, "Ralph, how did you come to be out there?"'

After a moment Finney made a strangled noise. Gamache turned to look. It was laughter. A soft, almost inaudible, chuckle.

'You called them mad. What did you mean?'

'Well now, that's just my perception, but I've seen men go mad before and I've thought about it quite a bit. What do we call madness?'

Gamache was beginning to appreciate that Finney spoke in rhetorical questions.

'Not going to answer?'

Gamache smiled at himself. 'Do you want me to? Madness is losing touch with reality, creating and living in your own world.'

'True, though sometimes that's the sanest thing to do. The only way to survive. Abused people, especially children, do it.'

Gamache wondered how Finney knew that.

'They've lost their minds,' said Finney. 'Not always a bad thing. But there's another expression we use to describe madness.'

A movement to his left caught Gamache's eye, a flapping. Looking over he saw Bean running down the lawn. *Fleeing?* Gamache wondered. But after a moment he realized the child was neither fleeing nor running.

'We say they've taken leave of their senses,' said Finney.

Bean was galloping, like a horse, a huge swimming towel flapping behind.

'The Morrows are mad,' Finney continued, either oblivious of the child or used to it, 'because they've taken leave of their senses. They live in their heads and pay no heed to any other information flooding in.'

231

'Peter Morrow's an artist and a gifted one,' said Gamache. 'You can't be that good an artist without being in touch with your senses.'

'He is gifted,' agreed Finney, 'but how much better would he be if he stopped thinking and started just being? Started listening, smelling, feeling?'

Finney sipped his now cool coffee. Gamache knew he should get up, but he lingered, enjoying the company of this extravagantly ugly man.

'I remember the first time I intentionally killed something.'

The statement was so unexpected Gamache looked over to the whittled old man to see what prompted it. Bert Finney pointed a gnarled finger at a point of land. Just drifting round it was a boat with a fisherman, alone in the early morning calm, casting.

Whiz. Plop. And the far-off ticking, like Bean's clocks, as the line was slowly reeled in.

'I was about ten and my brother and I went out to shoot squirrels. He took my father's rifle and I used his. I'd seen him shoot often enough but had never been allowed to do it myself. We snuck out and ran into the woods. It was a morning like this, when parents sleep in and kids get up to mischief. We dodged between the trees and threw ourselves onto the ground, pretending to be fighting the enemy. Trench warfare.'

Gamache watched as the elderly man twisted his torso, mimicking the movements of almost eighty years ago.

'Then my brother hushed me and pointed. Two chipmunks were playing at the base of a tree. My brother pointed to my rifle. I lifted it, took aim, and fired.'

Whiz. Plop. Tick, tick, tick.

'I got him.'

Bert Finney turned to Gamache, his eyes wild now, going every which way. It was hard to imagine this man being able to shoot anything.

'My brother cheered and I ran up excitedly. Very proud. I could hardly wait to tell my father. But the thing wasn't dead. It was gravely hurt, I could tell. It cried and clawed the air, then it stopped and just whimpered. I heard a sound and looked over. The other chipmunk was watching.'

'What did you do?' Gamache asked.

'I shot it again. Killed it.'

'Was that the last time you killed something?'

'For a long time, yes. My father was disappointed I wouldn't hunt with him after that. I never told him why. Perhaps I should have.'

They watched the man in the boat, the man, Gamache guessed, from the cabin across the lake.

'But I eventually killed again,' said Finney.

Bean galloped by again then disappeared into the woods.

'*Oh, I have slipped the surly bonds of earth*,' said Finney, watching the last flap of the bathing towel as it disappeared into the forest.

'Are they surly bonds?' asked Gamache.

'For some,' said Finney, still looking at the spot where Bean had been.

The fisherman's rod suddenly arched and the boat rocked slightly as the man, surprised, leaned back in his seat and started reeling in. The line protested, screaming.

Gamache and Finney watched, willing the fish to flick its head just right. To dislodge the hook tearing its mouth.

'How well did you know Charles Morrow?'

'He was my best friend.' Finney broke away, reluctantly, from the scene on the lake. 'We went through school together. Some people you lose track of, but not Charles. He was a good friend. Friendship mattered to him.'

'What was he like?'

'Forceful. He knew what he wanted and he generally got it.'

'What did he want?'

'Money, power, prestige. The usual.' Finney was drawn back to the fisherman and his arching rod. 'He worked hard and built a strong company. Actually, to be fair, he took over the family company. It was a small but respected investment firm. But Charles built it into something else. Opened offices across Canada. He was a driven man.'

'What was it called?'

'Morrow Securities. I remember he came to work one day laughing because little Peter had asked where his gun was. He thought his dad was a security guard. Very disappointed to find out he wasn't.'

'You worked for him?'

'All my life. He finally sold the company.'

'Why didn't he pass it on to his children?'

For the first time Bert Finney appeared uncomfortable.

The fisherman was leaning over the side of his boat, a net in hand, dipping it into the water.

'I believe he wanted to, but he just didn't think any of them would be suitable. Peter had far too much imagination, it would have killed him, said Charles, though he believed Peter would've been willing to try. He loved that boy's loyalty and his willingness to help. He was a very kind boy, Charles always said. Julia was already gone, off to BC and engaged to David Martin. Charles had very little time for poor Julia's husband, so that wasn't an option. Mariana? Well, he thought she could do it one day. He always said she had the best mind of any of them. Not, perhaps, the best brain. But the best mind. But she was busy having fun.'

'And Thomas?'

'Ah, Thomas. Charles thought he was smart and canny, both important.'

'But?'

'But he thought the boy was missing something.'

'What?'

'Compassion.'

Gamache thought about that. 'It doesn't seem like the first quality you'd look for in an executive.'

'But it is in a son. Charles didn't want Thomas quite that close.'

Gamache nodded. He'd finally gotten it out of Finney, but had Finney wanted him to ask, to push? Was this the reason Finney was sitting here? To steer the Chief Inspector towards his stepson?

'When did Charles Morrow die?'

'Eighteen years ago. I was with him. By the time we got him to the hospital he was dead. Heart attack.'

'And you married his wife.' Gamache wanted it to sound neutral. Not an accusation. And it wasn't one, it was simply a question. But he also knew a guilty mind was a harsh filter, and heard things unintended.

'I did. I've loved her all my life.'

Both men stared out to the lake. The fisherman had something writhing in his net. It was plump and shiny. As they watched he gently took the hook out of its mouth and held it aloft, by its tail.

Gamache smiled. The man who lived in the cabin across the lake was going to let the fish go. With a flash of silver the fish descended and struck the side of the boat.

The fisherman had killed it.

TWENTY

———

Armand Gamache walked off the wharf, leaving Bert Finney sitting in the Adirondack chair. On the grass the Chief Inspector turned round, looking for signs of the galloping child. But the lawn was empty and quiet.

His watch said seven thirty. Had Bean gone back into the Manoir?

This was the reason he'd gotten up so early, to see why Bean did. And now he'd managed to lose the child, in favour of a conversation with Finney. Had he made the right decision?

Gamache turned away from the lodge and took the trail that wound into and out of the woods, along the shores of Lac Massawippi. It was warm and he knew, even without the maître d's forecast, that it would be hot. Not the stifling heat and humidity before the storm, but still hot. Already the sun dazzled off the lake, blinding him if he looked too close and too long.

'Dream on, dream on,' a thin voice sang through the woods. Gamache turned and looked in, trying to adjust his eyes to the relative darkness of the forest in full leaf.

'Dream on, dream on.' The voice, reedy, reached an almost

237

shrieking pitch. He walked off the path, stepping on roots and unsteady rocks, his ankle almost twisting a few times. But he ploughed on, snaking his large body around living trees and climbing over dead ones until he reached an opening. It was astonishing.

A large circle had been cleared in the middle of the thick forest and planted with honeysuckle and clover. He wondered how he could have missed it, if only by following his nose. It was sweet almost to the point of cloying. The other sense he might have used was hearing.

The glade buzzed. As he looked closer he noticed the tiny, bright, delicate flowers bobbing. The clearing was alive with bees. Bees crawled into and out of and around the blossom-filled bushes.

'Dream on,' the voice sang from the other side of the bobbing bushes. Gamache decided on discretion and skirted the glade, catching sight as he did of half a dozen wooden boxes in the very centre of the circle.

Hives. These were honey bees at their morning feeding. The Manoir Bellechasse had its own hives.

At the far side he turned his back on the thousands of bees and stared once again into the woods. There he caught sight of colour flitting between trunks. And then it stopped.

Gamache ploughed indelicately through the forest until he was within yards of Bean. The child stood feet apart as though planted. Knees slightly bent, head tilted back, hands gripped in front as though holding something.

And smiling. No, not just smiling, beaming.

'Dream on, dream on,' Bean sang in a music-free voice. But a voice filled with something much richer than even music. Bliss.

Bean was the first Morrow he'd seen with a look of joy, of delight, of rapture.

Gamache recognized it because he felt those things himself, every day. But he hadn't expected to find them here, in the middle of the forest, in a Morrow. And certainly not from this child, marginalized, excluded, mocked. Named for a vegetable, asexual and rooted. Bean seemed destined for disaster. A puppy beside a highway. But this child who couldn't jump could do something much more important. Bean could be transported.

He sat for a long time, mesmerized, watching the child. He noticed thin white strings falling from Bean's ears and disappearing into a pocket. An iPod perhaps? Something was driving the concert he was listening to. He heard Louis Armstrong singing 'St James Infirmary Blues', then the Beatles' 'Let It Be', though it sounded more like 'Letter B'. And some tune without words that sent Bean galloping and humming in a whirl of activity. Every now and then Bean would kick back furiously then arch forward.

Eventually he snuck away, satisfied that Bean was safe. Better than safe. Unbelievable as it seemed, Bean was sound.

Agent Isabelle Lacoste stood by the yellow police tape, staring down at the place where Julia Martin had last lived, and died. The blades of grass had sprung back up, erect where yesterday they too had been crushed. Too bad people couldn't do the same thing, be revitalized after a rain and some sun. Spring back to life. But some wounds were too grave.

Lacoste was haunted by the sight of the body. She'd been in homicide for many years and had seen bodies in far more gruesome shape. What disturbed her, though, hadn't been

239

the stare on the victim's face, or even the statue imbedded in her chest. It was Julia Martin's arms. Flung out, open.

She knew that pose. She saw it each time she visited her mother. There on the steps of her modest east end Montreal home, her mother would be standing. Carefully turned out, always clean and proper. When they pulled up she'd open the door having stood just inside, waiting. She'd step onto the stoop and watch them park, then as Isabelle got out her mother's face would break into a smile. And her arms would open wide, in welcome. It seemed involuntary, as though her mother was exposing her heart to her daughter. And Isabelle Lacoste would head down the walk, picking up speed until finally she was enfolded in those old arms. Safe. Home.

And Lacoste did the same thing when her own children raced down the walk, and into her open arms.

It was just such a gesture Julia Martin had made in the moments before she died. Had she welcomed what was coming? Why had she opened her arms as the massive statue tilted on top of her?

Agent Lacoste closed her eyes and tried to feel the woman. Not the terror of her last moment, but the spirit, the soul of the woman. During each investigation Lacoste quietly went to the site of the murder, and stood there alone. She wanted to say something to the dead. And now, silently, she assured Julia Martin that they would find out who had taken her life. Armand Gamache and his team wouldn't rest until she rested.

So far they had a near perfect record, and she'd only had to apologize to a few spirits. Would this be one? She hated to bring negative thoughts to this moment, but this case disturbed Agent Lacoste. The Morrows disturbed her. But more even than that, the walking statue disturbed her.

Opening her eyes she saw the chief walking across the lawn and above the buzzing insects and chirps of birds she heard him humming and singing in his baritone.

'Letter B, Letter B.'

Jean Guy Beauvoir had slept fitfully. After putting in a few calls to British Columbia and getting some interesting answers he'd done what he knew he shouldn't. Instead of going to bed, or into the library to make more notes, on notepads, for God's sake, he'd gone into the kitchen.

Some of the young staff were just sitting down to eat, the rest were cleaning up. Beauvoir arrived as Pierre Patenaude bustled in. Chef Véronique's attention, momentarily on Beauvoir, shifted. As did Beauvoir's mood. He'd been buoyant, feeling again the strange desire to laugh or at least smile in her company. It was a gladness of heart he rarely felt. But that shifted as her attention shifted, away from him to the maître d'. And the Inspector surprised within himself an anger. A hurt. She seemed happy to see him, but happier to see the maître d'.

And why shouldn't she be? he told himself. *It's only natural.*

But the rational thought glanced off the hard feelings forming as he watched Chef Véronique smile at Patenaude.

What sort of man waits on others all his life? he wondered. *A weak man.* Beauvoir hated weakness. Distrusted it. Murderers were weak, he knew. And he looked at the maître d' with new eyes.

'*Bonjour*, Inspector,' the maître d' had said, wiping his hands on a dish towel. 'What can I do for you?'

'I was hoping for a cup of coffee and perhaps a small

241

dessert?' He turned and looked at Chef Véronique as he spoke. He could feel his cheeks burn slightly.

'*Bon, parfait*,' she said. 'I was just cutting some *poire Hélène* for Monsieur Patenaude. Would you like some?'

Beauvoir's heart raced and contracted at the same time, giving him a pain so sharp he wanted to press his fist into his chest. 'May I help?'

'You never help a chef in her own kitchen,' said Pierre with a laugh. 'Here's your coffee.'

Beauvoir took it reluctantly. This wasn't how he'd seen the encounter going. Chef Véronique would be alone in here. Washing up. He'd pick up a dish towel and dry as she washed, just as he'd seen the Chief Inspector do a thousand times after dinner at home. Unlike his own home. He and his wife ate in front of the TV then she took the dishes down and shoved them in the dishwasher.

He'd dry the dishes and then Chef Véronique would invite him to sit down. She'd pour coffee for both of them, and they'd eat chocolate mousse and talk about their days.

He certainly hadn't imagined sitting with the maître d' and five pimply Anglo kids.

Chef Véronique had cut them each a wedge of *poire Hélène*. Beauvoir watched as she put plump almost purple raspberries and *coulis* on each plate. One was larger than the other. Had more fruit, more custard. More rich pear pie on a dark chocolate base.

She'd put the plates in front of them. The larger one in front of the maître d'.

Jean Guy Beauvoir had felt himself grow cold. In the hot kitchen, on a hot summer's evening, he felt himself freeze over.

Now, in the bright, fresh, warm morning he felt hungover, as though he'd been drunk on emotion. Drunk and sick. But still, as he descended the wide stairs he felt himself pulled once again to the door into the kitchen. He stood outside for a moment, willing himself to turn round, to go into the dining room, or the library, or into his car and head home and make love with his wife.

The door suddenly swung open, knocking Beauvoir square in the face.

He fell back, swallowing with a massive effort the swear words that sprang to mind and tongue, in case it was Véronique who'd done it. For some reason, around her, he couldn't bring himself to swear. He shut his eyes against the pain and his hand flashed up and held his nose, feeling something trickle between his fingers.

'Oh, God, I'm so sorry.'

It was the maître d'.

Beauvoir opened his eyes and his mouth at the same time. '*Chalice*, look at this.' He stared down at his hand, covered in blood. Suddenly he felt a little lightheaded.

'Here, let me help.' The maître d' took Beauvoir's arm, but he shook it away.

'*Tabarnac!* Leave me alone,' he shouted, nasally, haemorrhaging swear words and blood.

'It wasn't his fault.'

Beauvoir stood still, not wanting this to be happening.

'You shouldn't be standing right in front of a kitchen door at mealtime. Monsieur Patenaude was simply doing his job.'

The foghorn voice was unmistakable, as was the tone. A woman defending someone she cared about. More concerned about the attack on the maître d' than the bleeding

243

policeman. That hurt more, far more, than the hard door to the soft nose. Beauvoir turned and saw Chef Véronique towering behind him, sheaves of paper in her beefy hand. Her voice had been hard, censorious, like his teachers at Catholic school when he'd done something particularly stupid.

Chalice, had he said *chalice*? And *tabarnac*? Now he felt really nauseous.

'*Désolé*,' he said, cupping the blood as it poured off his chin. 'I'm sorry.'

'What's happened?'

Beauvoir turned and saw Gamache walk through the door. He felt relief, as he always did when Gamache was in the room.

'It was my fault,' said Pierre. 'I opened the door and hit him.'

'What's going on?' Madame Dubois waddled over, concern on her face.

'Are you all right?' Gamache looked into Beauvoir's eyes. The younger man nodded. Gamache gave the Inspector his handkerchief and asked for more towels. After a moment he examined the damage, his large, sure fingers prodding Beauvoir's nose and forehead and chin.

'Right, nothing too bad. Your nose isn't broken, just bruised.'

Beauvoir shot a look of loathing at the maître d'. Somehow, Beauvoir knew, the man had done it on purpose. Somehow.

He went off and cleaned himself up, hoping to see in the mirror a heroic hockey player or a boxer wounded in the ring. What he saw was an idiot. A bloody idiot. After he'd changed he met the others for breakfast in the dining room. The Morrows were off in one corner, the police in another.

'Better?' asked Gamache.

'It's nothing,' said Beauvoir, catching Lacoste's amused look and wondering if everyone knew. Their *café au lait* arrived and they ordered.

'What have you found out?' Gamache asked Lacoste first.

'You were wondering, Chief, why Julia Martin exploded at the mention of a public washroom? I asked Mariana Morrow last night. Seems Julia had a huge blow-up with her father about that.'

'About a toilet?'

'Uh huh. It was the reason she went to BC. Seems someone wrote on the men's room wall in the Ritz that Julia Morrow gave good head. They even wrote the phone number. The family number.'

Beauvoir grimaced. He could just imagine how Mama and Papa Morrow would react to that. Men calling at all hours asking how much for a blow job.

'Apparently Charles Morrow saw it himself. Whoever did it knew exactly where to put it. You know the Oyster Bar?'

Gamache nodded. It was closed now but it'd been the favourite cocktail lounge for generations of Montreal Anglos. It was in the basement of the Ritz.

'Well, *Julia Morrow gives good head* was written in the men's washroom of the Oyster Bar. According to Mariana her father saw it then heard a bunch of his friends laughing about it. He went ballistic.'

'Who put it there?' Gamache asked.

'I don't know,' said Lacoste. It hadn't occurred to her to ask Mariana.

Their breakfasts arrived. Scrambled eggs with spinach and Brie for the Chief Inspector. A few maple-cured rashers of bacon lay over the eggs and a small fruit salad garnished the plate. Lacoste had ordered eggs Benedict and Beauvoir had the largest dish on the menu. A platter heaped with crêpes, eggs, sausages and back bacon sat in front of him.

A waiter left a basket of croissants along with a tray of home-made wild strawberry and blueberry *confitures*, and honey.

'Someone had it in for her,' said Lacoste, the hollandaise sauce dripping from her fork. 'Girls who don't give out are often labelled sluts by disappointed boys.'

'It's a terrible thing to do to a girl,' said Gamache, thinking of wispy Julia. 'How old would she have been? Twenty?'

'Twenty-two,' said Lacoste.

'I wonder if Thomas could have written it,' said Gamache.

'Why him?' asked Beauvoir.

'It would need to be someone who knew the phone number, knew Charles Morrow's habits, and knew Julia. And it would need to be someone cruel.'

'According to Mariana they're all cruel,' said Beauvoir.

'Could've been Thomas,' said Lacoste. She reached for a croissant, still warm from the oven, and cracking it open she spread golden honey on it. 'But that's thirty-five years ago. We can't judge the man by what the boy did.'

'True, but Thomas lied and told Julia we were talking about men's toilets when we weren't,' said Gamache. 'We were talking about washrooms in general. He wanted her to react. He wanted to hurt her, I know that now. And he did. He's still cruel.'

'Maybe it's a joke to him. Families have lots of in jokes,' said Beauvoir.

'Jokes are funny,' said Gamache. 'This was meant to hurt.'

'It's a form of abuse,' said Lacoste and beside her Beauvoir groaned. She turned to him. 'You think only a fist in a woman's face is abuse?'

'Look, I know all about verbal and emotional abuse, and I understand,' he said and meant it. 'But where does it end? The guy teased his sister about an event from years ago, and it's supposed to be abuse?'

'Some families have long memories,' said Gamache, 'especially for slights.'

He dipped a spoon into the honey and drizzled it on a warm croissant. He tasted it and smiled.

It tasted of fragrant summer flowers.

'According to Mariana their father wasn't so worried about whether Julia gave good head, but that everyone believed it,' said Lacoste.

'And Julia left because of that?' said Gamache. 'It's not trivial, I know, but was it actually enough to send her across the continent?'

'Hurt feelings,' said Lacoste. 'I'd rather have a bruise any day.'

Beauvoir felt his nose throbbing, and knew she was right.

Gamache nodded, trying to imagine the scene. Julia, who'd probably never put a foot wrong her whole life, is suddenly humiliated in front of all Montreal Anglo society. It might not be large, it might not be as powerful as it pretended, but it was where the Morrows lived. And suddenly Julia Morrow was branded a slut. Humiliated.

But the worst was to come. Instead of defending her, Charles Morrow, upright and upstanding and as immovable then as now, had attacked her as well, or at least failed to defend her. She'd loved him, and he'd stepped aside and let the hyenas have at her.

Julia Morrow had left. Gone as far from her family as she could. To British Columbia. Married David Martin, a man her father disapproved of. Divorced. Then come home. And been murdered.

'I spoke to Peter last night,' said Gamache and told them about his conversation.

'So he thinks Bert Finney killed Julia,' said Lacoste, 'for the insurance?'

'OK, suppose he did it,' said Beauvoir, after swallowing a piece of savoury sausage, dripping maple syrup. 'Again, he's like, a hundred and fifty. He's older than he weighs. How could he shove that huge statue off the pedestal? You might as well say that kid did it.'

Gamache took a forkful of scrambled eggs with Brie and stared out of the window. Beauvoir was right. But then, it wasn't any more likely that Peter or Thomas had done it. They were looking at an impossible murder. No one could have budged Charles Morrow, never mind shove him a foot or more until he'd tumbled. And if they did, it would have taken time and made noise. Julia wouldn't have just stood there and let it happen. But Charles Morrow, like the rest of his family, had been silent.

Besides, the statue scraping along the marble would have made not just noise but scratches and blemishes, but the surface was pristine.

Impossible. The whole thing was impossible. And yet it'd been done.

But another thought dawned and Gamache looked over to the family. Bean couldn't have done it. Finney couldn't have done it. Nor could Madame Finney or Mariana or even the men. Not alone.

But together?

'Peter's mistaken about Julia's life insurance,' said Beauvoir. He'd waited all breakfast to tell them his news. He soaked up the maple syrup with the last bit of crêpe. 'Madame Finney doesn't get her daughter's insurance.'

'Who does?' asked Lacoste.

'Nobody. She wasn't insured.' Ha, he thought, loving the looks on their faces. He'd had the night to absorb this unexpected news. The wife of the wealthiest insurance executive in Canada, uninsured?

'You need to speak to David Martin,' said Gamache, after a moment's thought.

'I have a call in to his lawyer in Vancouver. I hope to be speaking to him by noon.'

'Honoré Gamache?'

The name sped across the quiet room and landed on their table. Both Beauvoir and Lacoste jerked their heads up, then over to where the Morrows were sitting. Madame Finney was looking at them, a smile on her soft, attractive face.

'So Honoré Gamache was his father? I knew the name was familiar.'

'Mother, shhhh,' said Peter, leaning across the table.

'What? I'm not saying anything.' Her voice continued to pierce the dining room. 'Besides, I'm not the one who should be embarrassed.'

Beauvoir looked over at the chief.

Armand Gamache had a curious smile on his face. He looked almost relieved.

TWENTY-ONE

~

Clara had left the table. She'd heard enough. She'd tried to feel sympathy for Peter's mother, had tried to be compassionate and patient. But really, damn her, damn them all, thought Clara as she stomped across the lawn.

She could feel her heart racing and her hands trembling as they always did when she was enraged. And of course her brain didn't work. It had run away with her heart, the cowards, leaving her defenceless and blithering. Proving to the Morrows once again she was an ill-bred idiot. Because leaving the breakfast table early was rude, but apparently insulting other people wasn't.

The Morrows seemed to believe there was a special code that allowed them to say what they liked about others, deliberately within their hearing, without its being discourteous.

'Isn't that the ugliest baby you've ever seen?'

'You shouldn't wear white if you're fat.'

'She'd be prettier if she didn't scowl all the time.'

That last had been said about her, on her wedding day, as

she'd walked down the aisle smiling and joyful on her father's arm.

The Morrows could be counted on to choose the right fork and the wrong word. Their comments were always casual. And when confronted they'd look hurt, offended, perplexed.

How often had Clara apologized for being insulted?

And what Mrs Morrow had just said about Gamache's father was about as insulting as Clara had ever heard.

'It's all right, Jean Guy,' said Gamache a few minutes later as they drove down the rough dirt road towards the local cemetery and the man who made Charles Morrow. 'I'm used to it. Bert Finney told me he'd known my father at the end of the war. I suppose he said something to his wife.'

'He didn't have to.'

'My father isn't a secret, you know.' The Chief Inspector turned to look at Beauvoir, who stared straight ahead at the road, not daring to look at the boss.

'I'm sorry. It's just that I know what people think.'

'It was a long time ago, and I know the truth.'

Still, Beauvoir stared ahead, hearing the man beside him but also hearing the plummy, rounded voice of Madame Finney and the word that stuck in his head, that stuck in everyone's. That seemed attached forever to the name Honoré Gamache.

Coward.

'Clara, are you all right?'

Peter walked quickly across the lawn.

'I suppose you set your mother straight?' said Clara, staring

251

at him. His hair stuck out in all directions as though he'd run his hands through it over and over. His shirt was untucked and there were croissant crumbs clinging to his slacks. He stood silent. 'For God's sake, Peter, when're you going to stand up to her?'

'What? She wasn't talking about you.'

'No, she was smearing a friend of yours. Gamache heard every word she said. He was supposed to.'

'You didn't say anything.'

'You're right.' Clara remembered the tablecloth tucked into her waistband and giving the breakfast china a tug as she'd jerked to her feet.

All eyes were on her. Do it, they seemed to be saying. Humiliate yourself again.

And, of course, she had. She always did. She'd arm herself with the mantras 'One more day, just one more day' and 'It doesn't matter, it doesn't matter'. She'd meditate and surround herself with white, protective light. But eventually it all failed against the Morrow onslaught, and she'd be standing, quaking like an aspen, in front of them. Incensed, appalled and struck dumb.

And it'd happened again this morning, as Mrs Morrow had explained it all to her family.

'You've never heard the story?'

'What story?' Thomas had asked, thrilled. Even Peter seemed eager to hear it. It took the heat off him.

'Tell us,' said Peter, throwing Gamache into the fire so that he himself could escape.

'Irene,' Bert Finney warned. 'It was a long time ago. History.'

'This is important, Bert. The children should hear it.' She

turned back to them, and Clara, God help her, was curious herself.

Irene Finney looked down the table at them. She'd spent most of the night begging, praying, bargaining for sleep. For oblivion. For a few hours away from this loss.

And in the morning, when she awoke, her soft, pink, crusty cheek to the pillow, she'd lost her daughter again. Julia. Now gone, but she'd taken disappointment with her. No more birthdays forgotten, no more empty Sundays waiting for phone calls that never came. Julia at least would never hurt her again. Julia was safe. Safe now to love. That was what the void had coughed up. A dead daughter. But a beloved one. Finally. Someone safe to love. Dead, true. But you can't have everything.

Then Bert had returned from his morning walk with this wonderful gift. Something else to think about.

Honoré Gamache. Somehow the void had coughed him up as well. And his son.

'It was just before the war. We all knew Hitler had to be stopped. Canada would join with Britain, that was a given. But then this Gamache started giving speeches against the war. He said Canada should stay out of it. Said no good ever came of violence. He was very articulate. Educated.'

She sounded surprised, as though a beluga had graduated from Laval University.

'Dangerous.' She appealed to her husband. 'Am I wrong?'

'He believed what he was saying,' said Mr Finney.

'That only makes him more dangerous. He convinced a lot of others. Soon there were protests in the streets against going to war.'

'What happened?' asked Sandra. She looked up. The

253

ceiling was smooth. Swept clean by the Manoir staff without comment. Not a cookie left. Sandra couldn't help but feel sad for Bean and all that work. But Bean didn't seem bothered. In fact, Bean was riveted to the story.

'Canada delayed entering the war.'

'Only by a week,' said Finney.

'Long enough. It was humiliating. Britain in there, Germany brutalizing Europe. It was wrong.'

'It was wrong,' agreed Finney sadly.

'It was that Gamache's fault. And even when war was declared he convinced a lot of Quebecers to be conscientious objectors. Conscientious.' She loaded the word with loathing. 'There was no conscience involved, only cowardice.'

Her voiced lifted, turning the sentence into a weapon and the last word a bayonet. And across the room, the human target.

'He went to Europe himself,' said Finney.

'With the Red Cross. Never in the front lines. He never risked his own life.'

'There were a lot of heroes in the ambulance corps,' said Finney. 'Brave men.'

'But not Honoré Gamache,' said Irene Finney.

Clara waited for Finney to contradict her. She looked over at Peter, some jam on his ill-shaven cheek, eyes down. Thomas and Sandra and Mariana, eyes aglow. Like hyenas falling on prey. And Bean? The child sat on the tiny chair, feet planted firmly, gripping *Myths Every Child Should Know*.

Clara stood up, taking the tablecloth with her. Peter looked embarrassed. Causing a scene was so much worse than causing pain. Her hands trembled as she grabbed at the cloth and jerked it free. Her eyes were watering, with rage. But she could see the satisfaction in Mrs Morrow's eyes.

As Clara stumbled from the room, past Gamache himself, and out of the squeaking screen doors the words followed her into the wilderness.

'Honoré Gamache was a coward.'

'Monsieur Pelletier?'

'*Oui*,' came the shout from the rafters.

'My name is Armand Gamache. I'm with the Sûreté du Québec. Homicide.'

Beauvoir wished he could see the sculptor's face. It was his favourite part of any investigation, except for the arrest. He loved to see people's faces when they realized a couple of homicide officers were there. From the famed Sûreté.

But he was denied the pleasure. Pelletier was invisible, a voice from above.

'That would be about that statue,' came the disembodied voice. Another disappointment. Beauvoir loved passing on the gruesome details and seeing people pale.

'It would. Could you come down please?'

'I'm very busy. New commission.'

'Up there?' asked Gamache, craning his neck to see the man in the wooden rafters.

'Of course not up here. I'm fixing ropes to tie on to the piece, so it doesn't fall over.'

Gamache and Beauvoir exchanged glances. So statues did fall over. Could it be that simple?

With a start Beauvoir saw a scrawny man scuttle down the far wall of the old barn, like a spider. Only after the man landed softly did Beauvoir realize there was a makeshift rope ladder there. He turned to Gamache who'd also been watching, his eyes wide at the thought of anyone climbing up and down there.

Yves Pelletier was almost emaciated. He wore loose white shorts and a filthy undershirt, barely concealing his bony chest and ribs. His arms, though, were enormous. He looked like Popeye.

'Yves Pelletier,' he said with a broad townships accent, sticking his hand out. It was like shaking a hammer. This man seemed to be made of metal. All thin and hard and shining with perspiration. The barn was stuffy and hot. No air stirred and dust drifted thick in the sunbeams through the barn boards.

It smelled of old hay, concrete and sweat.

Beauvoir stood straighter and tried to look more manly in his soft leather shoes and trim linen shirt.

I have a gun, he told himself. *I have a gun and he doesn't.*

Threats came in different forms. He glanced over at the Chief Inspector who seemed completely at ease.

'What happened to you?' the sculptor asked Beauvoir, indicating his face.

Had Gamache not been there he'd have described the burning building filled with orphans, or the runaway car he'd stopped just before it ploughed into a pregnant woman, or the murderer he'd disarmed with his bare hands.

He decided to stay quiet and let the man imagine the heroics.

'Looks like a door hit you, son,' said Pelletier, turning round and leading them on a tour of his barn and out into the yard. It wasn't itself a graveyard, though it was right beside a large one.

'Customers,' laughed Pelletier, pointing to the headstones on the other side of his wooden fence. Rolling a cigarette he licked it and stuck it into his yellowed mouth. 'Can't make a living doing this shit. Wish I could, but being an artist doesn't pay the bills.'

He took a long drag, coughed and spat.

Someone less like an artist would be hard to find, thought Beauvoir.

'People hire me for those.' Pelletier waved towards the monuments and headstones. They wandered through the gate. Here and there a winged angel touched down. They were old, their wings worn.

Gamache stopped and took in the sight.

It was quiet, peaceful. But it also seemed alive. Every now and then a man or woman strolled from behind a tree. Only they weren't really moving. They were stuck in place, but somehow vibrant. They were statues.

Gamache turned and stared at their guide. The little man was picking a strand of tobacco off his tongue.

'You did these?'

'Except the angels. I don't do angels. Tried, but they never worked. Wings were always too big. People kept complaining about hitting their heads.'

This struck Beauvoir as funny and he laughed. The sculptor joined in and Gamache smiled.

The statues were all different sizes, all different moods. Some seemed filled with calm and gladness, some looked as though they were playing, some looked pained and some bitter. Not overt, just a hint, a hardness.

'What're they made of?' Beauvoir asked. Most were black and smooth and gleaming.

257

'Marble. Quarried not far from here.'

'But Charles Morrow wasn't made of this,' said Gamache.

'No, he was made of something else. I was going to use marble but after listening to people talk about him I changed my mind.'

'Who'd you talk to?'

'The missus, and his kids, but the one I spoke to most, who actually came here, was that ugly guy. If I ever did a sculpture of him I'd get complaints.' He laughed. 'But you know, I just might anyway, for myself.'

'Bert Finney?' asked Gamache, to be certain. Pelletier nodded and flicked his butt onto the grass. Beauvoir stepped on it.

'I knew you'd probably be coming so I looked up my notes. Wanna see?'

'*S'il vous plaît*,' said Beauvoir, who liked notes. They wandered back into the barn, which seemed gloomy compared to the lively cemetery. While Beauvoir read Gamache and the sculptor sat on a low wooden trough.

'How do you go about doing a sculpture?'

'Well, it's hard if I haven't met the person. Lots of those people I actually knew.' He waved casually towards the cemetery. 'In a small town you do. But Morrow I never met. So like I said, I spoke to his family, looked at pictures. That ugly guy brought a bunch of stuff. Quite interesting. So then I just let it kinda ferment, you know, until I get him. And one day I wake up and I have the guy. Then I get started.'

'What did you "get" about Charles Morrow?'

Pelletier picked at his calloused fingers and thought.

'You know those statues out there, the ones in the cemetery?'

Gamache nodded.

'They're not all the same size. Some people buy big ones,

some smaller. Sometimes it depends on their budget, but mostly it depends on their guilt.'

He smiled. Charles Morrow had been immense.

'I had the impression he wasn't missed. That the statue was more for them than him. A kind of replacement for grieving.'

There it was. So simple. The words drifted into the air to join the dry dirt in the sunbeams.

What could be worse? Dying, and not being missed.

Was that true of Charles Morrow, Gamache wondered.

'The family used words like prominent and respected, they even mailed me a list of boards he sat on. I half expected to get his bank balance. But there was no affection. I felt sorry for the guy. I tried asking what kinda man he was, you know? Father, husband, that sorta thing.'

'And what did they say?'

'They seemed offended by the question, as though it wasn't my business. Like I said, it's very hard to sculpt a man without knowing him. I almost decided to turn down the commission, though the money was so good it woulda killed me. But then this ugly guy shows up. Spoke almost no French and I don't speak much English. *He shoots, he scores.* That's about it. But we got along. That was almost two years ago. I thought about it and decided to sculpt the guy.'

'But who did you sculpt, monsieur? Charles Morrow or Bert Finney?'

Yves Pelletier laughed. 'Or maybe I sculpted myself.'

Gamache smiled. 'There's some of you in all your works, I'd expect.'

'True, but more perhaps in that one. It was difficult, troubling. Charles Morrow was a stranger to his family. They knew his outside but not his inside. The ugly man knew his inside. At least, I believe he did. He told me about a man who loved music, who'd wanted to be a hockey player, had played on his school team, but had agreed to go into the family business. Seduced by the money and the position. Ugly man's words, not mine. The ego. What a tyrant. My words, not his.' He smiled at Gamache. 'Happily, being a sculptor keeps my ego in check.'

'You might try being a police officer.'

'Have you ever been sculpted?'

Gamache laughed. 'Never.'

'If you decide you'd like to, come to me.'

'I'm not sure there's enough marble in that quarry,' said Gamache. 'What was Charles Morrow made of after all?'

'Well, now, there's an interesting question. I needed something special and money wasn't an issue so I searched and last year I finally found what I'd heard existed but never actually seen.'

Across the barn Inspector Beauvoir lowered the notes and listened.

'It was wood,' said the scrawny sculptor.

Of all the things Gamache thought he'd hear that wasn't one of them.

'Wood?'

Pelletier nodded. Gamache remembered reaching out and stroking Charles Morrow, trying to avoid the mud and grass and blood. He again felt the hard grey surface, undulating. It felt like sagging skin. But hard, like stone.

'Wood,' he said again, looking back at the sculptor. 'Fossilized wood.'

'All the way from British Columbia. Petrified.'

*

Agent Lacoste got off the phone with the coroner, made her notes then opened the strong box with the evidence. There wasn't much. Out of the box she pulled the packet of letters, tied with yellow ribbon, and the two crumpled notes on Manoir Bellechasse paper. Smoothing them out she decided to start there.

She found Madame Dubois first, behind her huge desk calling guests and cancelling reservations. After a minute or two the tiny hand replaced the receiver.

'I'm trying not to tell the truth,' she explained.

'What're you saying?'

'That there was a fire.'

Seeing Agent Lacoste's surprise she nodded agreement. 'It might have been better had I thought about it. Fortunately, it was a small, though inconvenient, fire.'

'That is lucky.' She glanced down at the rates card on the desk, and raised her eyebrows. 'I'd love to come back with my husband, one day. Perhaps for our golden wedding anniversary.'

'I'll be waiting.'

Agent Lacoste thought perhaps she would. 'We found these in the grate in Julia Martin's room.' She handed over the slips of paper. 'Who do you think wrote them?'

The two slips sat on the desk between the women.

I enjoyed our conversation. Thank you. It helped.

You are very kind. I know you won't tell anyone what I said. I could get into trouble!

'Perhaps one of her family?'

'Maybe,' said Lacoste. She'd thought about what the chief had said. About the exclamation mark. She'd spent much of the morning thinking about it. Then she had it.

'The words, certainly, could have been written by almost anyone,' Lacoste admitted to Madame Dubois. 'But this wasn't.'

She pointed to the exclamation mark. The elderly proprietor looked down then up, polite but unconvinced.

'Can you see any of the Morrows writing an exclamation mark?'

The question surprised Madame Dubois and she thought about it then shook her head. That left one option.

'One of the staff,' she said reluctantly.

'Possibly. But who?'

'I'll call the chambermaid assigned to her room.' Madame Dubois spoke into a walkie-talkie and was assured a young woman named Beth was on her way.

'They're young, you know, and most have never worked in jobs like these. It takes a while to understand what's appropriate, especially if the guests themselves aren't clear. We tell them not to be too familiar with the guests, even if the guests invite it. Especially then.'

After a longish wait a blonde girl, energetic and confident, though momentarily worried, came down.

'*Désolée*,' she said in slightly accented French, 'but Madame Morrow in the Lake Room stopped to talk to me. I think she might want to speak to you too.'

The proprietor looked weary. 'Another complaint?'

Beth nodded. 'Her sister-in-law's room was cleaned before hers and she wanted to know why. I told her it depended which end of the lodge we started at. She also thinks it's too hot.'

'I hope you told her that was Monsieur Patenaude's department?'

Beth smiled. 'I will next time.'

'*Bon*. Beth, this is Agent Lacoste, she's investigating the death of Julia Martin. She has a few questions for you.'

The girl looked disconcerted. 'I didn't do anything.'

It's not my fault, thought Lacoste. The cry of the young. And the immature. Still, she felt for the kid. Not more than twenty and being interviewed as a murder suspect. One day it'll make a great story, but not today.

'I don't think you did,' said Lacoste in good English. The girl relaxed a little, reassured by both the words and the language. 'But I'd like you to look at these.'

Beth did, then looked up, puzzled.

'I'm not sure what you want.'

'Did you write them?'

She looked astonished. 'No. Why would I?'

'Did you check the grate in Mrs Martin's room?'

'Not closely. Some guests light their fires even in summer. It's romantic. So I've gotten in the habit of just scanning it, making sure I don't need to lay another fire. Hers hadn't been lit. None of them have.'

'Would you notice if something had been put in there?'

'Depends. I'd notice if it was a Volkswagen or a sofa.'

Lacoste smiled at this unexpected humour. The girl suddenly reminded her of herself at twenty. Just finding her way. Vacillating between being impertinent and being obsequious. 'How about these, balled up?' Lacoste pointed to the papers on the desk.

Beth stared at them, considering. 'I might.'

'And what would you have done, if you'd seen them?'

'Cleaned them up.'

She thought Beth was telling the truth. She didn't think the Manoir kept workers who were lazy. The question was,

263

would Beth have noticed the papers or could they have sat there for days, even weeks, left there by long departed guests?

But she didn't think they had.

Why did Julia put most garbage into the wastepaper basket, but toss these into the grate? It was a bit like littering and Agent Lacoste suspected the Morrows thought themselves above that. They might murder, but they'd never litter. And Julia Martin was nothing if not courteous, to a fault.

So if she didn't put them there, somebody else had. But who? And why?

Gamache, Beauvoir and the sculptor Pelletier sat in the shade of a huge tree, grateful for the few degrees' relief it gave from the pounding heat. Beauvoir slapped at his neck and his hand came away with a smear of blood and a tiny black leg. He knew he was covered in bug bodies. You'd think, he thought, other bugs would get the message. But there was probably a reason blackflies didn't rule the world. Torment it, yes, but nothing else.

He slapped at his arm.

A rose bush planted beside a headstone looked in need of watering, its leaves droopy and yellowing. Pelletier followed Gamache's gaze.

'Thought that might happen soon. Tried to warn the family when they planted it.'

'Roses don't grow well here?' Gamache asked.

'Not now. Nothing'll grow now. It's twenty-five years, you know.'

Beauvoir wondered whether decades of snorting cement dust hadn't done something to this man's brain.

'What is?' asked Gamache.

'This tree. It's a black walnut.' The sculptor dragged his hammer hand over the furrowed bark. 'It's twenty-five years old.'

'So?' asked Beauvoir, hoping to get to the point.

'Well, nothing grows around a black walnut once it gets that old.'

Gamache reached out and touched the tree too. 'Why not?'

'Dunno. Something poisonous drops from its leaves or bark or something. But it's fine until it's twenty-five. Only kills things after that.'

Gamache removed his hand from the greyish trunk and returned his gaze to the cemetery, the sun dappling through the leaves of the killer tree.

'You carved a bird into the shoulder of the statue.'

'I did.'

'*Pourquoi?*'

'Didn't you like it?'

'It was charming, and very discreet. Almost as though it wasn't meant to be found.'

'Why would I do that, Chief Inspector?'

'I can't imagine, Monsieur Pelletier, unless someone asked you to.'

The two men stared at each other, the air suddenly crackling between them like a tiny summer storm.

'No one asked me,' the sculptor finally said. 'I'd gone through that,' he pointed to the rumpled dossier in Beauvoir's hands, 'and found a drawing of the bird. It was very simple, very beautiful. I etched it into Morrow, discreet as you say, as a little gift.'

He looked down at his hands, one picking at the other.

'I'd grown quite fond of Charles Morrow. I wanted him to have something to keep him company, so he'd be less alone. Something he'd kept close to him in life.'

'The footless bird?' said Beauvoir.

'The drawing's in there.' Again he pointed to the manila folder.

Beauvoir handed the folder to Gamache but said as he did, 'I didn't see anything like that in there.'

Gamache closed the folder. He believed him.

Like anything else in life, it's the things we can't have we most want, and suddenly Chief Inspector Gamache wanted that drawing of the bird very much indeed.

Beauvoir glanced at his watch. Almost noon. He had to be back for the call from David Martin. And lunch.

He touched his face gingerly and hoped she'd forgive him for swearing. She'd looked so shocked. Surely people swear in kitchens? His wife did.

'Looking at your sculpture of Charles Morrow I thought of Rodin,' said Gamache. 'Can you guess which one?'

'Not Victor Hugo, that's for sure. The Gates of Hell, perhaps?'

But the sculptor was clearly not serious. Then he thought about it and after a moment spoke quietly. 'The Burghers?'

Gamache nodded.

'*Merci, Patron.*' The strappy little man gave Gamache a small bow. 'But if he was by Rodin, the rest of the family would be by Giacometti.'

Gamache knew the Swiss artist with the long, lean, almost stringy figures, but he couldn't make out what Pelletier meant.

'Giacometti always began with a huge piece of stone,' Pelletier explained. 'Then he'd work and work. Refining and smoothing and chipping away anything offensive, anything that wasn't just right. Sometimes he did so much refining there wasn't anything left. The sculpture disappeared completely. All he had left was dust.'

Gamache smiled, understanding it now.

On the outside the Morrows were healthy, attractive even. But you can't diminish so many people without diminishing yourself. And the Morrows, inside, had all but disappeared. Empty.

But he wasn't convinced the sculptor was right. He thought there might be quite a bit of the Burghers in all of them. He saw all the Morrows, trudging along, chained together, weighed down by expectation, disapproval, secrets. Need. Greed. And hate. After years of investigating murders Chief Inspector Gamache knew one thing about hate. It bound you for ever to the person you hated. Murder wasn't committed out of hate, it was done as a terrible act of freedom. To finally rid yourself of the burden.

The Morrows were burdened.

And one had tried to break free. By killing.

But how had the murderer managed it?

'How can a statue come off its pedestal?' he asked Pelletier.

'I was wondering when you'd ask. Here, come with me.'

They walked further into the cemetery to a sculpture of a child.

'I did that ten years ago. Antoinette Gagnon. Killed by a car.'

They looked at the gleaming, playing child. Always young, perpetually happy. Gamache wondered whether her parents ever came, and whether their hearts stopped each time they turned the corner and saw this.

'Try to knock her over,' Pelletier said to Beauvoir.

The Inspector hesitated. The thought of knocking over a cemetery monument disgusted him. And especially a child.

'Go on,' said the sculptor. Still Beauvoir hung back.

'I'll try.' Gamache stepped forward and leaned against the small statue, expecting to feel the child scrape forward, or topple over.

She didn't budge.

He leaned harder then turned his back and shoved, feeling sweat break out on his body. Still nothing. Eventually he stopped and wiping his brow with his handkerchief he turned back to Pelletier.

'Is it fixed in place? A rod down the centre into the pedestal?'

'No. It's just heavy. Far heavier than it looks. Marble is. And petrified wood is heavier still.'

Gamache stared at the statue, about a quarter the size and weight of Charles Morrow.

'If one person didn't move the statue of Charles Morrow, could several?'

'At a guess I'd say you'd need twenty football players.'

The Morrows weren't that.

'There's one other thing,' said Gamache as they walked back to the car. 'The marble pedestal wasn't marked.'

Pelletier stopped. 'I don't understand.'

'I mean there were no marks on it,' said Gamache, watching the man's face. He looked genuinely upset for the first time. 'It was perfect, polished even.'

'The sides, you mean.'

'No, I mean the top. Where Charles Morrow stood.'

'But that's not possible. Just placing the statue on top of

the marble would mark it.' He was about to suggest Gamache hadn't looked closely enough, but decided this commanding, quiet man would have. Instead he shook his head.

'So how could the statue fall?' Beauvoir repeated.

Pelletier tilted his palms towards the blue sky.

'What's that supposed to mean?' asked Beauvoir, suddenly annoyed. 'God murdered Julia Martin?'

'He is a serial killer,' said Pelletier, without humour. After a moment's thought he spoke again. 'When I heard about what happened I asked myself the same question. The only way I know to get a statue that size off its pedestal is with ropes and a winch. Even in the time of Rodin that's how they did it. Are you sure that wasn't used to bring him down?'

He looked at Gamache who shook his head. Pelletier nodded.

'That leaves us with God.'

As they got in the car Beauvoir whispered to Gamache, 'You make the arrest.'

Pelletier walked back to the barn and Beauvoir put the car in gear.

'Wait, wait.'

They looked in their rearview mirror. The sculptor was running after them waving a piece of paper.

'I found this.' He shoved it through the window at Gamache. 'It was pinned to my board. I'd forgotten I'd put it there.'

Gamache and Beauvoir stared at the yellow, crinkled piece of paper. On it was a simple pencil drawing of a bird, without feet.

It was signed *Peter Morrow*.

TWENTY-TWO

—

'Glad I found you.' Mariana stumbled to catch up with her brother. 'I wanted to talk. It wasn't me, you know, who told Mother what you said to that cop. It was Sandra.'

Peter looked at her. She'd always been a crybaby, the tattle-tale.

'Fucking Sandra,' said Mariana, falling into step beside him. 'Always going behind people's backs. And Thomas, what a piece of work he's turned into. Snot. What're we going to do?' She stopped and whispered.

'What do you mean?'

'Well, someone killed Julia. It wasn't me, and I don't think it was you. That leaves one of them. If they'd kill Julia, they'll kill us.'

'Don't be ridiculous.'

'I'm not being.' She sounded petulant. 'I'm tired of all this crap. Tired of these reunions. Each is worse than the last, and this is the worst yet.'

'Let's hope.'

'I'm not coming back,' she said, yanking a flower from its

bush. 'No power on earth'll get me back to one of these. I'm tired of it all. All this pretending, yes Mother, no Mother, can I get you anything Mother? Who cares what the old bitch thinks anyway? She's probably disinherited us long ago. That Finney got her to do it, Thomas thinks. So why're we even bothering?'

'Because she's our mother?'

Mariana gave him a look and continued to shred the flower.

'I'd have thought,' said Peter, 'having a child of your own would make you more sympathetic to your own mother.'

'It has. It's shown me just how horrible our home life was.'

'Well, she was better than Father.'

'You think?' asked Mariana. 'At least he listened to us.'

'Right. And did fuck all. He knew what we wanted and ignored us. Remember that year we all asked for new skis for Christmas? He gave us mittens. He could've bought the ski hill and he gave us mittens. Why would he do that?'

Mariana nodded. She remembered. 'But at least Dad smelled the milk before he gave it to us. Mom never did.'

He smelled the milk and felt the bathwater, he blew on their hot food. They all thought it was disgusting. But a strange new thought started to form in a part of her brain that hadn't had a new thought in decades.

'Did you know, when I left home I found a note in my suitcase from him?' she said, another old memory staggering back.

Peter looked at her, amazed, and afraid. Afraid he was about to lose the one tiny scrap that was his alone. The cipher, the puzzle. The special code from his father.

Never use the first stall in a public washroom.

271

'Is Bean a boy or a girl?' he asked, knowing that would take Mariana off course.

She hesitated then went after the bait. 'Why should I tell you? Besides, you'll tell Mother.'

Her mother had stopped harping at Mariana about it years ago. Now there was silence, as though she no longer cared if she had a grandson or a granddaughter. But Mariana knew her mother, and she knew not knowing was killing her. If only it would hurry up.

'Of course I won't tell Mother. Come on, tell me.'

Mariana sure as hell knew enough not to tell Peter. Spot.

Peter watched Mariana think. Frankly, he didn't care whether Bean was animal, vegetable or mineral. He just wanted his sister to shut up, to not steal the only thing his father had given him alone.

But Peter knew it was too late. Knew that Father must have written the same note to all his children, and once again Peter felt a fool. For forty years he'd lugged that sentence around, thinking he was special. Secretly selected by their father because he loved and trusted Peter the most. *Never use the first stall in a public washroom.* All the magic had gone from it now. It sounded just stupid. Well, he could finally let it go.

He turned and stomped off in search of Clara.

'Peter,' his sister called after him. He turned back reluctantly. 'You sat in some jam,' she said, gesturing.

He walked away.

She watched him go, remembering the note her father had left. The note she'd memorized and was about to tell Peter about, as a peace offering. But he'd refused it, as he refused all offers of help.

You can't get milk from a hardware store.

It was a funny sort of thing for a father to tell a daughter. It seemed obvious. And then with all the superstores you could find milk in one aisle and hammers in the next. But by then she'd broken the code, and knew what her father had been trying to tell her. And what she'd just tried to tell Peter.

You can't get milk from a hardware store.

So stop asking for something that can't be given. And look for what is offered. She saw the fork of food, and the thin lips that rarely smiled at them, blowing on it.

Agent Lacoste walked along the shore of Lac Massawippi. It was hot, and made hotter by the sun shimmering off the water. She glanced around. Nobody. She imagined stripping off her light summer dress, kicking away her sandals, laying the notebook and pen on the grass, and diving in. She imagined how the refreshing water would feel as her perspiring body splashed into it.

Thinking about it actually made it worse, so she contented herself with taking her sandals off and walking through the shallows, feeling the cool water on her feet.

Then she spotted Clara Morrow sitting on a rock jutting into the lake. Agent Lacoste stopped and watched. Clara Morrow's hair was groomed under the sensible, floppy sun hat. Her shorts and shirt were neat, her face without smears or smudges or pastry. She was impeccable. Lacoste barely recognized her.

Lacoste got out of the water, wiped her feet on the grass and slipped her sandals back on. As she cleared her throat Clara started and looked over.

'*Bonjour.*' Clara waved and smiled. 'Come on over.' She patted the flat stone beside her and Isabelle Lacoste picked her way along the shore and out onto the rocks. The stone was warm on her bottom.

'Sorry to interrupt.'

'Never. I was just creating my next work.'

Lacoste looked around for the sketch pad. Nothing. Not even a pencil.

'Really? It looked as though—' She stopped herself, but not quite in time.

Clara laughed. 'As though I was doing nothing? It's all right, that's what most people think. It's a shame that creativity and sloth look exactly the same.'

'Are you going to paint this?' Lacoste indicated their surroundings.

'I don't think so. I was thinking about painting Mrs Morrow . . . Finney. Whatever.' Clara laughed. 'Maybe that'll become my specialty. Embittered women. First Ruth and now Peter's mother.'

But she always painted groups of three. Who would be the last bitter old woman? She hoped it wasn't herself, but at times Clara could feel herself slipping in that direction. Was that why she was fascinated by them? Maybe she knew that beneath her civilized and supportive exterior there lived a shrivelled, judgemental, negative old thing, waiting.

'Well, you had a series called the Warrior Uterus,' said Lacoste. 'About young women. Maybe this is the other end, so to speak.'

'I can call it the Hysterectomies,' said Clara. She also had the series on the Three Graces. Faith, Hope and Charity.

What would this series be called? Pride, Despair and Greed? The broken-hearted.

'Do you mind if I ask you a few questions?' asked Agent Lacoste.

'Fire away.'

'When you heard that Julia Martin had been killed, what did you think?'

'I was stunned, like everybody. I thought it was an accident. Still do, in some ways. I just can't figure out how that statue could've fallen.'

'Neither can we,' admitted Lacoste. 'The night she died there was a scene in the library.'

'Sure was.'

'Do you think that had anything to do with her death?'

'It does seem a coincidence,' Clara admitted reluctantly. 'I've watched the Morrows for twenty-five years. The angrier they get the quieter they get. They haven't really spoken in decades.'

Lacoste could believe it.

'But Julia, she was an outlier. Different. No, that's not right, not really different, but distant. She'd been away. I always think the Morrows have like a layer of polyethylene. They're dipped in it as kids, like Achilles. To protect them. Make them able to withstand high pressures and being dropped on their heads. And once a year they need to be close to Mother to kinda top it up. Get all buffed and polished and hardened again. But Julia had been away so long her coating had worn thin. It took a few days, but eventually she cracked. Exploded really. And said some things she didn't mean.'

'The Chief Inspector has the impression she meant every word.'

Clara was surprised, and thought about that.

'She might have meant it, but that didn't make what she said true.'

Lacoste nodded and consulted her notes. This was the delicate part.

'She accused your husband of being the worst. Of being,' she read from her notes, 'cruel, greedy and empty.'

Clara began to speak but Lacoste stopped her with a gesture. 'There's more. She said he'd destroy anything to get what he wanted.' Lacoste looked up. 'It doesn't sound like the Peter Morrow we know. What did she mean?'

'She was just trying to hurt him, that's all.'

'Did she?'

'Peter wasn't very close to her. I don't think he cared much about her opinion.'

'Is that possible?' Lacoste asked. 'I know we say we don't care, but they're family. Don't you think at some level he cared?'

'Enough to kill, you mean?'

Lacoste said nothing.

'The Morrows are used to wounding each other. Normally they do it more subtly. The stone in the snowball, the sting in the tail. You don't see it coming. You think you're safe.'

'Julia came home at a time of stress, to be with her family,' said Lacoste. 'She must've thought she was safe. But one of them got her.'

Clara said nothing.

'Who do you think did it?' Lacoste asked.

'Not Peter,' Clara said. Lacoste stared at her, then nodded and closed her book.

'Julia Martin said one other thing,' said Lacoste, getting

up. 'She said she'd finally figured out their father's secret. What did she mean by that?'

Clara shrugged. 'I asked Peter the same thing. He thinks she was just raving by then, trying to hurt. People do, you know. Like Mrs Morrow this morning and the terrible lies about the Chief Inspector.'

'She was talking about his father, not him.'

'But the hurt was directed at him.'

'Perhaps, but the Chief Inspector isn't easily hurt. Besides, you're mistaken. Everything she said about Honoré Gamache was true. He was a coward.'

Gamache and Beauvoir arrived back at the Manoir Bellechasse just as the call came from the Nanaimo Correctional Centre in British Columbia.

'You'll have to take it in there,' said Madame Dubois, pointing to the tiny office. Beauvoir thanked her and sat down behind the desk which seemed to be never used, the proprietor obviously preferring to be in the centre of activity.

'Monsieur David Martin?'

'*Oui.*'

'I'm calling about the death of your ex-wife.'

'Wife. We weren't divorced yet. Just separated.'

Beauvoir thought he must have fitted right in with the Morrows. Appropriate that he would end up in a corrections facility.

'I'm sorry for your loss.'

He said it by rote, but the man's response surprised him.

'Thank you. I still can't believe she's gone.' And he sounded genuinely sad. The first one so far. 'What can I do to help?'

'I need to know all about her. How you met, when you met, how well you know the family. Anything at all.'

'I didn't know the Morrows all that well. I saw them when I came back to Montreal, but even those visits tapered out. I know Julia was very upset by what happened.'

'What happened?'

'Well, when her father kicked her out of the house.'

'We'd heard that she left.'

There was a hesitation. 'Yes, I suppose that's right, but sometimes people can make your life such hell you have no choice.'

'Charles Morrow made his daughter's life hell? How?'

'He believed some malicious gossip. Well, I'm not even sure he believed it.' David Martin suddenly sounded exhausted. 'Someone wrote nasty stuff about Julia, her father saw it and got very angry.'

'Was it true what was written?'

He knew the story but he wanted this man's version.

'It said Julia gave good head.' The disgust was clear in his voice. 'If you'd ever met Julia you'd know it was ridiculous. She was gracious and kind. A lady. An old-fashioned word, I realize, but it described her. Always made others feel comfortable. And she adored her father. That's why his reaction hurt so much.'

'And her mother? What kind of relationship did she have with her?'

David Martin laughed. 'The further Julia moved away, and the longer she was gone, the better it got. Space and time. That's relativity for the Morrows.' But he didn't seem amused.

'You have no children?'

278

'No. We tried, but Julia didn't seem too keen. She did it for my sake, but once I realized she didn't really want them I stopped insisting. She was very wounded, Inspector. I thought I could make it better and look where it led me.'

'You're not saying you stole all that money and ruined so many lives for your wife?'

'No, that was greed,' he admitted.

'If you're so greedy, why wasn't your wife insured?'

There was another hesitation.

'Because I couldn't imagine her dying. Not before me. I'm older than her, I should've gone first. I wanted to go first. I could never take money from her death.'

'Do you know what's in your wife's will?'

'She might've made a new one,' Martin cleared his throat and his voice came back stronger, 'but the last I heard it all came to me, except for some bequests to charities.'

'Like?'

'Oh, the children's hospital, the animal shelter, the local library. Nothing very big.'

'Nothing to her family?'

'Nothing. I can't imagine they expected anything, but you never know.'

'How much money did she have?'

'Well, she might've had more but her father left most of his money to his wife when he died. The kids got just enough to ruin them.'

Now the disdain was clear.

'What do you mean?'

'Charles Morrow lived in terror his children would squander the family fortune.'

'Beware the third generation, *oui*, I heard,' said Beauvoir.

'His father had told him that, and he believed it. Each of the kids inherited about a million from their father, except Peter,' Martin continued. 'He declined his inheritance.'

'*Quoi?*'

'I know, foolish. He gave it back to the estate and it was split among his siblings and mother.'

Beauvoir was so surprised his formidable brain stopped for a moment. How could someone turn down a million dollars? He hated to think what he'd do for that money, and he couldn't begin to imagine what would make him turn it down.

'Why?' was all he could manage. Fortunately it was enough.

A chuckle came all the way across the continent. 'I never asked, but I can guess. Revenge. I think he wanted to prove to his father that he'd been wrong. That he of all the kids wasn't interested in his fortune.'

'But his father was dead.' Beauvoir didn't get it.

'Families are complicated,' said David Martin.

'My family's complicated, monsieur. This is just weird.' Beauvoir didn't like weird.

'How did you meet your wife?'

'At a dance. She was the most beautiful woman there, still was the most beautiful woman in any room. I fell in love and came back to Montreal to ask her father to let me marry her. He told me I was welcome to her. It wasn't very gracious. We didn't have much to do with each other after that. I'd actually tried to get them to reconcile, but after I met the family I lost enthusiasm for that.'

'Who do you think killed your wife?' Might as well ask.

'I don't honestly know, but I do know who I think wrote those terrible things in the men's room at the Ritz.'

Beauvoir already knew it was probably Thomas Morrow so he was uninterested in what came next.

'Her brother, Peter.'

Beauvoir was suddenly interested.

Peter strode into his brother's room, not bothering to knock. Best to be forceful, assured.

'You're late. God, you look a mess. Doesn't that wife of yours look after you? Or maybe she's too busy painting. What's it like to have a wife far more successful than you?'

Rattatatatat. Peter stood stunned. Once he recovered he knew this was his chance to stand up for Clara, to tell this smug, smarmy, smiling nemesis how she'd saved his life, given him love. How brilliant and kind she was. He'd tell Thomas—

'Thought so,' said Thomas, waving him into the room.

Silenced, Peter did as he was told, looking around as he entered. It was much more splendid than his room, the bed canopied, the sofa facing the balcony and the lake. The huge armoire was almost dwarfed by the scale. But Peter's eyes found the tiniest thing in there. Sitting on the bedside table.

Cufflinks. Left there, he knew, to be seen.

'We have to do something, Spot.'

'What do you mean?' With alarm Peter noticed crumbs on his shirt and quickly brushed them off.

'Someone killed Julia and that idiot of a detective thinks it was one of us.'

Now was his chance to stand up for Gamache, to tell Thomas what a remarkable man he was, astute, courageous, kind.

'Mother thinks he's trying to compensate for his father,' said Thomas. 'Must be hard to have a traitor and a coward for a father. For all the stuff we could say about the pater, he was no coward. Bully, perhaps, but no coward.'

'Bullies are cowards,' said Peter.

'That would make your friend's father both a bully and a coward. That's not a very nice thing to say, Peter. It's a wonder you have any friends at all. But I didn't ask you here to chat about you. This is about Julia, so please focus. It's obvious who killed her.'

'Finney,' said Peter, finding his voice again.

'Well done.' Thomas turned his back on Peter and looked out the window. 'Not that he didn't do us a favour.'

'Pardon?'

'Oh, come on, you can't tell me you haven't done the math. Four minus one?'

His voice was wheedling, insisting Peter answer a rhetorical question.

'What are you saying?'

'You're not really this thick, are you?'

'Mother might leave all her money to Finney,' said Peter. 'Julia's death doesn't mean we'll get a bigger inheritance. Besides, I don't care. Remember who turned down Father's inheritance? Money means nothing to me.'

And he knew Thomas couldn't argue. It was the one incontrovertible fact, bought for a million dollars. The thing that made him different, separated him from his siblings. They knew he'd refused the inheritance, but in true Morrow fashion had said nothing. And he'd said nothing, reserving the words for just this moment.

'Oh, come on,' said Thomas, his voice dripping reason. 'If it meant nothing to you you'd have taken the inheritance.'

'You're wrong,' said Peter, but the rock solid ground

282

beneath him shifted. The territory he'd bought in exchange for his inheritance, in exchange for security for himself and Clara, had proved worthless. He was sinking.

'Spot claiming not to care that Julia's death makes us richer?' said Mariana, stepping in without knocking. 'Three to inherit,' she sang to them.

'You're late, Magilla,' said Thomas.

'It's comforting, isn't it, knowing you'll be rich one day?' cooed Mariana. Peter could smell her stale perfume and powder and sweat. She smelled of decay.

'I don't care about those things, never have.'

'Now, that might work with Gamache. It might even work with Clara,' said Thomas. 'But we know you, Spot. We love fine things,' he looked around the room, 'and I bet your room's spartan compared to this.'

It was.

'But you're still the greediest of us,' Mariana finished her brother's thought.

'That's not true.' Peter raised his voice.

'Ah ha.' Thomas waggled his finger at his brother then raised it to his lips.

'Of course it's true,' said Mariana. 'Why do you think we call you Spot?'

Peter turned astonished eyes on her. He brought up his hands, to show them the paint spots tattooed there.

'My painting,' he said. But he could see in their faces he was wrong. Had been wrong all his life. Or had he? Had he known the truth all along, and denied it?

'We call you Spot because of the way you used to follow Father around,' said Thomas, his voice calm, explaining nicely this devastating fact. 'Like a puppy.'

'And what do puppies want?' Mariana asked.

'Affection,' said Thomas, 'and stroking. They want to be cuddled and told how wonderful they are. But it wasn't enough when Father said it to you. You wanted it all. Every ounce of affection he had. You hated it when he paid any attention to Julia. You were greedy then, Peter, and you're greedy now. Love, attention, praise, Spot. Good boy, Spot. And after Father died you turned to Mother. Love me, love me, love me, pleeeease.'

'And you shit on us because all we want from Mother is her money. We at least ask for something she can give,' said Mariana.

'You're wrong,' Peter exploded. His rage burst out of him with such force he thought the room would shake and tremble and shatter. 'I never wanted anything from them. Nothing.'

He screamed so loud the last word was barely audible. He thought he'd stripped his vocal cords. He looked around the room for something to throw. Mariana was staring at him, frightened. He liked that. But Thomas? Thomas was smiling.

Peter stepped towards him. He finally knew how to get that smile off his face.

'You want to kill me, don't you?' said Thomas, actually walking to meet Peter. 'I knew it. Always knew you were the unstable one. Everyone thought it was Julia or Mariana—'

'Hey—'

'But it's always the quiet ones. Isn't that what your neighbours in that dreary little village will be telling the CBC tomorrow? He always seemed so nice, so normal. Never a harsh word, never a complaint. You going to throw me off the balcony, Peter? Then there'll only be two of you to inherit. Will that be enough? Or should Mariana start worrying too? All the affection and all the money. The mother-lode.'

Peter could see himself tilting his head back and opening his mouth, and flames spewing out, like vomit. From the tips of his toes the rage would streak through his body, and shoot out, destroying everything around him. He was Nagasaki and Hiroshima, he was the Bikini Atoll and Chernobyl. He would annihilate everything.

Instead he clamped his mouth shut and felt the bitterness and bile burn in his throat and chest. He fought to shove the rage back in, stuffing it down there with anger and jealousy and fear and hate, hate, hate.

But Pandora's box wouldn't be shut. Not again. The demons had already escaped and were swirling around the Manoir Bellechasse, feeding and growing. And killing.

Peter turned a twisted, pinched face on Mariana.

'I might be a puppy, but you're something much worse, Magilla.'

He spat the last word in her fearful face. It felt good to see her afraid. Then he turned to Thomas.

'Magilla and Spot,' he said to the smug face. 'And do you know what we called you?'

Thomas waited.

'Nothing. You were nothing to us then and still are. Nothing.'

Peter walked out, feeling calmer than he had in days. But he knew that was because he was curled up in the back seat, and something else was driving. Something rancid and stinking and horrible. The something he'd hidden all his life. It was finally in charge.

TWENTY-THREE

⌐∼

Armand Gamache stood in what little shade the maple tree offered at high noon and stared once again at the white marble cube. The yellow police tape fluttered and the wretched hollow was still in the lawn.

Why had she been killed? Who benefited by Julia Martin's death?

She'd been dead almost two days now and he still didn't know why she'd been murdered, never mind how. He put his hands behind his back and stood very still, knowing something would come to him.

'Oh, *bonjour.*'

What had come to the Chief Inspector was the gardener, Colleen.

'You look deep in thought. I could come back.'

But she seemed reluctant to leave. He smiled and strolled over to her on the lawn. The two stared for a moment at the spot where Julia Martin had died. Gamache was silent, curious to see what Colleen would say next. After a minute or so she waved at the marble cube.

'The ants are gone. I'm glad. They were giving me nightmares.'

'You'll sleep easier with each passing day,' said Gamache.

Colleen nodded, then looked sadly at the flowers.

'I came to see how they were doing. I should've transplanted them earlier.'

Gamache looked at the flowers. Most were withered now. Beyond saving.

Then something occurred to him. Something that should have struck him much sooner.

'Why were you out here that morning?'

'Gardening,' she said.

He looked at her closely. 'But it was raining. Pouring. No one else was outside working. Why were you?'

Did her eyes widen slightly? Were her cheeks suddenly burning? Colleen was a blusher, he knew. Any attention was enough to bring it on. Best not to read too much into it. But still, she suddenly looked both guilty and furtive.

'I was gardening,' she insisted. 'It's best to move plants when it's wet and cool. They have a better chance to take. These seemed to need all the help they could get.'

They both looked again at the wilting flowers.

'Most of the other workers were inside, relaxing,' he pressed. 'I find it hard to believe you'd choose to be outside in the rain.'

'Well I was.'

'Why, Colleen? Tell me.'

He sounded so reasonable, so patient, she almost did. But at the last moment she closed her mouth. Instead of chastising or pushing this large man simply waited.

Colleen's lip trembled slightly, then her chin puckered and

her eyes narrowed. She looked down and her lank hair fell like curtains, hiding her face. What escaped was a sob.

'Nobody. Likes. Me. Here,' she gasped, fighting to thrust each word out. Shaking and crying, she brought her hands up to her face, to hide the tears that were too obvious. She looked, Gamache realized, exactly as she'd looked a few days earlier. On that very spot. Eventually the sobbing died down and quietly Gamache handed her his handkerchief.

'*Merci*,' she sputtered, between ragged gasps.

'People like you, Colleen.'

She raised her eyes to his.

'I watch and listen,' he continued. 'I read people. It's what I do for a living. Are you listening?'

She nodded.

'Those young women like you. If one good thing's come of all this pain, it's that you've found some real friends here.'

'Suppose,' said Colleen, again looking down. Then Gamache understood.

'How old are you?'

'Eighteen.'

'I have a daughter, you know. Annie. She's twenty-six. Married now, but much as she loves her husband he wasn't her first love. She met him one summer when she worked at a golf course. They were both caddies.'

Colleen's eyes were on the ground, her sneakered feet toeing the grass.

'Annie used to try to caddy in a foursome with Jonathan, but he wasn't interested. He had his own friends he hung around with and every night Annie would come home in tears. Even asked if I could speak to him, maybe show him my gun.'

She smiled a little.

Gamache's own smile faded. 'I think it was the most painful time of her life, and I think she'd say the same thing. It's terrible to love someone so completely and know they don't feel the same. It's very lonely.'

Colleen nodded and dropped her head again, crying quietly into the balled-up handkerchief. Gamache waited until she'd calmed. She offered him back the soggy square of cotton, but he declined.

'He loves someone else. He was always following her around, wanting to know all about her. Where she was from, what her home was like. All the things I wanted him to ask me, he was asking her.'

'Best not to torture yourself with it,' he said, gently but firmly. He was lucky, he knew. He'd married his first love. But he'd seen what unrequited love could do.

She sighed so hard Gamache expected to see the petals of the dying flowers flutter away.

After the young gardener left Gamache strolled back towards the *terrasse*, intending to go to the library for lunch and a meeting with his team. But partway there he caught sight of Peter Morrow standing on the wharf, staring at the lake.

He had a question for Peter. A question he wanted to ask the man in private.

Changing course he made for the dock, but as he did so he saw Peter reach back and fling something into the lake. A moment later he heard a plop and two rings appeared on the calm surface. Peter turned abruptly and marched off the dock, his feet thudding on the wood. Head down, he didn't even notice Gamache until he was almost upon the Chief Inspector.

'Oh, it's you,' said Peter, startled and not particularly pleased. Gamache noticed the ill-shaven face, the crumpled and partly tucked shirt, the stains on the slacks. Peter's courtesy and attire were equally ragged.

'Are you all right?'

'Just fine.' The sarcasm was impossible to miss.

'You seem haggard.'

'I just lost my sister, what do you expect?'

'You're quite right,' said Gamache. 'It was a thoughtless comment.'

Peter seemed to relax.

'No, I'm sorry.' He brought his hand up and it scraped along his sandpaper face. He seemed surprised not to feel the usual clean shave. 'It's a difficult time.'

'What did you throw into the lake?'

It was meant to help break the tension but it had the opposite effect. Peter's guard was up again as he turned angry eyes on Gamache.

'Do you have to know everything? Can't some things be private around you? Or maybe your father never taught you manners.'

He stomped away towards the Manoir then abruptly changed direction. Gamache saw why. Thomas Morrow came thundering out of the lodge, crossed the stone *terrasse* and hit the lawn running.

'What've you done with them? Peter, I'm going to kill you.'

Peter started running and then the chase was on. It was clear the Morrows made no habit of running and the sight of two men in late middle age inelegantly chasing each other around a manicured lawn at this Australian-rules reunion might have been funny had one not clearly been intent upon harm and the other not been terrified.

Gamache, who did make a habit of running, intercepted Thomas just as he was about to tackle Peter. Thomas writhed in Gamache's arms and suddenly Beauvoir was there, also gripping Thomas and finally wrestling him to the ground. Thomas scrambled up and flung himself again at Peter, who was now hiding behind the Chief Inspector.

'Stop it,' Gamache ordered, catching Thomas's shoulders in a jarring grip. He spoke with such authority it stopped Thomas more effectively than a punch.

'Give them to me, Peter,' Thomas growled, trying to catch Peter's eyes where he was cowering behind Gamache. 'So help me, I'll kill you.'

'Enough,' said the Chief Inspector. 'Back away, Mr Morrow.'

His deep voice was hard and even and meant to be obeyed.

Thomas Morrow backed up.

'What's this about?' Gamache looked from brother to brother. In his peripheral vision he saw Lacoste arrive. She and Beauvoir placed themselves behind respective brothers, ready to grab if need be. He also saw Bert Finney creak down the lawn beside Peter's mother. They stood behind Peter, out of his sight.

'He took my cufflinks.' Thomas pointed a trembling finger at Peter, but his eyes looked beyond his brother. To their mother.

'That's ridiculous. Why would I?'

'Oh, you don't really want me to answer that, do you, Spot? You stole them. They were in my room before you visited and now they're gone.'

'Is this true?' a voice behind Peter demanded.

Peter's expression went from rage to resignation and he closed his eyes slowly. Then he turned and faced his mother.

'I don't have them.'

Mrs Finney stared at him then slowly shook her head. 'Why? Why would you do this to us, Peter? I don't know how much more I can take. I've just lost my daughter and all you can think to do is fight with Thomas?'

'Mother.' Peter started forward then stopped.

'You're in my prayers.'

It was the insult she reserved for people beyond hope, and Peter knew it.

'Leave it, Thomas. If the cuffs are more important to him than family let him have them. I'll get you new ones.'

'That wasn't the point, Mother,' said Thomas, joining her.

'Not for you, no.' Mrs Finney walked back up to the Manoir, her husband on one side, her son on the other. And Peter left behind.

He tried to readjust his clothes then gave up and stopped moving completely. He seemed almost catatonic.

'We need to talk,' said Gamache, leading him by the elbow to a grove of trees and into the cool and restful shade. He sat Peter on a bench then sat beside him. 'You threw them into the lake.'

It wasn't a question, and Peter seemed almost relieved not to have to lie yet again.

'Why?'

Peter shook his head and shrugged. Words seemed too heavy, too much of a burden to produce. But Gamache waited. He was a patient man. His father had taught him that. Poetry and patience, and much else beside.

'Thomas always wore them,' said Peter finally, speaking to his hands clasped weakly between his knees. 'Clara once said that they were like Wonder Woman's bracelets, you know?'

Gamache actually did know. Another perk of having a daughter. He brought his arms up and crossed his wrists. Peter smiled a little.

'Power and protection was Clara's theory. She says everyone has them, but none more obviously than the Morrows. Mariana wears her shawls, Thomas has his cufflinks, Clara repeats her mantras, Mother wears her make-up, her "mask" as she calls it.'

'And you?'

Peter raised his hands. 'Did you not think it strange that this paint wouldn't come off?'

Gamache hadn't even thought about it, but now that he did it was true. All paint would come off skin, if you tried hard enough. None would stain permanently.

'When a family reunion comes along I stop scrubbing with turpentine and use normal soap. The oil paint stays on. After the reunion, when I'm back in Three Pines, I wash it off.'

Back in Three Pines, thought Gamache, picturing the peaceful village. Safe.

'Power and protection?'

Peter nodded. 'When Thomas or Mariana or Mother or anyone is getting at me I just look down at my hands,' he did so now, 'and I'm reminded that there's one thing I do well. Do better than anyone else in the family.' *Except*, came the whisper in his head, *Clara. Now Clara is a better artist than you.* 'I think maybe it's stopped working.'

'And you wanted to get rid of Thomas's charms too?'

293

Peter said nothing. It was close enough to the truth.

Gamache reached into the breast pocket of his jacket and carefully unfolded an old piece of paper. Peter reached out but Gamache withdrew it, not trusting the man with something so precious.

Peter's hand hovered in the air.

'Where'd you get that?'

Far from being angry or accusatory, his voice was full of wonder. He sounded like a little boy shown a pirate's treasure map, one hunted for and dreamed of for weeks and months, or, in the case of a grown man, years.

'From the artist who sculpted your father.'

Peter was barely listening, riveted on the drawing. It showed a noble, lively bird, its head cocked at an impertinent angle, its eyes gleaming. It threatened to fly off the yellowed page. Yet for all its vitality it was unfinished. It had no feet.

'You drew this,' said Gamache softly, not wanting to break too far into Peter's reverie.

Peter seemed to have entered the drawing and disappeared completely. Wherever it had taken him, it seemed a good place. Peter was smiling, his face relaxed for the first time in days.

'You must have been young when you drew this,' Gamache prompted.

'I was,' agreed Peter at last. 'I was maybe eight. I did it for Dad's birthday.'

'You were eight when you did this?' Now it was Gamache's turn to stare at the drawing. It was simple, elegant, not unlike Picasso's iconic dove. Almost a single line. But he'd captured flight, and life and curiosity.

'*Oh, I have slipped the surly bonds of earth*,' whispered Gamache.

Freedom.

Once, Peter knew, he had flown. Before the world grew too heavy. Now his art, instead of taking flight, did the opposite.

He looked again at the bird. The very first drawing he'd done on his own, without tracing. He'd given it to his father and his dad had picked him up and hugged him, and taken him all round the restaurant where they were eating, and shown the drawing to perfect strangers. Mother had made him stop but not before Peter had developed two addictions, to art and to praise. And specifically to the praise and approval of his father.

'When my father died I asked Mother if I could have that back,' said Peter, gesturing to the drawing. 'She told me he'd thrown it away.' Peter looked into Gamache's eyes. 'Where did you say you found this?'

'The sculptor, the one who did the statue of your father. Your father kept it. What is it?'

'It's just a bird. Nothing special.'

'It has no feet.'

'I was eight, what do you want?'

'I want the truth. I think you're lying to me.'

Gamache rarely lost his temper, and he didn't now, but his voice held an edge and a warning that even a Morrow couldn't miss.

'Why would I lie about a forty-year-old drawing of a bird?'

'I don't know, but I know you are. What kind of a bird is it?'

'A sparrow, a robin, I don't know.'

Peter was sounding exasperated. Gamache stood up

abruptly and refolding the paper he placed it carefully back in his breast pocket.

'You know I'll find the truth. Why are you trying to stop me?'

Peter shook his head and remained seated. Gamache started to walk away then remembered a question he'd meant to ask.

'You say you all have your talismans or mantras. What Clara called your power and protection. You didn't tell me what Julia's was.'

Peter shrugged. 'I don't know.'

'For God's sake, Peter.'

'Really.' Peter stood and faced Gamache. 'I didn't know her well enough. She hardly ever came back to reunions. This was unusual.'

Gamache continued to stare at him, then turned and walked out of the cool shade.

'Wait,' Peter called after him. Gamache stopped and let him catch up. 'Look, I have to tell you. I stole those cufflinks and threw them into the lake because my father gave them to Thomas. They went from first son to first son. I always thought maybe he'd give them to me. I know, it was stupid, but I'd hoped. Anyway, he didn't. I knew how much the cufflinks meant to Thomas.'

Peter hesitated, but plunged ahead anyway. It felt like walking off a cliff.

'They were the most important thing he has. I wanted to hurt him.'

'The way you wanted to hurt me just now when you talked about my own father?'

'I'm sorry I did that.'

Gamache stared at the dishevelled man in front of him. 'Be careful, Peter. You have a good spirit, but even good spirits stumble, and sometimes they fall. And sometimes they don't get up.'

TWENTY-FOUR

WHO BENEFITS?

Beauvoir wrote in very large, very clear, very red capital letters on the foolscap. Instinctively he wafted the magic marker under his nose as he surveyed his work.

Now that was art. Or, if not actually art, it was definitely beautiful. It represented structure and order, and both those things thrilled the Inspector. Soon they'd have a list, of names, of motives, of clues, of movements. They'd connect them all up. Some would be dead ends, some murky alleys, but some would be superhighways, and they'd follow those speeding clues to the end.

Inspector Beauvoir looked over at the Chief Inspector, his elbows on the dark wooden table, his large fingers intertwined, his eyes thoughtful and attentive.

And then what?

But Beauvoir knew the answer to that. When they'd gone as far as the known world took them, when he and Lacoste and all the other investigators could see no further, Chief Inspector Gamache stepped forward. He walked into the unknown. Because that's where murderers lurked. They might appear to walk in the same sun and drizzle, along the same grass and concrete, and even to speak the same language. But they didn't really. Chief Inspector Gamache was willing to go where few others could. And he never, ever asked them to follow him, only to help him find the way.

Both men knew that one day Beauvoir would step forward. And both men knew the burned and desolate spot Gamache sought wasn't exclusive to the murderer. The reason Armand Gamache could go there was because it wasn't totally foreign to him. He knew it because he'd seen his own burned terrain, he'd walked off the familiar and comfortable path inside his own head and heart and seen what festered in the dark.

And one day Jean Guy Beauvoir would look at his own monsters, and then be able to recognize others. And maybe this was the day and this was the case.

He hoped so.

Now he put the capped magic marker in his mouth and jogged it up and down like a giant red cigar, staring at the blank page, except for the expectant heading.

WHO BENEFITS?

'Well, David Martin does,' said Agent Lacoste. 'He doesn't have to pay alimony.'

Beauvoir wrote the name and the reason. He also wrote, *One less witness.*

'What do you mean?' asked the Chief Inspector.

'Well, at his trial she testified, but basically said she knew nothing about his business dealings. But suppose that wasn't true? I get the feeling these Morrows aren't very smart – in fact, they're so stupid they think they're smart. But they are cunning. And she grew up in a home where business was talked about, and she adored her father, so she probably paid attention.'

He stopped to gather his run-on thoughts. He was pretty sure this was leading somewhere. His colleagues waited.

There was a tap at the door and he strolled over to open it.

Lunch.

'Hello, Elliot,' said the chief as the lithe young waiter gave him a barbecued steak sandwich with sautéed mushrooms and caramelized onions on top.

'*Bonjour, Patron*,' the young man smiled, then beamed at Lacoste, who looked quite pleased.

He put a lobster salad in front of her. And Beauvoir got a hamburger and string fries. For the last twenty minutes they'd smelled the charcoals warming up in the huge barbecue in the garden, with the unmistakable summer scents of hot coals and lighter fluid. Beauvoir hadn't stopped salivating. Between that and the sweating he thought he should order a cold beer. Just to prevent dehydration. The chief thought that sounded good, as did Lacoste, and before long each had a beer in a tall frosted glass.

As he looked out of the French doors he saw the maître d' walk by with a platter of steak and shrimp from the barbecue, presumably for the Morrows.

'You were saying?' The Chief Inspector was looking at him.

Beauvoir took the burger with him to the foolscap.

'*D'accord*, the husband. Doesn't it seem as though he's been here the whole time?' said Beauvoir. 'I mean, even before the murder you said people were talking about him, telling you and Madame Gamache who Julia's husband was. It was as though the Morrows couldn't figure out if they loved him or hated him.'

'You're right,' said Gamache. 'He's been the uninvited guest.'

Beauvoir let that go, suspecting it must be a quote. Still, it was a good way of putting it. The one not necessarily wanted, not expected, not watched for or prepared for. The one, therefore, with the advantage.

'So many things come back to him.' Beauvoir circled Martin's name. It was easy, since it was the only name on the page so far. 'She was only here because of the divorce.'

'And his conviction,' said Lacoste. 'What was the case about anyway?'

They both turned to Gamache.

'You'll have to double check all this because it's been a few months since it was in the papers, but David Martin ran the Royale Assurance Company, a very old, very proud Canadian company that specialized in marine insurance. It started, I believe, in Nova Scotia more than a century ago, but moved to Vancouver as the shipping trade grew with the Pacific Rim.'

'Only shipping?'

'Not under Martin. He did two things, if I'm remembering right. He expanded into buildings and infrastructure. Bridges, dams, roads. But the most brilliant thing he did, and his downfall, was he decided to spread the risks. He created a thing called Partners.'

'Surely not the first business person to have partners,' Lacoste smiled.

'Very astute of you.' Gamache smiled back. 'But he spelled his with a capital P. It was like a pyramid scheme, though all perfectly legal, at first. He'd insure a bridge project, let's say, and get a bunch of companies to take some of the risk. They in turn would sell interests to smaller companies, and they'd sell on to individuals. All called Royale Partners.'

'And what would they get in return?' Lacoste asked, her lobster salad forgotten for a moment. This sort of Byzantine dealing fascinated her.

'They paid no money,' said Gamache, leaning towards her, remembering as he went. 'And they got a share of the company profits, which were huge. Most of the Partners became millionaires many times over.'

'But?' said Beauvoir.

'But they had to guarantee they'd pay for any loss.'

Beauvoir was lost. But Lacoste was with him.

'I understand,' she said. 'He sold some of the profits and all the risk. He was making hundreds of millions and wasn't in any danger if there was ever a huge claim.'

'Exactly. It worked for years, with everyone, even the smallest Partner, making a great deal of money. People were falling all over themselves to invest.'

'Did you?' Beauvoir asked.

'We were invited, but said no.'

'Smart,' said Lacoste.

'I'd like to think so, but it was really just fear. I can talk about it, and on some level I think I understand it, but honestly I don't. What I did understand was that if something went wrong we'd be ruined.'

'And something eventually went wrong?' asked Lacoste.

'Cigarettes,' said Gamache. 'One of the first things Royale Assurance under Martin expanded into was insuring the tobacco companies. They made enormous amounts of money out of the deals. Fortunes. But ten years ago a woman in Oregon sued Jubilee Tobacco after she developed emphysema.

She was sixty. Family history, her mother had died of it. The tobacco company won the first round and the woman died, but her husband took it further, and eventually it became a class action suit and two years ago the Supreme Court ruled that Jubilee Tobacco was liable.'

The door to the library opened and Sandra Morrow stepped in. Beauvoir deftly stepped in front of their lists and Gamache got to his feet and went across to her.

'May I help you?' he asked.

'No, thank you. I'm just here to find a book and settle in.'

She made to go around the Chief Inspector, who stepped in front of her.

'Excuse me,' she said, her voice frigid.

'I'm sorry, madame, but this room is no longer available for guests. I thought that was clear. If not, I'm terribly sorry for the confusion, but we need it as our headquarters.'

'Headquarters? You make it sound very grand. We're paying guests. And I paid to use this room too.'

'That won't be possible,' said Gamache, his voice firm but friendly. 'I understand your frustration, and I know it's a difficult time, but you'll have to go elsewhere.'

She gave him a look of such loathing it surprised even Beauvoir, who'd given and received a few of those looks in his life.

'I understand you need to investigate the death of my sister-in-law but you don't need this particular room. There must be bedrooms. Hers even. Smaller rooms. Surely the Manoir has a back office you could use. These are public rooms, for the guests.'

'Goodbye, Madame Morrow,' he said and held out his arm to indicate the door.

She looked at him closely.

'I know your type. You always take the best. You're a little man with a little power and it's made you a bully. I wonder where you get it from?'

She left.

Beauvoir shook his head. Just as he thought this Anglo-palooza couldn't get any weirder, Sandra Morrow did this.

'Where were we?' asked Gamache, regaining his seat and taking a sip of beer.

'Cigarettes,' said Lacoste, watching to see if Sandra Morrow's ragged little insults had resulted in even a flesh wound. But the chief looked superbly unconcerned.

'The Jubilee Tobacco case. I remember it,' said Beauvoir. 'All that stuff came out about the shit the companies are putting into cigarettes. My mother actually quit after watching a report.'

'Smart woman,' said Gamache. 'Lots of people quit.'

'And did that cause the crisis?' asked Beauvoir, lost again.

'No, they just turned to the developing world for their market. What brought Martin's house down around him was the discovery that long after they knew they were in trouble they continued to sell Partnerships, to offset their losses with the tobacco companies. Thousands of people were ruined. The small investors.'

Beauvoir and Lacoste were silent, thinking about that. Beauvoir, having spoken to Martin from prison, was surprised. He didn't seem like the sort to intentionally screw so many people, the small investors. Ma and Pop. Yet he had. Greed. That was the real jailer.

'Is it possible one of the Morrows, maybe even Charles Morrow, was a Partner?' Lacoste asked. 'Maybe they lost a fortune.'

'David Martin said the Morrows are worth about twenty million.'

'Dollars?' asked Lacoste.

'No, dog biscuits. Of course dollars,' said Beauvoir.

'But maybe they were worth a hundred million before all this,' said Gamache. 'Could you check it out?' he asked Lacoste.

Soon they had every other guest on the suspect list.

'Haven't exactly narrowed it down, have we?' Beauvoir smiled ruefully. 'They all had the opportunity, they all seemed to have motives for killing each other.'

'Julia said she'd figured out her father's secret,' said Lacoste. 'I think that's significant. I asked Clara about it.'

'And?' Gamache was curious.

'She wasn't helpful, in fact she was slightly unhelpful.'

'Really?'

Beauvoir stared at the list. Then at the other board. On it was a list of clues, facts, statements. The men's room graffiti. The two notes they'd found in the grate were tacked to it, and next to them a bird without feet.

And a series of questions:

Was the storm significant?

What had Julia figured out about her father?

Who wrote the notes in the grate?

Why did Julia keep the thank you letters from long ago?

Who wrote the graffiti on the men's room wall? Does it matter?

They had a long list for Who. For Why. But one word sat alone on the foolscap.

How.

How had that statue fallen? Nothing was written below the word, not even wild guesses.

'Oh, I have another name to add to the list,' said Beauvoir, scribbling the name slightly larger than the rest.

'Pierre Patenaude? The maître d'?' asked Lacoste.

'Of course him,' said Beauvoir.

'Why him?' asked Gamache.

'Well, he was out on the *terrasse* around midnight. He helped place the statue, so maybe he did something so that it would fall down. He worked in a cemetery as a kid, so he'd know about statues.'

'He'd know how to put them up, perhaps,' said Gamache reasonably. 'But not how to bring them down. He probably only learned how to cut grass around them, anyway.'

'He has access to all the rooms,' said Beauvoir, trying not to sound increasingly argumentative. 'He could've written the notes. Or maybe he didn't even give them to her. Maybe he just wrote them and crumpled them up and threw them into the grate knowing we'd find them.'

Two silent, staring faces greeted this burst of genius.

'On purpose,' he stressed. Still they stared. 'To misdirect. Oh, come on, he's a great suspect. He's everywhere and no one sees him.'

'You aren't suggesting the butler did it?' said Gamache.

'It's either him or the shopkeeper and his cleaning woman wife,' said Beauvoir, and cracked a smile.

The door opened and all three looked up. It was Elliot with a tray of fresh, sweet strawberries.

'We just picked them. And there's *crème fraîche*.' He smiled at Isabelle Lacoste, managing to make it sound like lubricant. 'From the nearby monastery.'

Even that sounded sexy.

They ate and stared at the lists. Finally, after scraping the last of the thick cream from the bowl, Beauvoir got up and walked again to their lists. He tapped one.

'Is this important?'

Who wrote the graffiti on the men's room wall? Does it matter?

'Could be. Why?' asked Gamache.

'Well, at the end of my conversation with David Martin he said he thought he knew who did it.'

'We know,' said Lacoste. 'Thomas Morrow.'

'No, Julia's husband thinks Peter did it.'

Beauvoir and Lacoste spent the rest of the afternoon checking backgrounds and movements. Armand Gamache went in search of Madame Dubois, though it wasn't a very long or difficult search. There she was, as always, in the middle of the reception hall at her shiny wooden desk looking as though it wasn't eighty degrees in the shade.

He sat in the comfortable chair opposite. She removed her reading glasses and smiled at him.

'How may I help you, Chief Inspector?'

'I've been puzzling about something.'

'I know. Who killed our guest.'

'That too, but I've been wondering why you put the statue where you did.'

'Ah, that is a very good question, and my answer will be riveting.' She smiled as she got up. '*Suivez-moi,*' she said, as though perhaps he wasn't going to follow her. They walked along the wide plank flooring to the screen door which clacked closed behind them. They were out on the veranda, shaded from the worst of the sun, but still hot. As she waddled by the planters on the edge of the porch she spoke, Gamache bending low, anxious not to miss a riveting word.

'When Madame Finney first approached me about the statue I declined. This was shortly after Charles Morrow died. She was still Madame Morrow then, of course. They'd stayed here often and I knew them quite well.'

'What did you think of him?'

'He was a type I knew. I'd never have married him. Too wrapped up in work and society and right and wrong. Not morals, of course, but things like dessert forks and thank you notes and proper clothing.'

'Forgive me, Madame Dubois, but all those things clearly matter to you, too.'

'They matter by choice, Chief Inspector. But if you showed up in a striped shirt and a polka-dotted tie I wouldn't ask you to change. Monsieur Morrow would have. Or he'd have made certain you knew it was offensive. He was easily offended. He had a very keen idea of his place. And yours.' She smiled at him.

'But there's always more to a person, and you say you got to know them quite well.'

'You're very clever. I suppose that's why they made you head of the Sûreté.'

'Only homicide, I'm afraid.'

'One day, monsieur. I will go to your swearing-in.'

'If you do, it will be Madame Gamache doing the swearing,' he said.

She stopped at the end of the veranda, where the wood was cut to accommodate the trunk of the large maple tree. She turned to look at him.

'I liked Charles Morrow. For all he was pompous he had a sense of humour and a lot of good friends. You can tell a lot about a man by his friends, or lack of them. Do they bring out the best in each other, or are they always gossiping, tearing others down? Keeping wounds alive? Charles Morrow despised gossip. And his best friend was Bert Finney. That spoke volumes about the man, *à mon avis*. If Monsieur Finney wasn't taken I'd have married him myself.'

Madame Dubois didn't turn away, didn't look down, didn't even look defiant as she made this remarkable statement. She looked simply truthful.

'Why?' Gamache asked.

'I like a man who does his sums,' she said.

'He was doing them on the dock this morning.'

'He's probably doing them now. He has a lot to count.'

'Twenty million, apparently.'

'Really? That many? He is a good catch.' And she laughed.

Gamache looked beyond her to the shade and the white marble that glowed even in the gloom. She followed his stare.

'You relented eventually, about the statue,' he said. 'You needed the money.'

'At first the Morrows insisted the statue go in one of those beds,' she indicated the main bank of roses and lilies between the lodge and the lake, 'but I refused. Even if the statue was a masterpiece it would still be a blemish there, and honestly I couldn't see the Morrows managing a masterpiece. As you might have noticed, the Morrows aren't exactly minimalists.'

'More maximalists, it's true.'

'So after much discussion we decided on this spot. It's discreet.'

'Hidden, you mean?'

'That too. And with luck the forest will grow around Charles Morrow and in twenty years he'll be swallowed up.'

'I can't see you allowing that, madame.'

She smiled at him a little sadly. 'No, you're right. Poor Charles had too much of that in his life. No, he'd have made a good home here. If he hadn't killed his daughter.'

Off in the middle distance they saw Pierre talking with one of the young workers. It looked like Elliot, though his back was turned to them. Pierre, though, saw them and waved.

'You spoke of friends,' said Gamache. 'It must be hard sometimes to be this far from a community.'

'You're thinking of Monsieur Patenaude?'

'And you. And Chef Véronique. The others come and go, I understand, the young workers like Elliot there.'

He'd turned and it was now clearly the young man. He seemed to be arguing with the maître d'.

'Some stay for a few seasons, but you're right. Most don't stay for more than a year. And our relationship with them isn't one of friendship. More like teacher and pupil or mentor and prisoner.'

She smiled. It was clear she saw this place as anything but a prison, but he could understand that some of the kids, perhaps Colleen, saw it as that. And couldn't wait to escape.

'Does it get lonely?'

'For me? Never. But I have my husband. He's in all the walls, and carpets, and flowers. He's in this maple.' She placed a tiny pink hand on the elephantine trunk. 'We planted it sixty years ago. I talk to him all the time and curl up next to him every night. No, I'm never lonely.'

'Is he?' Gamache indicated Patenaude.

'I must admit when he first came I didn't think he'd last long. Not used to hard work. But it suited him. He must have some *coureur du bois* blood in him. He took to the wilderness. And he had such wonderful manners our old maître d' quickly picked Pierre as his successor. Then Véronique showed up and our little family was complete.'

'Pierre seems to be having difficulty with Elliot,' said Gamache.

'Poor Pierre. I'm afraid that young man got up his nose the moment he arrived. He drifted in here in April and has caused nothing but problems ever since.'

'Why do you keep him?'

'Because he needs us. He's a good worker, has picked up French quickly. But he needs to learn self-discipline and self-respect. He demands attention, either by fighting or flirting.'

'I think he might have flirted with me.'

'Well, you probably started it,' she said and he laughed. 'He'll learn that he needn't do that, that he's good enough as he is. And he'll learn it from Pierre. Though perhaps not today.'

They watched as Elliot, clearly agitated, stomped up the dirt road. The maître d' watched him go, then slowly turned and made his way back, deep in thought. As the boss of occasionally difficult subordinates, Gamache felt for the man. And the boy.

'Agent Lacoste is very observant and intuitive.' He turned back to his companion. 'She believes Chef Véronique is in love with Pierre.'

'I'm afraid great powers of observation and intuition aren't necessary to divine that, Chief Inspector, though I'm sure she has both. Véronique's been in love with Pierre for years. And he, poor one, is oblivious.'

'Aren't you worried it'll cause difficulties?'

'I was at first,' she admitted. 'But after the first decade I relaxed. Frankly, it kept Véronique here, and she's a wonderful chef. But she'll never act on her feelings. I know that. She's the sort of extraordinary woman who gets enough fulfilment from loving. She doesn't need it in return.'

'Or maybe she's just afraid,' suggested Gamache.

Clementine Dubois gave him a Gallic shrug. '*C'est possible.*'

'But what if Pierre leaves?'

'He won't.'

'How can you be so certain?'

'He has nowhere to go. Do you know why we're all so happy here, monsieur? Because it's the last house on the road. We've tried everywhere else, and don't fit in. Here we fit. Here we belong. Even the kids who come to work are special. Seekers. And they stay as long as they choose. One day a few will decide to stay for ever. Like me. Like Pierre and Véronique. And then I can go.'

Armand Gamache stared down at the short, wizened woman with her hand on her husband. Then he stared out to the gleaming lake. Down the lawn there was movement and he noticed Irene Finney walking slowly across it, Bert by her side. And behind her walked Thomas, Mariana and finally Peter.

'Charles Morrow was a wonderful pianist, you know,' said Madame Dubois. 'Not just a technician, but he played with great spirit. We'd sit for hours on a rainy afternoon and listen to him. He always said Irene was like a major chord, and his children were the harmonics.'

Gamache watched them fan out behind their mother. He wondered whether the mother chord was maybe a little off, and the harmonics only magnified that.

Then another figure appeared briefly and disappeared

into the forest. A huge, hulking thing in overalls, gloves, boots and a hood. It looked like Frankenstein's monster, flat headed and hulking.

'Speak of the devil,' said Madame Dubois, and Gamache felt goosebumps spring up on his arms.

'Pardon?'

'Over there, that thing disappearing into the woods.'

'The devil?'

Madame Dubois seemed to find this extremely amusing. 'I like that, but no. Quite the opposite, really. That was Chef Véronique.'

'Hell of a sun screen.'

'Bee screen. She's our bee-keeper. Off to get honey for tea.'

'And beeswax for the furniture,' said Gamache with a smile.

That was why the Manoir Bellechasse smelled of decades of coffee and woodsmoke, and honeysuckle.

TWENTY-FIVE

⸺

Mariana Morrow plunked at the piano keys in the Great Room, glad of the peace.

Rich, she was going to be rich one day. As long as Mommy didn't leave everything to that Finney, and he didn't leave everything to some cats' home. Well, she'd done the best she could. She at least had produced a child. She looked over at Bean.

She regretted naming the child Bean, now. What had she been thinking? River would have been better. Or Salmon. Or Salmon River. No, too normal.

Bean had definitely been a mistake. Mariana's mother had been appalled at first, her only grandchild named after a vegetable. The only reason Mariana had had Bean baptized was to force her mother to listen to the minister declare, in front of the entire congregation, not to mention God, the name of Bean Morrow.

A glorious moment.

But her mother had proved more resilient than Mariana

had thought, like a new strain of superbug. She'd become immune to the name.

Aorta, maybe. Aorta Morrow. Or Burp.

Damn, that would've been perfect.

'And now, in the presence of this congregation, and before God, I give you Burp Morrow.'

Another opportunity missed. Perhaps it wasn't too late.

'Bean, dear, come to Mommy.'

Mariana patted the piano bench and the child walked over and leaned against it. Mariana thumped the bench with more force, but Bean didn't budge.

'Come on, Bean. Up you get. Sit beside Mommy.'

Bean ignored the thumping, glancing down at the ever-present book instead.

'Mommy, have you ever seen a flying horse?'

'Only once, dear. In Morocco after a particularly good party. I've also seen a few fairies.'

'You mean Uncle Scott and Uncle Derek?'

'I do. They fly sometimes, you know, but I don't think either could be called a stud.'

Bean nodded.

'Bean, do you like your name? I mean, wouldn't you like Mommy to change it for you?' She looked at the serious child. 'Why don't you jump?'

Bean, used to Mommy's verbal veers, followed easily. 'Why should I?'

'Well, people do. That's why we have knees, and arches on our feet. And ankles. Ankles are little wings, you know.'

She made fluttering actions with her fingers, but Bean looked sceptical.

'They don't look like wings, they look like bones.'

'Well, yours have probably fallen off. Disuse. It happens.'

'I think you jump enough for both of us. I like it here. On the ground.'

'You know what would make Mommy happy? If I could change your name. What do you think about that?'

Bean shrugged. 'Suppose. But you won't make it stranger than Bean, will you?'

The little eyes narrowed.

Chlamydia Morrow.

Very pretty. Too pretty, perhaps. Not quite right. Soon everyone would know if Bean was a boy or a girl and that little secret would be blown. The best way to infuriate Mother would be to give her only grandchild a really ridiculous name.

Mariana looked at the child, strange by even her family's standards.

Syphilis.

Mariana smiled. Perfect.

Syphilis Morrow. Leads to madness.

Jean Guy Beauvoir leaned back in his chair in the library and looked around. Not really taking in his surroundings, but feeling at ease. Normally he'd be making notes on his computer, checking messages, sending messages, surfing the web. Googling.

But there was no computer. Just a pen and paper. He chewed the pen and stared ahead, using his brain to make connections.

He'd spent much of the afternoon going over writing samples, trying to find out who'd written those notes to Julia. Someone had reached out to her, and from what little they were gathering about the lonely woman, she'd be almost incapable of not reaching back.

Had it killed her? Had she been murdered by her needs?

Beauvoir had had a need of his own. For the first hour and a half he'd concentrated on one suspect. The man he knew had done it. Pierre Patenaude. Far from being difficult to find, samples of his writing were everywhere. Notes on menus, staff rotation lists, evaluation forms and even French tests he'd given the young staff, trying to teach them that the night wasn't a strawberry and that flaming mice wasn't a menu option. It seemed the only thing the maître d' hadn't written were the notes to Julia Martin.

But after another hour of digging and comparing, of leaning over an old-fashioned magnifying glass taken from a display of butterflies, Beauvoir had his answer. He knew beyond doubt who'd written to Julia.

Bert Finney drew the curtains to block out the sun and watched as his wife undressed for her nap. Not a moment of any day went by when he wasn't astonished by his good fortune. He was rich beyond the dreams of avarice.

He was patient, but then he'd learned that years ago. And it had paid off. He was even willing to pick up after her, since it got him what he wanted. He gathered the clothes from the floor where she dropped them, trying not to notice the little gasps of pain coming from this tiny woman. Who felt so much, but mostly felt she couldn't show it. The only argument they'd ever had, and that only once, had been when he'd tried to persuade her to explain all this to the children. She'd refused.

And now Irene Finney stood naked in the centre of the

dim room, tears streaming down her cheeks. He knew they would end soon. They always did. But lately they'd been going on longer.

'What is it?' he asked, and knew immediately how ridiculous it sounded.

'Nothing.'

'Tell me.' He picked up her slip and bra and underwear and looked up into her face.

'It's the smell.'

And that might be true, but he thought it was more than that.

Irene Morrow stood at the Manoir Bellechasse sink, her young, pink hands ladling lukewarm water over Julia. Tiny Julia, so much more petite than Thomas, who was already bathed and in a huge white towel in Charles's arms. Now it was his baby sister's turn. Their room at the Manoir hadn't changed since she'd been going there as a girl herself. The same taps, the same black rubber stopper, the same buoyant Ivory soap.

Now her hands supported her baby in the sink, protecting her from the hard taps, holding her secure so she didn't slip. Making certain even the mild soap didn't get into the trusting eyes.

It would be perfect, if it hadn't been for the pain. Neuralgia they'd later diagnose, a women's problem her doctors had told Charles at the time. He'd believed them. So had she. After Thomas. But the pain had grown after Julia until she could barely stand to be touched, though she'd never admit that to Charles. Her Victorian parents had made clear two things: the husband must be obeyed, and she must never show weakness, especially to that husband.

And so she'd bathed her beautiful baby, and cried. And Charles had mistaken those tears as a sign of joy. And she'd let him.

And now Julia was gone, and Charles was gone and even the ruse of joy was gone, not even pretended to any more.

And all that was left was pain and a sink and old taps and the scent of Ivory soap.

'*Bonjour*, is this the clogging queen?'

'*Oui, c'est la reine du clogging*,' sang the cheery voice down the phone line. She sounded so far away and yet she was just over the line of mountains on the other side of the lake. In the next valley.

'Is that the stable boy?' Reine-Marie asked.

'*Oui, mademoiselle*.' Gamache could feel the laughter start. 'I understand your handsome husband has been called away on very important state business.'

'Actually, he's in detox. Again. The coast is clear.'

She was much better at this than he. Gamache always started laughing first and he did now.

'I miss you.' He didn't bother whispering, not caring who heard. 'Will you come for dinner tonight? I can pick you up in an hour.'

Arrangements were made, but before he left he met with the team. It was teatime and they sat balancing fine bone china cups and saucers and tiny plates with delicate doilies. On the table in front of them were notes on murder and crustless cucumber sandwiches. Lists of suspects and éclairs. Bits of evidence and petits fours.

'May I be mother?' Gamache asked.

Beauvoir had actually heard odder things from the Chief

Inspector so he just nodded. Isabelle Lacoste smiled and said, '*S'il vous plaît.*'

He poured and they took the food, Beauvoir counting to make sure he got his fair share.

As they ate they talked.

'OK,' said Isabelle Lacoste. 'I have the background information. First Sandra Morrow, née Kent. Affluent background. Father a banker, mother involved in volunteer activities. Born and raised in Montreal. Both parents dead. Inherited a modest amount by the time it was split among all the heirs and taxes were paid. She's a management consultant in the firm of Bodmin Davies, in Toronto. A junior vice president.'

Gamache raised his eyebrows.

'Not as impressive as you might think, sir. Almost everyone is called a junior vice president, except the senior VPs. She seems to have hit a glass ceiling a while ago.

'Her husband Thomas Morrow. Went to the Mantle private school in Montreal then McGill University. Barely scraped by with a general arts degree, though he made a few of the sports teams. Took a job at the Toronto investment firm Drum and Mitchell and he's still there.'

'He's the success story,' said Beauvoir.

'Actually, not,' said Lacoste. 'But you'd think so to hear him tell it.'

'To hear the whole family tell it,' said Beauvoir. 'They all point to Thomas as the success. Is he hiding something?'

'Doesn't actually seem all that big a secret. His office is a cubicle, he does a few million dollars' worth of business, but I understand in the investment world that's considered next to nothing.'

'He doesn't make that?'

'Not even close. No, that's his clients' money. According to his latest tax return he made seventy-six thousand dollars last year.'

'And he lives in Toronto?' Beauvoir asked. Toronto was a ridiculously expensive city. Lacoste nodded.

'Is he in debt?'

'Not that we could find. Sandra Morrow makes more than him, about a hundred and twenty last year, so between them they make almost two hundred thousand dollars. And as you discovered, they inherited over a million dollars from his father. That was a few years ago and I bet there's not much left. I'll keep digging.

'Peter and Clara Morrow we know about. They own their own cottage in Three Pines. He's a member of the Royal Academy of Arts in Canada. Very prestigious, but you can't eat the honour. They lived hand to mouth until Clara inherited money from their neighbour a few years ago. Now they're comfortable, though far from wealthy. They live modestly. He hasn't had a solo show in a few years, but he always sells out when he does. His works go for about ten thousand dollars each.'

'And hers?' asked Beauvoir.

'That's a little harder to say. Until recently she was selling her works for Canadian Tire money.'

Gamache smiled, seeing the wads of the store's credit bills they gave out with every purchase, like Monopoly money. He had a pile in his glove compartment. Perhaps he should buy an original Clara Morrow while he still could.

'But then her art started attracting more attention,'

Lacoste continued. 'As you know, she has a huge solo show coming up.'

'That brings us to Mariana Morrow,' said Beauvoir, taking a delicate sip of tea. He imagined Chef Véronique scooping the loose dried leaves into the pretty floral pot, then grasping the large iron kettle and pouring the steaming water in. For him. She'd know it was coming to him, and probably added an extra scoop. And trimmed the crusts from the cucumber sandwiches.

'Right, Mariana Morrow,' said Lacoste, turning the page of her notebook. 'Lives in Toronto too. In an area called Rosedale. I gather it's like Westmount. Very posh.'

'Divorced?' asked Beauvoir.

'Never married. This is the interesting part. She's self-made. Has her own company. She's an architect. Got a huge break right out of school. For her thesis she designed a small, energy efficient low cost home. Not one of those ugly concrete blocks, but something pretty cool. A place low income people needn't be ashamed to live in. She made a fortune from it.'

Beauvoir snorted. Trust a Morrow to make money from the poor.

'She goes all over the world,' continued Lacoste. 'Speaks French, Italian, Spanish and Chinese. She makes massive amounts of money. Her last tax form shows her income last year at well over two million dollars. And that's just what she declares.'

'Wait a minute,' said Beauvoir, almost choking on an éclair. 'You're saying that woman all wrapped in scarves who drifts around and is late for everything is a self-made millionaire?'

'More successful than even her father,' Lacoste nodded. She was secretly pleased. It gave her pleasure to think this most marginalized of Morrows was actually the most successful.

'Do we know who the kid's father is?' Beauvoir asked.

Lacoste shook her head. 'Maybe there isn't one. Maybe it was a virgin birth.'

She liked screwing with Beauvoir's head.

'I think I can guarantee you that's not true,' said Beauvoir, but a look at Gamache removed his smirk. 'Now, you're not telling me you believe it, Chief? I'm not going to be the one putting that in the official report. Suspects, Thomas, Peter, Mariana, oh yes and the Second Coming.'

'You believe in the first, don't you? Why not the second?' asked Agent Lacoste.

'Come on,' he sputtered. 'Do you really want me to believe the Second Coming is a child named Bean?'

'A bean is a seed,' said Gamache. 'It's an old allegory for faith. I have a feeling Bean is a very special child. Nothing is impossible with Bean.'

'Except to tell if it's a boy or a girl,' said Beauvoir, miffed.

'Does it matter?' asked Gamache.

'It matters in that all secrets in a murder investigation matter.'

Gamache nodded slowly. 'That's true. Often after a day or so it's obvious who's genuine and who isn't. In this case it's getting muddier and muddier. Thomas told us about a plant in the desert. If it showed itself for what it really was predators would eat it. So it learned to disguise itself, to hide its true nature. The Morrows are the same. Somehow, somewhere along the line they learned to hide who they really

323

are, what they really think and feel. Nothing is as it seems with them.'

'Except Peter and Clara,' said Agent Lacoste. 'I presume they're not suspects.'

Gamache looked at her thoughtfully.

'Do you remember that first case in Three Pines? The murder of Miss Jane Neal?'

They nodded. It was where they first met the Morrows.

'After we'd made an arrest I was still uncomfortable.'

'You think we arrested the wrong person?' asked Beauvoir, aghast.

'No, we got the murderer, there's no doubt. But I also knew there was someone else in Three Pines I felt was capable of murder. Someone who needed watching.'

'Clara,' said Lacoste. Emotional, temperamental, passionate. So much can go wrong with a personality like that.

'No, Peter. Closed off, complex, so placid and relaxed on the surface but God only knows what's happening underneath.'

'Well, I at least have some good news,' said Beauvoir. 'I know who wrote these.' He held up the crumpled notes from Julia's grate. 'Elliot.'

'The waiter?' asked Lacoste, amazed.

Beauvoir nodded and showed them the samples of Elliot's writing next to the notes. Gamache put on his half-moon reading glasses and bent over. Then he sat up.

'Well done.'

'Should I speak to him?'

Gamache thought about it for a moment then shook his head. 'No, I'd like to put a few more things together first, but this is interesting.'

'There's more,' said Beauvoir. 'He's not only from Vancouver, but he lived in the same neighbourhood as Julia and David Martin. His parents might have known them.'

'Find out,' said Gamache, rising and heading for the door to pick up his wife.

Elliot Byrne seemed to have breached the boundary set out by Madame Dubois. Had young Elliot conquered lonely and defenceless Julia Martin? What had he wanted? An older lover? Attention? Perhaps he'd wanted to finally and absolutely infuriate his boss, the maître d'.

Or was it simpler than that, as it often was? Did he want money? Was he tired of waiting tables for a pittance? And when he got money from Julia, did he kill her?

At the door to the library Gamache paused and looked back at the sheet of foolscap hanging up and the large red letters at the top.

WHO BENEFITS?

Who didn't benefit from Julia's death, he was beginning to wonder.

TWENTY-SIX

———

Reine-Marie laid down her fork and leaned back in the comfortable chair. Pierre whisked away the plate, which had the smallest dusting of strawberry shortcake crumbs left, and asked if there was anything else.

'Perhaps a cup of tea,' she said and when he'd left she reached out and squeezed her husband's hand. It was a rare treat to see him in the middle of one of his cases. When she'd arrived she'd said hello to Inspector Beauvoir and Agent Lacoste, both of whom were eating and working in the library. Then they'd wandered into the dining room, made up with crisp white linen and fresh flowers and gleaming silver and crystal.

A waiter placed an espresso in front of Gamache and a teapot in front of Reine-Marie.

'Did you know the Manoir makes its own honey?' Armand asked, noticing the amber liquid in a pot beside her teacup.

'Really? How extraordinary.'

Reine-Marie didn't normally take honey but decided to

try some with her Thunderbolt Darjeeling, dipping her little finger into the honey before stirring it in.

'*C'est beau*. It has a familiar taste. Here, try.'

He dipped as well.

Her eyes narrowed as she tried to figure it out. He knew, of course, what she was tasting but wanted to see if she'd get it.

'Give up?' he asked. When she nodded he told her.

'Honeysuckle?' She smiled. 'How wonderful. Will you show me the glade sometime?'

'With pleasure. They even polish the furniture with the beeswax.'

As they talked Gamache noticed the Morrows were at their table, though Peter and Clara weren't in their regular seats. They were relegated to the far end, with Bean.

'Hello,' said Reine-Marie, as they left the dining room for a stroll, 'how are you both?'

But she could see. Peter was wan and strained, his clothes dishevelled and his hair awry. Clara was immaculate, buttoned down and impeccable. Reine-Marie didn't know which was more disconcerting.

'You know.' Clara shrugged. 'How's Three Pines?' She sounded wistful, as though asking after a mythical kingdom. 'All ready for Canada Day?'

'Yes, it's tomorrow.'

'Really?' Peter looked up. They'd lost all sense of time.

'I'm going over tomorrow,' said Gamache. 'Would you like to come? You'll be in my custody.'

He thought Peter would burst into tears, he looked so relieved and grateful.

'That's right, it's your anniversary,' said Clara. 'And I hear there's a major new talent being unveiled at the clogging competition.'

Gamache turned to his wife. 'So Gabri wasn't kidding?'

'Sadly not.'

They made the arrangements and the Gamaches turned to go into the garden.

'Wait, Armand.' She laid a hand on his arm. 'Do you think we could pop in and compliment the chef? I'm dying to meet her. Would she mind?'

Gamache thought about it. 'Perhaps we should ask Pierre. I don't think it'd be a problem, but you never know. Wouldn't want to have to dodge cleavers.'

'Sounds like our clog-dancing training. Ruth's the coach,' she explained.

Gamache tried to catch Pierre's eye but the maître d' was busy explaining, or apologizing, to the Morrows.

'Come on, we'll just look in.' He took her hand and they pushed through the revolving door.

The place was chaos, though after a moment, shoved to the wall and clinging to it as waiters whizzed by balancing trays of glasses and dishes, Gamache could see the ballet. It wasn't chaos at all, but more like a river in full flood. There was a near frantic movement to it, but there was also a natural flow.

'Is that her?' Reine-Marie asked, nodding across the crowded room. She didn't dare point.

'That's her.'

Chef Véronique wore a white chef's hat and a full apron, and wielded a huge knife. Her back was to them. Then she turned and saw them. She paused.

'She doesn't look pleased to see us,' whispered Reine-Marie, smiling and trying to signal to the clearly annoyed chef that it was her husband's fault.

'Let's get out of here. Me first,' he said and the two scampered out.

'Well, that was embarrassing,' Reine-Marie laughed once they got outside. 'I'd watch your food from now on.'

'I'll get Inspector Beauvoir to taste it first,' he smiled. The reaction of Chef Véronique had surprised him. In the past she'd seemed in command and not particularly stressed. Tonight she seemed upset.

'Do you know, I think I've met her before after all,' said Reine-Marie, slipping her arm through her husband's, feeling his reassuring strength. 'Probably around here somewhere.'

'She's the one who tends the beehives, so maybe you have seen her.'

'Still,' said Reine-Marie, straightening up after sniffing the sweet perfume of a peony, 'she's quite singular. Hard to forget.'

The garden smelled of fresh-turned earth and roses. Every now and then she caught a slight scent of herbs wafting from the kitchen garden. But the scent she longed for, and caught as she leaned into her husband, was sandalwood. It was more than his cologne, he seemed to exude it. It was how every season smelled. It was how love and stability and belonging smelled. It was the perfume of friendship and ease and peace.

'Look.' He pointed into the night sky. 'It's Babar.'

He swirled his fingers around, trying to get her to see the elephant shape in the stars.

'Are you sure? It looks more like Tintin.'

'With a trunk?'

'What're you pointing at?'

The little voice came out of the darkness. The Gamaches squinted and then Bean appeared, carrying the book.

'Hello, Bean.' Reine-Marie bent down and hugged the child. 'We were just looking at the stars, seeing shapes.'

'Oh.' The child seemed disappointed.

'What did you think we'd seen?' Gamache knelt down too.
'Nothing.'

The Gamaches paused, then Reine-Marie pointed to the book. 'What're you reading?'

'Nothing.'

'I used to read about pirates,' said Gamache. 'I'd put a patch over my eye, a teddy bear on my shoulder' – Bean smiled – 'and find a stick for a sword. I'd play for hours.'

The large, commanding man swept his arm back and forth in front of him, fighting off the enemy.

'Boys,' said Reine-Marie. 'I was National Velvet, riding my horse in the Grand National race.'

She grabbed imaginary reins, tucked her head down, leaned forward and urged her steed over the very highest of fences. Gamache smiled in the darkness, then he nodded.

He'd seen that very pose before, recently.

'May I see your book?' He didn't hold out his hand, he simply asked. After a moment the child handed it to him. It was warm where Bean had clutched it and Gamache had the impression of small indents, as though Bean's fingers had melded with the hard cover.

'*Myths Every Child Should Know*,' he read, then flipped open the book. 'It belonged to your mother?'

Bean nodded.

Gamache opened it and let the leaves splay. He looked at Bean.

'The story of Pegasus,' he said. 'Shall I show you Pegasus in the night sky?'

Bean's eyes widened. 'He's up there?'

'He is.' Gamache knelt again and pointed. 'Do you see the four bright stars?' He put his cheek against the child's, feeling it soft and warm, then he lifted Bean's reluctant hand, until Bean relaxed and pointed along with Gamache. Bean nodded.

'That's his body. And down below, those are his legs.'

'He isn't flying,' said Bean, disappointed.

'No, he's grazing, resting,' said Gamache. 'Even the most magnificent of creatures needs a rest. Pegasus knows how to soar and chase and glide. But he also knows how to be at peace.'

The three of them stared at the stars for a few minutes, then they walked around the quiet garden and spoke of their days. Eventually Bean decided to go in and ask for a hot chocolate before bed.

The Gamaches linked arms again and strolled, then turned to walk back.

'Do you know who killed Julia Morrow?' she said as they approached the old lodge.

'Not yet,' he said quietly. 'But we're getting closer. We know who wrote the notes and we have an assortment of clues and facts.'

'Jean Guy must be very happy.'

'You have no idea.' In his mind's eye he saw the foolscap with its columns. And then, again, the one column without clues or facts, without even theories or guesses.

How.

They walked past the corner of the lodge and both instinctively looked at the white marble cube. Then a figure detached itself from the corner of the lodge. It was as though one of the logs had righted itself and decided to walk back into the forest. In the moonlight they watched the shadow make its way across the lawn, but instead of heading into the dark woods it turned towards the lake.

Bert Finney's steps echoed on the wooden dock and then were silent. Armand Gamache told Reine-Marie about Finney, and his father.

'And he told the others?' she asked.

Beside her Armand nodded. She looked up at the stars.

'Have you spoken to Daniel again?'

'I'll call him tomorrow. I wanted to give him time to calm down.'

'Him time?'

'Both of us time. But I'll call.'

Before they drove back they stopped in at the library to say goodnight.

'And don't let the Chief Inspector leave tomorrow without bringing a jar of Chef Véronique's honey,' she instructed Beauvoir.

'Her honey?'

'She's a bee-keeper too. Amazing woman.'

Beauvoir agreed.

As they drove back Reine-Marie remembered where she'd seen Chef Véronique before. It was most extraordinary and unexpected. She smiled and had opened her mouth to speak when he asked about the Canada Day festivities and soon she was describing the day the villagers had planned.

Once he'd dropped her off she realized she'd forgotten to tell him, but determined not to forget the following day.

*

When he got back to the Manoir Gamache found Agent Lacoste on the phone to her children and Jean Guy Beauvoir sipping espresso on the sofa surrounded by books. On bee-keeping.

Gamache wandered the shelves and before long he had an espresso, a cognac and a stack of books of his own.

'Did you know there's only one queen bee per hive?' asked Beauvoir. A few minutes later he broke into the chief's reading with another announcement. 'Did you know a wasp or hornet or queen can sting over and over but a worker bee can only sting once? Only honey bees have poison sacs. Isn't that amazing? When they sting it gets ripped out of them and stays in the victim. Kills the bee. They give up their lives for the queen and the hive. I wonder if they know they'll die.'

'I wonder,' said Gamache, who didn't really. He went back to his reading, as did Beauvoir.

'Did you know honey bees are the pollinators of the world?'

It was like living with a six year old.

Beauvoir lowered the book and looked at the chief, sitting on the sofa opposite reading poetry.

'Without honey bees we'd all starve. Isn't that amazing?'

For a moment Beauvoir imagined moving to the Bellechasse and helping expand Véronique's honey empire. Together they'd save the world. They'd be given the *Légion d'honneur*. Songs would be written about them.

Gamache lowered his book and stared out of the window. All he could see was his own reflection and that of Beauvoir. Two ghostly men reading on a summer evening.

'Bees form a ball and protect the queen if the hive is attacked. Isn't that beautiful?'

'It is.' Gamache nodded and went back to his reading. Every now and then Beauvoir would hear a murmur from the chief.

Oh, I have slipped the surly bonds of earth,
And danced the skies on laughter-silvered wings;
Sunward I've climbed . . . and done a hundred things
You have not dreamed of.

Beauvoir looked over and saw the chief, his eyes closed and his head tilted back, but his lips moving, repeating a phrase.

Up, up the long delirious burning blue,
I've topped the wind-swept heights . . .
Where never lark, or even eagle flew.

'Where's that from?' asked Beauvoir.

'A poem called "High Flight" by a young Canadian aviator in the Second World War.'

'Really? He must've loved flying. Bees love flying. Can cover long distances for food, if they have to, but they stay close to the hive if they can.'

'He died,' said Gamache.

'Pardon?'

'Says here the poet was killed. Shot down. The poem was quoted by President Reagan after the Challenger disaster.' But he'd lost Beauvoir to the bees again.

After a while Gamache put down the slim leather book of poetry and picked up the next volume. Peterson's field guide to North American birds.

They sat together for the next hour, the quiet punctuated by Beauvoir's bee bulletins.

Finally it was time for bed and after Beauvoir said goodnight Gamache took a final stroll in the quiet garden, looking up at the stars.

> *And, while with silent, lifting mind I've trod*
> *The high untrespassed sanctity of space,*
> *Put out my hand, and touched the face of God.*

TWENTY-SEVEN

⁓

The first of July, Canada Day, dawned misty and cool. It threatened rain. Armand Gamache looked across the breakfast table at Irene Finney. Between them sat her Earl Grey teapot and his *café au lait*. In the background waiters set up the morning buffet.

'When can I bury my daughter, Chief Inspector?'

'I'll call the coroner, madame, and let you know. I expect she'll release your daughter in the next day or so. Where will you have the funeral?'

She hadn't expected this question. To be asked about her family, yes. Herself, almost certainly. Their history, their finances, even their feelings. She'd been prepared for an interrogation, not a conversation.

'Is that really your business?'

'It is. We reveal ourselves in our choices. The only way I'll find your daughter's killer is if he reveals himself.'

'What an odd man you are.' It was clear Madame Finney didn't like odd. 'You really think where a murder victim is buried is a clue?'

'Everything's a clue. Especially where bodies are buried.'

'But you're asking me. Does that mean you suspect me?'

The woman in front of him was unflinching, almost daring him to press her.

'I do.'

Her eyes narrowed slightly. 'You're lying,' she said. 'You can't possibly suspect an eighty-five-year-old woman of pushing a several-ton statue onto her own daughter. But perhaps you've lost sight of reality. Must run in the family.'

'Perhaps. Frankly, madame, it is as likely that you did it as anyone. None of you could have shoved Charles Morrow from his pedestal, and yet it happened, I'm sorry to say.'

The less gracious she became the more gracious he grew. And she was quickly becoming very ornery indeed. Not a surprise to the Chief Inspector who knew she was of the type who could be both extremely courteous and excessively offensive.

'Thank you.' She smiled to the young waiter, then turned ice water eyes on Gamache. 'Go on. You were accusing me of killing my own daughter.'

'That isn't true.' He leaned forward, careful not to invade her personal space, but close enough to threaten it. 'Why would you say that? I can't imagine you aren't desperate to find out who really did it. So why aren't you helping?'

He spoke with curiosity, his voice calm and reasonable.

She radiated rage now. He felt his face would bubble and scald. And he knew why none of the Morrow children had ever been this close. And wondered, fleetingly, about Bert Finney, who had.

'I am trying to help. If you'd ask sensible questions I'll answer them.'

Gamache leaned back slowly and looked at her. Her face was etched with a network of tiny lines, like a glass that had just shattered and not yet collapsed. Small patches of pink marked her cheeks, making her even lovelier, more vulnerable. He wondered how many poor souls had been taken in.

'What are the sensible questions?'

This too surprised her.

'Ask about my family, ask about their upbringing. They wanted for nothing, you know. Education, sports. Ski trips in winter, tennis and sailing in the summer. And I know you think we gave them things.' She picked up the sugar bowl and thumped it down, a geyser of sugar leaping out and landing on the honeysuckle wood. 'And we did. I did. But we also gave them love. They knew they were loved.'

'How did they know?'

'Another foolish question. They knew because they knew. They were told. They were shown. If they didn't feel it that was their problem. What have they told you?'

'They've said nothing about love, but I haven't asked.'

'You ask me but not them? Blame the mother, is that it?'

'You mistake me, madame. When it comes time to blame, you'll know it. I'm simply asking questions. And you were the one to mention love, not me. But it's an interesting question. Do you think your children love each other?'

'Of course they do.'

'And yet they're strangers to each other. It doesn't take a detective to know they barely tolerate each other. Have they ever been close?'

'Before Julia left, yes. We used to play games. Word games. Alliteration. And I'd read to the children.'

'Peter told me about that. He still remembers those times.'

'Peter's an ungrateful man. I heard what he told you. That I'd be better off dead.'

'He didn't say that. We were talking about family dynamics and whether the children would continue to see each other after you're gone. He said it was possible they'd grow even closer.'

'Really? Why's that?'

She snapped it out, but Gamache thought he detected genuine curiosity.

'Because now they come to see you, and only you. They see each other as competition. But when you go—'

'Die, Chief Inspector. Don't you mean die?'

'When you die, they'll have to find a reason to see each other, or not. The family will either disappear or they'll grow even closer. That's what Peter meant.'

'Julia was the best of them, you know.' She was gliding the bowl back and forth across the spilled sugar as she spoke, not looking at him. 'Kind and gentle. She asked for almost nothing. And she was always such a lady. Her father and I tried to teach all of them that, to be little ladies and gentlemen. But only Julia understood. Beautiful manners.'

'I noticed that too. My father always said a gentleman puts others at ease.'

'Funny thing for a man who hurt so many people to say. He sure put himself at ease, letting others do the fighting. How does it feel to have a father so vilified?'

Gamache held her gaze then stared at the lawn sloping to the golden lake, and the dock. And the ugly old man doing his sums. The man who'd known his father. He longed to ask Finney about him. Gamache had been eleven when the police car had pulled up. He'd been staring out of the window, his soft cheek on the prickly back of the sofa. Waiting for his parents. Every other time they'd come home. But they were late.

He'd seen the car and known it wasn't theirs. Was it a slight difference in the sound? The tilt of the headlights? Or did something else tell him this wasn't them? He'd watched the Montreal police get out, put their hats on, pause, then start up the walk.

All very slowly.

His grandmother had also seen the car arrive, the headlights gleaming through the window, and had gone to the door to greet his parents.

Slowly, slowly he saw her walk, her hand outstretched for the doorknob. He tried to move, to say something, to stop her. But while the world had slowed, he had stopped.

He simply stared, his mouth open.

And then the knock. Not a sharp rap but something more ominous. It was almost a scratch, a gentle rub. He saw his grandmother's expression change in the instant before she opened the door. Surely his parents wouldn't knock? He'd run to her then, to stop her from letting this thing into the house. But there was no stopping it.

Before the officer had even spoken she'd shoved Armand's face into her dress, so that to this day when he smelled mothballs it made him gag. And he felt her large, strong hand on his back still, as though to keep him from falling.

All his childhood, all his teen years and into his twenties Armand Gamache had wondered why God had taken them both. Couldn't He have left one, for him? It wasn't a demand on his part or an accusation against a clumsy and thoughtless God, more of a puzzle.

But he'd found his answer when he'd found Reine-Marie, had loved and married her and loved her more each day. He knew then how kind God had been not to take one and leave the other. Even for him.

His eyes looked away from the lake and returned to the elderly woman in front of him, who'd just spewed her hurt all over him.

He looked at her with kindness. Not because he knew it would confuse or anger her further, but because he knew he'd had time to absorb his loss. And hers was fresh.

Grief was dagger shaped and sharp and pointed inwards. It was made of fresh loss and old sorrow. Rendered and forged and sometimes polished. Irene Finney had taken her daughter's death and to that sorrow she'd added a long life of entitlement and disappointment, of privilege and pride. And the dagger she'd fashioned was taking a brief break from slashing her insides, and was now pointed outward. At Armand Gamache.

'I loved my father then and I love him now. It's pretty simple,' he said.

'He doesn't deserve it. I'm sorry, but it's the truth, and I have to speak it. The truth will set you free.' She seemed almost sorry.

'I believe it,' he said. 'But I also believe it's not the truth about others that will set you free, but the truth about yourself.'

Now she bristled.

'I'm not the one who needs freeing, Mr Gamache. You refuse to see your father clearly. You're living with a lie. I knew him. He was a coward and a traitor. The sooner you accept that the sooner you can get on with your life. What he did was despicable. He doesn't deserve your love.'

'We all deserve love. And at times pardon.'

'Pardon? Do you mean mercy, forgiveness?' She made it sound like an oath, a curse. 'I'll never forgive the man who killed Julia. And if he's ever pardoned . . .' Her trembling hands released their grip on the sugar bowl. After a moment her voice steadied. 'We'd already lost so much time, you see. Stolen by David Martin. He didn't even want to come home to be married. Insisted they got married in Vancouver. And he kept her there.'

'Against her will?'

She hesitated. 'He kept her away. He hated us, especially Charles.'

'Why?'

'Charles was too smart for him, knew what sort of man David was. Not a gentleman.' She almost smiled. 'He always had a scheme. Always looking for the angle, the fast deal. Julia and Charles had had a falling-out. Perhaps you've heard?'

Her head lifted and her cunning blue eyes studied him. He nodded.

'Then you know how sensitive Julia was. Over-sensitive then. She left and met David Martin right away. When Martin heard her father was the financier Charles Morrow, well, he couldn't push for a reconciliation fast enough. Charles was thrilled at first, but then it became clear Martin only wanted him to invest in one of his schemes. Charles turned him down flat.'

'Both the deal and the reconciliation failed?'

'No, the deal went through but with other more gullible investors. But eventually he lost everything and had to start again. He never tired of badmouthing us to Julia. Turned her against us completely, especially her father.'

'But it didn't start with David Martin, it started long before that. With a slur written on the men's room wall of the Ritz.'

'You know about that, do you? Well, it was a lie. Filthy. With one purpose. To hurt Charles and drive a wedge between him and Julia.'

'But who'd want to do that?'

'We never found out.'

'Do you have your suspicions?'

She hesitated. 'If I do, I keep them to myself. Do you think I'm a common gossip?'

'I think if your family was attacked you and your husband would fight back. And you'd do everything you could to find out who'd done it.'

'Charles tried,' she conceded. 'We had our suspicions, but couldn't act on them.'

'Someone close to home?'

'This conversation is over.' She got up, but not before Gamache thought he saw her eyes dart away. Down the lawn. To the lake. And the ugly man almost enveloped by the mist around the dock.

Just as Gamache walked onto the dock a tiny figure flashed past, galloping across the lawn. Bean in flight, a Spider-Man towel flapping behind, hands gripping reins, a breathless whisper of a song, 'Letter B, Letter B,' barely sung and barely heard. Joyous, the child galloped over the grass then into the woods.

'See anything?' Gamache asked Finney and nodded to the binoculars.

'Don't really look any more,' admitted Finney. 'They're

more out of habit. In case anything unusual happens. Bean's asked me to keep an eye out for Pegasus, and I think I just saw him.'

Finney nodded to the now empty lawn and Gamache smiled.

'But I don't look for birds any more. Keep forgetting.'

'The martlet,' said Gamache, placing his large hands behind his back and staring onto the lake with its soft waves. Clouds were slowly moving in. 'Now there's an interesting bird. Used a lot in heraldry. It's thought to signify enterprise and hard work. The martlet's also meant to signify the fourth child.'

'Is that right?' Finney kept staring into the lake, but his lazy eye was energized, flitting here and there.

'Yes. I found a book last night about the Hundred Years War between England and France. At that time the first son of any family inherited, the second was given to the church, the third might make a good marriage, but the fourth? Well, the fourth had to make his own way.'

'Difficult times.'

'For martlets. And I remembered what Charles Morrow most feared about his own children, four of them as it turned out. He was afraid they'd squander the family fortune.'

'Foolish man, really,' said Finney. 'Kind and generous with everyone else, but harsh with his own.'

'You think? I'll tell you what I think. Yes, Charles Morrow was told by his own father to beware of the next generation, and he believed it. His one foolish decision. But sons tend to believe fathers. So Charles made another decision. A wise one this time. I think he decided to give his children something else, some other riches besides money. Something they couldn't waste. While he showered his wife and his friends with wealth and gifts.' He bowed slightly to Finney who acknowledged the gesture. 'He decided to withhold that from his children. Instead he gave them love.'

Gamache could see the ropy muscles of Finney's ill-shaven face clench.

'He thought a lot about wealth, you know,' said Finney finally. 'Obsessed with it, in a way. He tried to figure out what money bought. He never really figured it out. The closest he came was knowing that he'd be miserable without it, but honestly?' Finney turned his ravaged face on Gamache. 'He was miserable with it. It was all he could think of in the end. Would he have enough, was someone trying to steal it from him, would the children squander it? Made for very boring conversation.'

'And yet you yourself sit here and do your sums.'

'It's true. But I do it privately and don't impose on anyone.'

Gamache wondered if that was true. With Julia dead this man's sums just got a whole lot more interesting. Killing Julia could be considered an imposition.

'So whether because he was miserly or wise Charles Morrow decided he'd shower his children with affection instead of cash,' continued the Chief Inspector.

'Charles went to McGill, you know. He played on their hockey team. The McGill Martlets.' Finney paused, acknowledging the admission. 'He used to tell his children all about those games, but he'd tell them about the times he'd tripped on the ice or missed the pass or gotten smashed into the boards. All the times he'd messed up. To let the little ones know it was all right to fall, it was all right to fail.'

'They didn't like to fall?' asked Gamache.

'Most don't, but the Morrow kids less than most. So they risked nothing. The only one who could risk was Mariana.'

'The fourth child,' said Gamache.

'As it happens, yes. But of all of them Peter was the most fragile. He has an artist's soul and a banker's temperament. Makes for a very stressful life, being so in conflict with himself.'

'On the night she died Julia accused him of being a hypocrite,' Gamache remembered.

'They all are, I'm afraid. Thomas is the opposite of Peter. A banker's soul but an artist's temperament. Emotions squashed. That's why his music's so precise.'

'But without pleasure,' said Gamache. 'Unlike Mariana's.'

Finney said nothing.

'But I haven't told you the most interesting part about the martlet,' said Gamache. 'It's always drawn without feet.'

This brought a grunt from the old man and Gamache wondered if he was in pain.

'The sculptor Pelletier etched a martlet into the statue of Charles Morrow,' Gamache continued. 'Peter drew the same one for his father.'

Finney nodded and sighed. 'I remember that drawing. Charles treasured it. Kept it with him always.'

'Julia learned that from him,' said Gamache. 'Charles kept a few precious things with him and his daughter did the same thing. She kept a packet of notes with her always. They seem innocuous, mundane even, but to her they were her protection, her proof she was loved. She'd pull them out and read them when she felt unloved, which I imagine was often.'

Peter had said they all had armour, and this was Julia's. A bunch of frayed thank you notes.

'I know Charles was your best friend, but forgive me for saying this.' Gamache sat down so he could watch the older man's face, though it was nearly impossible to read. 'For all you say he loved his children, there doesn't seem to be much love back. Monsieur Pelletier had the impression Charles Morrow wasn't much missed.'

'You don't yet know the Morrows, do you? You think you do, but you don't, or you'd never have said that.'

It was said softly, without rancour, but the reprimand was clear.

'I was merely quoting the sculptor.'

Together they watched the dragonflies flitter and buzz around the dock.

'There was one other quality of the martlet,' said Gamache.

'Yes?'

'Do you know why it's always drawn without feet?'

Finney remained silent.

'Because it's on its way to heaven. According to legend a martlet never touches the earth, it flies all the time. I believe Charles Morrow wanted to give that to his children. He wanted them to soar. To find, if not heaven, then at least happiness. *Oh, I have slipped the surly bonds of earth*,' said Gamache. 'You quoted the poem "High Flight" when we first talked.'

'Charles's favourite. He was a naval aviator in the war. *And danced the skies on laughter-silvered wings*. Beautiful.'

Finney looked around, at the lake, the forest, the mountains. He opened his mouth then closed it. Gamache waited. Finally he spoke.

'You're very like your father, you know.'

The words went out into the world and joined the golden sunshine streaming through the gathering clouds and onto the water and the dock and warming their faces. The words joined the glittering waves and the bobbing insects and butterflies and birds and shimmering leaves.

Armand Gamache closed his eyes and walked deep into the shadows, deep into the longhouse where all his experiences and memories lived, where everyone he'd ever met and everything he'd ever done or thought or said waited. He walked right to the very back and there he found a room, closed but not locked. A room he'd never dared enter. From under the door there came not a stench, not darkness, not a moan of a terrible threat. But something much more frightening.

Light glowed from under that door.

Inside were his parents, he knew. Where young Armand had placed them. To be safe and sound. And perfect. Away from the accusations, the taunts, the knowing smiles.

All Armand's life Honoré had lived in light. Unchallenged.

The rest of the world might whisper 'Coward', 'Traitor', and his son could smile. His father was safe, locked away.

Armand put out his hand, and touched the door.

The last room, the last door. The last territory to explore didn't hold monstrous hate or bitterness or rancid resentments. It held love. Blinding, beautiful love.

Armand Gamache gave it the tiniest of pushes and the door swung open.

'What was my father like?'

Finney paused before speaking.

'He was a coward, but then you knew that. He really was, you know. It's not just the ravings of a mad Anglo population.'

'I know he was,' said Gamache, his voice stronger than he felt.

'And you know what happened later?'

Gamache nodded. 'I know the facts.'

He raced back down the longhouse, past the staring and astonished memories, desperate to get to the room and the door he'd been foolish enough to open. But it was too late. The door was open, the light had escaped.

He stared now into the most unsightly face in the world.

'Honoré Gamache and I had very different lives. We were on opposite sides very often. But he did the most extraordinary thing. Something I've never forgotten, something that I take with me even today. Do you know what your father did?'

Bert Finney didn't look at the Chief Inspector as he spoke, but Gamache had the impression of immense scrutiny.

'He changed his mind,' said Finney.

He struggled to his feet, wiping his balding head with a handkerchief and replacing the floppy hat Gamache had given him. He brought himself erect, achieving every inch of the height he still had, then turned and faced Gamache, who'd also risen and now towered over him. Finney said nothing, simply stared. Then his ugly, ravaged face broke into a smile and he put out his hand, touching Gamache on the arm. It was a contact like many Gamache had had in his life, both given and received. But there was an intimacy about this that felt almost like a violation. Finney locked eyes with Gamache, then turned and made his slow progress along the dock to the shore.

'You lied to me, monsieur,' Gamache called after him.

The elderly man stopped, paused, then turned, squinting

349

into the shafts of sun, made brighter by the shadows. He brought a quivering hand to his brow, to stare back at Gamache.

'You seem surprised, Chief Inspector. Surely people lie to you all the time.'

'It's true. It's not the lying that surprised me, but what you chose to lie about.'

'Really? And what was that?'

'Yesterday I asked my team to look into the backgrounds of everyone involved in this case—'

'Very wise.'

'*Merci.* They found that you were exactly as you claimed. Modest upbringing in Notre-Dame-de-Grace in Montreal. An accountant. Worked here and there after the war but jobs were scarce, so many men suddenly looking. Your old friend Charles hired you and you stayed on. Very loyal.'

'It was a good job with a good friend.'

'But you told me you'd never been a prisoner.'

'And I haven't.'

'But you have, monsieur. Your war record states you were in Burma when the Japanese invaded. You were captured.'

He was speaking to a survivor of the Burma campaign, of the brutal fighting and atrocious, inhumane captivity. Almost none survived. But this man had. He'd lived to be almost ninety, as though he was taking all the years stolen from the rest. He'd lived to marry, to have stepchildren and to stand peacefully on a dock on a summer's morning, discussing murder.

'You're so close, Chief Inspector. I wonder if you know how close you are. But you still have some things to figure out.'

And with that Bert Finney turned and walked onto the grass, heading off slowly to wherever men like him go.

Armand Gamache watched, still feeling the touch of the withered old hand on his arm. Then he closed his eyes and turned his face to the sky, his right hand just lifting a little to take a larger hand.

Oh, I have slipped, he murmured to the lake, *the surly bonds of earth*.

TWENTY-EIGHT

Gamache had a light breakfast of home-made granola and watched Jean Guy Beauvoir eat almost an entire hive of honey.

'Did you know honey bees actually flap their wings over the honeycomb and that evaporates water?' said Beauvoir, chewing on a mouthful of honeycomb and trying to look as though it didn't taste like wax. 'That's why honey is so sweet and thick.'

Isabelle Lacoste dabbed fresh raspberry jam on a buttery croissant and looked at Beauvoir as though he was a bear of very little brain.

'My daughter did a project on honey for her grade one class,' she said. 'Did you know bees eat honey and then throw it up again? Over and over. That's how honey's made. Bees' barf she called it.'

The spoon with a bit of honeycomb and dripping golden liquid paused. But adoration won out and it went into Beauvoir's mouth. Anything Chef Véronique touched was fine with him. Even bees' barf. Eating the thick, almost amber liquid gave him comfort. He felt cared for and safe near the large, ungainly woman. He wondered if that was love. And he wondered why he didn't feel this way with his wife, Enid. But he retreated from the thought before it could take hold.

'I'll be back mid-afternoon,' Gamache said at the door a few minutes later. 'Don't burn down the house.'

'Give our best to Madame Gamache,' said Lacoste.

'Happy anniversary,' said Beauvoir, holding out his hand to shake the chief's. Gamache took it and held it a moment longer than necessary. A tiny fleck of wax was hanging from Beauvoir's lip.

Gamache dropped the sticky hand.

'Come with me, please,' he said and the two men walked over the hard dirt drive to the car. Gamache turned and spoke to his second in command.

'Be careful.'

'What do you mean?' Beauvoir felt his defences swiftly rise.

'You know what I mean. This is a difficult enough job, a dangerous enough job, without being blinded.'

'I'm not.'

'You are, you know. You've become obsessed with Véronique Langlois. What is it about her, Jean Guy?'

'I am not obsessed. I admire her, that's all.' The words held an edge, a warning.

Gamache didn't budge. Instead he continued to stare at the younger man, so neat, so perfectly turned out, and in such turmoil. It was that turmoil that made him such a gifted investigator, Gamache knew. Yes, he collected facts and assembled them brilliantly, but it was Beauvoir's discomfort that allowed him to recognize it in others.

'What about Enid?'

'What about my wife? What're you suggesting?'

'Don't lie to me,' warned Gamache. From suspects, yes, it was expected, but from the team it was never tolerated. Beauvoir knew this and hesitated.

'I felt something for Chef Véronique early on, but it was ridiculous. I mean, look at her. Twice my age, almost. No, she fascinates me, nothing more.'

In a few words he'd betrayed his feelings and lied to his chief.

Gamache took a deep breath and continued to stare at the young man. Then he reached out and touched his arm.

'There's nothing to be ashamed of, but there is a lot to be aware of. Be careful. Véronique Langlois's a suspect, and I'm afraid your feelings for her are blinding you.'

Gamache dropped his hand and in that instant Beauvoir longed to fall into his arms, like a child. He was deeply surprised and ashamed of the nearly overwhelming urge. It was as though a hand was shoving him firmly from behind, towards this powerful, commanding man.

'I feel nothing for her,' he said, his voice hard.

'Lying to me is one thing, Jean Guy, but I hope you're not lying to yourself.' Gamache stared at him for a moment.

'Hello,' a cheerful voice called from down the drive.

The men turned and saw Clara and Peter walking towards them. Clara hesitated when she saw their faces.

'Are we interrupting?'

'Not at all. I was just leaving.' Beauvoir turned his back on the chief and walked swiftly away.

'Are you sure we didn't interrupt?' Clara asked as they drove away in Gamache's Volvo, towards Three Pines.

354

'No, we'd finished talking, *merci*. Looking forward to getting home?'

For the rest of the pleasant drive they talked about the weather and the countryside and the villagers. Anything but the case, and the Morrows they were leaving behind. Finally the car crested the hill and spread below them was Three Pines, its village green in the centre with small roads radiating off it, like a compass, or beams from the sun.

They drove slowly and carefully down the hill, as villagers streamed from their homes and sun-browned children in bathing suits ran unguarded across the road and onto the green, chased by bounding dogs. A small stage had been erected off to one side and already the barbecue pit was smouldering.

'Just drop us here,' said Clara, as Gamache drove up to Gabri and Olivier's bed and breakfast overlooking the village green. 'We'll walk over.'

She pointed, unnecessarily, to their place, a small red brick cottage across the green. Gamache knew it well. The low stone wall in front had rose bushes arching over it and the apple trees that lined their walk were in full leaf. On the side of the house he could see a trellis thick with sweet peas. Before he could get out of the car he saw Reine-Marie come out of the B&B. She waved at Peter and Clara then hurried down the stairs and into his arms.

They were home. He always felt a bit like a snail, but instead of carrying his home on his back, he carried it in his arms.

'Happy anniversary,' she said.

'*Joyeux anniversaire*,' he said, and pressed a card into her hand. She led him to the swing on the wide open porch. She sat but he looked at it, then up at the hook in the clapboard ceiling, anchoring it in place.

'Gabri and Olivier sit here all the time, watching the village. How do you think they know so much?' She patted the seat beside her. 'It'll hold.'

If it held the expansive and expressive innkeeper, thought Gamache, it'll hold me. And it did.

Reine-Marie pressed the thick hand-made paper between her hands, then she opened it.

I love you, it read. And beside it was a happy face.

'Did you draw this yourself?' she asked.

'I did.' He didn't tell her he'd worked on it most of the night. Writing verse after verse and rejecting them all. Until he'd distilled his feelings to those three words. And that silly drawing.

It was the very best he could do.

'Thank you, Armand.' And she kissed him. She slipped the card into her pocket and when she got home it would join the other thirty-four cards, all saying exactly the same thing. Her treasure.

Before long they were walking hand in hand on the village green, waving to the people tending the glowing embers around the stuffed lamb *au jus* wrapped in herbs and foil and buried before dawn. The *meshoui*, the traditional Québécois celebratory meal. For Canada Day.

'*Bonjour, Patron.*' Gabri clapped Gamache on the shoulder and gave him a kiss on each cheek. 'I hear this is a double celebration, Canada Day and your anniversary.'

Olivier, Gabri's partner and the owner of the local bistro, joined them.

'*Félicitations,*' smiled Olivier. Where Gabri was large,

356

effusive, unkempt, Olivier was immaculate and restrained. Both in their mid-thirties, they'd moved to Three Pines to lead a less stressful life.

'Oh, for Chrissake,' an old and piercing voice shot through the celebrations. 'It's not Clouseau.'

'At your serveess, madame,' Gamache bowed to Ruth and spoke in his thickest Parisian accent. 'Do you have a lee-sence for zat minky?' He pointed to the duck waddling behind the elderly poet.

Ruth glared at him, but a tiny twitch at the corner of her mouth betrayed her.

'Come along, Rosa,' she said to the quacking duck. 'He drinks, you know.'

'Good to be back?' Olivier passed Gamache and Reine-Marie an iced tea.

Gamache smiled. 'Always.'

They wandered the village, finally stopping at the café tables on the sidewalk outside the bistro to watch the children's races.

Peter and Clara joined them for a drink. Already Peter looked more composed.

'Happy anniversary,' said Clara, raising her glass of ginger beer. They all clinked.

'I have something I've been dying to ask,' said Reine-Marie, leaning over the table and laying a warm hand on Clara's. 'Is it possible to see your latest work? The one of Ruth?'

'I'd love to show it to you. When?'

'Why not right now, *ma belle*?'

The two women emptied their glasses and went off, Peter and Gamache watching them walk through the gate and up the winding path to the cottage.

'I have a question for you, Peter. Shall we walk?'

Peter nodded, suddenly feeling as though he'd been called into the principal's office. Together the two men walked across the village green, then by unspoken consent they climbed rue du Moulin and wandered along the quiet dirt road, a canopy of green leaves overhead.

'Do you know which stall that graffiti about your sister was written on?'

The question should have come out of the blue, but Peter had been expecting it. Waiting for it. For years. He knew eventually someone would ask.

He walked in silence for a few paces until the laughter from the village all but disappeared behind them.

'I believe it was the second stall,' said Peter at last, watching his feet in their sandals.

Gamache was silent for a moment, then spoke.

'Who wrote that graffiti?'

It was the hole Peter had skirted all his life. It had grown into a chasm and still he'd avoided it, taken the long way round so as not to look in, to fall in. And now it had opened up right in front of him. Yawning and dark, and everywhere. Instead of going away it had simply grown.

He could have lied, he knew. But he was tired.

'I did.'

For most of his life he'd wondered how this moment would feel. Would he be relieved? Would the admission kill him? Not physically, perhaps, but would the Peter he'd carefully constructed die? The decent, kind, gentle Peter. Would he be replaced by the wretched, hateful thing that had done that to his sister?

'Why?' asked Gamache.

Peter didn't dare stop, didn't dare look at him.

Why? Why had he done it? It was so long ago. He could remember sneaking into the stall. Could remember the clean, green metal door, the disinfectant smell that still made him gag. He'd brought his magic marker, and with that marker magic he'd done. He'd made his sister disappear. And he'd changed all their lives for ever with five simple words.

Julia Morrow gives good head.

'I was angry at Julia, for sucking up to my father.'

'You were jealous of her. It's natural. It would pass.'

But somehow the reassurance made it worse. Why hadn't anyone told him that decades ago? That there was nothing wrong with hating a sibling? That it would pass.

Instead, it stayed. And grew. The guilt had festered and turned rotten and had eaten a hole deep inside him. And finally, now, he could feel himself falling.

'Did Julia realize what you'd done, Peter? Is that what she was about to tell everyone?'

Peter stopped and looked at the Chief Inspector. 'Are you suggesting I killed my sister so she wouldn't tell?'

He tried to sound incredulous.

'I think you'd do just about anything to keep that secret. If your mother had found out that you were responsible for an act that left your family ridiculed and ruptured, well, God knows what she'd have done. Might have even written you out of her will. In fact, I think that's a distinct possibility. That mistake thirty years ago could cost you millions.'

'And you think I care about that? My mother's been throwing money at me for years and I send it all back, all of it. Even my inheritance from Father. I want none of it.'

'Why?' asked Gamache.

'What do you mean, why? Would you keep accepting money from your parents well into your adulthood? But, no, I forgot. You had no parents.'

Gamache stared at him, and after a moment Peter dropped his eyes.

'Be careful,' Gamache whispered. 'You're making hurting a habit. Spreading it around won't lessen your pain, you know. Just the opposite.'

Peter raised his eyes, defiant.

'My question stands, Peter. This isn't a pleasant chat between friends. This is a murder investigation and I'll know everything. Why do you refuse your mother's offers of money?'

'Because I'm a grown man and I want to stand on my own. I've seen Thomas and Mariana tug their forelocks and bow and scrape for money. Mommy bought Thomas his home and gave Mariana the seed money for her business.'

'Why shouldn't she? She has the money. I don't understand the problem.'

'Thomas and Mariana are slaves to it, slaves to Mommy. They love luxury and ease. Clara and I live hand to mouth. For years we could barely pay for the heating. But we're at least free.'

'Are you? Is it possible you're as obsessed with money as they are?' He held up his hand to stop Peter's angry interruption. 'If you weren't you'd accept it now and then. Thomas and Mariana want it. You don't. But it still runs your life. She still does.'

'Oh, and you're one to talk. Look at yourself why don't you? How pathetic is it to be a cop, to carry a gun when that was the one thing your own father refused to do? Who's compensating now? Your father was a coward, a famous one, and his son's famous too. For courage. At least my mother's alive. Your father's long dead and still he controls you.'

Gamache smiled, which angered Peter even more. This was his *coup de grâce*, the final thrust he'd kept in abeyance to be brought out and used only if things got desperate.

Now he'd dropped his bomb but Hiroshima remained, untouched, even smiling.

'I love my father, Peter. Even if he was a coward, he was still a great father, a great man, in my eyes if in no one else's. Do you know the story?'

'Mother told us,' he said sullenly.

'What did she say?'

'That Honoré Gamache rallied the French Canadians against the Second World War, forcing Canada to hesitate before entering and convincing thousands of young Quebecers not to sign up. He himself joined the Red Cross so he wouldn't have to fight.'

Gamache nodded. 'She's quite right. Did she tell you what happened then?'

'No, you did. He and your mother were killed in a car accident.'

'But there were many years in between. Near the end of the war the British Army marched into a place called Bergen-Belsen. I'm sure you've heard of it.'

The two men were walking again, down the shady lane, through the sweet summer air.

Peter said nothing.

'My father was with the Red Cross division assigned to go into newly liberated prisons. No one was prepared for what they saw. In Bergen-Belsen my father saw the full horror of what man was capable of. And he saw his mistake. He met it in the eyes of the men and women who'd waited for help that didn't come. From a world that knew what was happening and still didn't hurry. I was eight when he started telling me the stories. He knew as soon as he walked into Bergen-Belsen he'd been wrong. He should never have spoken against this war. He was a man of peace, that was true. But he also had to admit he'd been afraid to fight. And when he stood face to face with the men and women of Bergen-Belsen he knew he'd been a coward. So he came home and apologized.'

Peter kept walking, the smug smile plastered on his face. Carefully kept there to conceal his shock. No one had told him this. His mother, in relating the story, hadn't told them Honoré Gamache had changed his mind.

'My father got up in churches, synagogues, in public meetings, on the steps of the *Assemblée Nationale*, and he apologized. He spent years raising money and co-ordinating efforts to help refugees rebuild their lives. He sponsored a woman he'd met in Bergen-Belsen to come to Canada and live with us. Zora was her name. She became my grand-mother, and raised me after my parents died. She taught me that life goes on, and that I had a choice. To lament what I no longer had or be grateful for what remained. I was fortunate to have a role model that I couldn't squirm my way around. After all, how do you argue with the survivor of a death camp?'

Gamache actually chuckled, and Peter wondered at this man who'd lived every nightmare and was happy while Peter had every privilege and wasn't.

They walked out of the tunnel of maple trees and into the

light, dimmed by cloud. Both men stopped. Some fiddle music reached them.

'I don't want to miss Reine-Marie,' said Gamache.

They started making their way back.

'You were right. I knew my father would see what I'd written in the men's room. I knew he'd never use the first stall so I wrote it in the second. Not only did Father see it, but his friends did too.'

Their pace slowed almost to a stop.

'There was a terrible fight and Julia left. She loved Father, as you probably know, and couldn't forgive him for not loving her back. Of course, he did. That was the problem. He loved her so much he saw this as a betrayal. Not of the family, but of him. His little girl.'

Now they stopped. Gamache didn't speak. Eventually Peter continued.

'I did it on purpose. So that he'd hate her. I didn't want the competition. I wanted him all to myself. And she'd made fun of me. I was younger than her, but not by much. It was an awkward age. Eighteen. All gangly and unco-ordinated.'

'With pimples.'

Peter looked at Gamache with astonishment.

'How'd you know? Did Thomas tell you?'

Gamache shook his head. 'Peter's perpetually purple pimple popped.'

Peter inhaled sharply. Even after all these years he still felt the blade between his bones.

'Where'd you hear that?'

'Julia,' said Gamache, watching Peter closely. 'One night after dinner I was in the garden and heard someone repeating something over and over. Peter's perpetually purple—'

'I get it,' Peter cut him off. 'Do you know what it was?'

'Your sister explained it was a game you'd played as kids, but I didn't really connect it until this morning when your mother said you used to play word games with your father. Alliteration.'

Peter nodded.

'It was his way to try to make us feel like a family, I suppose, but it had the opposite effect. We became competitive. We thought the prize for winning was his love. It was excruciating. On top of that I had a terrible case of acne. I'd asked Julia if she knew of any creams I could use. She gave me some, but then later that night we played the game. The perpetually purple pimple. I said "popped" and thought I'd won. But then Julia said Peter's. Peter's perpetually purple pimple popped. Father roared and roared and hugged her. Made a big deal of it. She won.'

Gamache could see it. Young, awkward artistic Peter. Betrayed by his sister, laughed at by his father.

'So you plotted your revenge,' said Gamache.

'I wrote the graffiti. God, I can't believe what I did, all because of a stupid game. Something that just came out of Julia's mouth. She probably didn't even mean it. It was nothing. Nothing.'

'It almost always is,' said Gamache. 'So small no one else even sees it. So small you don't see it coming, until it smashes into you.'

Peter sighed.

They stood at the top of rue du Moulin. A group of fiddlers was playing away, softly, melodically, at first. Beside the stage Ruth waved her gnarled cane unexpectedly gracefully to the music. On the stage rows of dancers were lined up, kids in front, women in the middle, strapping men at the back. The music picked up steam and tempo and the dancers' feet fell with more and more insistence until after a minute or so the fiddlers were sawing away near maniacally, their arms flashing up and down, the music joyous and free, and the dancers' feet hit the floor in unison, stomping and tapping. But this was no display of traditional Irish dancing, where the upper torso is stiff and the arms like dead branches at their sides. These dancers, under the cane of Ruth Zardo, were more like dervishes, dancing and whirling and whooping and laughing, but always in rhythm. Their stomping feet shook the stage, the sound waves travelling through the earth, through the bodies of everyone in the village, up du Moulin, and into their chests.

And then it stopped. And there was silence. Until the laughter started, and the applause, to fill the void.

Peter and Gamache walked down and arrived just in time for the final clog dancing demonstration. It was a class of eight year olds. And Reine-Marie. The fiddlers played a slow Irish waltz while the dancers stumbled. One little boy edged his way to the front of the stage and did his own steps. Ruth thumped her cane at him, but he seemed immune to direction.

At the end Gamache gave them a standing ovation, joined by Clara, Gabri and finally Peter.

'Well, what did you think?' asked Reine-Marie, joining everyone at a picnic table. 'Be honest now.'

'Brilliant.' Gamache gave her a hug.

'Brought tears to my eyes,' said Gabri.

'It would have been better except Number Five there kept hogging the stage,' whispered Reine-Marie, leaning over, pointing at a beaming little boy.

'Shall I kick him?' asked Gamache.

'Better wait till no one's looking,' advised his wife.

The child sat at the next picnic table and immediately spilled a Coke in one direction and knocked over the salt shaker in the other. His mother made Number Five take a pinch of salt and toss it over his shoulder. Gamache watched with interest. Peter brought over a platter of hamburgers, slices of barbecued lamb and a pyramid of corn on the cob while Olivier put down a tray of beers and bright pink lemonades.

'For God's sake, *qu'est-ce que tu fais?* There're ants everywhere, and just wait. Wasps'll come and sting you.'

Mom grabbed the boy's arm and yanked Number Five to another table, leaving the mess for someone else to clean up.

'Everyone comes back for this week,' said Olivier, taking a long sip of cold beer and surveying the gathering. 'They arrive just before Saint-Jean-Baptiste and stay until after Canada Day.'

'How'd you celebrate Saint-Jean-Baptiste last weekend?' Gamache asked.

'Fiddlers, clogging and a barbecue,' said Gabri.

'Is Number Five a visitor? I've never seen him before,' said Reine-Marie.

'Who?' asked Olivier and when Reine-Marie nodded to her clogging mate he laughed. 'Oh, him. He's from Winnipeg. You call him Number Five? We call him Shithead.'

'For simplicity,' said Gabri. 'Like Cher or Madonna.'

'Or Gabri,' said Reine-Marie. 'Do you know, I've never actually heard the name Gabri before. Is it short for Gabriel?'

'It is.'

366

'But don't most Gabriels get called Gaby for short?'

'I'm not most Gabriels,' said Gabri.

'I'm sorry, *mon beau*.' Reine-Marie reached out to comfort the huge hurt man. 'I would never suggest you are. I've always liked the named Gabriel. The archangel.'

This went some way to smoothing Gabri's feathers. For a startled instant Reine-Marie could actually imagine full, powerful grey wings settling into place on Gabri's back.

'We have a son named Daniel, you know. And a daughter Annie. We chose names that would work in both English and French. Gabriel does too.'

'*C'est vrai*,' said Gabri. 'Gabriel I like but in school everyone called me Gaby. I hated that. So I made up my own name. Gabri. *Voilà*.'

'Hard to believe they called you Gaby,' said Olivier, smiling.

'I know,' said Gabri, not appreciating the sarcasm. But a moment later he caught Reine-Marie's eye with an amused look, confirming he wasn't nearly as oblivious or self-absorbed as he pretended.

They all watched as Shithead took a lick of his Coaticook ice cream, spilled more salt and again shot the Coke can across the table. It skidded over the salt, hit a bump and fell over. He started crying. Mom, after soothing him, took a pinch of spilled salt and tossed it over his shoulder. For luck. Gamache thought the only luck Number Five would have would be if his mother made him clean up after himself instead of moving each time he made a mess.

Gamache looked over at the first picnic table. Sure enough, ants and wasps swarmed over the sweet puddles of Coke.

'Hamburger, Armand?' Reine-Marie held out the burger,

then lowered it. She recognized the look on her husband's face. He'd seen something. She looked over but saw only an empty picnic table and a few wasps.

But he saw a murder.

He saw ants and bees, the statue, the black walnut, Canada Day and its counterpart Saint-Jean-Baptiste. He saw summer jobs and greed and the wickedness that would wait decades to crush Julia Morrow.

And he finally had something to write in that last column. How.

How a father had walked off his pedestal and crushed his daughter.

TWENTY-NINE

⁓

Armand Gamache kissed his wife goodbye just as the first huge drops of rain fell with a splat. No mist or atmospheric drizzle for this Canada Day. It was a day for plump, ripe, juicy rain.

'You know, don't you,' she whispered into his ear as he embraced her.

He pulled back and nodded.

Peter and Clara climbed into the Volvo like two shell-shocked veterans returning to the front line. Already Peter's hair stood on end.

'Wait,' Reine-Marie called just as Armand opened the driver's side door. She took her husband aside for a moment, ignoring the drops plopping all around them. 'I forgot to tell you. I remembered where I'd seen Chef Véronique before. You have too, I'm sure of it.'

She told him and his eyes widened, surprised. She was right, of course. And so many vaguely troubling things suddenly made sense. The world-class chef hidden away. The army of young English workers. Never older, never French.

Why she never greeted the guests. And why she lived, year round, on the shores of an isolated lake.

'*Merci, ma belle.*' He kissed her again and returned to the car, and the car returned to the road. Back to the Manoir Bellechasse.

As they turned the final corner of the dirt road they saw the old log lodge through the windshield wipers, and they saw a Sûreté vehicle parked on the winding drive. Then more police vehicles, as they got closer. Some Sûreté, some municipal police. Even a Royal Canadian Mounted Police truck. The drive was packed with vehicles parked higgledy-piggledy.

The chatting stopped in the car and it grew very silent, except for the clack, clack, clack of the wiper. Gamache's face grew stern and hard and watchful. The three of them dashed through the rain and into the reception room of the Manoir.

'*Bon Dieu*, thank God you're here,' said little Madame Dubois. 'They're in the Great Room.'

Gamache walked quickly.

At the opening of the door all eyes turned to him. There in the centre stood Jean Guy Beauvoir, surrounded by the Morrows, what looked like the entire staff of the Manoir, and men and women in assorted uniforms. A huge ordnance map was hanging from the fireplace mantel.

'*Bon*,' said Beauvoir. 'I believe you know this man. Chief Inspector Armand Gamache, the head of homicide for the Sûreté du Québec.'

There was a murmur and some nodding. A few of the officers offered salutes. Gamache nodded back.

'What's happened?' Gamache asked.

'Elliot Byrne is missing,' said Beauvoir. 'It was noticed sometime between the breakfast and the luncheon service.'

'Who reported it?'

'I did.' Chef Véronique stepped forward. And as Gamache looked at her he wondered how he hadn't seen it before. Reine-Marie was right. 'He wasn't there for the breakfast service,' the chef was explaining, 'and that was unusual but not unheard of. He'd worked dinner the night before and sometimes their schedule gives them the next breakfast off. So I didn't say anything. But he should have been there to set up for lunch.'

'What did you do?' asked Gamache.

'I spoke to Pierre, the maître d',' said Véronique.

Pierre Patenaude stepped forward, looking shaken and worried.

'Shouldn't we be looking for him?' he asked.

'We are, monsieur,' said Beauvoir. 'We have calls out to police and the media, to the bus and train stations.'

'But he might be out there.' Pierre waved outside, where rain was now pouring down the windows, making the outside world distorted and grotesque.

'We'll form search parties, but first we need information and a plan. Go on.' Gamache turned to Beauvoir.

'Monsieur Patenaude managed a quick search of the bunks and the grounds, to make sure Elliot wasn't sick or hurt or maybe just goofing off,' said Beauvoir. 'Nothing was found.'

'Were his clothes gone?' asked Gamache.

'No,' said Beauvoir, and their eyes locked for an instant. 'We were just about to form search parties for the surrounding area.' Beauvoir addressed the room. 'Everyone who wants to volunteer please stay. The rest, please leave.'

'Can I help?' Little Madame Dubois, dwarfed by the sequoia-like RCMP officers, stepped forward.

'You can help me, madame,' said Gamache. 'Carry on.' He nodded to Beauvoir, and to everyone's astonishment the Chief Inspector took Madame Dubois's arm and they left the Great Room.

'Coward.' The whispered word in the Morrow voice slid off Gamache's back and to the floor, where it evaporated.

'What can I do, monsieur?' she asked when they arrived in the outer office.

'You can find me Elliot's employment application and whatever information you have about him. And you can place these phone calls.'

He jotted down a list.

'Are you sure?' she asked, perplexed by the list, but seeing his face she didn't wait for an answer.

He walked into the library and closed the door. In the hallway he heard the trooping of heavy feet as the searchers prepared to go out into the rain. Not a storm, but the rain and wind would make the ground sodden and slippery. It was going to be miserable.

After making a few more notes he looked up and stared out of the window. Then he quickly walked out of the French doors and through the rain across the lawn, towards a group of searchers just entering the woods. They were wearing bright orange coats, supplied by the local hunt and game society, who were also volunteering. Each team would have a police officer and a local hunter. The last thing they needed was to lose the searchers. It happened. How often had the lost reappeared and the searchers disappeared, only to be found as bones years later. The Canadian wilderness didn't give up her territory or her dead easily.

The rain was coming down in torrents, hitting them

sideways. Everyone was anonymous in the orange covers, slick with rain.

'Colleen?' he shouted, knowing with their hoods up all they'd hear was the din of the rain pelting their heads. 'Colleen!'

He grabbed a promising shoulder. A young man Gamache recognized as a porter turned round. He looked frightened and uncertain. Water dribbled down Gamache's face, into his eyes and down his cheeks. He smiled reassuringly at the young man.

'You'll do fine,' he shouted. 'Just stick close to them.' Gamache pointed to two large orange coats with bold duct tape X's on their backs. 'And if you get tired, tell them. You're not to hurt yourself, *d'accord*?'

The young man nodded. 'Are you coming with us, sir?'

'I can't. I'm needed somewhere else.'

'I understand.'

But Gamache saw the disappointment. And he saw fear lick the boy. And he felt horrible. But he was needed elsewhere, though he needed to find the young gardener first. 'Is Colleen in your group?'

The young man shook his head then ran off to catch up with the others.

'*Sacré*,' whispered Gamache, standing alone now on the soaked lawn, his own clothes unprotected and wet through. 'Idiot.'

He spent the next few minutes striding into the woods, asking each group he found whether the gardener was with them. He knew the standard search pattern, had co-ordinated enough searches himself not to be worried about losing the searchers. He was worried about something else. About

Elliot, missing. About Elliot, whose clothing was still in his modest wooden cupboard in the small bunkroom.

'Colleen?' He touched another orange shoulder and saw another little leap as some poor kid's movie nightmare came momentarily true. As they turned he knew they expected to see Freddy Krueger or Hannibal Lecter or the Blair Witch. Huge, terrified eyes met his.

'Colleen?'

She nodded, relieved.

'Come with me.' He shouted to the team leader he was taking the young gardener from the search, and while the others trudged deeper into the woods Gamache and Colleen emerged onto the lawn and jogged towards the refuge of the lodge.

Once inside with towels to dry off Gamache spoke.

'I need to know a few things, and I need you to be honest.'

Colleen looked well beyond being able to lie.

'Who do you have the crush on?'

'Elliot.'

'And who do you believe he had feelings for?'

'Her. The woman who was killed.'

'Julia Martin? Why do you say that?'

'Because he was always hovering around her, asking questions.'

She brought the soft towel to her wet face and gave a good scrub.

'Like what, Colleen? What did he want to know?'

'Stupid things. Things like what her husband did and where they lived and whether she sailed or hiked. Whether she knew Stanley Park and the yacht club. He'd worked there once.'

'Did he know her, do you think, from Vancouver?'

'I heard them laughing once that he probably served her a martini there, just as he was serving her one in Quebec.'

Colleen clearly didn't see the humour.

'You talked about ants,' he said more gently. 'The ones that gave you nightmares. Where were they?'

'All over.' She shivered at the memory of ants crawling all over her.

'No, I mean in real life, not your dream. Where did you see the ants?' He tried not to let his anxiety show, and deliberately kept his voice even and calm.

'They were all over the statue. When I was trying to transplant the sick flowers I looked up and the statue was covered with ants.'

'Now, think carefully.' He smiled and took his time, even though he knew time was fleeing before him, racing away. 'Were they really all over the statue?'

She thought.

After what seemed hours she spoke. 'No, they were at the bottom, all over his feet, and the white block. Right where my head was.'

And he could see the young gardener kneeling down, trying to save the dying plants, and coming face to face with a colony of scampering, frenzied ants.

'Was there anything else there?'

'Like what?'

'Think, Colleen, just think.' He was dying to tell her, to quickly lead her to it, but he knew he couldn't. Instead he waited.

'Wasps,' she said finally. And Gamache exhaled, unaware he'd been holding his breath. 'Which was funny because

375

there wasn't a nest. Just wasps. That kid, Bean, said it was a bee sting, but I'm sure it was a wasp.'

'Actually, it was a bee,' said Gamache. 'A honey bee.'

'But that's ridiculous. Why would a honey bee be there? Their hive's all the way across the property. Besides, all the flowers around there were sick. A bee wouldn't be attracted to them.'

'One last question. Agent Lacoste says you kept saying it wasn't your fault.' He quickly held up a steady hand to reassure her. 'We know it wasn't. But I need to know why you said it.'

'Elliot and Mrs Martin were talking on the other side of the statue. Laughing and kinda flirting. I was so angry. It was horrible to have to see them every day. I was working there and they obviously hadn't seen me, or didn't notice. Anyway, I stood up and put my hand on the statue. It moved.'

She lowered her eyes and waited for the inevitable laughter. He'd never believe her. Who would? What she'd said was laughable, which was why she hadn't said anything about it before. How could a statue move? Yet it had. She could feel it grinding forward even now. She waited for him to laugh, to dismiss what she'd just said as ridiculous. She raised her eyes and saw him nodding.

'Thank you,' he said softly, though she wasn't convinced he was talking to her. 'It's too late to join the others on the search. Perhaps you could help me.'

She smiled, relieved.

While Gamache took a couple of calls Madame Dubois put through he asked Colleen to call the Correctional Centre in Nanaimo, BC. 'Tell them Chief Inspector Gamache needs to speak to David Martin, urgently.'

Gamache spoke to the Musée Rodin in Paris, the Royal Academy in London and the Côte des Neiges cemetery in Montreal. He'd just hung up when Colleen handed him her phone.

'Mr Martin's on the line.'

'David Martin?' Gamache asked.

'It is. Is this Chief Inspector Gamache?'

'*Oui, c'est moi-même.*' He continued in rapid French, and received answers in equally rapid French. Very quickly Gamache found out about Martin's early life and career, his early bankruptcies, his investors.

'I need the names of all your early investors.'

'That's easy. There weren't that many.'

Gamache scribbled the names as Martin dictated them.

'And they lost everything they'd invested with you?'

'We all did, Chief Inspector. No need to shed huge cow tears for them. Make no mistake, they were out for the main chance as well. It wasn't charity. If the companies had hit big they'd have made a fortune. It's business. I went bankrupt, and some of them did too. But I picked myself up.'

'You were young and without responsibilities. Some of them were older with families. They didn't have the time or energy to start again.'

'Then they shouldn't have invested.'

Gamache rang off and looked up. Irene Finney and Madame Dubois were standing in the room, side by side, with the same expression on their faces now. Behind them Colleen, like a 'before' version of these elderly women, stood fresh and plump but with the same look on her face.

Fear.

'What is it?' He stood.

'Bean,' said Mrs Finney. 'We can't find Bean.'

Gamache paled.

'When was the last time you saw Bean?'

'Lunch,' said Mrs Finney, and they all checked their watches. Three hours. 'Where's my grandchild?'

She looked at Gamache as though he was responsible. And he knew he was. He'd been slow, allowed himself to be misdirected by his own prejudices. He'd accused Beauvoir of being blinded by emotion, but he had been too.

'You sit here, safe and warm with the old women and children,' hissed Mrs Finney. 'Hiding here while others do the difficult work.'

She was shaking with rage, as though the fault line had finally spread too wide and she'd tumbled in herself.

'Why?' Gamache whispered to himself. 'Why Bean?'

'Do something, man,' Mrs Finney shouted.

'I need to think,' he said.

He placed his hands behind his back and started to walk with a measured pace, around the library. In disbelief they watched. Then finally he stopped and turned, reaching into his pocket.

'Here, take my Volvo and park it across the drive. Are there other ways in and out of the property?' He tossed his keys to Colleen and walked rapidly to the door, Mesdames Dubois and Finney following and Colleen dashing into the rain.

'There's a service road,' said Madame Dubois. 'Little more than a track, at the back. We use it for heavier equipment.'

'But it puts out onto the main road?' asked Gamache. Madame Dubois nodded. 'Where is it?'

She pointed and he dashed into the rain and climbed into

the huge RCMP pickup, finding the keys in the ignition, as he expected. Soon he was clear of the lodge, heading down the service road. He had to find a narrowing of the woods where he could leave the truck and seal off the property.

The murderer was still with them, he knew. As was Bean. He needed to keep them there.

He parked the truck across the track and was just jumping out when another vehicle rounded the corner in his wake and skidded to a stop. Gamache couldn't see the driver's face. The bright orange hood put it in shadow. It looked as though a spectre was driving the car. But Gamache knew it was no spirit, but flesh and blood behind the wheel.

Spinning tyres spewed mud and dead leaves as the car strained to back up. But it was sunk into the mud. Gamache raced forward just as the door opened and the murderer leapt out and began running, the orange raincoat flapping madly.

Gamache skidded to a halt and thrust his head into the car. 'Bean?' he shouted. But the car was empty. His heart, thudding, stopped for a moment. He turned and raced after the orange figure, just disappearing into the lodge.

Within a moment Gamache also plunged through the door, pausing only long enough to tell the women to lock themselves in the inner office and to get on the walkie-talkie to tell the others to return.

'What about Elliot?' Colleen shouted after him.

'He's not in the woods,' said Gamache, not looking back. He was looking down, following the line of drips, like transparent blood.

Up the polished old stairs they went, along the hall, and puddled in front of one of the bookcases.

The door to the attic.

He yanked it open and took the stairs two at a time. In the dim light he followed the drops to an opening. He knew what he'd find.

'Bean?' he whispered. 'Are you here?' He tried to keep the anxiety out of his voice.

Stuffed cougars, hunted almost to extinction, stared glassy eyed at him. Little hunted hares, moose and delicate deer and otters. All dead, for sport. Staring.

But no Bean.

Downstairs he heard boots and masculine voices, raised. But in this room there was only a hush, as though a breath had been held for hundreds of years. Waiting.

And then he heard it. A slight thumping. And he knew what it was.

Ahead of him a square of light and water hit the floor. The grimy skylight was open. He scrambled towards it, and stuck his head out. And there they were.

Bean, and the murderer, on the roof.

Gamache had seen terror many times. On the faces of men and women newly dead, and those about to die, or believing they were. He saw that look now, in Bean's face. Mouth covered with tape, book clutched in little tied hands, feet dangling. Gamache had seen terror, but never like this. Bean was literally in the clutches of the murderer, standing on the very peak of the rain-slick metal roof.

Without thinking Gamache clutched the sides of the skylight and hoisted himself through, his feet immediately slipping on the wet metal. He fell on one knee, feeling the jar.

And then the world started to spin and he grabbed hold of the edge of the open skylight. He could barely see, blinded by the rain in his eyes and the sheer panic in his head. It shrieked at him to get off the roof. Either through the hole into the attic, or over the edge.

Do it, shove yourself off, his howling head pleaded. Do it.

Down below people were yelling and waving and he dragged his eyes up.

To Bean.

And Bean too looked into the face of terror. The two of them stared at each other, and slowly, with wet, trembling hands, Gamache dragged himself to his feet. He took a tentative step along the peak of the steep roof, one unhappy foot on either side. His head spinning, he kept himself low, so that he could grab hold. Then he shifted his eyes, from Bean, to the murderer.

'Get away from me, Monsieur Gamache. Get away or I'll throw the kid over.'

'I don't think you will.'

'Going to risk it? I've killed already. I have nothing to lose. I'm at the end of the world. Why'd you block the roads out? I could've gotten away. By the time you found the child tied up in the attic I'd have been halfway to . . .'

The voice faltered.

'To where?' Gamache called, over the moaning wind. 'There was nowhere to go, was there? Don't do this. It's over. Bring Bean to me.'

He held out unsteady arms, but the murderer didn't budge.

'I didn't want to hurt anyone. I'd come here to forget it all, to get away. I thought I had. But seeing her again—'

'I understand, I do.' Gamache tried to sound reassuring, reasonable. Tried to keep the tremble from his voice. 'You don't want to harm a child. I know you. I know—'

'You know nothing.'

Far from being frightened, the murderer seemed almost calm. A panicked, cornered murderer was a terrible thing, and the only thing worse was a calm one.

'Bean,' Gamache said, his voice steady. 'Bean, look at me.' He caught the child's panicked eyes, but could tell Bean wasn't seeing anything any more.

'What're you doing? No! Get down!' The murderer suddenly grew agitated, and looked beyond Gamache.

The Chief Inspector turned carefully and saw Beauvoir climbing through the skylight. His thumping heart calmed, for an instant. Beauvoir was there. He wasn't alone.

'Tell him to get down.'

Beauvoir saw the horrific scene. The murderer standing like a lightning rod in the storm, holding the horrified child. But the most horrifying was the chief, who was looking at him with eyes so grave. Frightened, his fate sealed, and knowing it. A Burgher of Calais.

Gamache lifted his hand and gave Beauvoir the signal to withdraw.

'No, please,' Beauvoir rasped. 'Let me come too.'

'Not this time, Jean Guy,' said Gamache.

'Get away. I'll toss the kid over.' Bean was suddenly thrust into space, the murderer barely holding on. Even with tape over the child's mouth Beauvoir could hear the scream.

With one last look, Beauvoir disappeared, and Gamache was alone again, with a dangling Bean and the murderer and the wind and rain that buffeted them all.

Bean struggled in the murderer's arms, twisting to break free and letting out a high-pitched, strangled shriek, muffled by the tape.

'Bean, look at me.' Gamache stared at Bean, willing himself to forget where he was, trying to trick his traitor brain into believing they were on the ground. He wiped the fear from his own face. 'Look at me.'

'What're you doing?' the murderer repeated, staring at Gamache with suspicion and clutching the squirming child.

'I'm trying to calm the child. I'm afraid Bean'll knock you off balance.'

'It doesn't matter.' The murderer hoisted the child higher. And Gamache knew then the murderer was going to do it. To throw the child over.

'For God's sake,' Gamache pleaded. 'Don't do it.'

But the murderer was beyond listening to reason. For reason had nothing to do with what was happening. The murderer now heard only a very old howl.

'Bean, look at me,' Gamache called. 'Remember Pegasus?'

The child calmed slightly and seemed to focus on Gamache, though the squealing continued.

'Remember riding Pegasus into the sky? That's what you're doing now. You're on his back. Can you feel his wings, can you hear them?'

The moaning wind became the outstretched wings of the horse Pegasus, who gave a powerful beat and took Bean into the sky, away from the terror. Gamache watched as Bean slipped the surly bonds of earth.

Bean relaxed in the murderer's arms, and slowly the big book slipped from the small, wet fingers and hit the roof, sliding down and launching into the air, the leaves spreading like wings.

Gamache glanced down and saw frenzied activity, arms

waving and pointing. But one man held his arms out-stretched, to catch someone falling from the heavens.

Finney.

Gamache took a deep breath and looked briefly beyond Bean, beyond the murderer, beyond the chimney pots. To the tree tops, and the lake and the mountains.

'This is my own, my native land!'

And he felt himself relax, a little. Then he looked further. To Three Pines, just on the other side of the mountains. To Reine-Marie.

Here I am, can you see me?

He stood up, slowly, a firm hand on his back steadying him.

'Now, higher, Bean. I've seen you take Pegasus higher.'

Below, the men and women saw the three figures, the Chief Inspector standing upright now in the driving rain and the other two, melded as though the murderer had sprung tiny arms and legs from the chest.

Beside Finney the book thudded to the ground, leaves outstretched and flattened. And in the sobbing wind they heard a far-off song in a deep baritone.

'Letter B, Letter B,' it sang, to the tune of the Beatles' 'Let It Be'.

'Oh, God,' Lacoste whispered and raised her arms too. Beside her Mariana was staring, numb and dumb and uncomprehending. Everything else could fall, she saw it all day, every day. Except Bean. She stepped forward and raised her arms. Unseen beside her, Sandra lifted her hands towards the child. The precious thing, stuck on the roof.

Bean, hands now free of the book, brought them together in front. Clutching reins, eyes staring at the big man opposite.

'Higher, Bean,' Gamache urged. *Wheeled and soared and swung*, said a voice in his head, and Gamache's right hand opened slightly, to grasp a larger, stronger one.

The child gave a mighty yank and kicked Pegasus in the flanks.

Shocked, Pierre Patenaude let go and Bean fell.

Armand Gamache dived. He sprang with all his might and seemed to hover in the air, as though expecting to make the other side. He strained, reached out his hand, and touched the face of God.

THIRTY

~

Gamache's eyes locked on the flying child. They seemed to hang in mid-air then finally he felt the fabric of Bean's shirt and closed his grip.

Hitting the roof he scrambled for purchase as they started skidding down the slick steep side. His left hand shot up and gripped the very top of the roof, where skilled hands had battered and connected the now tarnished copper hundreds of years earlier. And had placed a ridge along the peak of the roof. For no reason.

Now he was hanging down the side of the metal roof, clinging on to the copper ridge with one hand, and Bean with the other. They looked into each other's eyes and Gamache could feel his grip firm on the child, but slipping on the roof. He could see, in his peripheral vision, frantic activity below, with shouts and calls and screams that seemed another world away. He could see people running with ladders, but he knew it would be too late. His fingers were tearing away from the roof and he knew in another instant they would both slide over the edge. And he knew if they fell he'd land on top of the child, as Charles Morrow had done. Crushing what lay beneath. The thought was too much.

He felt his fingers finally lose contact with the ridge, and for a blessed and surprising moment nothing happened, then the two of them started over.

Gamache twisted in one final effort, to heave the child away from him and towards the open arms below. Just then a hand gripped his from above. He didn't dare look, in case it wasn't real. But after a moment he looked up. Rain fell into his eyes and blinded him, but he still knew whose hand held his in a grip from long ago, and long ago lost.

Ladders were quickly raised and Beauvoir scrambled up, taking Bean and handing the child down, then crawling up onto the roof and supporting the Chief Inspector with his own young body.

'You can let go now,' said Beauvoir to Pierre Patenaude, who was clinging to Gamache's hand. Patenaude hesitated a moment, as though he didn't yet want to release this man, but he did and Gamache slid gently into the younger man's arms.

'All right?' Beauvoir whispered.

'*Merci*,' Gamache whispered back. His first words in his new life, in a territory he hadn't expected to see, but one that stretched, unbelievably, before him. 'Thank you,' he repeated.

He allowed himself to be helped down, his legs shaking and his arms like rubber. Once on the ladder he turned and looked up, into the face of the person who'd saved him.

Pierre Patenaude looked back, standing upright on the roof as though he belonged there, as though the *coureurs du bois* and the Abinaki had left him there when they'd departed.

'Pierre,' a small but firm voice said in a conversational tone. 'It's time to come in.'

Madame Dubois's head poked out of the skylight. Patenaude looked at her and stood straighter. He put his arms out and tilted his head back.

'*Non, Pierre*,' said Madame Dubois. 'You are not to do that. Chef Véronique has made a pot of tea and we've lit a fire so you won't get a chill. Come down with me now.'

She held out her hand and he looked at it. Then, taking it, he disappeared into the Manoir Bellechasse.

Five of them sat in the kitchen of the Manoir. Patenaude and Gamache had changed into dry clothes and were wrapped in warm blankets by the fire while Chef Véronique and Madame Dubois poured tea. Beauvoir sat beside Patenaude, in case he made a run for it, though no one expected him to any more.

'Here.' Chef Véronique hesitated a moment, a mug of tea in her large grip. It hovered between Gamache and Patenaude, then it drifted over to the maître d'. She handed the next one to Gamache with a small, apologetic smile.

'*Merci*,' he said, taking the tea in one hand. His left he kept under the table, flexing it, trying to get the feeling back. He was chilled, more from shock he knew than from the rain. Beside him Beauvoir put two heaping spoons of honey into Gamache's tea and stirred.

'I'll be mother today,' Beauvoir said quietly, and the thought stirred something inside the younger man. Something to do with this kitchen. Beauvoir put the teaspoon down and watched Chef Véronique take the seat on Patenaude's other side.

Beauvoir waited for the sting, the anger. But he felt only giddy amazement they were together in this warm kitchen, and he wasn't kneeling in the mud, trying to force life back into a broken and beloved body. He looked over at Gamache, again. Just to make sure. Then he looked back at Chef Véronique and felt something. He felt sadness for her.

Whatever he'd felt for her before was nothing compared to what she felt for this man, this murderer.

Véronique took Patenaude's trembling hand in her own. No reason to pretend any more. No reason to hide her feelings. 'Ça va?' she asked.

It might have been a ridiculous question, given what had just happened. Of course he wasn't all right. But Patenaude looked at her with a little surprise, and nodded.

Madame Dubois brought Beauvoir a cup of hot, strong tea and poured one for herself. But instead of joining them the elderly woman stepped back from the table. She tried to block out the other two and see only Véronique and Pierre. The two who'd kept her company in the wilderness. Who'd grown up and grown old here. One had fallen in love, the other had simply fallen.

Clementine Dubois had known Pierre Patenaude was full of rage when he'd arrived as a young man, more than twenty years earlier. He'd been so contained, his movements so precise, his manners so perfect. He hid it so well. But ironically it had been his decision to stay that had confirmed her suspicion. No one chose to live this deep in the woods for so long without reason. She knew Véronique's. She knew her own. And now, finally, she knew his.

This was the first time Véronique and Pierre had held hands, she knew. And probably the last. Certainly the last time they'd all gather round this old pine table. And discuss their days.

She knew she should feel horrible about what Pierre had done, and she knew she would, in a few minutes. But for the moment she only felt anger. Not at Pierre, but at the Morrows and their reunion and at Julia Martin, for coming. And getting murdered. And ruining their small but perfect life by the lake.

Madame Dubois knew that was unreasonable and unkind, and certainly very selfish. But for just a moment she indulged herself, and her sorrow.

'Why did you kill Julia Martin?' Gamache asked. He could hear people moving about outside the swinging doors into the dining room. A Sûreté agent was stationed at the door, not to stop anyone from leaving the kitchen but to stop anyone from entering. He wanted a few quiet minutes with Patenaude and the others.

'I think you know why,' said Patenaude, not meeting his eye. Since looking into Chef Véronique's eyes a minute earlier he'd been unable to raise his own. They'd been cast down, staggered by what he'd met in her gaze.

Tenderness.

And now she held his hand. How long had it been since someone had held his hand? He'd held other people's hands, at celebrations when they sang 'Gens Du Pays'. He'd comforted kids homesick and afraid. Or hurt. Like Colleen. He'd held her hand to comfort her when she'd found the body. A body he'd made.

But when was the last time someone had held his hand?

He cast his mind back until it hit the wall beyond which he could never look. Somewhere on the other side was his answer.

But now Véronique held his cold hand in her warm one. And slowly his trembling stopped.

'But I don't know why, Pierre,' said Véronique. 'Can you tell me?'

Clementine Dubois sat down opposite him then and the three again, and for the last time, entered their own world.

Pierre Patenaude opened and closed his mouth, dredging the words up from deep down.

'I was eighteen when my father died. A heart attack, but I know it wasn't that. My mother and I had watched him work himself to death. We'd had money once, you know. He was the head of his own company. Big home, big cars. Private schools. But he'd made one mistake. He'd invested in a young man, a former employee. Someone he'd fired. I was there the day he'd fired the man. I was just a kid. My father had told me that everyone deserved a second chance. But not a third. He'd given this man a second chance, then fired him. But Dad liked this young man. Had kept in touch. Had even had him over for dinner after firing him. Perhaps he felt guilty, I don't know.'

'He sounds a kind man,' said Madame Dubois.

'He was.' Patenaude's eyes met hers and he was surprised, again, by tenderness. Had he always been surrounded by it, he wondered. Was it always there? And all he'd seen were the dark woods and the deep water.

'He gave this man his personal money to invest. It was foolish, a kind of madness. The man later claimed my father and the others were as greedy as he was, and maybe that was true. But I don't think so. I think he just wanted to help.'

He looked at Véronique, her face so strong and her eyes so clear.

'I believe you're right,' she said, squeezing his hand slightly.

He blinked, not understanding this world that had suddenly appeared.

'The man was David Martin, wasn't it?' said Véronique. 'Julia's husband.'

Patenaude nodded. 'My father went bankrupt, of course. Lost everything. My mother didn't care. I didn't care. We loved him. But he never recovered. I don't think it was the money, I think it was the shame and the betrayal. We never expected Martin to pay Dad back. It was an investment, and a bad one. It happens. Dad knew the risks. And Martin didn't steal the money. But he never said he was sorry. And when he made his fortune, hundreds of millions of dollars, he never once contacted Dad, never offered to pay him back. Or invest in his company. I watched Martin get rich and my father work and work trying to rebuild.'

He stopped talking. There seemed nothing more that could be said. He couldn't begin to explain how it felt to watch this man he adored sink, and finally go under. And watch the man who'd done this rise up.

Something new had started growing in the boy. Bitterness. And over the years it ate a hole where his heart should have been. And finally it ate all his insides so that there was only darkness in there. And a howl, an old echo going round and round. And growing with each repetition.

'I was happy here, you know.' He turned to Madame Dubois, who reached her old hand across the table and touched his arm.

'I'm glad,' she said. 'And I was happy to have you. It seemed a kind of miracle.' She turned to Véronique. 'A double blessing. And you were so good with the young staff. They adored you.'

'When I was with them I felt my father inside me. I could almost hear him whispering to me, telling me to be patient with them. That they needed a steady but gentle hand. Did you find Elliot?'

He asked Beauvoir beside him, who nodded.

'Just got the call. He was at the bus station in North Hatley.'

'Didn't get far,' said Patenaude, and he smiled despite himself. 'He never could take direction.'

'You told him to run, didn't you? You tried to frame him, monsieur,' said Beauvoir. 'Tried to make us believe he'd killed Julia Martin. You found the notes he'd written her and you kept them, deliberately tossing them into the grate, knowing we'd find them there.'

'He was homesick. I know the signs,' said Patenaude. 'I've seen it often enough. And the longer he stayed the more angry and frustrated he got. But when he found out Julia Martin was from Vancouver he clung to her. At first it was inconvenient for me. I was afraid he'd figure out what I was doing. Then I saw how I could use it.'

'You'd have let him be arrested for your crime?' Véronique asked. She wasn't, Beauvoir noticed, accusing, not judging. Just asking.

'No,' he said, tired. He rubbed his face and sighed, coming to the end of his energy. 'I just wanted to confuse things, that's all.'

Beauvoir didn't believe him, but he thought Véronique did. Or maybe she didn't, and loved him anyway.

'Is that why you took the child?' asked Madame Dubois. They were in dangerous territory now. Killing Julia Martin was one thing. Who, honestly, didn't want to kill a Morrow

393

every now and then? Even framing Elliot she could understand, perhaps. But dangling that child from the roof?

'Bean was insurance, that's all,' said Patenaude. 'To add to the confusion, and in case Elliot came back. I didn't want to hurt Bean. I just wanted to get away. None of this would have happened if you hadn't tried to stop me,' he said to Gamache.

And everyone in the comfortable, warm room glimpsed Pierre Patenaude's small world, where wretched actions could be justified, and others blamed.

'Why did you kill Julia Martin?' Gamache asked again. He was bone tired but he had a distance to go yet. 'She wasn't responsible for what her husband did. They weren't even married at the time.'

'No.' Patenaude looked at Gamache. They both looked very different from less than an hour ago, on the roof. The fear was gone from Gamache's deep brown eyes, and the rage from Patenaude's. Now they were two tired men, trying to understand. And be understood. 'When I first realized who she was I felt kind of numb, but as the days passed I just got angrier and angrier. Her perfect nails, her styled hair, her teeth.'

Teeth? thought Beauvoir. He'd heard many motives for murder, but never teeth.

'Everything so perfect,' the maître d' continued. As he spoke his voice sharpened and sculpted the gentle man into something else. 'Her clothes, her jewellery, her manners. Friendly but slightly condescending. Money. She shouted money. Money my father should have had. My mother.'

'You?' Beauvoir asked.

'Yes, even me. I got more and more angry. I couldn't get at Martin, but I could get her.'

'And so you killed her,' said Gamache.

Patenaude nodded.

'Didn't you know who he was?' Beauvoir asked, pointing at the Chief Inspector. 'You killed someone right in front of the head of homicide for Quebec?'

'It couldn't wait,' said Patenaude, and they all knew the truth of it. It had waited too long. 'Besides, I knew you'd come eventually. If you were already here it didn't much matter.'

He looked at the Chief Inspector. 'You know, all David Martin had to do was say he was sorry. That's all. My father would have forgiven him.'

Gamache got up. It was time to face the family. To explain all this. At the door to the dining room he turned and watched as Pierre Patenaude was led through the back door and into a waiting Sûreté vehicle. Chef Véronique and Madame Dubois stared out of the screen door as it clacked shut behind him.

'Do you think he would have really thrown Bean off the roof?' Beauvoir asked.

'I believed it then. Now, I don't know. Perhaps not.'

But Gamache knew it was wishful thinking. He was only glad he was still capable of it. Beauvoir stared at the large, still man in front of him. Should he tell him? He took a breath, and walked into the unknown.

'I had the strangest feeling when I saw you on the roof,' he said. 'You looked like a Burgher of Calais. You were frightened.'

'Very.'

'So was I.'

'And yet you offered to come with me.' Gamache cocked

his head slightly to one side. 'I remember. And I hope you remember, always.'

'But the Burghers died, and you didn't.' Beauvoir laughed, trying to break the unbearable moment.

'Oh, no. The Burghers didn't die,' said Gamache. 'Their lives were spared.'

He turned back to the door into the dining room, and said something Beauvoir didn't quite catch. It might have been *merci*. Or mercy. Then he was gone.

Beauvoir put out his hand to shove the swinging door and follow the chief, but hesitated. Instead he walked back to the table where the women stood still staring out of the back door and into the woods.

In the dining room he could hear raised voices. Morrow voices. Demanding answers, demanding attention. He needed to join the Chief Inspector. But he needed to do something first.

'He could have let them die, you know.'

The two women turned slowly to look at him.

'Patenaude, I mean,' Beauvoir continued. 'He could have let Chief Inspector Gamache and Bean die. But he didn't. He saved their lives.'

And Chef Véronique turned to face him then with a look he'd longed for, but no longer needed. And inside he felt a deep calm, as though some old debt had been paid.

THIRTY-ONE

'Paradise lost,' said Chief Inspector Gamache, taking his place, naturally, at the centre of the gathering, a raised hand hushing the Morrows. 'To have it all and to lose it. That's what this case was about.'

The room was packed with the Manoir staff, police officers and volunteers. And Morrows. Reine-Marie had hurried over from Three Pines when she heard what had happened and was sitting quietly off to the side.

'What's he talking about?' whispered Sandra loudly.

'A poem by John Milton,' said Mrs Finney, sitting upright next to her husband. 'It's about the devil being cast out of heaven.'

'That's right,' said Gamache. 'The fall from grace. The tragedy in Milton's poem was that Satan had it all and didn't realize it.'

'He was a fallen angel,' said Mrs Finney. 'He believed it was better to rule in hell than serve in heaven. He was greedy.' She looked at her children.

'But what's heaven and what's hell?' asked Gamache. 'It

depends on our point of view. I love this place.' He looked around the room and out of the window, where the rain had now stopped. 'For me it's heaven. I see peace and quiet and beauty. But for Inspector Beauvoir it's hell. He sees chaos and discomfort and bugs. Both are true. It's perception. *The mind is its own place, can make a heaven of hell, a hell of heaven,*' Gamache quoted. 'Early on, even before the death of Julia Martin, I knew there was something wrong. Spot and Claire, the odious missing family members, became Peter and Clara, two gentle, kind friends of ours. Not without their flaws,' Gamache held up his hand again to head off Thomas's catalogue of Peter's faults, 'but at their hearts good people. And yet they were denounced as vile. I knew then this was a family at odds with reality, their perception skewed. What purpose did it serve?'

'Does there have to be a purpose?' asked Clara.

'There's a purpose to everything.' Gamache turned to her, sitting next to Peter. 'Thomas was seen by the family as an accomplished pianist, linguist, businessman. And yet his playing is workmanlike, his career is mediocre and he can't speak French.

'Mariana's business is flourishing, she plays the piano with passion and skill, she has an extraordinary child and yet she's treated like the selfish little sister who can't do anything right. Peter is a gifted and successful artist,' Gamache walked along the room to Peter, dishevelled and bleary, 'in a loving marriage with many friends. And yet you're perceived as greedy and cruel. And Julia,' he continued. 'The sister who left and was punished for it.'

'She was not,' said Mrs Finney. 'She chose to leave.'

'But you forced her out. And what was her crime?'

'She shamed the family,' said Thomas. 'We became a laughing stock. *Julia Morrow gives good head.*'

'Thomas!' snapped his mother.

They'd been cast out of society. Mocked and ridiculed. Paradise lost.

And so, they'd taken their revenge on the good child.

'It must've been hard for Julia to come to the reunion,' said Mariana. Bean was on her lap for the first time in years, feet dangling inches off the ground.

'Oh, please,' said Thomas. 'Like you care, Magilla.'

'Stop calling me that.'

'Why should I? You might fool him,' he looked at Gamache, 'he doesn't know you. But we do. You were selfish then and you're selfish now. That's why we call you Magilla. So you'll remember what you did to Father. He asked one thing of you, to kiss him when he got home. And what did you do? You stayed in the basement watching that ridiculous TV show. You preferred a cartoon gorilla to Father. And he knew it. And when you'd finally come to kiss him you were crying. Upset at being made to do something you didn't want to. You broke his heart, Magilla. Every time I call you that I want you to remember the pain you caused him.'

'Stop it.' Mariana stood. 'It. Was. Never. The. Cartoon.'

The words jerked out as though fighting with her, desperate to stay inside. 'It. Was. The. Cage.'

No sound came out of Mariana now. She stood silent, her mouth open, a fine line of drool dripping down, like clear honey. Bean squeezed her hand and Mariana started to breathe again, in sobs and whoops, like a newborn, slapped.

'It was the cage. Every day I'd rush home from school to

watch Magilla the Gorilla in his cage. Praying that today he'd find a home. He'd be adopted. And loved.'

Tilting her head back she stared at the beam above her head. She saw it tremble, a fine spill of dust and plaster raining down. She braced herself. And then it stopped. The beam held fast. It didn't fall.

'And that's why you design beautiful homes for the homeless,' said Gamache.

'Mariana,' said Peter softly, approaching her.

'And you,' said Thomas, his words springing up between Peter and his sister, stopping him. 'You're the most devious of all. You who had everything wanted more. If there's a devil in this family it's you.'

'Me?' Peter said, stunned by the attack, vicious even by Morrow standards. 'You're saying I had everything? What family did you live in? You're the one Mother and Father loved. You got everything, even his—' He stopped, remembering the plops and the two circles radiating on the calm lake.

'His what? His cufflinks?' Thomas vibrated with rage, his hands shaking as he thought of the frayed white dress shirt hanging in the closet upstairs. His father's old shirt that Thomas had taken the day he'd died. The only thing he'd wanted. The shirt off his back. That still smelled of him. Of rich cigars and spicy cologne.

But now the links were gone. Because of Peter.

'You have no idea, do you?' Thomas spat. 'You can't even imagine what it's like to have to succeed all the time. Father expected it, Mother expected it. I couldn't fail.'

'You failed all the time,' said Mariana, recovered. 'But they refused to see it. You're lazy and a liar and they thought you could do no wrong.'

'They knew I was their only hope,' said Thomas, his eyes never wavering from Peter. 'You were such a disappointment.'

'Peter never disappointed his father.'

It was a voice the Morrows rarely heard. They turned to look at their mother, then beside her.

'He never expected you to excel, Thomas,' Bert Finney continued. 'And he never wanted anything except for you to be happy, Mariana. And he never believed those things written on the bathroom wall about Julia.'

The old man struggled to his feet.

'He loved your art,' he said to Peter. 'He loved your music, Thomas. He loved your spirit, Mariana, and always said how strong and kind you were. He loved you all.'

The words, more dangerous than any grenade, exploded in the middle of the Morrows.

'That's what Julia figured out,' said Finney. 'She realized that was what he'd meant when he withheld money and gifts. She who had it all knew how empty those things were, and that anything of value she'd already been given. By her father. Love, encouragement. That was what she wanted to tell you.'

'Bullshit,' said Thomas, returning to sit beside Sandra. 'He kicked her out of the house. How loving was that?'

'He regretted that,' admitted Finney. 'Always regretted not defending Julia. But he was a stubborn man, a proud man. He couldn't admit he was wrong. He tried to apologize, in his way. He reached out to her in Vancouver, when he found out she was engaged. But he let his dislike of Martin ruin it. Charles needed to be right. He was a good man, plagued by a bad ego. He paid a high price for it. But it doesn't mean he didn't love you all. Including Julia. It just meant he couldn't show it. Not in the way you wanted.'

Was that the thing to be deciphered, wondered Peter. Not the words of the strange message, but the fact of the message itself?

Never use the first stall in a public washroom.

Peter almost smiled. It was, he had to admit, very like a Morrow. They were nothing if not anal.

'He was cruel,' said Thomas, not wanting to let go.

'Your father never stopped searching for the person who wrote that graffiti. He thought that way he could show Julia how much he cared. And in the end he found him.'

There was silence then, until the small clearing of a throat broke it.

'That's not possible,' said Peter, standing up and smoothing his hair. 'Father never said anything to me about it.'

'And why would he?' demanded Thomas.

'Because I was the one who wrote the graffiti.' He didn't dare look at his mother.

'Yes,' said Finney. 'That's what your father said.'

The Morrows stared, speechless.

'How'd he know?' asked Peter, feeling light headed, slightly nauseous.

'It was written in the second stall. Only you and he knew about that. It was his private gift to you.'

Peter inhaled sharply.

'I wrote the graffiti because she'd hurt my feelings. And because I wanted Father to myself. I didn't want to share him with anyone. I couldn't stand that Father loved Julia. I wanted to destroy that. And I did.'

'Have you not heard a word I said?'

Bert Finney now commanded the room, Gamache willingly ceding his place.

402

'It wasn't yours to destroy. You claim too much for yourself, Peter. Your father loved your sister all his life. You couldn't destroy that. He knew what you'd done.'

Finney stared at Peter and Peter pleaded with him to stop there. Not to say that last thing.

'And he loved you anyway. He loved you always.'

Paradise lost.

It was the most devastating thing Finney could have said. Not that Peter was hated by his father. But that he'd been loved all along. He'd interpreted kindness as cruelty, generosity as meanness, support as tethers. How horrible to have been offered love, and to have chosen hate instead. He'd turned heaven into hell.

Gamache stepped forward and took charge of the room once again.

'The seed for a murder is often planted years earlier,' said Gamache. 'Like the black walnut tree, it takes that long to grow and become toxic. That's what happened here. I made a huge mistake at the very beginning. I assumed the murderer was a member of the family. It almost cost Bean's life.' He turned to the child. 'I'm so sorry.'

'You saved my life.'

'How kind of you to see it that way. But I made a mistake. A massive one. I was looking in the wrong direction.'

'What made you suspect Patenaude?' asked Clara.

'This was such an unusual case,' said Gamache. 'It wasn't the who that got me, or even the why. It was the how. How had the murderer killed Julia Martin? How could that statue have fallen, and without scratching the pedestal? Remember the day of the unveiling you went for that boat ride?' Gamache asked Peter. 'We were on the dock and Bean came tearing down the lawn.'

'Stung by a wasp,' said Peter.

'Not a wasp, a bee,' said Gamache. 'A honey bee.'

'I'm sorry,' said Clara, 'but how could it matter if it was a bee or a wasp?'

'The fact it was a honey bee gave Patenaude away. It was the fatal clue, the one thing he had no control over. Let me explain.'

'Please,' said Mrs Finney.

'The Manoir Bellechasse has its own hives, over there.' He waved into the forest. 'Chef Véronique planted a grove of honeysuckle and clover and put the hives in the middle. Honey bees can fly a great distance to get food, but if it's close they don't bother. She put the honeysuckle there so the bees wouldn't leave the glade and disturb the guests. And for years it worked so well we didn't even know they were there.'

'Until Bean got stung,' said Peter, perplexed.

'Frankly I don't know the difference between a bee sting and a wasp,' Gamache admitted. 'But Inspector Beauvoir became quite interested in honey bees.' He didn't say why. 'According to him a wasp never leaves its stinger, neither do other bees. They can sting over and over. But a worker honey bee can sting only once. As it stings it leaves a barb and a tiny poison sac and that kills the bee. Bean's stings still had a barb and a poison sac in them. Bean hadn't been in the glade when stung, but was all the way across the property.' He arched his arm over from the forest until his hand was pointing in the opposite direction. 'Bean was stung while playing around the pedestal for the statue. What would a honey bee be doing there, so far from the honeysuckle grove? Especially since all the flowers there were dying, killed by the black walnut?'

'What was the bee doing there?' asked Madame Dubois, puzzled.

'It was one of those tiny mysteries, an inconsistency that nags. A murder investigation is full of them. Some are important, some are just the messiness of everyday life. This turned out to be crucial. I finally got it yesterday at the Canada Day picnic.'

'Really?' said Clara, remembering the lunch, the whole village out on the green, the kids hyper on a diet of Coaticook ice cream, cream sodas and toasted marshmallows.

'What did you see that we didn't?' asked Reine-Marie.

'I saw bees and ants attracted to the puddles of Coke, and I saw spilled salt,' he said.

'So did I,' said Peter, 'but they didn't tell me anything.'

'Do you remember how the Coke spilled?'

'The little boy shoved it across the table,' said Peter, remembering.

'He shoved it across the spilled salt,' clarified Gamache. 'Your mother did much the same thing when we spoke this morning.'

Peter turned astonished eyes on his mother.

'I did no such thing.'

Gamache walked over to the sideboard and picked up a delicate china sugar bowl. 'May I?' he asked Madame Dubois, who nodded. He then took the linen tablecloth off one of the dining-room tables, revealing a wood surface underneath. It was antique pine and rough to the touch. Taking the top off the sugar bowl he turned it upside down.

'Have you lost your mind?' demanded Mrs Finney.

But she joined everyone else, now crowded round the table, with its pyramid of granular white sugar. Gamache smoothed it out, until it covered half the dark wood surface.

'This morning as we talked on the *terrasse* you held a sugar bowl much like this one,' the Chief Inspector said to Mrs Finney. 'When you were agitated you moved it back and forth, across some sugar that had spilled.'

'I was never agitated.'

'My mistake,' said Gamache. 'Perhaps animated would be a better word.'

Mrs Finney looked unhappy with the choice.

'The point is, the bowl glided across the sugar.' He demonstrated, sweeping it gently back and forth. 'That boy at lunch did something similar with his pop can, though not nearly as gracefully. He simply shoved the can across the spilled salt, like this.'

Gamache put the sugar bowl at one end of the wooden table and shoved it forward. It skidded across the top and stopped at the edge.

'Now, watch what happens on the other half, the part of the table without sugar.'

He tried it again, but this time the china bowl barely moved, catching the rough wood and stopping short.

'This was how the murder was done.'

Gamache looked into faces no wiser. In fact, considerably more perplexed.

'I placed a call this afternoon to the Musée Rodin in Paris and spoke to an archivist there who'd heard about the technique. A worker at the Côte des Neiges cemetery had also heard of it, but they haven't used it for years. It's a trick for moving statues.'

'Are we still talking about the Coke can?' asked Peter. 'Or the sugar bowl?'

'We're talking about the statue of your father. Pierre Patenaude worked one summer in a cemetery and he saw them placing statues. Some of the older workers still used this technique back then.'

Gamache took the sugar bowl and pushed it across the table again. This time it didn't stop at the edge, but fell off the side. Beauvoir caught it just as it fell.

'*Voilà*,' said Gamache. 'Murder. According to the Musée Rodin, when they placed the Burghers of Calais on top of the pedestal, they put a cushion of sugar on it first, so they could adjust the statue an inch here or there, turn it slightly. Just before the statue of your father arrived Pierre Patenaude did the same thing. He poured a layer of sugar over the base.'

'That must've taken a lot of sugar,' said Clara.

'It did. He'd been hoarding it for days. That was why the Manoir unexpectedly ran out. He'd been stealing it. Remember how white the pedestal is?'

They nodded.

'The maître d' guessed a layer of white sugar wouldn't be noticed, especially since he'd shooed everyone away, leaving just Madame Dubois and the crane operator, both of whom would be busy concentrating on other things.'

They could see it all. Charles Morrow hoisted off the flatbed truck, tied tight and strung up, all eyes staring, breaths held and prayers said that he wouldn't fall. And then, slowly, slowly, he was lowered to his pedestal.

'Even at the unveiling we didn't notice,' said Clara. 'What we did see were wasps.'

'Attracted by the sugar,' said Gamache. 'Wasps, honey

bees, ants. Colleen the young gardener has nightmares about the ants and I assumed she meant she'd seen ants crawling over the body. But she didn't. In fact, the coroner even told us the heavy rain meant there were no ants. Colleen saw the ants before the statue fell, on the pedestal and feet.' He looked at Colleen, who nodded. 'The cushion of sugar had attracted every insect for miles around. When I saw the wasps and ants at the spilled Coke I realized they were attracted to something sweet.'

'A honey bee,' said Peter, shaking his head. 'I wonder if Patenaude realized how damning that was?'

'Such a small thing, a bee. Imagine that giving away a murderer,' said Clara.

'The real brilliance of this old sugar technique is that it's time sensitive,' said Gamache. 'One good rain, the sugar dissolves and the statue subsides onto its pedestal, to stay there forever.'

'But suppose it hadn't rained,' asked Peter. 'What then?'

'Hose it off, simple. Colleen might have noticed, but probably not with the shock of the discovery.'

'But still, it didn't have to be Pierre,' said Madame Dubois. 'Any one of us could have hoarded that sugar.'

'It's true. He was the most likely, but I needed more. And I got it from Gabri, when he told us about his name. Short for Gabriel, of course. You told him about our own children's names that also work in both French and English.'

'I remember,' said Reine-Marie.

'That was a clue. That and the turn of phrase "everyone comes back for this week". You only "come back" if you're from here to begin with. David Martin told Inspector Beauvoir that he'd come back to Montreal a few times. Come back. I'd presumed he was English, from British Columbia, but suppose he was a Montrealer and his name was Da-veed Mar-tan?' Gamache gave it the French pronunciation. 'When I returned to the Manoir one of the calls I made was to Martin. He confirmed he was from Montreal, and that a François Patenaude had been involved in an early, disastrous investment.'

He told them then what the maître d' had told them in the kitchen.

As he spoke Beauvoir looked over and saw Chef Véronique standing at the kitchen door, listening. And he suddenly knew who she was, and why he'd cared for her.

THIRTY-TWO

The rain had stopped, but the grass underfoot was sodden. Sun shot through the clouds and beamed onto the lake, the lawn, the vast metal roof. Their feet squelched as the two couples and Beauvoir walked across the Manoir lawn towards the circle of chairs newly dried by the young staff.

'What do you think will happen to the Bellechasse?' Reine-Marie asked, holding her husband's hand but talking to Clara.

Clara paused and glanced back at the grand and solid lodge. 'This was built to last,' she said finally, her eyes catching a gleam on the old roof. 'And I think it will.'

'I agree,' said Gamache.

Elliot Byrne was standing on the *terrasse*, setting out tables for dinner and directing some of the younger staff. He seemed a natural.

'How are you doing?' Reine-Marie asked Beauvoir, on her other side, as he batted away at the cloud of biting blackflies that had descended upon him.

'Did you know who she was?' he asked.

'Chef Véronique? As soon as I saw her,' said Reine-Marie.

'Though I knew her by another name, she's unmistakable, even after all these years. I used to watch her. Our kids were raised on her recipes.'

'So was I,' said Beauvoir, and he coughed up a bug. 'Sorry.' He smiled ruefully at Madame Gamache.

The swarming flies and buzzing receded, and he could again smell the Vicks VapoRub, could taste the flat ginger ale and the crackers. He could feel the lumpy sofa and the soft blanket as he lay feverish, a sick day off school. Beside him sat his mother, gently rubbing his cold feet, as together they watched her favourite show on Radio Canada.

'*Bonjour, mes enfants*,' said the beefy young woman in the wimple. 'Bless you for joining me. Let's just hope I don't burn the kitchen down today. Mother Superior is still angry about that frying pan I forgot on the gas last week.'

And she'd laugh. She had a laugh like a French horn and a voice like a root vegetable.

Soeur Marie Angèle and her famous cooking show. *Midi Avec Ma Soeur.*

It had become required viewing for young mothers across Quebec. Some to laugh at the old-fashioned, drab woman, no older than themselves really, who taught them how to make a perfect blancmange or *rouille* or *poire Hélène*. She seemed like something from another era. But below the laughter was admiration. Soeur Marie Angèle was a gifted cook who loved what she did, and did it with humour and excitement. There was a simplicity and certainty about her in a Quebec changing so rapidly.

Beauvoir could again hear his mother's laughter as Ma Soeur made even the most complicated recipes seem easy and clear.

411

Enrolment in nunneries spiked, as did sales of her popular cookbooks, with the plain, happy woman in a habit with crossed baguettes on the cover.

How could he not have seen?

But there was a troubling edge to his memories. And then he remembered. The scandal when Soeur Marie Angèle suddenly left. In headlines and talk shows, in the streets and kitchens of Quebec, there was one topic. Why would Soeur Marie Angèle suddenly quit? And not just the show, but the order?

She'd never answered that. She'd simply taken her frying pans and vanished.

Into the wilderness, and here, Beauvoir knew, she'd finally found peace. And love. And a garden to tend and honey to harvest and people she cared for to cook for.

It was a small and perfect life. Away from the glare, away from scrutiny.

All the troubling little mysteries became clear. Why this wonderful chef was content to stay at the Manoir Bellechasse when she could work in the finest restaurant in Quebec. Why the Manoir employed only English kids, from other provinces.

So that her secret would be safe. Her peace unviolated. No one would recognize Chef Véronique as the infamous Ma Soeur who'd left the order like a thief in the night. And come here, to be taken in and protected by the fierce Madame Dubois. Her new Mother Superior.

'Why do you think she left the order?' he asked Reine-Marie, as they strolled down the lawn.

She paused to think about that. 'Depends what you believe,' she said.

'What do you believe?'

'I believe this is where she belongs. For some, I suppose, this would be the wilderness. You walk ten feet into the woods and you're lost. But for others this is heaven. Why look for the divine in a cold and cramped nunnery when you could be here? You can't tell me God doesn't have a home on this lake.' She smiled at Beauvoir. 'Not a very original answer. But the simplest one.'

'The blancmange of answers?' he asked and she looked at him, surprised, and laughed.

'Like Quebec itself. Just keep stirring until everything smooths out.'

Paradise regained.

On the other side of the gardens Bean and Mariana were playing. They'd packed up and were preparing to leave, after one more flight through the gardens.

'Mom, Mom, you're Pegasus. Run. Fly.'

'Pegasus is resting, dear. Grazing. See.' Mariana pawed the ground with a weary hoof.

She'd placed all of Bean's clocks in the suitcase, then gone into the washroom to pack her toiletries. When she'd returned she saw, to her dismay, the clocks scattered once again around the room.

'What's all this, Beano?' she asked, trying to sound casual.

Bean zipped up the small, nearly empty valise. 'Don't think I need them any more.'

'Why not?'

'You'll make sure I wake up. Won't you?'

'Always, my dearest,' said Mariana. And now she watched her strange little child prance around the sweet garden.

'I guess even Pegasus needs to rest,' said Bean, hands in

front, gripping the reins and leaning back and forward, steadying a mighty steed.

The Morrows and Gamaches sat but Beauvoir remained on his feet.

'I need to get home. Will you be all right?' he asked the chief.

Gamache stood up and nodded. 'Will you?'

'Better than ever,' said Beauvoir, scratching the bites on his neck.

'Let me walk you to your car.' Gamache touched Beauvoir on the arm and the two walked back across the lawn. Side by side.

'One thing still bothers me, and I know it bothers Agent Lacoste,' said Beauvoir as they approached his car. Lacoste had accompanied Patenaude into the Sûreté headquarters in Montreal, but had asked the Inspector to clear up one question that even Patenaude couldn't answer.

'Why did Julia open her arms, as the statue fell?'

Gamache opened the car door for his junior.

'I don't know.'

'No, really, sir. Why would she? I know you can't possibly know for sure, but what do you think? Just a guess.'

Gamache shook his head. How many times, he wondered, had Julia imagined her father with her once again? Her father embracing her. How often, in the quietest moments, had she indulged the fantasy of strong arms around her? Of his scent, the rub of his suit? Had she longed for it? Was she standing beside his statue imagining it once again, forgiving and forgiven meeting at last? And as he moved towards her, had she failed in that last moment to distinguish real life from longing?

'I don't know,' he repeated, and walked slowly back across the moist, fragrant lawn, his right hand clasped almost closed.

'May I join you?' Mariana plopped into an Adirondack chair. 'This playing Pegasus is exhausting. At least Magilla lived in a cage. Much more restful.'

Bean joined them and a waiter, sent by Elliot, came to ask if they wanted anything. Bean and Mariana ordered soup while the others asked for pots of tea and sandwiches.

Reine-Marie reached into her purse. 'I have something for you,' she said to the child. Bean's eyes grew wider.

'A present?'

Reine-Marie handed Bean the gift and soon the wrapping was off and Bean looked at Reine-Marie, amazed.

'How'd you find it?'

Bean opened *Myths Every Child Should Know* and eagerly turned to the chapter on the flying horse.

'Myrna?' Clara asked, thinking of their friend who ran the new and used bookstore in Three Pines. Reine-Marie nodded.

'What are the chances she'd have that book?' asked Clara.

'Oh, she has everything,' said Peter.

Clara nodded, but also suspected what she'd find in the front of the book in round, childish letters. A little boy's name and maybe a drawing. Of a footless bird.

'Tell me about Pegasus,' said Reine-Marie. Bean leaned against her, opened the book and starting reading. Across the table Mariana blew softly on her child's hot soup.

'Why did you say you weren't a prisoner?'

Gamache had seen Beauvoir off then made his way back

415

to the others. His body ached and he longed for home, a hot bath, and to crawl into bed beside Reine-Marie. But as he slowly walked back he paused, and changed course. To the dock. There he took his place beside the old man. It seemed natural now to stand side by side.

'I wasn't a prisoner,' Finney said. 'You were right, I was in a Japanese prison camp, but I wasn't a prisoner. It's not semantics, you know. It's an important distinction. Crucial.'

'I believe you.'

'I saw a lot of men die there. Most men. Do you know what killed them?'

Starvation, Gamache thought to say. Dysentery. Cruelty.

'Despair,' said Finney. 'They believed themselves to be prisoners. I lived with those men, ate the same maggot-infested food, slept in the same beds, did the same back-breaking work. But they died and I lived. Do you know why?'

'You were free.'

'I was free. Milton was right, you know. The mind is its own place. I was never a prisoner. Not then, not now.'

'What sums do you do, when you come here? You don't count birds, and I don't think you count money.'

Finney smiled. 'You know what money buys?'

Gamache shook his head.

'I'm an accountant and I've spent a lifetime counting money and watching the people who have it. Do you know what I've decided? The only thing money really buys?'

Gamache waited.

'Space.'

'Space?' Gamache repeated.

'A bigger house, a bigger car, a larger hotel room. First class plane tickets. But it doesn't even buy comfort. No one complains more than the rich and entitled. Comfort, security, ease. None of that comes with money.'

He walked slowly off the wharf, his feet echoing slightly.

'Your father was a hero, you know. He had the courage to admit he was wrong. And to change. He hated violence, hated killing. It's interesting that his son would have a career bringing killers to justice. But be careful, young Armand. His cross isn't yours. You don't need to avenge every death.'

'It's not death that angers me,' said Gamache. 'It's suffering. It angered my father too. I don't consider it a cross, never a burden. Perhaps it's a family trait.'

Finney looked at him closely.

'You asked what I count each evening and each morning. What I counted each day in prison while better men withered and died. Do you know the sums that I do?'

Gamache stood still, in case moving would scare this man off and he'd never have his answer. But he knew he needn't worry. This man was afraid of nothing.

'I count my blessings.'

He turned and saw Irene on the *terrasse*, as though he'd sensed her there.

'We're all blessed and we're all blighted, Chief Inspector,' said Finney. 'Every day each of us does our sums. The question is, what do we count?'

The old man brought his hand to his head and removed his hat, offering it to Gamache.

'No, please, keep it,' said Gamache.

'I'm an old man. I won't need it again, but you will. For protection.'

Finney handed him back his hat, the hat he'd bought at the same time he'd bought one for Reine-Marie, after her

417

skin cancer scare. So that she wouldn't feel foolish in her huge, protective hat. They'd be foolish together. And safe together.

Gamache accepted the hat.

'You know the Mariana Islands, sir? They're where the American troops left to liberate Burma. The Marianas.'

Finney stopped then looked over to the four chairs, one of which contained a young woman and her child, both very unlike the other Morrows.

'Now, I'd like to tell you a story,' said Reine-Marie when Bean had finished excitedly telling the adults about Pegasus. 'It's about Pandora.'

Beside her Peter made to get up. 'I don't think I need to hear this again.'

'Come on, Peter, stay,' said Clara, taking his hand. He hesitated then sat back down, squirming in his seat, unable to get comfortable. His heart raced as he listened to the familiar tale. Once again he was on the sofa at home, struggling to find and hold his space next to his brother and sisters, not to be tossed off. And across the room their mother sat, upright, reading, while Father played the piano.

'This is for Peter,' she'd say, and the others would snicker. And she'd tell them about Pandora who lived in Paradise, a world without pain or sorrow, without violence or disease. Then one day Zeus, the greatest of the gods, gave Pandora a gift. A magnificent box. The only catch was that it should never be opened. Every day Pandora was drawn to the box and every day she managed to walk away, remembering the warning. It must never be opened. But one day it was too much for her, and she opened the box. Just a crack. But it was enough. Too much.

Out flew all the winged horrors. Hate, slander, bitterness, envy, greed, all shrieked and escaped into the world. Disease, pain, violence.

Pandora slammed the box shut, but it was too late.

Peter wriggled in his chair, feeling the panic crawling like ants over him. Just as he'd wriggled on the sofa, his brother and sisters pinching him to keep still. But he couldn't.

And he couldn't now. His eyes fell on the glowing white thing in the perpetual shade of the black walnut, the tree that kills. And Peter knew that despite what Gamache might believe, that box had opened on its own. And horrors had been unleashed. It had tilted and dropped his father on Julia. Crushing. Killing.

He heard Reine-Marie's voice again.

'But not everything escaped. Something lay curled at the very bottom of the box.'

Bean's eyes were wide. Peter stopped twitching and stared.

Something was left in the box? This was new. His mother hadn't mentioned this.

'At the very bottom, underneath everything else, one thing sat and stayed. Didn't flee.'

'What was it?' asked Bean.

'Hope.'

'Here, let me help.' Peter reached for his mother's suitcase.

'Bert can do it, or one of the porters.'

'I know they can, but I'd like to.'

'Suit yourself.'

He carried her case out of the door. Thomas and Sandra were leaving, without saying goodbye. Thomas did honk his horn. To say goodbye or warn Peter out of the way?

'Bert's bringing the car,' said Mrs Finney, staring ahead.

'Will you be all right?'

'Of course I will.'

'I'm so sorry about the graffiti, Mother. I never should have done it.'

'That's true. It was a terrible thing you did.'

Peter waited for the 'but'.

Irene Finney waited for the car. What was taking Bert so long? He'd pleaded with her in their room as they packed to tell the children everything. To explain why she never held them, never hugged them. Never gave or accepted kisses. Especially that. To explain the pain of neuralgia, that any touch, even the lightest, was excruciating.

She knew what they thought. That she was cold. Couldn't feel. But in fact she felt too much. Too deeply.

But she was raised never to admit a flaw, a failing, a feeling.

She looked over at Peter. Holding her valise. She opened her mouth, but the car appeared just then. She stepped back from the void.

'Here he is.'

Without a backward glance she got in the car and left.

You can't get milk from a hardware store.

Mariana had told Peter about the note Father had left her. Maybe, thought Peter, if we put all our notes together, the code would be complete. But then he smiled and shook his head. Old habits. There was no code, and he had his answer.

His father had loved him.

As he watched his mother disappear into the woods he wondered if he could ever bring himself to believe that she loved him too. Perhaps one day, but not today.

He walked back to Clara, knowing not everything had left. One thing remained.

Reine-Marie found her husband on the dock, his floppy hat restored, his slacks rolled up and his feet dangling in the clear cool waters.

'I almost lost you today, didn't I?' She sat beside him, catching the aroma of rosewater and sandalwood.

'Never. Like the Manoir, I'm built to last.'

She smiled and patted his hand, and tried not to think about it.

'I finally got through to Daniel in Paris,' said Gamache. 'I apologized.'

And he'd meant it.

'I told him if he wanted to name his son Honoré he had my blessing. He was right. Honoré is a good name. Besides, his child will make his own way. Like Bean. I'd thought it cruel naming the child Bean, that it helped explain the child's unhappiness. But Bean isn't unhappy at all.'

'It could have been worse,' said Reine-Marie. 'Mariana could have married David Martin.'

'How would that make it worse?'

'Bean Martin?'

Gamache laughed, low and rumbling. 'It's an amazing thing to know your child has more courage than you.'

'He's his father's son.'

They looked across the lake, lost in their own thoughts.

'What are you thinking?' she asked quietly after a few moments.

'I'm counting my blessings,' he whispered, looking at her in her floppy hat. 'Daniel told me something else. They found

421

out today the sex of their child and they've decided on a name.'

'Honoré?'

'Zora.'

'Zora,' said Reine-Marie. She reached for his wounded hand and together they did their sums.

It took some time.

ACKNOWLEDGEMENTS

I have a few people to thank for this book. The first and foremost, as always, is my kind and gentle husband Michael. It took me a lot longer than it should have to realize that Armand Gamache isn't simply my fictional husband, he's my real husband. Indeed, without even realizing it I based Chief Inspector Gamache on Michael. A man who is content and knows great joy, because he's known great sorrow. And mostly, he knows the difference.

I'd also like to thank Rachel Hewitt who curates the sculpture collection at the Royal Academy in London.

Hope Dellon, of St Martin's Minotaur and Sherise Hobbs of Headline are my editors and worked to make this book what it is. I owe them both a huge debt, as I do the most wonderful agent in the world, Teresa Chris. She is very wise.

I owe a great debt to Lise Page, my assistant, who patiently tends gardens in the summer and tends to us the rest of the year. Everything she touches flourishes. And she rarely finds the need to use fertilizer.

And finally Jason, Stephen and Kathy Stafford who own

and run Manoir Hovey in the village of North Hatley, Quebec. The Manoir Bellechasse is inspired by Hovey Manor, and by the many, many wonderful days and nights we've spent there. If you read this book and then visit Hovey you'll notice that it is far from an exact replica – of the Inn or the lake. But I hope I have, at least, captured the feel of Manoir Hovey. In fact, Michael and I love it so much we got married in the tiny Anglican Chapel in North Hatley many years ago, then had a two-day wedding party at Hovey.

Bliss.

Though, as Stephen has pointed out, they happily do not have nearly the number of blackflies as the fictional Manoir Bellechasse. Nor, it must be said, nearly the number of murders.

If you enjoyed *A Rule Against Murder*,
read on for the beginning
of the next Gamache case,
The Brutal Telling!

ONE

~

'All of them? Even the children?' The fireplace sputtered and crackled and swallowed his gasp. 'Slaughtered?'

'Worse.'

There was silence then. And in that hush lived all the things that could be worse than slaughter.

'Are they close?' His back tingled as he imagined something dreadful creeping through the woods. Towards them. He looked round, almost expecting to see red eyes staring through the dark windows. Or from the corners, or under the bed.

'All around. Have you seen the light in the night sky?'

'I thought those were the Northern Lights.' The pink and green and white shifting, flowing against the stars. Like something alive, glowing and growing. And approaching.

Olivier Brulé lowered his gaze, no longer able to look into the troubled, lunatic eyes across from him. He'd lived with this story for so long, and kept telling himself it wasn't real. It was a myth, a story told and repeated and embellished over and over and over. Around fires just like theirs.

It was a story, nothing more. No harm in it.

But in this simple log cabin, buried in the Quebec wilderness, it seemed like more than that. Even Olivier felt himself believing it. Perhaps because the Hermit so clearly did.

The old man sat in his easy chair on one side of the stone hearth with Olivier on the other. Olivier looked into a fire that had been alive for more than a decade. An old flame not allowed to die, it mumbled and popped in the grate, throwing soft light into the log cabin. He gave the embers a shove with the simple iron poker, sending sparks up the chimney. Candlelight twinkled off shiny objects like eyes in the darkness, found by the flame.

'It won't be long now.'

The Hermit's eyes were gleaming like metal reaching its melting point. He was leaning forward as he often did when this tale was told.

Olivier scanned the single room. The dark was punctuated by flickering candles throwing fantastic, grotesque shadows. Night seemed to have seeped through the cracks in the logs and settled into the cabin, curled in corners and under the bed. Many native tribes believed evil lived in corners, which was why their traditional homes were rounded. Unlike the square homes the government had given them.

Olivier didn't believe evil lived in corners. Not really. Not in the daylight, anyway. But he did believe there were things waiting in the dark corners of this cabin that only the Hermit knew about. Things that set Olivier's heart pounding.

'Go on,' he said, trying to keep his voice steady.

It was late and Olivier still had the twenty-minute walk through the forest back to Three Pines. It was a trip he made every fortnight and he knew it well, even in the dark.

Only in the dark. Theirs was a relationship that existed only after nightfall.

They sipped Orange Pekoe tea. A treat, Olivier knew, reserved for the Hermit's honoured guest. His only guest.

But now it was story time. They leaned closer to the fire. It was early September and a chill had crept in with the night.

'Where was I? Oh, yes. I remember now.'

Olivier's hands gripped the warm mug even tighter.

'The terrible force has destroyed everything in its way. The Old World and the New. All gone. Except . . .'

'Except?'

'One tiny village remains. Hidden in a valley, so the grim army hasn't seen it yet. But it will. And when it does their great leader will stand at the head of his army. He's immense, bigger than any tree, and clad in armour made from rocks and spiny shells and bone.'

'Chaos.'

The word was whispered and disappeared into the darkness, where it curled into a corner. And waited.

'Chaos. And the Furies. Disease, Famine, Despair. All are swarming. Searching. And they'll never stop. Not ever. Not until they find it.'

'The thing that was stolen.'

The Hermit nodded, his face grim. He seemed to see the slaughter, the destruction. See the men and women, the children, fleeing before the merciless, soulless force.

'But what was it? What could be so important they had to destroy everything to get it back?'

Olivier willed his eyes not to dart from the craggy face and into the darkness. To the corner, and the thing they both knew was sitting there in its mean little canvas sack.

But the Hermit seemed to read his mind and Olivier saw a malevolent grin settle onto the old man's face. And then it was gone.

'It's not the army that wants it back.'

They both saw then the thing looming behind the terrible army. The thing even Chaos feared. That drove Despair, Disease, Famine before it. With one goal. To find what was taken from their Master.

'It's worse than slaughter.'

Their voices were low, barely scraping the ground. Like conspirators in a cause already lost.

'When the army finally finds what it's searching for it will stop. And step aside. And then the worst thing imaginable will arrive.'

There was silence again. And in that silence lived the worst thing imaginable.

Outside a pack of coyotes set up a howl. They had something cornered.

Myth, that's all this is, Olivier reassured himself. Just a story. Once more he looked into the embers, so he wouldn't see the terror in the Hermit's face. Then he checked his watch, tilting the crystal towards the fireplace until its face glowed orange and told him the time. Two thirty in the morning.

'Chaos is coming, old son, and there's no stopping it. It's taken a long time, but it's finally here.'

The Hermit nodded, his eyes rheumy and runny, perhaps from the woodsmoke, perhaps from something else. Olivier leaned back, surprised to feel his thirty-eight-year-old body suddenly aching, and realized he'd sat tense through the whole awful telling.

'I'm sorry. It's getting late and Gabri will be worried. I have to go.'

'Already?'

Olivier got up and pumping cold, fresh water into the enamel sink he cleaned his cup. Then he turned back to the room.

'I'll be back soon,' he smiled.

'Let me give you something,' said the Hermit, looking around the log cabin. Olivier's gaze darted to the corner where the small canvas sack sat. Unopened. A bit of twine keeping it closed.

A chuckle came from the Hermit. 'One day, perhaps, Olivier. But not today.'

He went over to the hand-hewn mantelpiece, picked up a tiny item and held it out to the attractive blond man.

'For the groceries.' He pointed to the tins and cheese and milk, tea and coffee and bread on the counter.

'No, I couldn't. It's my pleasure,' said Olivier, but they both knew the pantomime and knew he'd take the small offering. '*Merci*,' Olivier said at the door.

In the woods there was a furious scrambling, as a doomed creature raced to escape its fate, and coyotes raced to seal it.

'Be careful,' said the old man, quickly scanning the night sky. Then, before closing the door, he whispered the single word that was quickly devoured by the woods. Olivier wondered if the Hermit crossed himself and mumbled prayers, leaning against the door, which was thick but perhaps not quite thick enough.

And he wondered if the old man believed the stories of the great and grim army with Chaos looming and leading the Furies. Inexorable, unstoppable. Close.

And behind them something else. Something unspeakable.

And he wondered if the Hermit believed the prayers.

Olivier flicked on his flashlight, scanning the darkness. Grey tree trunks crowded round. He shone the light here and there, trying to find the narrow path through the late summer forest. Once on the trail he hurried. And the more he hurried the more frightened he became, and the more fearful he grew the faster he ran until he was stumbling, chased by dark words through the dark woods.

He finally broke through the trees and staggered to a stop, hands on his bent knees, heaving for breath. Then, slowly straightening, he looked down on the village in the valley.

Three Pines was asleep, as it always seemed to be. At peace with itself and the world. Oblivious of what happened around it. Or perhaps aware of everything, but choosing peace anyway. Soft light glowed at some of the windows. Curtains were drawn in bashful old homes. The sweet scent of the first autumn fires wafted to him.

And in the very centre of the little Quebec village there stood three great pines, like watchmen.

Olivier was safe. Then he felt his pocket.

The gift. The tiny payment. He'd left it behind.

Cursing, Olivier turned to look into the forest that had closed behind him. And he thought again of the small canvas bag in the corner of the cabin. The thing the Hermit had teased him with, promised him, dangled before him. The thing a hiding man hid.

Olivier was tired, and fed up and angry at himself for forgetting the trinket. And angry at the Hermit for not giving him the other thing. The thing he'd earned by now.

He hesitated, then turning he plunged back into the forest,

feeling his fear growing and feeding the rage. And as he walked, then ran, a voice followed, beating behind him. Driving him on.

'Chaos is here, old son.'